THE FINAL MINUTE

Also By Simon Kernick

The Business of Dying
The Murder Exchange
The Crime Trade
A Good Day to Die
Relentless
Severed
Deadline
Target
The Last 10 Seconds
The Payback
Siege
Ultimatum
Wrong Time, Wrong Place
Stay Alive
Dead Man's Gift

Simon
Kernick
THE
FINAL MINUTE

CENTURY

Published by Century 2015

2 4 6 8 10 9 7 5 3 1

First published in Great Britain in 2015 by
Century
Random House, 20 Vauxhall Bridge Road,
London SW1V 2SA

www.randomhouse.co.uk

Addresses for companies within The Random House Group Limited can
be found at: www.randomhouse.co.uk

The Random House Group Limited Reg. No. 954009

A CIP catalogue record for this book
is available from the British Library

HB ISBN 9781780890777
TPB ISBN 9781780890784

The Random House Group Limited supports the Forest Stewardship Council®
(FSC®), the leading international forest-certification organisation. Our
books carrying the FSC label are printed on FSC®-certified paper. FSC is
the only forest-certification scheme supported by the leading environmental
organizations, including Greenpeace. Our paper procurement policy can be
found at:
www.randomhouse.co.uk/environment

Printed and bound by CPI Group (UK) Ltd, Croydon, CR0 4YY

For Nick. Here you go!

One

I've been worried that I'm not who they say I am for a while now.

It started a week or so back after I fell down the cellar steps en route to getting a bottle of red wine and smacked my head on the stone floor. They kept me in the local hospital overnight as I was showing the symptoms for mild concussion, and ever since they let me out, things haven't felt quite right.

To be honest, the whole set-up here's pretty odd. According to my sister, she's been looking after me at her house for over two months now, and that feels about right, although it's impossible to tell for sure because the days just seem to drift into one another in a kind of soft fog. The thing is, I'm not sure whether I'm being paranoid or not. When you've got no long-term memory you're as helpless as a young child, which means you've got to trust the people around you. And particularly those whose job it is to bring your memory back – like the man sitting opposite me across the room.

Dr Bronson's a big, dapper man at the wrong end of his fifties with a quite magnificent mane of black hair, tinged with silver, and a long, thoughtful face that would have been described as ruggedly handsome a few years back but which is now beginning to lose its fight with gravity. Even so, you can still imagine that he'd have his pick of single ladies of a certain age. He has that kind of gravitas, but at the same time he also gives off the impression that he doesn't take himself too seriously – not if the clothes he's wearing today are anything to go by, anyway. His latest adornment is a tweed three-piece suit, a red bow tie that matches the rims of his glasses, well-worn brown brogues, and loud pink socks.

'So how have you been, Matt?' he asked me, his voice soft, yet sonorous and reassuring. We'd been seeing each other twice a week every week here at my sister's, and this had always been his opening line.

'OK, I guess. Nothing much changes really.' Which up until a few days ago had been the truth. Now, though, I was less sure.

'I sense you're looking a little despondent today,' he remarked. 'Don't lose hope, whatever you do. Recovery from the kind of immense brain trauma you suffered takes time. Sometimes months. Sometimes years. We've both got to be patient through this process.'

The brain trauma he was referring to was my car accident. Early one morning some months back, I was driving in a semi-rural stretch of Hampshire when my car left the road, went down an embankment, and hit a tree. For some reason I wasn't wearing a seatbelt, which possibly saved my life, because I was thrown clear of the car, straight through the windscreen, and was twenty feet away from it when it burst into flames. I was in a coma for three months, and when I woke up my life was this.

A blank slate.

Without doubt, the most lonely feeling in the world.

'I know, I know,' I said, with more than a hint of exasperation. 'It's just we don't seem to be making any real progress.'

'Well we are,' he countered firmly. 'We've managed to get you to remember growing up with your sister; the camping trips with the family when you were a boy. We're slowly piecing together your childhood, Matt. And we're using that as a foundation to allow us to reconstruct the memories of adulthood, and finally get your memory back altogether. When people suffer from the kind of amnesia you do, the memories often come back very slowly, starting with the earliest first. We may never solve the mystery of what you were doing on the road that night, we may never remember the few months of your life prior to the accident, but we will return your life to you, Matt. You have to believe that. It's like a box we've simply got to prise open.'

I sighed. 'I'm trying.'

'So nothing's come to you since we last spoke?'

I paused. Did I tell him or didn't I? 'Everything we talk about here is confidential, isn't it? It can't go any further than these four walls?'

He gave me a strong, reassuring smile. 'Exactly. I'm bound by oath not to repeat anything you tell me to anyone. Has something come back to you then?'

I paused again. Because the thing was, I didn't entirely trust Dr Bronson. It was hard to say why. He acted genuine enough, but maybe that was the problem: he came across like an actor playing a part. Yet maybe that was what all therapists were like with their patients. In the end, I bit the bullet, figuring I didn't have anything to lose by telling him. 'I've had a dream.' *Jesus, the dream.* I took a deep breath. 'The same one, twice in the last four nights.'

'Did you write everything down like I suggested?' Dr Bronson always suggested. Never told.

'I didn't have to. I can remember the whole thing vividly. And it was exactly the same both nights. I never have recurring dreams. I never really dream. But this . . .'

Now, suddenly, Dr Bronson looked really interested. He wrote something down on his yellow A4 notepad. 'Tell me about it. Start from the beginning and take me through every detail. You know, we might have a breakthrough here, Matt.'

That, worryingly, was what I was afraid of. I took a deep breath. Then I began.

'I'm in an unfamiliar house. The lights are on and it's night. The dream starts with me standing outside a half-open door. I push it open all the way and I notice that I'm wearing gloves. The lights are on inside the room and I feel a sense of terrible foreboding as I walk slowly inside.

'The room's a mess. A lamp's been knocked over and a glass of wine's been spilled on the carpet. But my attention's focused on a naked woman who's lying sprawled out on her back on a huge double bed. She's dead and the sheets round her head are covered in blood. As I get closer, I can see she's been beaten over the head with something and I'm pretty sure her throat's been cut too. She's young, somewhere in her twenties, with long dark hair and curves in all the right places, and I feel a pang of something I can't quite put my finger on. It's more than sadness, but it's not quite guilt. I touch the skin of her neck with a gloved finger, feeling for a pulse, but to be honest, I already know she's dead, because I can actually smell the odour of shit in the air, and she's not moving at all. Her eyes are closed and it looks like she's asleep, but when I put a hand to her mouth, I can't feel any breath.

'I turn and leave the room, still feeling this strange pang. Then I'm back in the hallway of this house. It's a big, flashy-looking place, with marble flooring and arty paintings on the walls – you know, the sort that are all bright patterns, but not actually of anything. Everything screams money, and everything looks pristine and brand-new.

'I walk down the hall, and it's then that I hear a noise behind me. I'm scared, I know that, and I turn round quickly.' I stopped speaking for a moment. I could hear my heart quickening as I recalled the scene. 'That's when I see her. She's blonde, dressed in black lace underwear – a bra and panties, nothing else – and she's sitting on the floor against the wall. I wonder what she's doing. And then she turns her head my way, very slowly, and I get a look at her face properly for the first time. And you know what? She's utterly beautiful, like the most beautiful woman I've ever seen in my life, and I get this really strong physical hit in my gut. But the thing is, she's hurt. There's a gaping wound on the side of her head and it's bleeding all over her hair and down on to her shoulder. And her eyes are wide and staring.'

I paused again because the memory was bringing back that same feeling in my gut, making me breathe in short, rapid starts. I was beginning to sweat too. I couldn't work out whether it was excitement at the fact that I could actually picture this scene, and that it felt real, or something else. I shut my eyes, trying to remember everything as it happened, trying to hold the memory absolutely still amid the fog inside my brain.

'Take your time,' said Dr Bronson. He said something else too, but I didn't hear it. I was too busy concentrating.

I took a deep breath. 'And then this girl's eyes focus as she sees me properly for the first time, and her expression changes. First, it's surprise. Then shock. And then something else.'

'What?'

My insides tightened. This was why I hadn't wanted to talk to him about it, but I ploughed on regardless. 'Fear. She's looking at me and she's frightened. But it's more than that. She's absolutely terrified. I can see it in her eyes. And it's me she's terrified of, even though I don't know why.' I took another deep breath. 'Then I turn away from her and I catch my reflection in a full-length mirror. I look different. It's me, but at the same time it's not me. My face is thinner, and my cheekbones are more pronounced. My hair's shorter too. But it's the expression I'm wearing that I really notice. It's cold. Hard. There's no humanity there. And yet inside I'm feeling all these emotions.'

'What kind of emotions?'

'I'm not sure exactly. I know I feel angry for some reason. And panicky too, like I'm caught up in something running out of control. But it's not just that.' I took a moment to think hard, trying to take myself back into the dream. I pictured the blonde girl again. Her deep blue eyes, the gentle curve of her lips. And immediately I knew what it was. 'Infatuation,' I told him, a certainty in my words. 'I'm in love with this woman. And not just in the dream. I've met her before. I know her.' I emphasized the last three words, almost spat them out.

'Try to think, Matt,' said Bronson soothingly. 'Where do you know her from?'

Once again I concentrated, summoning up every ounce of willpower as I tried to squeeze out anything important that might be drifting on the misty edges of my subconscious. But nothing happened, and the effort tired me. I shook my head, picked up the glass of water on the table next to me and took a big gulp. 'Right now, that's all I can tell you.'

'We often find with amnesiacs that dreams take on a very realistic quality precisely because real memories are so scarce,' said Dr Bronson.

'It felt real.'

'Were there any differences between the two dreams? Any details that were in one but not in the other? You see, Matt, it's very rare to have exactly the same dream twice.'

'It was exactly the same one,' I said emphatically. 'Down to the last detail. I told you, I've never had a recurring dream before and I don't even dream that much. I mean, what is there to dream about? My subconscious is a pretty empty space so it's not like I've got a great deal of available material. But this was different. Very different.'

'Well, we know that at some point before your accident you were a police officer in London,' Dr Bronson ventured. 'Could the dream have something to do with anything you worked on?'

'I really don't know,' I said, because I didn't. I had no memory at all of being a police officer. According to Jane, my sister, on whom I relied for most of my information about my past, I worked in uniform in London for approximately five years, having had a career change from being a teacher. I was unmarried, had no steady girlfriend, and no one knew where I was going, where I'd just been, or why I was carrying no ID when the car I was driving careered off the road on that fateful night five months earlier.

Wiping out everything I'd ever known.

'This is where the hypnotherapy really helps us,' said Dr Bronson, leaning forward. 'Let's put you under and see if we can extract some more from this dream. See where it leads us.'

Part of the way through each of our sessions, Dr Bronson engaged in hypnotherapy with me. In other words, he put me into a trance. I never remembered anything about this part of the session; it remained a blank space, like my memory. I knew it was meant to be a way of pulling up memories from deep in my subconscious because Dr Bronson always told me so. Except he'd turned up nothing, other than some images from my child-hood that were so vague I wasn't even sure they were real.

Part of me wanted to cooperate, to find out what this dream related to, but I was scared of where it might lead. Because if it was based on real events, then I was somehow involved – either directly or indirectly – in a murder. But my caution ran deeper than that. I was feeling less and less comfortable allowing Dr Bronson to put me in a position where I was completely vulnerable.

'I'm sorry, Doc, I don't think I can handle it today,' I said, suppressing a fake yawn. 'I don't feel too good, to be honest. I could do with lying down.'

'It would really help if you could stay awake for the next half an hour, Matt. This is all for your own good.'

He was eyeing me with suspicion now. I didn't want to upset

him because it was possible I was wrong, and right then he was still the best hope of getting my old life back.

'Come on,' he said. 'We've got a real opportunity here, and you know one of the things I like about you is how determined you always are to cooperate. This could be a real opening for us.'

He leaned across and turned me gently so I was facing him. He was looking into my eyes now, his own eyes magnified by the lenses in his glasses, and suddenly an insistent voice coming from somewhere inside told me to get out of there.

I relied on my instincts. These days I had nothing else.

'I'm sorry, Doc,' I said, breaking free from his gaze and putting some distance between the two of us. 'I honestly feel really sick.'

'You'll feel better once I get you under.'

His voice was more insistent now, and I didn't like the expression on his face. It was no longer comforting and avuncular. Although he was attempting to hide it behind a tight smile, there was an almost desperate eagerness there.

'No,' I said, shaking my head and trying to look as ill as possible. 'I don't think I will.'

Dr Bronson's eager expression disappeared and was replaced with a disapproving one which I guessed he reserved for his most uncooperative patients. 'Are you still taking your medication?' he asked.

'Of course I am,' I told him, which strictly speaking was true. As it happened, I didn't have much choice in the matter. Because of the seriousness of my memory loss, Jane had brought in a live-in male nurse called Tom who was there to help look after me, and it was Tom who gave me the medication. He always watched me put the pills in my mouth and waited while I swallowed them with a glass of water. He then checked inside my mouth just to make sure they'd gone down. He always did it in a friendly way, with a few laughs, like we were mates rather than patient and carer, but lately I'd been watching him more closely – subtly of course, because I didn't want to raise any suspicion – and the more I saw of him, the less he convinced me in his role. He was a big guy, early to mid-thirties, with a hard, lived-in face, the chiselled jaw of the naturally fit, and a scar on his chin. He reminded me of one of those buff actors they use in the war movies I watched a lot these days. Plus he'd taken up with my sister – I heard them humping at night occasionally – which couldn't be that ethical, and wasn't the behaviour I'd necessarily expect from a nurse. Although what the hell did I know any more? Anyway, in the past week I'd decided that I had to find a way to keep the pills out of my system, because that same gut instinct that was at work in this room was telling me in very loud words that they were hindering, not helping, my condition.

It wasn't a decision I'd come to easily. I'd been totally reliant on Jane, Tom and Dr Bronson. They were my crutch, my defence against a dark, foreboding outside world in which I was a complete stranger. Put bluntly, they were all I'd got.

But were they really helping me? I just didn't know.

So I formulated a plan. I knew I couldn't get out of taking the medication, not with Tom standing over me, but whenever I could, I'd let the tablets lodge in the space between my cheek and gum and get rid of them afterwards. This was no easy feat though, so in the majority of instances I had to swallow and then, when Tom had gone, slip out to the toilet, make sure no one was within earshot, and make myself throw up as quietly as possible. Then

I'd clear up after myself, spray a bit of air freshener around and return to my room, leaving no one any the wiser.

So far my memories hadn't started to come back, but I had experienced flashes of déjà vu. Visions of childhood – of kissing a girl; of riding a bike – flitted across my consciousness like wraiths, barely showing themselves before fading once again into the darkness. But they'd been getting more frequent.

And now the dreams had started, and I was beginning to think there was a connection in there somewhere.

Dr Bronson was talking about the importance of taking my medication, but I was no longer listening. I needed to get out of this room. It was suddenly oppressive.

I got unsteadily to my feet, deliberately swallowing hard. 'Jesus, I think I might throw up.'

For a big man, Dr Bronson moved fast, shoving his chair backwards so he was out of range of anything I sent his way. Turning away, I made a pretence of staggering from the room and out into the hallway.

I could hear Jane and Tom talking quietly in the kitchen. They must have heard me because Jane popped her head round the open door and gave me a puzzled smile.

'Everything all right, Matt?' she asked.

I told her what I'd just told Dr Bronson and hurried up the stairs in the direction of the bathroom and my bedroom.

'Oh dear,' she said as I went. 'Let me get Tom to make something up that'll calm you down.'

'It's OK,' I called back over my shoulder. 'I just need a lie down.' And, as I spoke the words, I thought two things. One: my sister looks absolutely nothing like me. She has red hair where mine's dark; pale, freckled skin where mine's touching olive; a short, petite build compared to my much taller, more solid frame. No obvious similarities at all. That was the first thing. The second was more worrying. I fancied her. I really did. I'd felt that way almost from the first time I clapped eyes on her after waking from my coma. When she'd told me who she was, I'd been shocked. Honestly. I'd thought the feeling might go away, but it hadn't. In fact, in the absence of any other women in my life, it had got stronger. I didn't even like to look at her any more. And as for Tom, I was jealous as hell of him.

When I got to my room, I opened the door and shut it loudly again, but without going inside. Then I waited a minute before creeping back to the top of the stairs and listening to the whispering voices downstairs in the hall. The three of them were talking quietly but I could hear only snatched phrases uttered in tense, businesslike terms. 'How much longer?' I heard my sister hiss, just a little too loudly, and there was an irritation in her tone that was a marked contrast to her usual friendly, caring manner around me. It was pretty obvious she was talking about how much longer she was going to have to look after me, and it made me flinch because I'd grown used to relying on her, and it wasn't nice to hear what she really thought.

I thought I heard the doc say something about being close, then the voices faded away as they went into the kitchen.

I stood stock-still, wondering what the hell I thought I was doing skulking there in the shadows. It made me feel like a naughty child, listening in on something I shouldn't.

And in that moment I experienced a sudden, perfectly clear vision of me as a young boy standing behind a half-open door listening to my parents shout at each other. And there's someone standing next to me, older and bigger, and as I turn to him I can't make out his face but that doesn't matter because in that moment I know without a shadow of a doubt that it's my brother.

And of course there was only one problem with that. I wasn't meant to have a brother.

Two

My sister's house was a big, rambling place built some time round the turn of the last century, when things were built to last, and set on an isolated stretch of peninsula on the mid-Wales coast. My bedroom was tucked away at the back of the house, about as far away from Jane's room as it was possible to get, which I'd assumed was so I wouldn't be able to hear her and Tom at night. Unfortunately it hadn't worked. It was a sparsely furnished space, and had probably been a kid's room once, with a single bed, a couple of pictures on the wall, and an old photo of my parents on the bedside table. They were both dead now: my father of a heart attack in 1997, my mother of breast cancer five years later. Dr Bronson told me that I should look at the photo every day because it might jog a memory at any time – he'd even made me bring it into some of the sessions – but all I'd ever seen was two strangers staring back at me.

Until now. As I sat down on the bed, the vision of my brother already fading, and stared at the photo, there was just a flicker of familiarity about them – that sense that I'd seen them somewhere before. It was vague, but it was something.

There was a knock on the door. It was Jane.

I lay down on the bed, putting on a suitably unwell expression, and told her to come in.

She stepped inside, bearing a cup of tea and a sympathetic smile. 'Are you OK?'

I sat up, and gave her a weak smile. 'I'm a little better now.' I was about to tell her I could do with some fresh air but I held back. If I told her I wanted to go for a walk she'd insist on either she or Tom accompanying me in case I got lost in the woods that seemed to stretch for miles around this place, and couldn't find my way back. That was what they always said, as if I was some helpless kid.

'I brought you this.' She put the tea on the bedside table next to the photo of our parents, and I breathed in the faint scent of her perfume. My sister was an attractive woman. At thirty-six, she was three years younger than me, but she could easily have passed for thirty. With her clear, porcelain skin and petite build, she had a fragile, almost doll-like look, but there was also a confidence about her, a sense of quiet strength, that I imagined appealed to a lot of men. I know it appealed to me.

She also looked absolutely nothing like either of my parents.

I thanked her and picked up the photo. 'Tell me about Mum and Dad.'

So she told me. About how they met at a dance; how they married after a whirlwind romance; how Dad worked long hours running a small print business and Mum looked after the two of us; how we spent our holidays camping down in Cornwall, and occasionally in France. And as she talked the smile on her face looked both pretty and genuine. It felt like she was recounting real experiences, and yet I remembered none of them. I asked her to describe our old house in Sutton, and she did. In detail too. I tried to picture it, but couldn't. I'd asked her a couple of weeks ago whether she could take me there and show me the street we used to live on in case it jogged some long-forgotten memories. She'd seemed to think it was a good idea, as had Dr Bronson, but we'd never actually gone, and neither of them had mentioned it in the past few days.

'You're going to get better, Matt,' she said, touching my arm briefly before stepping away from the bed as if she thought I might grab her at any moment if she stayed put. Of course I'd never mentioned the fact that I occasionally had inappropriate thoughts about her, nor had I ever put any of those thoughts into action. If anything I was very much the other way, avoiding any physical contact, just in case. But I wondered then if she had an inkling that my view of her wasn't entirely brotherly.

I sighed. 'Yeah, I know. I'm sure I will eventually. But it just seems to be taking a long time.'

'Dr Bronson said there's been some progress this week. That you might actually be getting the first memories back.'

I wasn't sure that it was entirely ethical for Dr Bronson to be discussing my condition with Jane, especially as he always liked to inform me that anything I said would never go further than the four walls of my sister's study where we always had our meetings, but I let it go. 'I've had a few,' I said, 'but nothing

16

substantial.' There was no way I was going to tell her anything about the dream, and I was hoping that the doc hadn't either. I didn't want my sister thinking I was some kind of psycho.

'He also says you didn't want to do the hypnotherapy today,' she added, wearing a vaguely reproachful look.

I raised an eyebrow. 'Did he now?'

'You know, you've got to trust him, Matt. It's costing me a lot of money to hire his services – these things don't come cheap. He's one of the best therapists in the country. So please, try to cooperate.'

'I will.'

'He's still here if you want to see him. It seems daft for him to come all this way from London and not manage to get a full session in with you. Especially when you've been making progress.'

'I don't think I can face it today. I'm sorry, Sis.'

'It costs me six hundred pounds every time he comes here,' she said, the frustration showing on her face.

I didn't want to upset her, and I could see I was doing a pretty good job of that, but there was no way I was going under today. 'Well, as I said, I'm sorry, but I'm really not feeling up to it.'

She breathed out loudly in a show of exasperation and, with an angry shake of the head, left the room, shutting the door behind her with something close to a slam.

I'd never seen Jane like that before. She always went out of her way to be nice to me. But then, I thought, I'd always cooperated in the past, and now I was standing up to her. I remembered her words to the doc earlier: *How much longer?* They hadn't sounded like those of a caring sister.

I looked down at the cup of tea and decided there was no way I was going to drink it. God alone knew what Jane had put in there but I was sure it was more of the drugs they'd been feeding me these past two months, the ones that had always seemed to sap my energy. The irony right now was that, far from feeling sick, I actually felt better physically than at any time since I'd arrived here.

A thought struck me then with absolute clarity. I had to get out of this house. I needed to breathe in some fresh air, to walk and to think.

To remember.

I waited for a few minutes until I heard Dr Bronson's car pulling away on the gravel driveway, then got up and went over to the old-fashioned sash window. I flicked open the catch as far as it would go, which was only about eighteen inches. The view looked straight out on to a beech tree, the outer branches of which were tantalizingly close.

Not even thinking about it, I crawled through the gap in the window and manoeuvred myself round so that I was half in and half out, before slowly letting myself down so I was hanging from the ledge. At this point I had no choice but to drop. The distance from my feet to the grass was probably about eight feet. It was a long way, especially given that spending the last few months sitting around had left me seriously unfit, but it was too late to worry about that now and I felt an unusual sense of exhilaration as I let go, as if I was finally doing something worthwhile after a lifetime of wasted opportunities.

I hit the ground hard and rolled on to my side, gritting my teeth against the jarring pain in my Achilles tendons. I lay still for a couple of seconds, waiting for the pain to subside before slowly getting to my feet and peering in through the utility room window. The door was open and I could see into the kitchen where Jane was talking with Tom. He was leaning back against a worktop nodding as she spoke to him animatedly, moving her hands a lot. She looked stressed. Tom didn't. He looked calm. But then he always did. He was a big man with a big presence, the kind of guy who didn't need to raise his voice to get what he wanted. As I watched, he put a hand on her shoulder and smiled. The gesture seemed to calm her, and she leaned up and kissed him, jabbing me with a most unwelcome shard of jealousy.

But at least they hadn't noticed me. I turned and ran across the lawn, into the welcoming embrace of the trees. I didn't know where I was going, or how long I was going to go there for, but it just felt good to be out of that house, which had seemed to resemble a prison more and more these days.

As soon as I was well into the trees I slowed to a walk, taking in the sounds and smells around me. It was a sunny, warm mid-September day with a feel of summer about it. Jane had lived out here on the peninsula for ten years now, ever since the death of her husband. He was older and had left her a lot of money in his will, and she'd decided to come here to retreat from the world. She'd shown me photos of the husband – apparently we'd met a few times over the years, and he'd liked me – but needless to say, I had no memory of him whatsoever.

I hated what I'd become. An invalid, a slave to the vagaries of my mind, a husk of a man with nothing to talk about and, apart from a woman who may or may not have been my sister, a nurse who looked like a soldier, and a shrink who I wasn't at all sure wanted to cure me, no one in the world to talk to.

I was completely and utterly alone.

Gingerly, I touched the four-inch scar that ran in a flattish diagonal line from the tip of my hairline across my forehead before turning down towards my left temple. It was the width of a child's fingernail and a direct result of the injury that had made me lose my memory. No one knew what I'd been doing out on the road that night. The car I was in hadn't been my own. No one knew whose it was. It had been so badly burned out that it was impossible to ID from the plates; apparently even the serial number had been erased by the flames. The fact that I'd been carrying no ID on me when I'd been found unconscious and alone twenty feet away, following an anonymous 999 call, only added to the mystery. It was only when Jane reported me missing and actually started contacting hospitals that she'd managed to find me, over a week later – which now, when I thought about it, seemed a pretty big coincidence.

I had other scars too on various parts of my body, at least two of which didn't look like the result of any kind of an accident (and which Jane hadn't been able to explain either), but I was always drawn to the one on my head. It was a little tender to the touch after the tumble in the cellar, and still looked too new to be a scar. I kept it hidden from the world under a floppy fringe but I inspected it regularly – five, ten, twenty times a day, as if I was hoping that I'd look one day and it'd be gone, and my memory miraculously returned to me.

I heard someone call my name from somewhere back in the direction of the house. It was Tom, and there was an urgency in his voice. So they'd discovered I was missing. That had been quick. I wondered if Tom had gone up to make sure I'd drunk the tea and discovered me gone.

The Final Minute

I broke into a run. I knew it was never a good idea to piss Tom off. One time I hadn't wanted to take my medication. I'd genuinely felt sick and had asked him if he minded me doing it in my own time. He said he'd wait, and I'd said there was no need, he could trust me. But he'd insisted, and not in a nice way either. His exact words, delivered in slow, harsh tones that seemed to require all his self-control, were: 'My job's to make sure you take those fucking pills, so that's what I'm going to do. OK with you?' I'd looked in his eyes then and seen a coldness there that made me think that nursing had definitely been a poor career choice for him. It had also made me decide against arguing.

But I was going to risk his wrath now because I wanted to be alone. No, scotch that. I *needed* to be alone.

I quickened my pace. Within the space of a minute I got a burning sensation in my lungs and my breaths turned into long, laboured pants, but even so, I felt good. I was alive. I was free. Even if it was just for a few hours. Unfortunately, the woods didn't provide much cover. Plus, Tom was a hell of a lot fitter than me so it wasn't going to take him long to catch up. And then he was going to be mighty pissed off. I could hear him continuing to call my name. He was still some distance away but not as far as I was expecting, and there was an edge to his voice now.

I needed to make a choice. I could skirt the edge of the woods heading in the direction of the mainland. I'd walked there before with Jane. There was a farm about half a mile down with a number of outbuildings and a rundown garden which offered plenty of hiding places, but there was no guarantee I'd get there before Tom ran me down. Alternatively, I could head left and make for the end of the peninsula where the land tumbled down sheer cliff faces to the sea; but it was too exposed out there, and that made me wonder what the hell I was thinking about, running away like this. It wasn't like there was anywhere for me to go. I had no money. No friends. Nothing. I was always going to have to head back to the house eventually.

And yet my gut was telling me that I'd never get better if I stayed there.

I came to the edge of the woods. Ahead of me was a stretch of wild grassland about a hundred yards long that ran to the edge of a cliff. I'd stood there a number of times taking in the view of the bay and the headland beyond. It was a wild, isolated place, barely touched by civilization, with only a handful of whitewashed cottages dotted across the horizon. Today the sky was a hazy pale blue with a handful of clouds drifting across it, bathed in the gentle rays of a bright sun.

But there was no time to enjoy the view. At least not yet. I glanced back over my shoulder and, seeing no immediate sign of Tom, ran across the grassland in the direction of the cliff edge, careful to avoid the bumps of knotted grass and rabbit holes that littered the route but keeping as fast a pace as I could muster. Halfway across I looked round again. Still no sign of him. I was going flat out now, and as I reached the edge I slowed up and looked down. On this stretch of the peninsula, the cliff was actually more of a grassy, rock-strewn slope that meandered down to the sea in several angled steps before becoming sheer for the last thirty or so feet. It was steep enough of course, but if you fell, you were likely to roll rather than hurtle through the air.

The Final Minute

Carefully, I climbed down a short way, resting my feet on rocks a couple of feet apart so that my head was level with the top and I could peer over without being seen.

I didn't have to wait long for Tom to appear out of the trees. He was at almost the exact same spot where I'd emerged but I could tell he hadn't seen me. He looked round angrily and called out my name again, real frustration in his voice. Then he did something I really didn't expect. He started walking purposefully in my direction, like he knew exactly where I was, even though he couldn't have seen me. Only the top of my head was visible, and even that was obscured by the long grass. And yet still he kept coming.

I looked down. I suppose one of the advantages of amnesia is that you can't remember whether you had certain phobias or not, like a fear of heights. I was guessing I didn't because the view below didn't disorientate me. About twenty feet down the land flattened a little for a couple of yards before dropping again, and there was a tangled gorse bush there that I could hide behind so that Tom wouldn't be able to see me from the top. It looked safe enough, so I started to clamber down the slope.

Which was the moment it all went wrong. The rock my right foot was resting on came loose at the same time that I lifted my left, and suddenly I had lost my balance and was falling backwards through the air. I was doing an aerial somersault, and the ground, in the shape of wind-bleached rocks jutting through the grass, was racing up to meet me. I threw out my arms to break the fall, hit the gorse bush, its thorns ripping at my flesh, and then landed hard and bounced on to my side, coming perilously close to the edge of the ledge.

But for once I avoided banging my head. Groaning in pain, I crawled under the gorse bush so I could no longer be seen from the top of the cliff and lay still. I could hear Tom calling my name again, but at last he stopped and turned away.

I got myself comfortable and settled in to wait until he'd finally given up the search for me, already shutting my eyes and thinking about a nap.

Three

Carl Hughie, known simply as Mr H to those who worked under him, or owed him favours, had three bad habits – smoking, gambling and prostitutes – and he was currently indulging in all three. The prostitute was in the hotel bathroom getting herself ready and Mr H, dressed only in the complimentary bathrobe, was sitting in a tub chair making a phone bet with Ladbroke's, a copy of the *Racing Post* spread out on his lap, while puffing away on one of his cheap cigars. Life at that exact point was good.

In his own way, Mr H was a powerful man. He had access to the machinations of the establishment, and his star, like that of the man he ultimately reported to, was rising fast. At fifty, and a lifetime bachelor, he was still young enough to enjoy it. The woman in the bathroom was costing him a grand for the night – a sum that would have been well out of range of his official salary but which he could now easily afford. And by God she was worth it. Her name was Magdalena and she could do things to a man he hadn't even known existed.

Unfortunately, as he placed his last bet, he saw a photo of a grey-haired man appear on the TV screen on the far wall, with a caption underneath saying that two British nationals had been murdered in St Lucia.

Mr H recognized the man in the photo immediately and, grabbing the remote, he turned the sound right up. The man's name was Maurice Bufton and, according to the news report, he'd been killed alongside his twenty-year-old daughter at his villa in a suspected burglary gone wrong. There were also unconfirmed reports that Bufton had been tortured before he died.

Mr H knew immediately this wasn't a burglary gone wrong. Bufton, now retired and living the ex-pat life, possessed a piece of important information, and Mr H would have bet anything that this information had been forcefully extracted from him. All of which meant he now had a real problem on his hands.

Magdalena appeared in the bathroom doorway wearing only a baby-doll nightie, a pair of five-inch heels and a very inviting smile, but she might as well have been wearing a boiler suit and comedy face mask for all he cared. 'Get some clothes on and grab a drink in the bar,' he said with a dismissive wave of his hand. 'I've got some business that needs dealing with.'

She pouted but knew better than to argue with a client. He took out his phone and waited while she got dressed and left the room.

He gave it thirty more seconds before making the call.

'What is it?' his boss demanded.

'They've taken out Bufton.'

There was a long silence at the other end of the phone. 'Are you sure it's them?'

'They're calling it a burglary gone wrong on the news but the report said he'd been tortured, which seems like too much of a coincidence to me.'

Mr H's boss sighed. 'This is a real problem. We can't lose our man. Not until we've found out what he knows.'

'What do you want me to do?'

'Call the house where they're holding him. Tell them to sedate him and take him away for a few days where they can lay low. But sort it. And sort it soon. And get that bloody psychotherapist to work a bit faster. We need that information.'

Mr H was a fixer. He had good contacts; he got things done; and best of all, he didn't worry too much about who got hurt in the process. It made his services very expensive and, luckily for him, his boss had very deep pockets. But he also knew that all that would count for nothing if he messed up on something as important as this. He needed to make a lot of new plans very fast. But first he needed to get the house evacuated.

The mobile reception out on the coast was awful so he stubbed out his cigar and called the landline, waiting while it rang and rang and rang.

He looked at his watch: 7.30 p.m. Someone should have been there. Taking a deep breath, willing himself to stay calm, he called again.

But there was still no answer.

Four

I awoke with a sudden start.

I was lying on my back staring up at a darkening sky, the final orange glow of the sun just inside my field of vision. For a few seconds I was completely disorientated before I finally realized where I was. I looked at my watch. Eight o'clock. Jesus, I must have been out for three hours. I hadn't been sleeping well lately and I guessed I was just making up for it. I'd been dreaming too. Short, dramatic bursts of activity that might have been memories. And then again might not have been. It was very hard to tell.

Below me I could hear the sound of the sea lapping against the rocks, and the occasional cry of one of the seagulls that lined the cliffs on this coast. But there was no sign of Tom anywhere.

I tried to remember the dreams and compartmentalize them for later analysis, but the effort was too much and I gave up as other thoughts came into play. I was cold, and I was hungry. And frightened of being alone. Whatever their motives, Jane and Tom were the only people looking out for me right now and I had a sudden urge to be back in the warmth of the house eating a decent meal. I'd take whatever flak they threw at me and examine my admittedly limited options after that.

But first I had to climb to the top of this cliff in poor light. I stared up, thinking it looked a pretty scary prospect. If I fell again, I probably wouldn't be so lucky next time, and it was a long way down to the sea. But the need to get home was so powerful that I started up it without hesitation.

Fifteen minutes later, the house loomed in front of me. It was a beautiful place, built from local stone, and surrounded on all sides by well-tended lawns. It might have been in need of modernization both inside and out but, even so, it still possessed a certain grandeur. Both floors were lit up and the curtains were drawn in all the windows, but there was no sign of anyone.

I didn't own a key – Jane had always said there was no need – so I went round the back of the house and peered through the window into the kitchen. The lights were on but the room was empty and there were no used pans or crockery left over from dinner, which meant they were probably out trying to track me down. Unfortunately, I had no way of contacting them. They both had mobile phones but, needless to say, I didn't. We'd talked about getting me one in case I ever got lost but, like so many things round here, no one had ever quite got round to doing it.

The back door was unlocked, however, and I stepped inside, wondering how I was going to do this. There was no point going in silently like some naughty schoolboy. I was a man after all, and I hadn't actually done anything wrong. So I called out Jane's name as I walked through the kitchen, trying to sound as jaunty as possible, as if me disappearing like this was the most natural thing in the world.

I heard footsteps and a second later a woman I didn't know appeared in the doorway. She looked like one of those lean, fit Californian women who populated the TV programmes I watched. She had an athletic figure, golden, sun-kissed skin, and naturally blonde hair tied back in a ponytail. It was no surprise that when she started speaking her accent was unmistakably American.

'You must be Jane's brother, Matt,' she said with a big, confident smile as she came towards me and put out a hand. She must have seen the confusion on my face because she immediately added, 'I'm Pen, an old friend of hers from college. She didn't tell me her brother was so hot.'

I must have been vain in my past life because that part got me straight away. I smiled back as we shook hands, thinking I liked this girl already.

'We're just in the lounge,' she continued. 'I'm sorry, I'm a bit of a prankster. I wanted to give you a shock. Jane says you deserve it, running away like that this afternoon. I think you scared her. Did she tell you I was coming tonight?' Pen didn't stop talking as she led me across the hallway to the lounge door, and I was thinking there was a real charisma about this girl and maybe, if she was single, it would be nice to get to know her.

It only began to dawn on me that something wasn't quite right when she opened the door and moved aside to let me go first, as if she owned the place.

Which was when I saw Jane.

The Final Minute

At least I think it was Jane. It wasn't that easy to tell. The woman I was looking at was sitting in a chair in the middle of the room facing the door. She'd been bound to the chair with black duct tape and her head was slumped forward. She was wearing a navy blue towelling robe that looked vaguely familiar and did a good job of camouflaging the worst of the blood: all but one of the fingers on her left hand were missing. A few feet away, lying on his side next to the TV in just a pair of nuthugging briefs, was Tom. There were two holes in his back, thick blood trailing from each one like tears, and more blood caking the hair on the back of his head.

I took in all this in the space of a split second, and then I felt something hard and metallic being pushed into the base of my skull and the pretty American woman called Pen hissed, 'Inside,' giving me a hard shove.

As I stumbled in, trying to make sense of what I was seeing, I caught movement out of the corner of my eye and the next second I received a single hard blow to the side of my head, which sent me sprawling into a chaise longue. The initial pain immediately dissipated, replaced by a sense of shock as the adrenalin flooded my body. My vision blurred as I sat back up, then settled as I saw the man who'd hit me for the first time. He was huge. A man mountain dressed all in black, with big dark eyes that watched me coldly, like a lizard inspecting prey. I was nothing to him and he was letting me know it.

In front of me, Pen picked up a crumpled apron from behind one of the chairs and put it on. It was white and liberally spattered with fresh blood. Then she pulled on gloves and screwed a silencer to the end of her pistol, before turning to the big man. 'OK, let's find out what he knows.'

31

The big man reached down and yanked me to my feet, grabbing me in a headlock so I was facing his accomplice.

I could just about see Jane's corpse, and I felt an overwhelming sense of sadness. She'd seemed so alive such a short time ago, and now she was gone. The woman who'd looked after me these past two months. The closest person I had in the world.

'You're sad about your sister,' said Pen. 'Don't be. She's not your sister. She didn't even know you before you had your accident. But I think you guessed that, didn't you? This is all a set-up. You, her, the guy who's meant to be nursing you. You're being kept here, like you're in storage. Do you want to know why? Because I can tell you if you do.'

I took a deep breath. The man's grip was strong, and my head was throbbing like hell, but I was as alert now as I could ever remember. 'Yes,' I said. 'I do.'

'Good. You cooperate with us and I'll tell you everything. But I'm going to be completely honest with you here, Matt, because it's easier that way. Tonight's the last night of your life. There's nothing we can do about that. You know too much.'

Which was an irony if ever I'd heard one. 'I don't know anything,' I told her, trying, with not much in the way of success, to sound as calm as possible. 'I can't remember a damn thing about my life before here. You know about my accident, so you should know that.'

'I know all about you, Matt. Jane and I have been having a long chat. She didn't want to talk at first. Understandably, her first loyalty's to her employer.'

'Who's her employer? I need to know as much as I can. That way maybe I can help you.'

'But she talked in the end,' Pen continued, ignoring my question completely. 'Because everyone does. We've all got a threshold, beyond which we simply give in. You're going to give in tonight, Matt. You're going to tell us everything you know – because I suspect you know a lot more than you're letting on.'

I started to tell her I was happy to give in straight away but a huge hand was clamped over my mouth.

She put a finger to her lips. 'Shh. I'm going to make you an offer, Matt. Answer my questions quickly and honestly, and it'll all be over in the blink of an eye. All the confusion and pain of this life will disappear, and you can finally sleep.'

Her words took on a hypnotic quality and for a moment I could relate to what she was saying. An end to this continuous living nightmare. Sleep.

But no. I still had too many questions.

'Or you can die choking and bleeding, covered in snot, begging for the agony to stop. Like this.' She grabbed Jane's head by her hair and lifted it up, while the big guy yanked my head round so I had to look.

But it wasn't Jane I was looking at. It was a torn bloody doll. I wanted to throw up when I saw what they'd done to her eye. And suddenly I was absolutely terrified.

She lifted her phone and pointed it at my face, and I realized she was filming me. 'So, question one,' she said. 'And the most important one of all. Where are the bodies?'

I swallowed, fear pulsing through me in intense, crippling waves. 'I don't know what you're talking about. I really don't. Whose bodies?'

She smiled, but she didn't look so pretty now. There was

a cruelty in the way her lips curled up at the ends. 'I think you know whose bodies we're talking about. You might have been able to fool these people' – she gestured in the direction of Tom's and Jane's corpses – 'but I'm a very different proposition.'

'I'm telling you the truth, I swear it. I remember absolutely nothing before the accident.'

Except now I did remember something.

Something I didn't want to admit to anyone.

Pen shrugged. 'We'll soon find out.' She put the gun down on one of the chairs and picked up a small, very sharp knife that looked like it would have no trouble removing a finger. Or an eye. She went over to Jane, slashed the tape binding her to the chair in one swift, savage movement, then yanked her out of the chair and dropped her to the floor as if she was nothing more than a bag of rubbish. She turned to me. 'Your turn.'

I felt my heart lurch in my chest. It was hard to believe that this was happening to me. That I was about to be tortured by a cold-hearted sadistic bitch and her sidekick to extract information I simply didn't have. That very soon I was going to die in agony without ever knowing who I really was.

Which was when I noticed movement behind her. It was Tom. The big lug might have taken a headshot but it had clearly missed his brain. His legs were moving slowly but perceptibly, as if he was waking up, and he was trying to lift his head.

The guy holding me noticed it as well and his grip loosened. 'Shit,' he said aloud.

Pen turned round to see what he was referring to and, grunting something, picked up the gun and went over to where Tom lay.

With her back to me, I knew this was my chance. I either took it or I died. It was that simple.

Without warning, I slammed my head back into the guy holding me. We were pretty much exactly the same height and I connected perfectly with the bridge of his nose. Nothing broke, but he let out a low grunt, and before he had time to right himself, something happened that surprised me: pulling an arm free, I reached round behind, positioned the side of my thumb beneath his nose and pushed upwards with all the power I could muster.

This time he let go of me completely as he struggled to get away from my grip. Turning, I punched him once, very hard, again on the nose; then, before he could regain his balance, I pulled him round so that he was between me and Pen, making myself as difficult a target for her as possible. I caught a brief glimpse of her trying to get a shot in without hitting her accomplice, a startled look on her face, and then I was running in a crouch towards the huge bay window that looked out on to the front lawn.

I dived into it, shoulder first, at the point where the curtains meet, just as a shot rang out with an angry hiss. The window exploded outwards and the next second I landed in the flower-bed, my body crunching on the glass beneath me as I rolled over, trying to get as far from the window as possible. Adrenalin was fuelling me totally now and I was up on my feet in an instant. But there was a carefully honed instinct for survival too – one I'd never realized I had. Somehow I knew not to make a dash straight across the lawn towards the trees because I'd be far too easy a target that way. Instead, I crouched down so I couldn't be seen through the windows and ran round the edge of the house towards the back, counting on the fact that in the confusion they weren't going to know where I was heading. As soon as I was level with the kitchen, I sprinted the short distance across the back lawn and into the trees without looking back.

I kept running, fear and real determination driving me on. Pen had confirmed that Jane wasn't my sister, but the burning question I now had was why had I been set up like this?

Five

I was following the woods round the northern side of the house in the general direction of the road that led off the peninsula when I heard a car starting somewhere off to my right, and I guessed they were trying to cut me off.

I stopped, getting my breath back, and watched through the trees as a car – a big black four-wheel-drive, its headlights off – made its way slowly along the driveway some forty yards away, making very little noise. It was impossible from this distance to see whether there were two people inside it or not, and as I watched it disappeared from view into the woods. The problem now was that it was positioned between me and the mainland. If I were them, I'd have had one person trying to pick up my trail from the house, and the other parking the car and doubling back through the woods to trap me that way. At their widest point the woods were only a hundred yards across, and there weren't that many places to hide. And out here in the middle of nowhere, time was on their side.

Unless . . .

I had an idea. I found a spot among some ferns in a shallow dip behind a tree, where I had a good view in both directions, and lay down flat on my stomach, listening out for sounds of footfalls on the breeze. I was a good fifty yards from the house and well hidden enough that I wasn't going to be seen unless they actually walked into me.

I waited there for twenty minutes, the pain from where the big guy had hit me gradually subsiding to little more than a thick, dull ache, like a hangover. During that time I heard and saw nothing suspicious. So it was clear they weren't trying to catch me in a pincer movement. Which meant they were waiting for me to make my move.

Time might have been on their side, but it was on mine too. I waited another twenty minutes. There was a shallow glass cut on my hand but that was the only obvious injury from my dive through the window. Then again, there was still so much adrenalin pumping through me that I could have been cut in a dozen places and not have felt a thing. I was still shocked. Not only at what had happened to Jane and Tom but also at the way I'd reacted when I'd seen my chance of escape. I hadn't frozen with fear. I'd fought back.

Something else too. More important. I'd known what I was doing. Some deep-seated instincts had taken over and I'd fought like a pro. I felt like I'd had fights like that before, with my life in imminent danger, and yet nothing in my supposed background would have suggested it.

My need to find out who I was became desperate, and I knew where my best bet for information lay. Back in that house. I'd explored it whenever I'd had a chance in the past two months, wanting to discover all I could about my situation, but Jane and Tom had both kept their rooms locked at all times, and I got the feeling that I never found out any more than they wanted me to find out. Now, though, I was free to hunt down anything I could.

Darkness had settled completely now, and the first stars were appearing in the sky, bathing the woods in an unwelcome blue light. Somewhere off in the trees an owl hooted plaintively. Otherwise the night was perfectly silent. I sniffed the cool air, my eyes scanning the undergrowth in both directions, knowing this could be a trap. An inner voice told me to keep waiting. I was a patient man, but there was an urgency about my situation now. It was clear I'd been involved in something major prior to my accident.

Where are the bodies?

Who am I?

I gave it another twenty minutes, figuring that, even with time on their side, Pen and her accomplice had still committed two murders and so couldn't remain here for ever. Then, moving inch by inch, I raised myself up to my full height and stepped out from behind the tree.

Nothing moved. I waited a couple of beats before starting back towards the house, moving slowly and carefully, looking round all the time, knowing that I was taking a huge risk but concluding that in the end what the hell did I have to lose. I had no life. No memory. Two of the three people who knew me were dead, and I'd probably never see Dr Bronson again. It was as if I didn't exist, which should have been a terrible feeling, but it wasn't. With nothing to lose, I suddenly had everything to gain.

I stopped at the edge of the treeline looking towards the kitchen and the rear of the house. It seemed amazing that it was only about an hour earlier that I'd entered the house that way, and in that time my whole world had changed.

If Pen or her accomplice were still in the house, he or she would almost certainly assume I'd come through the kitchen door, as I had last time. It was the only unlocked entrance and the closest to the woods. Deciding not to risk it, I moved slowly through the trees round towards the side of the house, passing the double garage where the cars were kept. Seeing nothing untoward, I ran across the lawn, over to the far lounge window. The curtains were drawn so, keeping to the shadows, I crept round to the window I'd leapt through earlier. My momentum had caused the whole frame to come out and broken glass littered the flowerbed and the grass beyond. Now exposed to the breeze, the curtains billowed a little but didn't give me a view into the room. I looked over my shoulder to check there was no one creeping up behind me, then put my ear close to the fabric and listened.

All was silence.

This was where I was going to have to take a big risk. For all I knew, one of my pursuers could be just the other side of the curtains waiting for me to show my face. I could be dead in the next few seconds. My heart was beating hard in my chest and I had to steady my breathing to prevent it being audible.

Slowly, very slowly, I parted the curtains a few inches. This time I could smell the death in the room. It came at me in a pungent, sour wave, like meat left out to rot in the hot sun, and I had to fight off nausea. I couldn't see the bodies from the angle I was at, but the room looked empty. After taking another look behind me, I parted the curtains a few inches more, lifted my leg over the window sill and climbed inside.

I'd done a good job of being silent, and the carpet beneath my feet was thick enough to muffle my footfalls as I crept further inside.

I looked over at the two corpses. There was a second hole in the back of Tom's head where Pen must have shot him again, just to make sure, and this time he was actually dead. It seemed ironic that he'd saved my life by refusing to die quietly – a fact I was sure would have annoyed him if he'd known anything about it. Still, I felt an odd pang of gratitude.

Jane lay on her side where she'd been pulled from the chair, one arm sprawled behind her in an almost flamboyant gesture. Her gown had fallen open, revealing a full, shapely breast – a sight that looked so wrong against the terrible damage to her face. She'd been a fraud. But why? What had been her motive? I felt a familiar wave of frustration as I moved across the carpet, stopping at the half-open door to look round it.

Which was when I saw Pen.

She was standing in the hallway, leaning against the wall with her back to me, watching the kitchen door, the gun down by her side. As I'd anticipated, she was waiting to see if I'd come in the back way again. Twelve feet separated us, but the hallway floor was polished mahogany and it creaked. If I tried to creep up behind her, I'd never make it.

And then, as I watched, she turned round in my direction.

Thankfully her movement was casual enough to give me time to pull my head back behind the door without being spotted.

I heard her yawn and, as I watched through the narrow half-inch gap between the door and its jamb, she turned back round again, and sighed wearily. Clearly she was tired of waiting around. The problem was, I was just going to have to stay put and keep quiet until she decided I wasn't coming back.

A minute passed. Then two. I considered retreating towards the window and hiding behind the chaise longue where I'd be less exposed if she decided to come back into the room, but before I could make my decision, I heard the crackle of static. Through the gap in the door I could see that Pen had a two-way radio in her free hand.

'I'm not sure how much longer we should give it,' she whispered into it. 'The phone keeps ringing, and that's not a good sign.'

Which was a surprise to me. The landline rarely rang. Once a week at most. The only times I answered, it was people trying to sell me stuff.

I heard a male voice talking back but couldn't hear what he was saying, then she was speaking again. 'OK,' she hissed, 'pick me up in ten minutes.'

She replaced the radio in her jacket and then, without warning, turned and strode into the lounge.

I didn't even have time to be scared. As she came past the door, barely a foot away from me, I shot out of my hiding place, grabbed her gun arm at the wrist with one hand and wrapped my free arm round her neck, my fingers pressing decisively into soft skin. It was as if I was being piloted by my subconscious. She barely had time to grunt before she went limp in my arms. I let her fall to the floor, grabbing the gun at the same time. She lay still and I pointed the gun at her head, my finger tensing on the trigger as a cold rage bubbled up inside me.

My first instinct was to kill her, but as I looked at her lying motionless on the floor, her eyes closed, her expression peaceful, my rage dissipated. I patted her down, quickly locating the knife she'd used on Jane in her jacket pocket. I took it, along with the radio, but couldn't find the duct tape. I had no idea how long she'd be unconscious for. For all I knew she could have been faking, but I felt a lot safer now I had a gun. Her partner was coming to pick her up in ten minutes – about nine now – so I was going to have to hurry.

I removed the batteries from the radio and threw it across the room, then raced up the stairs, no longer bothering to stay quiet. Straight away, I saw that Jane's bedroom door was half open. She and Tom had clearly been caught unawares by their killers and, given the fact they were half naked, it was a fair bet that they'd been in bed.

My suspicions were confirmed the moment I stepped inside. The bed, a giant four-poster that looked like it could sleep five comfortably, was unmade, the sheets chaotic, and there were clothes and shoes strewn across the floor where passion had clearly got the better of them. Even after everything else that had happened today, the sight made me jealous. I had many vague recollections of being intimate with women. But I couldn't picture any of their faces. Nor could I remember anything about any of them. They were like ghosts. I knew I'd enjoyed their nakedness though, and yearned for it again.

I picked up Tom's jeans and rifled through the pockets, finding a wallet and a mobile phone. I checked the wallet. A hundred and eighty pounds in cash, a couple of credit cards and a driving licence in the name of Robert Thomas Berman, with a photo of Tom looking suitably sour-faced. According to the licence he lived in South London, in the SE24 postcode. It struck me then that I'd never known his last name, and had never bothered asking. Ours wasn't that kind of relationship.

I turned my attention to Jane's clothes and started going through them. Her jeans pockets were empty but her handbag was on the dressing table and when I went through that, I got hold of another mobile phone and a purse. This time there was no cash but there was a driving licence and credit cards in the name of a Ms Alison Wolfrey. The address on the licence was London again.

I shoved everything of value into my pockets and then started on the drawers in the bedside table, quickly finding the keys to Jane's BMW convertible, which she kept locked in the garage, presumably in case I ever got an urge to take it for a spin.

I was just forcing them into a pocket when the home phone rang, its sound blasting through the house. There was a handset on the bedside table, just next to my ear, and the ringing startled me. Holding the gun, I checked the landing and the stairs to make sure Pen wasn't creeping up on me, then closed the bedroom door and went over to the phone. I stared at it as it continued to ring then, taking a deep breath, I picked up.

'Hello,' I growled, trying to emulate Tom's brusque, gravelly tones.

'Tom?' snapped a man's voice in a neutral, educated accent. He sounded stressed.

'Yeah.'

'Put Alison on.'

'She's not here.'

'Where the hell is she? She's not answering her phone.'

'She's out walking,' I told him, growing naturally into my role as a liar, although not necessarily a mimic. 'You know the reception's not very good round here.'

'And where have you been? I've been phoning this number for the last hour.'

'I was outside too.'

'Our man's still safe and sound, isn't he?'

I guessed that 'our man' meant me. I almost said, 'Yes I am, and by the way, who the hell am I?' But I didn't. 'Yeah, he's still here.'

'Get him out of there. Now.'

I glanced over towards the door, keeping the gun trained on it. 'What's going on?'

'The location's been compromised. Don't ask me any more questions. Grab our man, get him out of there, and set fire to the place. We don't want to leave any evidence anyone was ever there. Understand?'

There were a million more questions I wanted to ask but I knew that now wasn't the time. 'Sure. I'm on it.'

'If you can't find Alison, leave her. We can find her later. And be quick. We haven't got much time.'

He rang off and I put down the phone, going over what he'd just said. I remembered it pretty much word for word. The irony was that I had a great short-term memory, but on its own, it wasn't going to help me find out why I was being treated like some hugely valuable commodity – a man with priceless information I didn't even know myself.

I was still pondering that as I approached the bedroom door, gun in hand.

And that was when I smelled it.

Smoke. It seemed like someone was already ahead of the man on the phone in deciding to torch the place.

I yanked open the door and jumped to one side, just in case someone was waiting there to ambush me. But the landing was empty and the air acrid. I could hear the angry crackle of burning wood as I ran over to the top of the stairs. Smoke was pouring down the hallway from the direction of the front door, while flames gouted through the open lounge door. Unfortunately, there was also a thick black cloud of smoke billowing out of the kitchen as well, effectively trapping me up here. I cursed myself for leaving Pen alone down there. She must have regained consciousness and, rather than tackle me now that I had her gun, decided to burn me alive.

Already the smoke was making it hard to breathe, and Jane's house was all wood panelling, so it was going to go up like a tinderbox.

Putting a hand over my mouth, I ran back to my bedroom. At least I knew I could get out that way. I shut the door behind me, cutting off the worst of the smoke, and went over to the window I'd sneaked out of earlier. Someone had been up here and shut it, so I opened it again quietly. I took a quick look out into the night and didn't see anything untoward, so unscrewed the gun's silencer and chucked it on the bed, before shoving the gun down the front of my jeans, saying a silent prayer for it not to go off accidentally, and climbing out the window, leaving my bedroom and the only life I really knew behind, for ever.

This time I didn't hang about but dropped immediately to the ground, rolling over in the grass and gritting my teeth silently against the pain of the impact.

Still I didn't see anyone. I could make for the safety of the trees and wait for my pursuers to leave, because they were going to have to now they'd set the house on fire. Even in an isolated place like the peninsula the fire would be seen for miles around, and already the flames were beginning to take hold. But the thing was, I didn't want to be anywhere near this place when the police and fire brigade turned up, because I'd have a lot of very awkward questions to answer and no real means of answering them. It seemed best then, now that I had the keys to Jane's BMW, to make a getaway on wheels. I knew I could drive. I had plenty of vague memories of being behind the wheel of a car and I'd got Jane to let me have a go in the BMW with her in the passenger seat a couple of weeks back (even though she'd taken a lot of persuading). I could remember what to do perfectly.

I got to my feet, pulled the gun from the front of my jeans and moved across the grass in the direction of the detached garage on the other side of the house, listening out for any signs of danger. As I rounded the corner, the garage appeared in front of me twenty feet away. I looked round quickly, then ran across to the door, keys in my spare hand, unable to stop my shoes from crunching on the gravel. I found the right one, unlocked the door and, as quietly as possible, lifted it up on to its runners. At that moment, I didn't want to look round, just in case someone was creeping up on me, gun in hand, ready to put a bullet in my head. It was almost better not to know.

But I did look.

And saw the big man in the shadows of the burning house, maybe fifteen yards away. In his black clothes he was almost invisible in the darkness and smoke, but it was definitely him. And he was definitely pointing a gun at me, his arm perfectly steady. I couldn't see Pen anywhere, but knew she wouldn't be far away.

'Stay where you are and drop the gun,' he called out, because he knew I'd seen him and I assumed he needed to get closer to get a better shot at me. This was the first time he'd spoken and, like Pen, he had an American accent.

For a second I didn't move. Then, as he took a step forward and called out the words 'He's here' over his shoulder, I leapt into the welcome darkness of the garage, swinging the gun up behind me and giving the trigger a hard squeeze. The gun kicked as I fired three times in his general direction, hoping to put him off balance, before fumbling for the car key. I knew Jane pressed a button to turn off the central locking but it was hard to tell which one it was in the darkness and I could hear rapid footsteps on the gravel.

I ducked down behind the car as a shot whistled past before ricocheting off the back wall. I pressed one button on the key, then another, and the lights on the BMW flashed. A second shot flew through the garage, dangerously close to my head, so using the car as cover I fired off another shot towards my attacker, forcing him to jump to one side, temporarily out of sight.

I threw myself inside the car. The driver's seat was way too far forward and my knees were virtually hitting my chest, but that was the least of my worries. I turned on the engine, yanked the car into drive, thanking God that at least part of my memory was working, then accelerated out of the garage, grabbing the gun with my free hand and keeping my head down, tensing for the inevitable ambush.

It came almost immediately. As I shoved my foot flat on the floor and the tyres ripped up gravel, I saw the guy loom to my left, gun outstretched, already firing. Glass broke, and I actually felt the heat from the bullet as it passed just in front of my face. More bullets hissed through the car's interior, their sound partially muffled by the silencer on his gun, but I had no time to be scared. Instead, I opened up with my own gun, the noise of its retorts tearing through my ears. He was barely ten feet away from me and he was a big target, so even in a moving car it was hard for me to miss.

And I didn't. I wasn't sure how many times I hit him, but I saw him fall, and then I was turning away and concentrating on where I was driving.

That was when I saw Pen running out towards me from the side of the house. Her face was a mask of pure rage, and she was holding something in both hands. I just had time to process that it was a stone statue and then she was hurling it at the windscreen with a force I really wasn't expecting. I swung the wheel away from her reflexively but the statue still hit the windscreen on the passenger side, smashing a fist-sized hole in the glass before bouncing off across the bonnet.

The car skidded off the driveway and on to the lawn, and I swung it round as I came to the front of the house, giving Pen as wide a berth as possible, before accelerating towards the trees and the mainland. The car my assailants had come here in was directly in front of me, blocking the exit, so I drove through a flowerbed to avoid it, then slowed up, lowered my driver's-side window, leaned out with the gun and put a bullet in their front tyre, grinning as it deflated with a fart-like hiss. I inched forward and pulled the trigger again, aiming at the rear tyre this time. But nothing happened. I was out of bullets. No matter. I'd slowed them down enough to put some miles between us. The gun was no use to me now so I wiped the handle with my shirt, remembering what the criminals did in all the cop shows I watched (or maybe from experience, I still wasn't quite sure), and dropped it out of the window.

In my rear-view mirror, I could see Pen running round the front of the house, holding a gun herself this time, and moving at a good pace. I slammed my foot on the accelerator as she pulled the trigger, tearing up some more of the flowerbed before coming back on to the drive, and within seconds I'd put thirty, then forty yards between us, and then the woods opened up to greet me and I knew that, at least for now, I was safe.

There was something else too.

I felt good.

Six

Pen de Souza screamed a curse into the clear night sky as she watched the car, and their target, disappear into woodland at the end of the driveway.

There was no point trying to follow him. She'd seen him put the bullet in the tyre. She cursed again, knowing she should have put a bullet in his kneecap the moment he'd first walked in the door. After all, they'd only needed him to answer one question: 'Where are the bodies?'

Neither she nor her partner, Tank, had any idea of the identity of the bodies in question, nor did they want to know. In their line of business, knowing too much made you dangerous to the client. They had been tasked to get exact coordinates of the bodies' location, make a mental note of them (not write anything down), and when it was established that the target was telling the truth, kill him.

And they'd failed on all counts. Pen felt the bitter taste of it in her mouth. She wasn't used to failure. In the five years she and Tank had worked together, no target had ever escaped them. The combination of planning and guile they used had ensured that. With her pretty, girl-next-door looks and ready smile, Pen could disarm the most suspicious of people – men and women – while Tank provided the brute force to back her up. Yet tonight it hadn't worked, and Pen had been humiliated when the target had caught her off-guard – *her!* And in a choke-hold of all things! Thankfully, he'd been foolish enough to leave her alive and unsecured, which would end up being a mistake on his part. Far worse, though, was what he'd done to Tank. Her man.

She turned and ran back past the burning house to where Tank was sitting up on the grass, rubbing his chest. 'Are you OK, babe?' she asked, crouching down beside him and putting a hand on his shoulder, thanking Lady Luck with all her heart that he'd been wearing a flak jacket. She didn't know how she would ever cope if she lost him.

Tank nodded slowly, giving her a tight smile. 'Yeah, I'm all right. He got me twice in the chest – good shots too, especially for a guy moving. I'm lucky the jacket held from that range. I'm guessing you didn't get him.'

She shook her head. 'He got away. And he put a bullet in one of our tyres.'

Tank grunted. 'The guy's no idiot. He didn't panic, he knows some good moves, and he can shoot straight under pressure. I didn't think he'd be that good.'

'Right now, I'm just glad you're all right.' Pen put her arms round him and hugged him close.

'I'm always all right, baby, you know that.'

He kissed her hard on the mouth and she kissed him back, her breathing quickening, because he always did that to her. She was thankful that he didn't blame her for the plan they'd used. It had been her idea to lure the target into the room with the two people they'd already killed, because she preferred to interrogate subjects when they were terrified but otherwise uninjured: it tended to be easier to get a proper answer out of them that way. Tank hadn't been so keen, but he'd gone along with it, which was one of the many things she loved about him: he took responsibility for his actions, which was not a trait she'd found in many men over the years. Except this time the plan had backfired, and Pen swore to herself that she wouldn't make the same mistake twice.

Reluctantly, she broke away from the kiss and they both got to their feet, walking hand in hand back to the stolen Shogun they'd arrived in.

'We're not going to get him now, are we?' said Tank, pulling the spare wheel from the boot, along with a box containing the equipment to change it with.

'Oh, we'll get him,' said Pen coldly.

She looked back over her shoulder towards the house. Flames were sprouting from the windows now, and the fire was lighting up the night sky. It was a beautiful sight but one that, even out here in the middle of nowhere, was going to attract the attention of the authorities soon enough.

Pen took out the wheel brace and gave Tank a big smile. 'And when we do, I'm going to tear him apart limb from limb for what he did to you.'

Seven

There was no way I could drive too far in a car riddled with bullet holes. The windscreen was still just about holding, but a spider's web of cracks had spread out from the hole where the statue had hit, and I had a feeling it wasn't going to last much longer. Also, I really didn't want to draw attention to myself. I'd just shot a man, and left behind a burning house with two corpses inside. So I needed to come up with some kind of plan.

I was back on the mainland now, driving through a mix of fields and patchy woodland. The land here was still very rural, with only the occasional house popping up on either side of the road. I'd been down this way a handful of times when I'd gone clothes shopping with Jane in Pembroke, the nearest major town to the house, and knew there was a village somewhere along this road. A couple of minutes later it appeared on my left-hand side, a sprinkling of brick-built houses – some rendered grey, some white – nestled in the faint copper glow of streetlamps. Civilization. It filled me with a relief I really shouldn't have been feeling. I was lost and alone. I had no past, and as a direct result, I had no future. I could hand myself into the authorities, but what would that mean? Life in an institution. Or maybe even life in prison if they didn't believe my story of what had happened back at the house. I couldn't tolerate that. I had to find out who I was.

But first things first. There was a pub across the road from the village, its sign lit up and swinging gently in the sea breeze. I turned in and drove round the back, parking the car in a dark corner under a large tree.

I sat back in the seat and closed my eyes, breathing slowly and steadily, allowing myself to calm down. My head still ached dully from where I'd been hit, but I hadn't sustained any real damage. My hands had stopped shaking too, which surprised me. I'd almost died only a matter of minutes ago, and at least one of the people trying to kill me was still out there, but the shock I should have been experiencing simply wasn't kicking in.

I thought back to the dreams I'd had when I was asleep on that exposed ledge. Visions of terrible violence; of staring into the eyes of men I was trying to kill, and who were trying to kill me, our faces so close we breathed in each other's sweat; of being held down in a cold, dark room while different men stood above me, with cleavers and axes, and mad, terrifying expressions, like monsters in a child's nightmare. And that big, strange house from earlier dreams, with its marble floors and abstract artwork on the walls, and its corpses and dying women littering the rooms and hallway . . .

I could conjure up every one of those images, and the thing was, they felt real. As if they'd definitely happened. Scattered pieces of a nightmarish puzzle that seemed to be my past life. Yet I was supposed to have been a police officer. Police officers didn't get involved in the things I was dreaming about. No one did.

I sat in the car another ten minutes. During that time I heard two separate sets of sirens coming past on the road, heading in the direction of the peninsula, and when I looked out of the car window I thought I could see a faint orange glow on the horizon. It was then I realized that I needed a drink. I still had Tom's wallet with his money, and by now Pen and her buddy would have made themselves scarce. It might not have been the best use of the cash I had, but after what I'd been through that day, I figured I deserved a cold beer.

The moment I walked in the door, I knew that in my past life I'd been a pub man. The bitter smell of the hops, the steady buzz of conversation, the clink of glasses on wood, the booze-fuelled laughter. It all felt so familiar. I'd done up my jacket and tried to tidy myself up, but I still looked far too much like a man who'd got himself into trouble recently, although I doubted whether too many of the drinkers would guess that I'd almost been killed at least twice tonight.

It had just turned 9.30 and the pub was busy. The punters were mainly male and of all ages, ranging from the barely legal to the barely alive, with a sprinkling of wives and girlfriends mixed in. Most of them looked my way as I walked over to the bar, and some blatantly stared. I ignored all of them and ordered a pint of Foster's because, just like I knew how to handle a car, I instinctively knew that this was my drink of choice in a pub.

The barman was red-faced with a near-white handlebar moustache that made him look like a walrus. He inspected me like I was some kind of alien life form masquerading as a human being. 'English,' he said dismissively, and I wasn't sure whether he meant it as an insult or a question.

I took it as a question. 'Yeah,' I said, looking him in the eye. 'I guess I am.'

He turned away without another word and poured the pint, and I paid him with cash from Tom's wallet before moving to the end of the bar as far out of the way as possible and taking a long gulp of the beer. It tasted good. I'd drunk beer back in the house a couple of times (although Jane had always discouraged it, claiming it wouldn't be good for my recovery), but it tasted a lot better out of a tap. Or maybe it was simply the sense of freedom I was tasting.

There was a folded, crumpled newspaper on the corner of the bar. It didn't look like it belonged to anyone so I picked it up and leafed through it. Jane never kept papers in the house. She always referred to them as media propaganda, so I tended to get what news I got from the TV – not that I'd been paying much attention of late. The pages were filled with stories of disaster, murder, cheap politics and the drunken antics of young, strangely artificial-looking celebrities I didn't recognize. It was only when I got to the features section towards the back that I came across something that caught my eye. It was an interview with a woman called Tina Boyd. There was a photo of her sitting behind a neat desk looking at the camera. She was what you'd describe as striking – late thirties, dark hair cut just above the shoulders, good-looking, with nicely defined cheekbones. If it hadn't been for her eyes, I'd have had her down as an actress or businesswoman, but there was a hardened glint in them that gave her away as someone who'd seen too much.

Having been drawn to her photo, I read the article. She talked about her career as a detective in various branches of the Met, during which time she'd been kidnapped, shot twice, come under suspicion for murder, and earned herself the nickname the Black Widow because her colleagues seemed to have a habit of dying around her. Luckily for them it seemed she'd left the force for good now and was working as a licensed private detective in London. She spoke briefly about the case she was currently working on, the hunt for a twenty-eight-year-old woman who'd been missing for almost six months, and appealed for help in finding her. At the bottom of the article was a small photo of the missing woman's face. She was blandly pretty, with perfect features that seemed to have been taken from an artist's mould, but a mould that had clearly been used plenty of times before, because she looked exactly the same as all the small-time female celebs who peppered the rest of the paper. But there was also something familiar about her.

I squinted in the dim light of the bar, bringing the paper closer to my face. I stared at the photo for a good five seconds, wondering if I was mistaken or not.

But I wasn't.

I took a deep breath and steadied myself, finding it difficult to believe what I was seeing. Because the woman in the photo was one of the two women in my recurring dream, the one lying naked and dead on the bed. Which simply confirmed for me something I already suspected. That it wasn't a dream.

It was a memory.

*

There were details about Tina Boyd's website at the bottom of the article which I ripped from the page, shoving the piece of paper in my pocket. Now at least I had a plan of action. I needed to find Tina Boyd and speak to her. If she was as good a detective as the article suggested, maybe she could help to unlock my memories.

But, as I stood there, oblivious to the noise of the conversations around me, I wondered if this was really such a good move because I was becoming increasingly worried about what I might find out. I remembered Pen's question back at the house as she'd pointed the gun at me: 'Where are the bodies?' Did I really want to know? And was it me who'd killed them?

'Fancy buying me a drink?' said a voice beside me. It was husky and female, with the hint of a slur, and accompanied by a heady smell of perfume.

I turned to see a larger lady with thick, lustrous curls of black hair, a bust that was pushing the tight top she was wearing to the absolute limits, and way too much make-up.

'I haven't seen you round here before,' she continued, leaning just a little too hard on the bar. 'What's your name?'

Good question. I didn't even know that for sure. 'Matt.'

'I'm Lucy. I live across the road.' She seemed to notice the mark on my face where I'd been hit by the big guy and ran a finger gently along it in a pretty suggestive manner. As she leaned in closer, I could smell the booze on her breath, and something else not quite so pleasant. 'What happened to your face?'

'I hit it on a door earlier,' I said, leaning back.

A part of me was tempted to keep talking to her. I liked the idea of some female company, and wasn't really too bothered where it came from, but I could see a group of three guys in their twenties staring over at me with less than friendly looks on their faces. Another siren blared outside as the vehicle it belonged to came past, and the pub was temporarily illuminated by a flashing blue light. It was time to put some more distance between me and the burning house.

'Come on lover, how about that drink?' she said, with what I think was meant to be a sultry pout.

'Another time,' I said, finishing my drink.

Her expression darkened. 'Not good enough for you, am I?'

'It's not that. I just need to be somewhere, that's all.'

'Well fuck you then.' She turned away and banged her glass on the counter to get the barman's attention.

The three young guys were looking at me with downright hostility now, so I decided to beat a retreat. There was a payphone in the corridor outside the main bar with a notice board pinned with business cards just above it. I found the number for a local taxi service and dialled it. There was no way I could risk driving Jane's car to Pembroke Station, not when it was peppered with bullet holes and with part of the windscreen missing.

An old guy answered on about the tenth ring and I told him where I was and where I wanted to go. He sounded like he'd just woken up but said he was just down the road and would be at the pub in a few minutes.

As I put down the phone, I heard the door to the main bar open and the three young guys who'd been staring at me emerged. The one in the front was the biggest. He was wearing a tight T-shirt and hooded top and looked like he spent a lot of time in the gym.

'What are you doing in here?' he demanded, jutting out his chin as he came towards me.

'Nothing,' I said. 'I'm just leaving.'

'You insulted our mate in there. Who do you think you are, eh? Strolling in here like you own the place.'

As he drew closer, his friends crowding in behind him like school kids egging him on, I stepped back and noticed that I'd automatically raised my arms so my hands were resting on my chest, palms inward. It wasn't an aggressive gesture, but it was clearly a defensive one.

'Look, I don't want any trouble,' I told him, and started to back away.

'Well fuck off then,' he said, coming towards me.

I didn't like turning my back on them but figured it would be best just to leave as quickly as possible. When I walked out the door into the cool night air, though, I heard them coming out behind me.

'See, you're a fucking coward as well, running away like that,' continued the big guy.

As the adrenalin coursed through me, my mind computed the various possibilities. Out in the open, they'd be able to come at me simultaneously from three sides. Even if I was in top condition, I wouldn't stand much of a chance; tired, out of shape, and having already had more than my fair share of injuries today, I'd be annihilated.

So I swung round fast, while he was still in the doorway with his mates behind him, and punched him twice in the face with two lightning-fast jabs that surprised me as much as him. He fell back against the guy behind him, but I didn't stop. Instead, an intense, all-consuming rage seemed to sweep across me, and before he could recover I'd driven him back inside the building and was all over him, landing a rapid succession of blows.

He went down, and his mates both jumped out of the way as he crashed to the floor. I could see he was already beaten. His eyes were vacant and blood was pouring from his mangled nose, but the rage didn't leave me. I was loving this sudden feeling of power. I wanted to hurt this bastard. To make him pay. So I took a step back and kicked him hard in the face, my shoe connecting perfectly with the underside of his chin, shunting him along the floor.

Now he was no longer moving and, just as quickly as it had arrived, the rage left me, and I stood there panting with exertion. The whole attack – because that was what it pretty much had been, an attack – had lasted no more than ten seconds and been carried out in complete silence as I'd channelled my anger as effectively as possible, like I knew exactly what I was doing.

I turned my gaze on the other two, neither of whom had made any move to intervene, and who both suddenly looked very pale. 'Either of you two want any trouble?' I asked.

They both shook their heads.

'Good. Then get your friend some help, and be careful who you pick your fights with next time.'

This time they both nodded.

'Who the fuck are you?' asked one of them in tones that came dangerously close to awe.

'I have no idea,' I told him, and left them to it, thinking that I might have made a mistake by drawing attention to myself like that. It was becoming clear to me I had a pretty vicious temper when provoked, and it was something I was going to have to learn to control, and fast.

Thankfully, when I walked outside this time, the taxi had

pulled up. I clambered in the back, gave him a friendly smile, and told him my destination.

As he pulled away, I looked back over my shoulder and saw a group of irate and shocked-looking locals pour out of the pub door into the car park. Then, just as quickly, they disappeared as we turned a corner.

It was time to find Tina Boyd.

Eight

'I'm doing everything I can to find your daughter, Mr Donaldson,' said Tina Boyd, leaning forward in her office chair and looking the man opposite her directly in the eye so he would know she wasn't trying to avoid any of the difficult questions. It was only nine a.m. but Alan Donaldson had been waiting for her when she'd arrived that morning with her regular takeaway double espresso and blueberry muffin from the coffee shop round the corner. He was half an hour early. Tina had been hoping to enjoy breakfast in peace in her cramped little office, as she did every morning, but she hadn't kicked up a fuss or told him to come back later, as she might have done if he'd been anyone else (client or not).

But Alan Donaldson was a broken man. You could see it in the haunted, pained expression in his eyes, in the way the brightness seemed to have left them; in the greying pallor of his skin and the hollowness of his cheeks. He must have been handsome once,

Tina was sure of that. There were traces of the easy charmer about him, and Tina had known a few of them in her time. His face was lean and sculpted with the remnants of a strong, well-defined jaw, and he still had the tall, confident bearing that suggested a man used to getting his own way.

But things hadn't worked out for him. Exactly one week earlier he'd come in to see her and explained how, fifteen years earlier, his wife, tired of his constant infidelities, had thrown him out of the family home. Donaldson hadn't wanted to go. In fact he'd begged to stay, but his wife had had enough and so, conceding defeat, he'd moved in with the girl he'd been seeing. This had angered his wife no end and, according to his version of events, she'd turned his two children, Ben and Lauren, against him, and his relationship with them had become steadily more distant.

Both kids had ended up going off the rails, although Ben had managed to get himself back on track, go to university and get a law degree, before emigrating to Canada. He hadn't spoken to his father in ten years. Lauren, though, the apple of her father's eye (his own description), had gone from one bad relationship to another, her good looks meaning she had no shortage of suitors. She'd had affairs with married men, used them until she grew bored; had been used herself by boyfriends whose abuse of her sometimes bordered on the physical; had fallen in with all the wrong sorts of people, and eventually moved to London. Donaldson had tried to keep in touch but he couldn't bear to see what was happening to his daughter, and her anger towards him was palpable. She'd make arrangements to see him but be out when he turned up at her flat; she'd ignore his calls. Eventually they'd lost touch.

Donaldson now lived alone, the last of his girlfriends long since gone. His ex-wife – the children's mother – had died three years ago. Since then, he himself had been diagnosed with advanced prostate cancer, and was a man desperate to make amends and find peace with his children. Except there was a major problem. Ben was still refusing to speak to his father and, more worryingly, Lauren had gone missing.

That was where Tina came in. She was a private detective with a high profile, although not too much in the way of results as yet, but Donaldson clearly had faith because he'd hired her to find Lauren, and told her that money was no object.

No object or not, Tina wasn't a miracle worker. She felt sorry for Donaldson. He'd been responsible for his own downfall but, even so, she wanted to do whatever she could to reunite him with his daughter, which was why she'd done the interview in the *Mail* the other day, insisting that they focus at least part of it on Lauren's disappearance and publish a photo of her.

'I'm working on a number of leads at the moment,' she told him, 'but it's never easy finding someone if they don't want to be found.'

'I understand,' said Donaldson, trying to keep the disappointment out of his voice.

'Did you know that your daughter changed her name by deed poll just over a year ago?'

'Really?' He looked shocked. 'I know she's still very angry with me but I didn't think she'd resort to changing her name. What does she call herself now?'

'Lauren Marano.'

He looked puzzled. 'I don't know where she got that from.'

Tina shrugged. 'Maybe she thought it sounded exotic. It's

interesting because I've scoured the net to see if I can find any online presence for a Lauren Marano. It's quite an unusual name, but there's no sign of anyone under that name looking like your daughter. And I can't find her under her old name either.'

'But Lauren's always had a Facebook page. She wouldn't let me friend her but I know she had one.'

'She doesn't any more. I've been in contact with Facebook trying to find out whether they've taken down a page used by a Lauren Marano or Donaldson, and when, but so far I haven't had any meaningful response, and they're not obligated to help me.'

'Do you think it's a bad sign that her page isn't up any more?' Donaldson asked uncertainly.

'Not necessarily, although it does make it harder to track down her current whereabouts, especially as I've got no forwarding address from her last place. I've been in contact with all the utility companies trying to track her location down that way but it's slow work.'

'Did you manage to get hold of Ben?'

This was where things got more worrying. 'Yes I did,' Tina answered. 'Ben's been in contact with Lauren periodically over the past three years, but he hasn't spoken to her since the beginning of April. He had a postal address for her but she left there over a year back, around the time she changed her name. Ben's tried the mobile number and the email he's got for her, but the number's out of service, and she hasn't replied to his messages.'

Tina saw the pained look in his eyes. 'Look, Mr Donaldson, it's important not to worry too much yet. Lauren could have just fallen off the radar. People do that all the time. Did you know that more than a hundred thousand people go missing every year in this country? And most of them just turn back up when they're good and ready.'

Donaldson nodded slowly. 'Yes, I did know that. The police were at great pains to point it out to me. But I also know that two thousand of those hundred thousand never turn back up. I'll be honest with you, Tina. I'm very worried about Lauren. She's always been a girl who's easily led, and there are some horrible people out there.'

'I know that as much as anyone,' said Tina, smiling to soften her words.

'I know you do. It's why I came to you in the first place. You don't have children, but I know you care. I trust you to do everything you can to find my daughter.'

Over the years Tina had built up a reputation as a maverick operator, someone prepared not only to bend the rules, but to ignore them entirely if the mood took her. At one time that reputation had been at least partly justified, but she'd changed now, and had no desire to further sully her reputation. Having said that, she was prepared to pull out all the stops to find Lauren because she was a lot more concerned about her than she was letting on. She didn't like the fact that Ben, the one person Lauren had had fairly regular contact with, could no longer get hold of her. Ben was worried too: it had been he who'd initially reported her missing to the police. Tina had spoken to the officer who was supposedly dealing with the case and, though he'd expressed sympathy, he didn't appear to be trying too hard to find her. After all, Lauren was simply one of thousands.

'I'm hopeful the newspaper interview will throw up a few leads,' she told Donaldson now. 'They used the photo you gave me of Lauren in it, and I've had a number of calls from people claiming to know her, so I'm following up on those.' As it happened, Tina had received far fewer calls than she'd have liked, and most of the callers had either been or sounded like cranks. But one had stood out. A young woman called Sheryl had left a message for Tina earlier that morning saying she'd been a friend of Lauren and had information that might be of help. So far Tina hadn't managed to track her down, but at least she represented a possibility. 'I can prepare a full progress report if you like,' she continued.

He managed a smile. 'It's fine. I trust you.'

'You didn't have to come in, you know. I know it's a bit of a journey for you.'

'I prefer to do business face to face. Would you mind if we scheduled another meeting for next week, in case you haven't had any news by then?'

Tina nodded, knowing it would make him feel better. 'Of course.' She put it in the diary and walked with him to the door.

He paused with the door open and looked at her with an expression that looked a lot like sympathy. 'You know, I've had a lot of regrets in my life,' he said. 'There are so many things I'd have done differently. But – and forgive me if I'm speaking out of turn on this – if there's one piece of advice I could impart, it's live your life as you want to, take the opportunities when you see them. Don't wait for life to come to you.'

'Don't worry, I have lived the life I wanted to,' she said, knowing she was lying. 'I'll keep you posted about progress.'

They shook hands and she watched as he walked down the road in the direction of Paddington Station, his gait slow and painful.

Once upon a time he'd been a man with hopes and dreams, but circumstances and age had brought him down, and Tina wondered if she too would end up like that. It was obvious he'd seen the sadness that dwelt in her. Either he was very observant or she needed to learn to hide it better.

She dismissed the thought and lit a cigarette, staring out across the street towards the railway lines and the A40 flyover, with the high-rise blocks of the Warwick Estate looming up behind them. It wasn't an inspiring view. Nothing about her office was particularly inspiring. It was a cramped room on the ground floor of a decaying pre-war terrace in Bayswater about half a mile west of Paddington Station, but it had the advantage of having parking round the back, and it was central. She lived a good forty minutes' drive away on a good day, in a village just inside the M25 near Potters Bar, and in truth she could easily have worked from home. But, for Tina, home was her sanctuary, a place where she shut out the world, and all the darkness within it, and she had no desire to sully her personal space with the work she did. So this arrangement was the next best thing.

She could hear her office phone ringing. She thought about letting it go but knew she couldn't turn down work. So, taking a last drag on the cigarette, she stubbed it in the outside ashtray the building's smokers had clubbed together to buy, then walked back inside.

'Is that Tina Boyd?' asked a man's voice when she picked up.

'Speaking.'

There was a long pause, and Tina wondered if it was another crank caller.

'My name's Matt Barron, and I need you to help me find a killer.'

'You need the police for that, Mr Barron.'

'They're not going to believe my story.'

'Then talk to a lawyer.'

'That's not going to work either. Listen, I know how this sounds—'

'Good. Because it sounds like you're wasting my time.'

'I'm not, I promise. But it's a long story, and it's one I'd rather tell in person.'

Tina sighed. She could easily have said no. And for a long time afterwards she wished she had. But in that moment she was intrigued because maybe she hadn't changed so much after all. In the end, PI work was a lot more dull and laborious than she'd been expecting and this, at least, might provide something in the way of excitement. And if this guy was a crank, then she'd break out the pepper spray and the truncheon from her desk drawer and deal with him that way.

'OK,' she said, looking at her watch. 'Come here for midday.'

Nine

The world's a frightening place when you've got no one, and no means of supporting yourself. You feel cornered the whole time, as if whichever way you turn, you're going to encounter some insurmountable obstacle that'll keep forcing you backwards. The euphoria of escaping my assailants the previous night had now disappeared entirely, replaced by a strong sense of fear and hopelessness, and I was counting on Tina Boyd helping me, because right now she felt like the only thing standing between me and oblivion.

First impressions weren't that great, though. Her office was in a row of grime-stained terraces in a deserted litter-strewn street, opposite a construction site where the buildings had been thoughtfully levelled to provide a view of the train lines. I guess it was good business sense never to show your potential clients how much profit you were making out of them, but it seemed Tina might have been going a bit too far the other way.

The Final Minute

Once I'd paid the cab driver, I was down to my last twenty pounds, which was going to please Tina no end. Not only had I sounded like some kind of loon when I'd talked to her on the phone, I couldn't pay her either.

But at least I was clean. I'd thought about sleeping rough somewhere after I'd got off the train at Paddington at close to midnight, but had quickly given up that idea when I'd stepped on to the concourse and felt the bite of the wind. I'd found a cheap guesthouse on an adjacent street, paid cash for the room, and had managed to have a warm shower and a short, but thankfully dreamless, sleep.

I rang the buzzer at the front of the building, feeling strangely nervous, and waited for Tina to come to the door. She gave me an appraising look through the glass that didn't fill me with a great deal of confidence, before opening up. The photo in the paper hadn't lied: she was an attractive woman of about my age, not as tall as I'd been expecting, but there was the shoulder-length dark hair and the pretty, angular face that reminded me of an actress I'd seen on TV recently but couldn't put a name to. It was her eyes that really caught my attention, though. They were hard and dark, the expression in them coolly inquisitive, but there was something else there too, a vulnerability she couldn't quite hide, even though it was clear she was trying hard.

I fancied her immediately.

Then she frowned and said something that really shocked me. 'Sean? What on earth are you doing here?'

For a couple of seconds, I couldn't speak. I stared at her. She stared at me.

'My name's Matt – Matthew – Barron,' I said uncertainly. 'At least that's what I've been told. I was in a car accident. It left me in a coma for three months.' I lifted up my fringe to reveal the scar. 'And now I can't remember a thing about my life before.' I felt a sudden twinge of hope, because at least Tina had recognized me. 'I need you to help me piece together what's happened to me.'

She tried hard not to look at me as if I was insane but didn't quite manage it. 'I'm not sure I'm the right person to help you. You need to see a doctor.'

'Look, people are trying to kill me, and I have no idea why. Let me at least tell you my story. Or what I know of it. Please.'

Tina sighed. 'OK, you'd better come in,' she said, with far too much reluctance for my liking.

She led me down a narrow hallway about five degrees colder than the air outside and into her office. It was smaller than I'd expected of someone who could get a full-page spread in a national newspaper, with a big desk covered in paperwork and folders, a couple of chairs and two filing cabinets taking up most of the available space.

She took one of the chairs. I took the other.

'You obviously know me,' I said. 'Can you tell me who I am? Because I honestly don't have a clue.'

Tina looked thoughtful. 'Before I tell you anything, I want you to go through everything that's happened to you, and why you think there are people trying to kill you.'

I could tell she was sceptical of my story, and who could blame her? But I was there now and I had to lay everything on the line. So I did. Beginning with the accident, covering everything I could think of, and finishing with the events of the previous night. And even as I recounted it, I realized how outlandish the whole thing sounded. Credit to Tina, she didn't interrupt, and she kept her expression neutral. But she didn't take any notes either, which didn't exactly bode well.

'So, let me get this straight,' she said after I'd finished talking. 'You've been staying at the house of a woman who claimed to be your sister, but because of your amnesia you didn't know if it was your sister or not, and then last night a man and a woman with guns turn up, the woman tells you Jane's not your sister, kills her and the nurse, asks you a question you have no idea the answer to, and then they try to kill you as well. However, you fight back and actually manage to shoot one of your assailants during your successful escape.' She paused, looking at me. 'Is that a fair summary?'

I shrugged. 'Yes. Pretty much. Look, there must be some way of checking whether or not I'm telling the truth. They set fire to the house with the bodies inside. Maybe there's been a news report.'

'Maybe.' She let the word hang in the air for a couple of seconds, waiting, it seemed, for me to admit that it was all a crock of shit; but when I didn't say anything, she sighed. 'I'll have a look. Give me the location again.'

'The nearest town's Pembroke. The house is about ten miles away.'

I waited while Tina typed away on her PC keyboard. 'OK,' she said eventually, 'there's a report here on a local news website saying a house was destroyed in a fire last night twelve miles north-west of Pembroke, but there's no mention of any bodies.'

'There will be, I promise.'

'You said you were in a car accident. Have you got the exact date?'

'It was early April. I don't know the exact date, but it was in north Hampshire, and I was taken to Basingstoke Hospital afterwards. I was in a coma for three months. But there was no ID on me when I crashed, and they couldn't trace the car I was driving either. It was too burned out.'

'So how did you end up being Matthew Barron?'

'When I woke up from my coma in the hospital, my sister was there. She told me who I was. She even had a driving licence with that name and my photo on it. Not that I ever saw that again.'

'Which is strange, isn't it? Not only that you had no ID, but this woman claiming to be your sister knew how to find you.'

'Apparently she rang round all these different hospitals after I went missing. When she found me, she visited almost every day until I recovered. And then she was the one who signed me out.' I remembered the day I'd been discharged from the hospital; how strange it had been, leaving with a woman who was a complete stranger to me, and yet one whom I'd found myself trusting implicitly. She'd been so smiley and chatty, so happy that I was recovering and coming to stay with her, and even now, after everything that had happened, it made me wonder if I was wrong about her.

Tina was tapping away on the keyboard again. Eventually she stopped and sat back in her seat. 'OK, I've found a local news article about a car accident in April on the A31. The driver was taken to hospital with serious injuries, and the car destroyed. The date was the eighth.'

'That sounds about right.'

'Let me have a look at that driving licence.'

'I haven't got it. I didn't find it in the house. But I did collect these.'

I fished out the two licences I'd liberated from Tom and Jane's belongings, and handed them over, explaining whose they were.

Tina carefully examined them, then put them down on her desk.

'Now it's your turn,' I said, trying to keep the emotion out of my voice. 'You say you know who I am. Tell me. Please.'

Tina adjusted her position in the chair so she was more upright, and looked me in the eye. 'You've got a rough, round scar on your stomach, haven't you? And another on your thigh?'

I nodded. 'Yes, I do. Jane always told me they'd come from the accident, but I was never sure – they looked too old.'

'They are. They're bullet holes.'

I could feel the excitement building. It lasted all of about three seconds, until Tina spoke again.

'Your name's Sean Egan,' she said, an accusing note now in her voice. 'And you're a rapist.'

Ten

Tina watched Sean Egan as he sat dead straight in his seat, a look of utter shock on his face. He didn't seem to be faking it either. She'd genuinely pole-axed him with the news. It had been a shock to her too, seeing him turn up out of the blue after five years, claiming he didn't even know who he was.

'I . . . I . . .' He exhaled loudly, then stopped.

'You used to be an undercover police officer,' Tina continued. 'Our paths crossed on a job once. You even saved my life. You look a little different, but it's definitely you.' She shook her head. 'Jesus, Sean. What happened to you?'

'That's what I need you to find out.' He shook his head. 'A rapist? Do you remember the details?'

'I remember reading about it at the time. It was one of those date rape cases. You met a married woman in a bar. Her husband was away and you went back to her place – which is something that neither of you denied. It's what happened next that was the problem. The woman claims she had second thoughts – apparently she felt guilty – and asked you to leave. Except you didn't. She says you knocked her about and forced her to have sex, then when you were done, you left.' There was something else that Tina didn't add. That at the time Sean had been living with his pregnant partner. For the moment, she didn't want to give him that information. He had enough on his plate already, and Tina had an idea that Sean's ex probably wouldn't be overkeen on hearing from him right now.

He put his head back and stared silently at the ceiling.

Tina Googled the words 'sean egan rape police officer', clicking on the first link. 'It seems the jury didn't believe your story, Sean. You were sentenced to four years. The judge called you a predatory offender who couldn't accept being told no.'

He looked bewildered. 'But I wouldn't do that. It's not like me.'

'How do you know that? You can't remember. Look, is there anything about this that sounds familiar? You went to prison. That must have been a brutal experience for a rapist who's also a former police officer.'

He sighed, rubbing his face and eyes in frustration. 'No, right now I can't remember a thing. Are there any details of what happened after my release?'

She added the word 'release' to the original batch and searched again, scanning through the results. 'No, nothing. But that's not surprising. No one's interested in a story about a criminal getting out. They like it to be the other way round. You were only put away just over three years ago so, clearly, if you had your accident five

79

months ago, you were released pretty early for a violent offender, and I can't find any mention of an appeal anywhere.'

'Was I still a police officer when I supposedly raped this woman?'

'No. You resigned at the time I knew you, five years back. You'd been on an unofficial job in which a lot of people got killed, and you were very lucky to escape charges. You were known as being a pretty volatile character, Sean. There's no question about that.'

'But I saved your life?'

'Yes,' she said. 'You saved my life.' She remembered the incident well enough. Would always remember it. His appearance might have changed, but as she stared at him now she caught a glimpse of the man he'd once been: young, good-looking, with a gleam in his eye, and something of the bad boy about him. She'd fancied him at the time, but had steered clear. Sean had been trouble then, and it was clear that, one way or another, he was trouble now.

'I'm not a bad man, Tina,' he said.

'You know, Sean, I've met a lot of bad men who said that.'

'But you knew me. Was I bad?'

'I didn't think so, no. But I wouldn't bet my house on it.'

He shook his head. The pain and confusion on his face still looked genuine, and Tina had to work hard to resist feeling sorry for him.

'Can you tell me what I was involved in when our paths crossed?' he asked.

'It'd be easier to let you read up about it. I'll download everything I can on your background and print it off for you to take away.'

He made an exasperated gesture. 'Take it where? I've got nowhere to go. I don't know anyone. I've got no family, no friends, no money. I'm completely alone.'

'You need to go to A and E, tell them you're suffering from amnesia. Give them your name and they'll be able to help you. I'll make some calls and try to locate family members, but that's all I can do for the moment.'

'But, Tina, there are people who want to kill me,' he said, looking her right in the eye. 'I don't know why but they do. I want to hire you to help me find out what's going on. When they had me at gunpoint back at Jane's house, the female killer asked me "Where are the bodies?" I have no idea what she meant but I need to find out.'

Tina had to admit she was tempted by this. She was pretty confident that Sean was telling the truth, and whatever had happened to him was a hell of a lot more interesting than the usual kind of jobs she got involved in. But she also knew that helping him could throw up a lot of complications and problems she really didn't need right now. 'You need to go to the police, Sean, and tell them what you've told me. You said you witnessed a double murder, and potentially killed a man in self-defence. It's your duty to report it.'

'But they're not going to believe me, are they? I had enough trouble convincing you. I'm an ex-con. If I tell them the two people who've been looking after me for the past two months were murdered by a pair of contract killers with no obvious motive, with no witnesses . . . well, I don't think I'd have a hope in hell of convincing them it wasn't me who was the killer.'

'And if I don't report this conversation to the police, then I put myself in a very precarious legal position,' Tina countered.

'Help me find out who I am, Tina. When I know my history, and what happened to me before the accident, I'll happily go to the police and tell them everything. And I won't mention you either.'

'I'm already working on a case.'

'I know you are. I read about it in the paper. It's why I decided to contact you. I think the missing girl might be connected to what's happened to me.'

Tina frowned, sceptical again suddenly. 'How?'

'I told you I stopped taking my medication after I hit my head. Since then I've had the same dream twice. And it's so real that I'm sure it happened. It involves me being in a house with a dead woman, and another very badly injured one. I don't know who they are, or why I'm there, but I can picture both their faces perfectly, and I believe that the girl who's dead is the one you're looking for.'

'Jesus Christ, Sean. Can you hear how this is sounding?'

'Of course I can. But when I was talking to the psychotherapist, Dr Bronson, about it yesterday, he was suddenly way more interested in me than he had been before. In fact he was desperate to put me under hypnosis so he could get more details. And it doesn't feel like a coincidence that the people who came to the house last night wanted to know about the location of some bodies.'

Tina exhaled loudly. 'If you're lying . . .'

'I'm not. I swear it.'

Tina wondered what the hell she might be getting into. She thought of Alan Donaldson then, and his desperate desire to be reunited with his missing daughter, how she'd felt so sorry for him as he'd sat where Sean was sitting now. And now this stranger from her past had turned up and told her he'd seen Lauren in a dream, and that she was dead. Sean had real powers of persuasion too. She remembered that about him from the first time round. They'd hardly known each other but, unlike most men, he'd really got under her skin. He was looking at her intently now, and she knew just how dangerous someone like him could be. But his story was seductive, and it appealed to that self-destructive part of her she'd been working so hard these past years to suppress, but which never truly went away.

'OK,' she said, 'I'll help you.'

And with those words she set herself on a path whose final destination would haunt her for a long, long time to come.

Eleven

The man Sean Egan knew as Dr Bronson was sitting in the gloomy living room of his cramped London flat smoking a cigarette and sipping from a large tumbler of whisky. His real name was Robert Whatret, and he'd made a mess of his life. He couldn't blame it on one mistake either. There'd been many, and they'd all had different names.

There'd been a time when he had a thriving private therapy practice giving him an annual income in the several hundreds of thousands; an attractive, articulate wife he could be proud of; homes in London, Berkshire and the Dordogne. He'd had it all. But in the end, it had never been enough. Robert Whatret was a sex addict. It didn't matter that he and his wife had shared a healthy, active sex life. It didn't matter that he'd truly loved her. If there was an available woman – fat, thin, young, old, pretty, ugly, it really didn't matter – he'd try to get her to have sex with him. The fact that he knew his behaviour was manic and addictive, and the result of insecurity and low self-esteem originating from childhood, didn't help at all. In fact, it simply made his guilt and self-loathing worse. In his youth he'd had numerous affairs and one-night stands, all of which had been intensely exciting at the time but had invariably left him feeling empty afterwards. He was careful, though, and during that whole period his wife had never found out.

The problems had really begun when he'd grown older and his looks had begun to fade. His sexual needs, however, hadn't. In fact, they seemed to become more urgent, and more extreme, as he tried to fill the emotional void inside himself. A large part of his work was based around the process of hypnotherapy, and the majority of his patients were women, providing him with an ideal opportunity. He would send selected patients into a deep trance and then, while they were under, he'd take advantage of them. It started as fondling, but he found the thrill so intense that he quickly progressed to far more serious sexual assaults. As before, he got away with it for a long time, even though it soon became clear that certain patients suspected something was amiss. Several stopped seeing him altogether.

In the end it was inevitable that he'd be caught, although the circumstances couldn't have been worse. Rather than report her suspicions to the police, one of the patients – a very attractive, middle-aged blonde with severe OCD called Adele, who was clearly a lot brighter than Whatret had anticipated (he tended to target those he perceived to be more vulnerable and less intelligent) – approached Whatret's wife and told her what she thought was going on. According to what Whatret had since pieced together, Adele didn't want to get involved in pressing charges or testifying in court, but she did want him stopped if he was abusing his position.

Mrs Whatret hadn't needed much persuading that her husband was up to no good and had planted a hidden camera in his office. Unfortunately for Whatret, in a supreme piece of misfortune that wiped away all the good luck that had kept him out of trouble so far, his very first appointment after that was with one of his favourites – Estelle, a buxom fifty-five-year-old with intimacy issues dating back to an abusive stepfather who, ironically, given that she hadn't had full sex in more than a decade, gave an incredible blowjob while under hypnosis. The hidden camera had been placed in the perfect position to capture the two of them in high definition as Estelle sat on the couch fellating him.

Mrs Whatret had been intending to use any evidence the camera garnered to secure a decent settlement in a divorce, but she'd been so mortified by what she saw that she'd gone straight to the police, who'd arrested Whatret in his offices the same day (thankfully he'd been with a male patient at the time). What had followed had been entirely predictable: professional disgrace, divorce, the loss of what was left of his assets in damages claims, and eventually a three-year prison sentence.

Since his release more than two years earlier he'd come close to suicide on more than one occasion, and had begun to hit the bottle in earnest. Funnily enough, that had cured him of his desire to chase women. He no longer had the inclination or the energy, and he would almost certainly have succumbed to his suicidal inclinations by now if it hadn't been for the mysterious job offer he'd received a few months earlier.

The Final Minute

Whatret had never met his employer. He knew him only as Mr H, and they only ever spoke on the phone. Mr H wanted him to carry out a particular, and highly illegal, form of therapy on a patient living in Wales. Ordinarily Whatret would have turned down the job immediately, having no desire to see the inside of a prison again. But the money was big. Very big. Mr H had left an envelope containing ten grand in cash for him at a deposit box in Hendon, and that was just the retainer. He received another thousand in cash for each of his twice-weekly trips to Wales, plus travelling expenses, and in the absence of anything else, other than state benefits that barely covered the cost of cheap food, it was his only lifeline.

Now, though, sitting in his flat on a threadbare sofa and staring at the cobwebs on his nicotine-stained ceiling, with only his thoughts and his fears for company, Whatret wished he'd never got involved. The guilt was playing havoc with him, as it always did. He had no wish to be complicit in keeping a vulnerable man in a mentally impaired state while he tried to extract information from him, but this was exactly what he was being paid to do. And when he finally did extract that information, what then? He had a bad feeling that once he and Matthew Barron were no longer of any use to Mr H, their days might well be numbered.

But was there any other option? He was finished anyway. He might as well try to enjoy his money while he still could. He took another sip of the whisky – he'd splashed out on Black Label – and wondered what he was going to do with his day.

Which was when the phone rang.

Straight away he knew who it was. Steeling himself, he picked it up.

'We've got a problem,' said Mr H in that matter-of-fact tone of his. 'Barron's gone.'

Whatret tensed, not liking the sound of this at all. 'Gone where?'

'We don't know. The two people looking after him are dead, and the house is burned down. Do you know anything about any of this?'

'Of course not,' said Whatret, trying to keep the nerves out of his voice. 'I went to see him yesterday as usual, and everything was fine when I left.'

'I'm assuming you haven't yet got the information out of him.'

'I'd have called if I had.' He had been given a number to call the moment Barron told him what Mr H needed to hear, but so far that prize had eluded him. 'I'm getting close, though.'

'That's not much use to us now he's gone AWOL, is it? You've had two months to get it out of him, and you've failed.'

'It's not easy, Mr H. Barron experienced a catastrophic head injury and you've asked me to find out things that he was involved in literally hours before the accident happened. Those memories aren't going to come back to him just like that. They may never do.'

'That's not what I want to hear.' There was a real edge to Mr H's voice now. 'How long is his amnesia going to last without his medication and your . . . therapy?' He spoke the last word as if it was some kind of voodoo.

Whatret knew that lying now wasn't going to help him. He sighed. 'His memories will start to come back. I've had to work very hard to suppress the older ones. With the type of retrograde amnesia Mr Barron's suffering from, those memories closest to the time of the injury will be the ones that come back last.' He didn't bother adding the 'if at all' this time, knowing it wouldn't help. 'But everything else – those from his childhood, his twenties, his thirties – they'll all start returning.'

'How long will it take?'

'It's impossible to tell. Retrograde amnesia isn't a predictable condition. It depends on the individ—'

'How long?'

This was why Whatret hated dealing with laymen. They had no concept of the complexity of the workings of the various parts of the brain. They just wanted easy answers. 'Without the drugs and regular hypnotherapy, the first memories, the long-term ones, will start coming back almost immediately. It's possible – not probable, but possible – that he'll be remembering a lot of his adult life within days.'

He heard Mr H curse down the other end of the line.

'There are certain things he'll never remember, of course,' Whatret added hurriedly. 'I spent a long time during the hypnotherapy implanting false memories in Barron's mind, and also making sure he never remembers some things. I followed your instructions to the letter in that regard.'

'The problems will come when he finds out who he really is. Then he becomes extremely dangerous to us.'

Whatret had no idea who the 'us' were, nor did he want to know. He had a strong feeling that the less information he had the better it would be for his long-term health. 'It'll take time for Barron to piece things together,' he assured Mr H. 'He's been in a state of perpetual confusion for the past two months. At the moment, he's pretty helpless.'

Mr H was silent for a few moments. 'If he was being held against his will by people who were prepared to torture him, how much could he reveal?'

Jesus, thought Whatret, *what am I getting involved in here?* 'He doesn't know much. Certainly not the information you want from him.' But even as he spoke these words, he experienced a niggling doubt. Barron had been dreaming about the incident in the house with the murders. It wasn't a complete stretch for him to have remembered what had happened afterwards. But there was no way he could tell Mr H this. Instead he said, 'He won't reveal anything about that night. He knows nothing about it. So, do you think he might have been kidnapped?'

'We don't know yet,' said Mr H. 'But we believe he's still alive.'

'Am I going to be all right?' asked Whatret. 'I mean, after what happened to the other two?'

'You'll be fine. Sit tight and keep your phone with you at all times. We may well need you.'

The line went dead, but as Whatret stared at the receiver, he had a terrible feeling that he wasn't going to be all right. He was in far too deep with some very dangerous people. Worse, he was expendable.

Mr H put the phone down and shook his head angrily, frustrated with the continued lack of results.

He was certain that Sean Egan, a man with information that could be worth tens of millions of pounds hidden somewhere in his addled brain, was still alive and had made it out of the house where he was being held without being compromised by the people who'd come to kill him.

So now he needed to be located and taken out of circulation.

It was time to put the contingency plan into action.

Twelve

I tried to persuade Tina to let me stay at her place but, unsurprisingly, she was having none of it. I could hardly blame her. I looked a mess, my story sounded insane, and, as far as she was concerned, I was a rapist. It hardly made me ideal house-guest material.

The revelation about the rape had hit me hard. I didn't see myself as an aggressive or violent man, and the idea of forcing myself on a woman felt completely alien to me. Yet the problem remained that because I didn't know who I really was, I had no idea whether I was capable of such an act. I'd always acted honourably around Jane, even if my thoughts had been impure at times, but maybe that had been because I relied on her to look after me and didn't want to risk ruining things between us. Or, of course, because I believed she was my sister. In the end, I was left with the cold, hard facts that not only could I be the rapist Tina had said I was, I could also have been responsible for the killing in that house in my dream.

Until I got my memory back, anything was possible.

But at least with Tina on board I had a chance of finding out the truth, however unpalatable it might be.

We were now in her car on the way to the local hospital so that I could hand myself over to the Accident and Emergency department. I didn't want to go but didn't see that I had an alternative. Tina had given me a mobile phone with her number in it so we could contact each other at any time. She'd made me protect it with a passcode, and had told me that if I needed to call her I should phone and leave her a message and she'd call me right back. When I'd asked why her answer had been blunt. 'No offence, Sean, but I don't want to be associated with you, and I need to protect myself in case this phone falls into the wrong hands.'

I could see her point so I didn't complain. To be fair, Tina had been good to me under the circumstances. She'd also lent me a hundred pounds she'd drawn from the cashpoint, and had treated me to a ham baguette from the local sandwich shop. Since I was the one who was meant to be paying her, I was pretty grateful.

'What do you think they're going to do with me?' I asked her as we waited for the lights up ahead to change. The sky had turned a heavy, brooding grey and it had begun to spit with rain.

She shrugged without looking at me. 'I don't know. They might keep you in for observation, or more likely they'll get you sent to a specialist psychiatric unit, or a care home. Either way, you'll have a roof over your head.'

'And what are you going to do in the meantime?'

'I'll make some enquiries into your background. I've still got a lot of contacts in the force and I should be able to fill in some of the missing pieces in your story. I'll also see if you have any family members you can stay with, but the problem is that if you're right, and there are people after you, you might be putting them in danger.'

I shook my head wearily. 'I have so many unanswered questions. Not the least of which is why does someone want me dead?' I felt the familiar wave of frustration surging over me, followed by a deep, bitter gloom as I pondered the hardest question of all. 'And what kind of man am I?'

This time Tina put a sympathetic hand on my arm. 'We'll find out the answers, Sean. It might take some time but we'll get there. I've got the licences you took from your sister and your nurse, and they've given me something to go on. The info I've printed off for you might help too. It doesn't give you a full picture of your life, or your career, by any means. A lot of what happened to you, particularly where your path crossed with mine, was kept out of the public domain, but again, it's a start.'

I looked down at the dozen or so sheets of A4 paper I was holding, and wondered whether anything in there would drag back memories from the abyss, and whether I actually wanted them to.

The lights turned green and we made a turn before pulling up beside a very modern high-rise building with funky blue windows.

Tina pulled up on the road outside where a big red sign said Accident and Emergency. 'OK, this is St Mary's Hospital A and E. You go up the pedestrian walkway and it's on the right.'

Now that it came to it, I didn't want to leave her. 'What if they take my phone and I can't get hold of you?' I said, not liking the edge of panic in my voice. 'Look, I don't want to sound needy, Tina, or weak, but right now . . . right now, I have no one except you.' I felt a well of emotion building in me as I spoke the words, and I actually thought that – God forbid – I was going to cry. I hadn't cried at all during my time at Jane's; I think the drugs they'd been feeding me had put paid to any emotional outbursts. But now I was having to use every ounce of my willpower to hold back the tears. 'You can't imagine what it's like being me. This city; these streets; this hospital. They all scare the hell out of me.'

'I can't pretend to know what you're feeling, Sean, and I can only imagine how horrible it must be having no memory, but St Mary's is a world-class hospital and the people here will be able to help you.'

I knew she was right, and that begging to stay with her wasn't going to help. The well of emotion receded as quickly as it had appeared. 'Sure, OK. But please keep in contact.'

I started to get out of the car but Tina put a hand on my arm again. 'Wait.' She reached into the glove compartment and took something out of what looked like a jewellery box. 'Take this, but keep it hidden.' She handed me a small plastic coin-shaped object.

I inspected it. 'What is it?'

'It's a miniature tracking device. It means I can find out your exact location to the nearest five metres wherever you are, so if you lose the phone, or it gets taken away, I can still find you.'

'Jesus,' I said. 'That's impressive.' Which it was.

'And it's an expensive piece of kit too, so don't lose it. The battery life's only forty-eight hours, so after that time we'll have to work out what to do, but hopefully things will have settled by then.'

I leaned down and slipped it into my sock, figuring that was as inconspicuous a place as any. 'Thanks, Tina. I really appreciate this.'

She looked at me but didn't smile. 'Don't let me down, Sean.'

I nodded, and stepped out into the rain.

Thirteen

Tina's next appointment was with Sheryl Warner, the girl who'd rung earlier in the day to talk about Alan Donaldson's daughter, Lauren, having seen the piece in the *Mail*. It seemed the two of them had been friends, and after a short conversation with her, Tina had decided that she was well worth visiting.

On the drive to her house, she thought about Sean Egan. The problem was she couldn't make up her mind about him. She was almost certain he wasn't lying about what had happened to him (although the dream in which he'd described Lauren appearing seemed too coincidental), and he'd never struck her as the kind of man who'd rape a woman. But Tina had learned from her long career in the police that seemingly charming, balanced people were capable of doing some terrible things when the mood took them, and Sean had certainly proved capable of violence during that very short space of time he'd been in her orbit all those years

back. He'd taken the law into his own hands by unofficially infiltrating a gang of armed robbers and being directly involved in the
kidnap of a murder suspect. The murder suspect and all the gang,
with the exception of Sean, had ended up dead, and although he'd
not been charged in connection with the events, it didn't mean
he hadn't been responsible for at least some of the killings. It
crossed her mind to report what Sean had told her to her former
colleagues in the police. After all, by his own admission he had
important information about two murders, and if she didn't say
anything she was leaving herself open to charges of perverting
the course of justice and assisting an offender.

Even so, she decided that for now she'd keep quiet and play
things by ear. It would be useful to talk to the woman who'd
accused Sean of rape, and whose evidence had put him behind
bars, but it wouldn't be easy. Like all rape victims, the woman
had lifelong anonymity and Tina would have to pull some strings
with old contacts if she was going to track her down. And then
what? Even if Sean was completely innocent, the woman was
never going to admit it. That was the problem with date rape: it
was one person's word against another. And yet Tina knew she'd
feel better about working with Sean once she'd at least had the
chance to talk to the woman who, as far as a jury was concerned,
had been his victim.

Sheryl Warner lived at the southern end of Camden Town,
close to Morningside tube station. Tina knew the area well. It
wasn't far from where she'd lived for a while with her then
boyfriend, a fellow cop called John Gallan; there was an Italian
restaurant called Conti's they'd both liked just off the high street.
That had been the last time she'd lived with anyone, and it was a

long time back now. John had been dead eight years, and it made her wonder where the time had gone, and what she'd be doing in another eight years.

There was no parking near the flats so Tina found a spot on a meter a few streets away. It had been raining but the sky was now beginning to clear. Her route took her past the street where Conti's was and she couldn't resist a glance to see if it was still there. But it was gone, replaced with a coffee shop that looked to be doing a roaring trade, and in a way that pleased Tina because she knew that seeing Conti's as she remembered it, with its traditional red and white chequered tablecloths and empty wine bottles lining the walls, would have just made her sad.

Sheryl's flat was on the first floor of a large townhouse opposite a well-kept park. At first glance it all looked very nice, like an estate agent's photo, but a closer look revealed that the park was clearly a hangout for drunks, and barely twenty yards from Sheryl's front door, but just out of sight, was a dilapidated pre-fab pub that looked more like a fortress, backing on to a huge highrise estate. As was so often the case in London, Tina thought: turn a corner into the next street and everything changes.

After being buzzed in, Tina climbed a creaking staircase that smelled vaguely of damp. Before she could knock on the door at the top it was opened by a petite blonde girl in her mid-twenties looking effortlessly pretty and cool in a pink vest, grey track pants and thick socks. She smiled widely, revealing newly whitened teeth that were a bit too big for her mouth. 'Hi Tina,' she said in a voice that veered dangerously close to cutesy. 'Nice to meet you.' She stuck out a hand, and Tina shook it. 'Come in.'

Sheryl led her into a spacious living room that smelled of perfume and cigarettes and looked like it could use a decent spring clean, and plonked herself down on the sofa, gesturing for Tina to take a seat in the armchair next to it.

'Excuse the mess, I had a late one last night.'

And it was a mess too, with cups, crockery and half-full ashtrays dotted around on all available surfaces, and a lot of strewn clothes. The curtains were closed too and all the lights were on, which gave the place a claustrophobic feel.

Tina removed a top from the chair and placed it on the carpet before sitting down, thinking that at three o'clock in the afternoon the excuse that you hadn't had time to clear up didn't really wash.

As was her habit, she got straight down to business. 'When was the last time you saw Lauren Donaldson?'

'Not for a long time now.'

'Can you be more specific?'

She giggled. 'I'm not very good with dates.'

'Try,' said Tina. 'This is a missing person we're talking about.'

Sheryl looked taken aback by her tone but didn't argue. Instead she pulled a face of intense concentration, like a kid. 'Well, it was quite a few months ago. Probably March, April? She was in a club with Jen. Jen was a good friend of hers. They used to hang out a lot.'

'Has Jen got a last name?'

She thought about it for a moment. 'Jones. Yeah, Jen Jones.'

Tina wrote it down.

'Sheryl, I've had real trouble finding the latest address for Lauren. Do you know where she was living when you last saw her?'

'She was living with Jen. I went up there once after a party last summer. Their flat was in Chalk Farm, not that far from here. To be honest, I was pretty wasted so I can't remember the exact address.'

'Do you have any idea where I can find Jen?'

Sheryl shook her head. 'No. I haven't seen her for a long time either. I think the last time I saw her she was with Lauren.'

Tina was beginning to wonder if she was wasting her time here. 'So how did you know Lauren?'

'We met at a party a couple of years ago. We kind of hit it off and arranged to meet afterwards. We used to be part of the same scene.'

'And what kind of scene was that?'

'It's like a party scene. You go to different clubs and parties . . . you know.'

'So it was a social circuit?'

'Yeah,' said Sheryl unconvincingly. 'I suppose.'

'Can you give me the names of any of the other people on this circuit who'd know Lauren?'

'Erm . . . God, I don't know.'

'How many of you were there on this party circuit of yours? Because it's interesting, no one else has contacted me regarding Lauren's disappearance.'

'I think some people probably want to remain anonymous.'

Tina felt her antennae prick up. This was what often happened in detective work. You dug slowly, bit by bit, and sometimes it seemed like you weren't getting anywhere. Then you struck something interesting, and potentially valuable. 'Why would that be?'

Sheryl seemed uncomfortable for the first time. She grabbed a packet of cigarettes from the table beside her and lit one, offering the pack to Tina, who waved it away. She'd smoked two cigarettes on the way down here and that was enough for now.

Sheryl took a short drag on the cigarette, as if she didn't really enjoy it, before looking at Tina through the smoke. 'Look, can I ask you a question? What do you think happened to Lauren?'

'I don't know,' said Tina, 'but I'm worried about her. She hasn't been seen for months; her Facebook page seems to have been taken down; her phone's out of service. Her brother, who seems to be the only person she used to talk to regularly, hasn't been able to get hold of her since early April.'

'Is that Ben? She always talked about him. He was the only one of her family Lauren liked.' She took another half-hearted drag on the cigarette. 'You know, I'm worried about her too. I tried calling her a few times but, like you said, her phone's dead.'

'Have you tried Jen's?'

'Once. I didn't know her as well as Lauren. But her phone was dead too. I said to people that I hadn't seen them, but no one seemed that bothered. It was like they just weren't there any more, and everything just moved on. It's like that on the party scene really. People drift in and out.' She paused. 'You're not a cop any more, are you?'

'No, I'm not. Anything you tell me will be treated with the utmost confidentiality. All I'm interested in is finding Lauren.' And this woman Jen, Tina thought. That she too seemed to have disappeared around the same time was coincidental to say the least.

'There are a lot of drugs at some of the parties I go to,' continued Sheryl. 'Rich guys too. Guys who buy you things, take you away to nice places. And, you know, if they're good to you, you're good to them.'

'I think I understand.'

'One of the guys who kind of organizes a lot of the parties, he sometimes approaches girls and asks if they want to make some extra money.'

'Doing what?'

'You know, escort work. He asked me a couple of times but I didn't want to do it. But I think Lauren might have been doing some. She always seemed to have a lot of cash.'

'Can you tell me the name of this guy who organizes these parties?'

'He's still a friend of mine. What are you going to do to him?'

'I'm just going to talk to him, that's all. I'm sure he'll want to help.'

Sheryl pulled a face. 'I don't know if he will. I asked him about Lauren before, and he didn't want to talk about her then. He just said he hadn't seen her in a while and that was it, you know?'

Tina leaned forward in her seat, fixing Sheryl with a serious look. 'I won't tell him we spoke, and I'll make sure your name never gets mentioned, but if your friend knows something about Lauren, I need to find it out.'

'Seriously, you don't want to mess him about. He knows people.' Sheryl emphasized the 'knows'. 'Once there was a black guy after him for money over something and he ended up getting shot.'

Tina had no idea if this was true or not, and didn't much care. 'Don't worry about me, I can handle him.'

Sheryl smiled. 'Yeah, that's what I like about you. You look like you don't take shit off guys.'

'I don't take it from anyone. And nothing'll happen to you. You've got my word on that.'

Sheryl sighed. 'His name's Dylan Mackay. I've got his phone number if you want it.'

Tina knew that if she phoned him, she'd get nowhere, but she took it anyway. 'Do you have an address for him?'

Sheryl shook her head. 'I've never been to his house, but I think it's in Kensington somewhere.'

'I'll find him,' said Tina, making a note of the details. 'Do you have any up-to-date photos of Lauren and Jen?'

'Yeah, I've got a few on my Facebook page.' She looked round on the sofa until she found an iPad in a pink case.

Tina waited while she logged on to her account, thinking that it was an empty life this girl led, stuck in a messy flat on her own, going to parties with people she didn't really know and who didn't really care about her. She needed to get out and do something different – although the irony of this thought, given her own solitary existence, was not lost on Tina.

'Look, here's one of the three of us,' said Sheryl, coming over and planting herself on the arm of Tina's chair. She leaned in with the iPad so they could both see the screen.

The picture was a good one of the three women. They were clearly at a party, all wearing pretty but very revealing dresses, their faces made up like they were trying just a bit too hard, all grinning at the camera. Sheryl was on the left. She was holding a full glass of champagne and had her arm round Lauren's shoulders. Lauren's grin was more of a playful pout, and she looked the worse for wear. Tina's gaze settled on the woman on the right. This was Jen, and with her peroxide blonde hair and thick, luscious lips she was the sexiest-looking of the three, and definitely the most worldly-wise. Even her smile looked calculated. Tina had no doubt she was a leader rather than a follower.

'That was taken at China White's,' said Sheryl proudly. 'I remember it was a good night.'

Tina looked at the date on the post: 28 March. It immediately struck her that this was only eleven days before Sean had his car accident.

'Was this the last time you saw them?' she asked.

'You know what? I reckon it might have been. In fact, yeah, I'm sure it was.'

The timing concerned Tina but she kept it to herself. 'Have you got any photos of Dylan?'

'A couple, I think.' She took back the iPad and scrolled through until she found a picture of a good-looking guy of about thirty taken at yet another party. He was tanned, with dark curly hair, and carried a look of money and breeding. Tina disliked him immediately.

She got to her feet and handed a business card to Sheryl, thanking her for her time. 'Could you download both those photos and email them to me, and any others you've got of Lauren and Jen?'

'Sure,' said Sheryl, walking Tina to the door, 'but don't forget to keep me out of everything with Dylan.'

Tina reiterated that she would, but as she walked back down the staircase, she wondered if she'd be able to keep her word. If she started asking questions it wouldn't take too long for Dylan to suspect Sheryl of having a hand in it, and Tina doubted if she'd stand up too well under questioning. But there was nothing she could do about that. Her priority was to find Lauren.

Or perhaps more likely, what had happened to her.

Fourteen

St Mary's A and E was busy and loud, and most of the chairs in the open-plan waiting room were occupied by the walking wounded, and quite a few who didn't look too ill at all.

It had taken me a good few minutes to explain to the receptionist what was wrong with me. Acute amnesia, it seemed, wasn't a regular problem round here, or an emergency. Things also weren't helped by the fact that there was no National Health number for a Matthew Barron, and I didn't want to give her my real name, so I just shrugged and acted dumb. In the end, she'd made me fill out a form (which hadn't taken long), and told me to take a seat along with everyone else.

I'd found an empty chair at the end of a row, next to an old man who smelled of compost and opposite a harassed-looking mum, who was trying with only limited success to prevent her two-year-old son from making a beeline for the exit. Somehow, I couldn't blame him.

While I sat there waiting, I leafed through the pile of information on my background that Tina had given me. It didn't take long to find revelations that came as a real shock. The first thing I found out was that I had indeed had a brother. The second thing was that he'd died twenty years earlier. His name was John and he'd been a veteran of the first Gulf War. At the age of twenty-one, during the height of the fighting to oust Saddam Hussein's forces from Kuwait, the armoured personnel carrier he'd been travelling in had been hit by friendly fire from an American A10 fighter plane, and John had ended up with extensive burns to his face and body. He'd survived the attack but had been invalided out of the army and, according to the report I read, was unemployed and suffering from PTSD when he died four years later.

I tried to remember all this. There was a vague familiarity to the words I was reading, but once again there was nothing definite I could cling to. They had a black and white face-shot of John as a young man, and I stared at it for a long time. In the photo he was wearing a small, almost nervous smile, as if he was trying to find the right pose. He didn't look that much like me. His hair had been cut short, military-style, and he had a round, boyish face with dimples and rosy cheeks. I thought he looked familiar, but I wasn't sure whether this was an actual memory or just my mind playing tricks on me.

There was another photo of him, this time lying in a hospital bed with his face obscured by bandages. The sight made me feel sick. My brother, young and fresh-faced in the first photo, burned beyond recognition. I didn't want to see any pictures showing the injuries, and thankfully there weren't any. I didn't want to read about his death either, but I had to know what had happened to him, and to the rest of my family.

John's death had been both dramatic and tragic. According to the newspaper article Tina had supplied me with, he'd just finished his morning shift in the charity bookshop where he did voluntary work and was en route to buy a sandwich for lunch when he walked straight into an armed robbery. Two masked gunmen were holding up a cash delivery van outside a branch of NatWest while their getaway driver sat in a car nearby, revving his engine. Rather than keep a safe distance, John, it seemed, had gone steaming in, chasing the gunmen as they ran for the car. He'd rugby-tackled one of them but the robber John had targeted was a big guy and had managed to throw him off. At this point the second gunman had come over, shotgun raised, and even though John had been down on his knees, with his hands raised in surrender, the gunman had shot him once in the head from point-blank range, killing him instantly.

My brother.

It was hard to read the article. It was even harder when I saw the words that, according to eyewitnesses, the gunman had said to John just before he shot him.

'Oi, freak!'

A simple, harsh statement epitomizing how little the gunman had thought of him. A man who'd suffered terrible injuries in the service of his country, and who'd just been trying to do the right thing, only to be shot down like a dog by a piece of dirt who couldn't resist mocking him before he pulled the trigger.

It made me sick. It made me angry.

More importantly, it made me remember.

Oi, freak! Those words came vomiting out of the dark, inaccessible recesses of my mind, and suddenly I was transported back to a dark crematorium where a grim-looking bald-headed priest was delivering a eulogy on all the positive things John had achieved in his short life, all the good he'd done. I was standing in the front row, and I could feel the tears stinging my eyes. They weren't tears of sadness either. They were tears of frustration. As I stood there staring at the priest, not listening to his pointless words, I was full of rage at the injustice of what had happened to my brother. And then I saw with perfect clarity my mother and father, standing next to me, holding hands, my mother in a black dress and coat, my father in a loose-fitting suit and cheap black tie that looked older than he was.

I knew it was my parents. They were the same as the people in the photo in my bedroom at Jane's place, which made me wonder where Jane had got it from. I was certain too, without looking at any of the other articles on my lap, that they were both now dead. But, though the thought should have filled me with grief, it didn't. Instead I felt a weird sense of elation. Slowly, inch by brutal inch, my memory was coming back.

'Jordan, no!'

Awoken from my reverie, I looked up to see the hyperactive two-year-old boy grabbing at the papers on my lap. His mum got up, wrapped him in a bear hug and dragged him back to her seat. The kid struggled, but in vain.

'Sorry about that,' she said from behind his flailing body. 'He's a bit bored.'

I smiled. 'No problem. I think we all are.'

'He can be a bit of a handful, but he's a good lad really,' she continued, but I was no longer listening.

My attention was focused on two men in suits and raincoats who'd just come in through the main doors. One was tall and wiry with a pile of thin, unruly grey hair whose sole purpose seemed to be to try to cover his otherwise bald pate, and just looked like a rather windswept combover. I put him at around fifty but he could have been a few years older. The other was a couple of inches shorter but a lot broader. He had thick black hair and an even thicker full-face black beard, making it difficult to know what was going on behind there, but he had sharp eyes that quickly scanned the room, stopping on me for just one second too long before continuing on their way. He was about forty, and looked like the kind of guy you didn't want to get in an argument with.

Straight away I knew they were police officers. They just had that air of authority about them. I also knew they were here to see me, even though neither was now looking my way. I wondered if Tina had reported my story to her former colleagues, but quickly dismissed the idea. She wasn't that kind of woman. She wouldn't go behind my back.

Then I wondered if I was being paranoid, but when I looked up again I saw the two guys talking to two uniformed security guards.

Acting as casually as possible, I put all the A4 papers on the chair next to me, covered them with a newspaper, and started to get to my feet.

The four of them had split up now and were walking purposefully down either side of the row of chairs, coming at me in a pincer movement.

For a second I thought about making a run for it, but there was only one set of double doors into the room and the four of them had them well covered.

'Mr Barron?' said Combover as they surrounded me. His voice sounded vaguely familiar – as did so much in my life recently. 'My name's DI Carl Jones, and this is DC Brian Smith.' Combover produced a warrant card which he flipped open just long enough for me to see a photo of him alongside the Metropolitan Police insignia, before he made it disappear like some cheap magician. 'We need to speak to you down at the station.' He leaned forward and took my arm – not roughly, but not exactly gently either. 'Please come quietly because we don't want to make a scene.'

'Can I ask what this is about?' I said as they moved in closer.

'We'd rather not discuss it in here. Now, if you just put your hands behind your back for us, we're going to handcuff you for your own safety.'

His tone was calm and reasonable, as if he was talking to a misbehaving kid, but I wasn't fooled. Something was wrong here, I could tell. The problem was, what did I do about it? It was four against one and, although the two security guards didn't look like they'd pose much threat, I could tell the bearded cop would be a real issue. His hands were touching the lapels of his suit jacket ready for any sudden move, and he was staring at me intently.

'It's OK,' I said. 'I don't need handcuffs. I'm happy to come along quietly.'

'It's for your own safety, sir,' continued Combover, a pair of handcuffs suddenly materializing in his hand.

'Am I under arrest?' I asked, thinking there was no way I was going to allow them to cuff me voluntarily.

'We will arrest you if we have to.'

'On what charge?'

'Murder,' he said, loud enough for several of the people in the waiting area to hear. I heard Jordan's mum gasp from behind the wall of bodies surrounding me. The security guards visibly stiffened, and the tension in the room was suddenly ratcheted up a couple of notches.

'Look,' I told them, 'there must be some mistake. I haven't killed anyone.'

As I said this, I gave Combover a hard shove and swung round fast, trying to make a break for it.

But I'd missed my chance. Blackbeard had clearly been expecting exactly that kind of move from me, and he grabbed me in a bear hug, driving me forward into the chairs. His weight, plus the weight of the two fat security guards, meant I didn't have a chance. I sank to my knees before being pushed face first on to the hard floor so I was lying on my front. I struggled, terrified of where these guys were going to take me, but it was no use. I was helpless. I felt my wrists being forced together and the cuffs roughly applied.

'These men aren't police!' I blurted out, but I could hardly breathe under all that weight and my words were barely audible.

'Come on, Mr Barron, this isn't helping,' said Combover, crouching down next to me. 'All we want to do is talk to you.'

I tried to look up at him, but in the position I was being held in I could only see his shoe. He continued to talk to me, and I stopped struggling, but the next second I felt my shirt being lifted ever so slightly from behind – presumably by Blackbeard – followed by a sharp prick.

I started struggling again, trying to speak, but this time no words came out and I suddenly felt dizzy and weak, as if all my energy was leaking out of me.

'I think we can take it from here, gents,' said Combover as he and Blackbeard lifted me to my feet.

I could hardly stand now and the two of them had to hold me upright. I also noticed that Combover picked up the bundle of papers Tina had given me.

'Is he all right?' asked one of the security guards.

'He's just play-acting,' answered Blackbeard, speaking for the first time, his voice gruff. 'He's renowned for doing this. Can you get us a wheelchair for him?'

The guard pushed past, giving me an uncertain look as he did so. I tried to catch his eye, because if these guys were police officers, they were definitely the dodgy kind. No cop injects a prisoner with a debilitating drug while trying to restrain him. But the guard had already looked away, and now all my efforts were concentrated on trying to stay awake and on my feet.

A few seconds later, the guard came back with a wheelchair and the two detectives bundled me into it. Combover continued talking to the two guards, and as I sat there in the seat, unable to move, I saw all the waiting people staring at me as if I was some kind of circus exhibit. But as I met their gazes they seemed to melt into one another until they became a single watery blur, and my eyes seemed to close involuntarily.

I felt myself being wheeled through the A and E double doors and out into the fresh air, and then Combover leaned down so his mouth was right by my ear. 'Who gave you all this stuff, Sean?' he hissed, hitting me on the side of the head with the bundle of papers.

The Final Minute

So he knew my real name. I wasn't surprised. Everyone I was meeting at the moment seemed to know a lot more about me than I did. I didn't answer his question. I couldn't have even if I'd wanted to. The power of speech had now well and truly left me.

'You'd better not have done anything stupid,' he whispered. 'Because I'm telling you, you're just as much use to us dead as you are alive.'

And on that cheery note, I fell asleep.

Fifteen

Pen de Souza despised men. They'd mistreated her from the very beginning. Her father had started it. A frustrated alcoholic who thought the world owed him a living, he blamed everyone else for the fact that he was a nobody and had taken his anger out on the two people closest to him – Pen and her mother. Pen's childhood had been a sickening blur of beatings and mental and sexual abuse. Her mom had tried to escape from him many times, but it never worked. She always went back, trailing Pen on her arm, taken in by his repeated empty promises that this time things would be different.

He'd first raped Pen when she was ten years old. She hadn't been Pen then. Her name had been . . . No, she wouldn't even repeat the name of the person she used to be. That person was gone. He said that if she told her mom what he'd done, he'd kill both of them. It was to be their little secret, and if she did what she was told, he'd treat her like a princess. He didn't treat her like a princess. He raped her again, even though she begged him not to. Pen couldn't remember how many times it had happened after that. She didn't like to dwell on it. She didn't like to dwell on any part of her childhood, except for the day when, aged fifteen, she finally fought back.

It was a hot, dry afternoon. Her mom was out and the bastard was drunk, and Pen knew what was coming before it happened. She could feel and smell the tension in the air, and he was watching her in that sneaky way of his.

When he came at her, his movements lumbering and awkward, a lopsided smile on his face, she'd acted instinctively, grabbing an empty Coors bottle from the sideboard. She remembered perfectly the look of surprise on his face and the way the smile faded as he saw her expression. She'd struck him hard round the side of the head. The bottle didn't break but it was a good hit and, as he fell to his knees, one hand pawing at the blood that was already soaking his hair, she'd danced out of his line of sight and brought the bottle down with everything she had on the top of his skull. It shattered then, leaving a broken, jagged neck in her hand, and suddenly she was filled with a sense of power she'd never experienced before. She'd smiled then, and when the bastard had looked up and seen that smile, his eyes had widened in fear. 'Please don't, Princess,' he'd pleaded drunkenly, his eyes half closed as the blood poured from the deep cut on his head. But there'd been no mercy in Pen that day, or on any other day since. Mercy was for the weak. And she would never be weak again.

In a single flash of movement, she'd raked the broken bottle down his face, splitting open his flesh as if it was a ripe watermelon, before slicing off the top half of his left ear, absorbing the delicious sound of his screams, revelling in the pain she was inflicting.

She could have killed him then. She'd wanted to desperately. All it would have taken was a single deep slash across the throat and that would have been the end of his pathetic, hollow life. But Pen was no fool. She knew that it might not be looked upon as justifiable homicide by a judge, and that she could end up spending years in prison, and he wasn't worth sacrificing a part of her life for. So she'd thrown the bottle in the trash and left the bastard bleeding on the floor while she called her mom at work to tell her what had happened.

Foolishly, Pen had thought her mom would understand, but the stupid weak bitch was so much in his thrall that she'd driven straight home, taken one look at her husband's ruined face and burst into tears as she cradled him in her arms. She'd called an ambulance, tried everything to clean up his wounds, and when Pen had tried to explain what had happened and why, her mom had screamed that she was no daughter of hers, that she was the spawn of the Devil and she never wanted to speak to her again.

As soon as he'd recovered, her father pressed charges like the piece of shit he was, and Pen had been arrested. At her trial for assault and battery, her own mother had backed up her father's story that he'd never laid a finger on his daughter, that she was making up her stories of abuse. The judge, a sour-faced old man who probably wore ladies' underwear under his robes, had told Pen she was a cold, sadistic young woman with anger issues and had sentenced her to five years in juvenile prison. It was the second of the many betrayals perpetrated on her by men, but those were other stories, not to be dwelt upon right now. And anyway, now she'd found Tank. He was the only man she cared about, because he was so different from all the rest. They were soulmates; they understood everything about each other; they were one.

Pen was still getting over the fact that she'd come close to losing him the previous night when she and Tank walked over to where a middle-aged man in a suit stood next to his car, holding a briefcase. They were in the middle of a disused airstrip west of London, and it was drizzling with rain.

'What happened last night?' demanded the man in the suit, not bothering with any introductions, even though this was the first time the three of them had met. 'I hear the target got away. That's not what my client's paying you for.' He addressed Tank as he spoke, but the sleazy bastard couldn't help molesting Pen with his eyes.

Both she and Tank had been expecting exactly this kind of question, and had prepared accordingly, but it was Pen who answered, staring down the man in the suit as she spoke. 'I don't know how, but he must have known we were coming. He wasn't in the house when we arrived. We found out from the two looking after him that he'd gone absent without leave late that afternoon, and they didn't know where he was. They also told us that they'd been using a hypnotherapist to try to get the location of the bodies from him but they'd had no success. Apparently the target's suffering from acute amnesia.'

The man in the suit grunted. 'But he's got enough sense to escape from you two.'

'He didn't come back in the house. We heard him stealing a car from the garage, attempted to stop him, but weren't able to.'

'So you're saying it's not your fault?'

Pen remained coolly impassive. 'No, it's not our fault. First of all, it was a rush job, and they're always the riskiest kind. Secondly, the target knew something was wrong before we arrived. There was no way we could have planned for that. So we neutralized the two witnesses and burned the place down.'

The man in the suit nodded slowly as he digested this information, unable to resist another glance at Pen's chest. 'We need the target killed urgently. I don't care how you find him, but find him. Don't bother with the interrogation. We've moved beyond that now, and if he's still suffering from amnesia, he won't divulge anything to anyone else. Just kill him, and kill him fast.'

'We don't have enough information about him,' said Pen, 'and we're operating in a foreign country. It's not going to be easy.'

The man in the suit reached into his briefcase, removed a slim A4 card folder, and handed it to Pen. 'I've got a full dossier on the target's background in there. His real name's Sean Egan and we'll be using all our contacts to help you track him down. But it's essential that he dies before he has a chance to impart the information he's holding.'

'Are you sure he has the information you think he has?'

'Oh, he's got it. The accident may have made him forget it temporarily but his memory will come back at some point, and when it does he'll realize the importance of what he knows. Kill him, and my client's prepared to pay you an extra half a million dollars, on top of the generous sum he's already paying for the job. But fail and he'll be . . .' He paused, as if searching for the right words. 'Very upset indeed.' He let the words hang in the air, so that they were in no doubt of their meaning.

Pen knew the identity of the client. Not only was he a ruthless killer himself but he had immense wealth and resources to back him up. It was she who'd accepted the job, and it was she who took responsibility for it now. 'We'll find him,' she said simply. She nodded to Tank and they turned and walked back to their car in silence. They were taking a big risk agreeing to find a man on the run, but Pen was already thinking about the extra money and the possibility of finally retiring with her lover and living out the rest of their days in a state of bliss.

Kill Sean Egan, and that dream came a whole lot closer. It was all the motivation she needed.

As they got back in the car, Pen squeezed Tank's arm and kissed his massive shoulder through the material of his jacket. 'It's time to hunt, baby,' she whispered, feeling a frisson of excitement.

Sixteen

When I woke up I was in darkness. From the sound of the engine, and the fact that I was crouched in the foetal position and being banged about a fair amount, it didn't take me long to work out that I was in a car boot. My head felt heavy and thick and I experienced a rush of panic as I remembered what had happened to me. I was in the hands of the two men who were meant to be cops but who clearly weren't, and wherever they were taking me, it wasn't going to be good.

I also found out something else about myself that I didn't know: I was claustrophobic. I experienced an immediate rush of sweat-inducing panic as I lay there in the darkness. My hands were still secured behind my back, and I could hardly move. I wanted to cry out but stopped myself. I had to calm down. It was pitch black in the boot and it smelled of dirt and oil, but sooner or later they were going to let me out, and until that time I had to concentrate on thinking of a way out.

The car was moving erratically, with plenty of slowing down and speeding up and going round sharp bends, so I guessed we were out in the country somewhere. I had no idea how long I'd been out for. It could have been five minutes, it could have been five hours – it was impossible to tell. I wondered how they'd tracked me down to the hospital. The fact they weren't legitimate cops meant Tina had had nothing to do with it, and no one else could possibly have known where I was.

But these guys, whoever they were, had known.

It struck me then that maybe at some point during my stay at the house in Wales I'd been fitted with a tracking device similar to the one Tina had given me. That would also explain the fact that Tom had seemed to know where to look for me the previous day. I realized with a sinking feeling that it was probably in my watch. I could feel through the cuffs that I was still wearing it, but when I turned over and managed to lie on my front I could no longer feel the mobile Tina had given me in my front pocket. So they'd clearly searched me, and now they had a phone and a load of articles about my past history that I was going to have to try to explain away without involving Tina.

There was one thing in my favour though, and that was the fact that the tracker Tina had given me had been well hidden in my sock. I was almost certain they wouldn't have searched me there, which meant there was a chance she could still find me if she decided to look. It wasn't much to cling to, of course, but then beggars can't be choosers.

For the next half an hour or so I concentrated on breathing slowly, ignoring my nausea and the fact that I was lying trapped in darkness, as the car continued its meandering journey. I thought about my brother, John. A good man who'd been murdered for trying to do the right thing. I focused on trying to remember more about growing up with him. It was hard, but slowly, very slowly, tiny video clips of memories popped up in my consciousness. John and me fishing at the side of a narrow river as kids; John teaching me to ride a bike on the road outside a vaguely familiar family house; John in his army uniform with the woman I believed to be my mother kissing him on the cheek while I looked on, feeling incredibly happy and proud.

My brother. The man I'd forgotten. The man who'd been dead twenty years.

A conflicting mix of emotions swirled through me. Happiness that my memories were coming back, but a sense of gloom and frustration that the people I most cared about were long gone, and that no one had replaced them. And fear too, because I had no idea what was going to happen next.

The car slowed and turned down a bumpy track. It hit a pothole and I banged my head on the boot lid. A minute later, the car turned again, then stopped. One of the doors opened and I heard the faint clatter of gates being opened, then we were moving again, but only for a few seconds this time before the car came to a halt and I heard the engine being turned off.

I closed my eyes, deciding that for the moment feigning sleep was my best bet to avoid answering any awkward questions.

The lid flew open and I was manhandled out. I kept my body floppy and fell on to my side, eyes still shut.

'Listen, you fuck, get up. We know you're awake.' The voice belonged to Blackbeard, and he sounded angry.

I didn't respond, and it was Combover who spoke next, his

voice calmer: 'Come on, Sean. We only gave you a very small amount of anaesthetic. The effects would have worn off a while ago, so play-acting's not going to help you.'

Again I saw no advantage in responding, so I didn't.

Unfortunately, this turned out to be a bad move because a couple of seconds later I felt an excruciating pain as one of them – I strongly suspected it was Blackbeard – kicked me very hard right in the balls.

My eyes shot open and I was unable to stop myself from crying out. The pain was horrible, and I rolled round on the hard gravel surface, wanting to clutch the affected area but unable to, with my hands cuffed behind my back. I also got my first glimpse of where I was. I could see the bottom of a large wooden building about twenty yards away, with trees and greenery beyond. Birds sang and the sun had even managed to fight its way through the clouds, which somehow made the whole thing far worse.

'I told you the fucker was bluffing,' said Blackbeard, and the next second I saw his foot come hurtling towards me. He caught me right in the gut. The blow hurt, but it was nothing compared to my nuts, which felt like they'd been driven back into my bladder and were now permanently jammed in there.

It was a bit late to continue feigning sleep now so I manoeuvred myself into the foetal position, bringing up my knees and lowering my head to make myself as small a target as possible, as Blackbeard brought his foot back to deliver another kick.

'All right, that'll do,' said Combover. 'He's softened up enough. Now, get up, Sean.' He leaned down and hauled me up by the scruff of my neck.

I didn't bother resisting this time and managed to clamber

unsteadily to my feet, seeing my surroundings properly for the first time. The building I'd seen while I was lying on the ground was an old pitched-timber barn that backed on to open fields. Opposite it across the dusty, lightly gravelled yard was a dilapidated building that might have been a workshop or farmhouse but had clearly been empty for some time. A further outbuilding stood next to it, and behind that was a wall of mature oak trees, blocking any further view. The place was deserted and, aside from the birdsong and the faint hum of traffic in the distance, there were no sounds at all. Even if I screamed my head off, no one would hear me. It wasn't a pleasant thought.

The sun was starting to set and there was a slight chill in the air. I guessed the time was between six and seven, and as the two of them frogmarched me across the yard to the barn, I wondered when, or indeed if, I was ever going to see the sun again.

Combover used a key to unlock the heavy padlock on the barn's double doors, and as they opened and I was led inside, I caught a very distinct smell of something stale and unpleasant.

There was nothing in the barn but a few empty diesel barrels lined up against one wall and a metal chair in the middle of the room, which looked like it had been clamped to the floor. Two chains about six inches long, with metal restraints attached, hung from each arm; two further sets of chains and restraints were coiled by the chair's front legs. An orange plastic bucket sat next to the chair and I noticed that there was a thin trail of something dark and dried running down the bucket to the concrete floor, and several dark stains dotted about the chair in an irregular pattern. It wasn't hard to guess what the stains were, or what this contraption was used for, and I temporarily forgot the pain in my balls as

I realized with an injection of adrenalin and fear that I was here to be tortured.

'Christ, it stinks in here,' grunted Blackbeard as they removed the restraints they'd put me in back at the hospital and shoved me down in the chair.

For a split second I thought about making a break for it before they had a chance to strap me in, but the thought disappeared as Combover produced a small revolver from somewhere inside his suit and pointed it at my head. 'Don't even think about it, Sean,' he said with a smile that created laughter lines around his amused blue eyes.

That was the thing about Combover when you looked at him closely. He looked and sounded like a nice, trustworthy, eminently reasonable guy, the sort who would do everything he could to avoid inflicting pain. It was, I had to admit, a great act, and even as he pointed a gun at me I found it difficult to dislike him too much. But somehow I also knew he'd use it if he had to.

'The thing is, we're always one step ahead of you,' he continued as Blackbeard applied the chains to make sure I wasn't going anywhere. 'You need to remember that. And if you want to get out of here in one piece, you need to do exactly as you're told. Understand?'

I nodded, but my attention was once again drawn to the bucket. There were two pairs of pliers of different sizes propped up inside, and a thick, dried-up pool of blood at the bottom. I could see what looked like a sprinkling of tiny yellow stones amid the blood, and it took a couple of seconds for me to realize that they were teeth. I felt my mouth go dry. 'Sure,' I said weakly.

'Good. We want to do this as smoothly and stress-free as possible.' Combover nodded to Blackbeard, who'd finished strapping me to the chair now. 'Would you mind waiting outside for a few moments? I want to speak to Sean alone.'

Blackbeard muttered something under his breath, but did as he was told.

When the barn door had closed behind him, Combover sighed deeply, carefully smoothed his hair so it covered the majority of his bald patch, then looked down at me with a sympathetic expression. He'd lost the gun without me noticing, but then he seemed to have the magician's knack for making things materialize and disappear at will. 'I won't bullshit you, Sean. And I don't want you to bullshit me either. If you answer my questions truthfully, there may be a way out of this for you. I'm not guaranteeing anything, but if you give us the information we need, it's possible you'll be allowed to live.'

Now it was my time to sigh. 'For some reason, I don't feel too optimistic you'll keep your side of the bargain.'

'The only reason to kill you would be to make sure you keep your mouth shut, but you've already got an extremely good reason to do that.'

'Oh yeah? What's that then?'

'Because you're implicated in mass murder,' he said simply.

I thought of my recurring dream then, and immediately pictured the body of the dead woman on the bed – the woman Tina Boyd was searching for – and the beautiful blonde propped up against the wall, bleeding. And the fear in her eyes as she saw me approaching her.

'You're not saying anything, Sean. That's because you

remember, isn't it?' He was still smiling, but there was nothing pleasant about it now.

I shook my head. 'I don't know what you're talking about. I really don't. I've been suffering from amnesia.'

'So you don't know who you are then?'

I was exhausted, both physically and mentally, but even so, I knew he was trying to catch me out here, and there was no way I was going to give up Tina. 'I remember my name,' I told him. 'It came back to me today. That's why I printed all that stuff about me off the internet.'

'Where did you print it off?'

'In an internet café in Paddington near the hospital where you picked me up. How did you find me, by the way?'

'Don't try to turn this around, Sean. You answer the questions, not me.'

'And I am answering them.' The pain in my groin had faded to a dull, insistent ache, and I realized almost with surprise that I was desperately thirsty. 'Can I have a drink of water please?'

He shook his head. 'Not until you start telling the truth. And right now, I don't think you are. Because for a man with full-on amnesia, you seem to be remarkably self-sufficient. Where did you get the phone you had on you?'

'I bought it in a phone shop.'

'Why?'

'Because I thought I might need it,' I snapped, feigning annoyance at the way the conversation was going.

I'd been in this kind of situation before, I was sure of it. Having to think on my feet under pressure; having to talk for my life. I was good at it too. I remembered that Tina had said at one time

I'd been an undercover cop, and the printed-off documents had confirmed it. The problem was, the man I was trying to convince almost certainly knew my background too.

Combover produced the phone from his pocket. 'What's the code to open it?' he asked casually.

I feigned puzzlement, knowing that I couldn't let him have it, because then he'd have Tina's number. After a few seconds' silence I shook my head wearily. 'Jesus, I can't remember.'

'Fuck you, Sean. I told you not to try to put one over on me.'

'I'm serious. Jesus, with everything else that's happened these past twenty-four hours I'm surprised I can remember anything. I'm sorry. Maybe it'll come back to me.' I sighed loudly.

Combover's expression softened a little. 'Tell me what happened last night back at the house in Wales.'

Something dawned on me then. The reason why Combover's voice seemed vaguely familiar. 'It was you who phoned the house, wasn't it? And told me to get out. You thought you were talking to Tom.'

'I told you to answer the questions. What happened last night?'

I told him the exact truth as it had happened, starting from me returning to the house from my walk, and leaving nothing out.

When I'd finished, Combover nodded slowly, as if this all made sense, which I guess to him it did. Unfortunately, very little of it did to me.

'The people who tried to kill you are very dangerous, and very ruthless. They want the same information from you that we do. The location of the bodies.'

'Whose bodies?' I asked, trying to rid my mind of the images from my dream. The images of death and fear.

'I think you know, Sean, and if you don't, then I'd advise you to try very hard to remember.'

'Can you at least give me some idea of what's going on? It might help.'

'I'll tell you this. The people trying to kill you are a threat to national security. If they find out where these bodies we're talking about are, it puts them in a position of great power. It also means that, as the only person who knows their location – and somewhere in your head, Sean, I can promise you that you do hold that information – you are an extreme danger to them. As a result, they will move heaven and earth to kill you. If we find those bodies first, it'll ruin them – and that will immediately remove the threat to your life. So, if you can tell me the answer to that question, there's every chance you'll get an opportunity to start a new life away from here. That's a pretty big incentive to start talking.'

'It is,' I said, 'but at the moment I honestly can't help you.' Whether Combover was lying or not was irrelevant. If I'd had the information, I'd have given it to him, if only for a glass of ice-cold water. One way or another, I just wanted this nightmare to end.

Combover looked disappointed, as if he'd put his trust in me and I'd somehow let him down. 'I'm going to call your therapist, Dr Bronson. He's going to come here and you're going to let him put you under, and see if we can get to the truth that way. I know he hasn't been successful so far, but this time you're going to work with him like you've never worked before. Because be in no doubt, Sean, your life depends on it. And if we don't get what we want that way, we'll have to start using more direct methods.'

He glanced down at the bucket just so I wasn't in any doubt what he meant by that.

'I'm telling the truth. I promise.'

'Well, we'll soon find out. My colleague's going to take over from me now while I phone Dr Bronson, and I'll be straight with you. He's going to hurt you. I'm afraid he enjoys inflicting pain far too much. However, he's also a professional, so firstly he'll make sure you're conscious and able to work with the good doctor when he arrives, and secondly he'll stop the minute you start actually telling us what we want to hear.'

'But I can't tell you what you want to hear if I don't know what the hell it is!' I said, the desperation in my voice all too real. I didn't think I could handle any more pain, and I felt the fear getting the better of me. 'Please. I'll do everything I can to cooperate. And can I just have a drink of water?'

Combover shook his head dismissively and turned away. 'Try not to scream too much,' he said over his shoulder as he walked out of the door, leaving me alone and helpless.

Seventeen

It didn't take Tina long to find an address for Dylan Mackay, the man who'd supposedly asked Lauren and her friend Jen if they wanted to do escort work, and who, according to Sheryl, seemed so keen to forget Lauren had ever existed. In Tina's experience it didn't take long to find anyone if they weren't making much effort to hide themselves, and Dylan was clearly not too bothered about keeping a low profile. It made it easier that he also owned his own property. According to the Land Registry, there were only two homeowners in Kensington with the name Dylan Mackay, and having taken down their details and full names, a simple Google search quickly brought up the Facebook photo she'd seen in Sheryl's flat of the good-looking young man with the dark curly hair and arrogant pose. She needn't have asked for a copy after all because his privacy settings were obviously non-existent. He was even on LinkedIn, which was somewhat ironic, given the paucity of his CV. It brought a smile to Tina's face to be reminded how foolish some people could be in allowing themselves to be plastered all over the internet for all to see, particularly if they were involved in things they shouldn't be. Sheryl had suggested that Dylan was some kind of pimp, and Tina couldn't see why she'd lie. A quick credit check had revealed that, although Dylan's flat was worth upwards of seven hundred grand in the current, hugely inflated London property market, his mortgage was four hundred thousand, and he had a credit card and other debts totalling a further one hundred and twenty grand, and these were just the ones listed. So Dylan clearly needed money, which to Tina's mind enhanced his value as a decent lead.

She looked at her watch. It was twenty past six. She could pay him a visit now but it was the middle of rush hour, and there was no guarantee that he'd be there. He struck Tina as the kind of guy who didn't get up too early in the mornings, so she decided to leave it until tomorrow.

She thought of Sean then, and wondered what had happened to him. It had been a good four hours since she'd dropped him off at the hospital and she hadn't heard anything. She considered trying the mobile she'd given him, but concluded it was probably safer to check the tracker he was carrying. It wasn't that she was paranoid, but she didn't want anyone knowing she was working with Sean, not when he'd already admitted to her that he'd been indirectly involved in two murders. By rights, Tina should have reported what he'd told her to the police, since conversations between private detectives and clients weren't covered by the same laws of confidentiality that lawyers enjoyed. But for the moment she was prepared to give him the benefit of the doubt, as long as he kept his distance.

She accessed the website that tracked the device's movements, keyed in its ID number, and felt a jolt of surprise when she saw its location. The red light was flashing in a semi-rural area about five miles north-west of junction 18 of the M25, on the Hertfordshire/Buckinghamshire border. She zoomed in as far as she could go and frowned when she saw a collection of buildings that made up a place called Cherry Tree Farm.

What the hell was he doing there? Tina went through the possible explanations. Sean had been seen by a doctor in A and E and, with severe amnesia diagnosed, he'd been sectioned under the Mental Health Act and had been taken to a secure facility to be evaluated in more detail. She didn't buy that, though. Firstly, Cherry Tree Farm didn't look big enough to be a mental health facility. Secondly, it was almost impossible for Sean to have arrived there that quickly, not with all the paperwork that would have been needed. Thirdly, he was unlikely to have been sectioned. He might have amnesia, but he was very much in control of his faculties.

The only other innocent explanation she could think of was that he'd got cold feet and left A and E before they'd seen him. But even if he'd done that, why on earth would he have gone to an isolated farm in the middle of nowhere? And how would he have got there? A taxi in rush-hour traffic, taking in a big chunk of north-west London, would probably cost more than the hundred pounds Tina had lent him. It was possible that some memory had come back which linked him to the farm and that was why he'd gone there, but to Tina that too seemed hugely unlikely.

Which left only one alternative. Something was wrong, and Sean was in trouble.

Just in case the tracker and Sean had somehow parted company, Tina grabbed her mobile and dialled the hospital, asking to be put through to a Mr Matthew Barron.

The receptionist asked her what ward he was on.

'I don't know. I dropped him off at A and E this afternoon. He's got amnesia. Is it possible to check whether he's been admitted? I was going to come down and visit him.'

As she waited for the receptionist to check, she wandered outside and lit a cigarette, taking a long, much-needed drag.

'I'm afraid no one under that name's been admitted,' said the receptionist, coming back on the line.

Tina asked her to check that he hadn't been admitted under the name Sean Egan. The receptionist wasn't happy but she eventually acquiesced, although when she came back on the line, Tina wasn't surprised to hear that there was no patient under that name in the hospital either.

She thanked the receptionist and ended the call, wondering what to do now. She was hungry and tired but she couldn't just leave things like this. If Sean hadn't left the hospital voluntarily, then that meant he'd been taken by someone. It struck her then that the people who'd been holding him in Wales could have fitted him with a tracking device of their own. It might have been on a watch, or it might even have been fitted internally if they'd known what they were doing, and had access to the real high-tech devices. Either way, she should have thought of it.

Still, it was too late to worry about that now. She stubbed out the cigarette and went back inside.

The Final Minute

It was time to take a drive to Cherry Tree Farm and hope that Sean was still there.

And still alive.

Eighteen

Robert Whatret was sitting in his front room watching the news on TV and not really concentrating too much, when the phone rang.

He felt a familiar sense of dread when he saw that the call was from a withheld number. With a shaking hand, he put the phone to his ear.

'We've got our man back,' said Mr H.

'Thank goodness,' said Whatret, not quite sure what this meant for him.

'We're holding him at a location just out of town. It should be about an hour's drive for you at this time of night. I'm going to text you the location at the end of this call. You need to get over here right away.'

'I've been drinking.'

'How much?'

'I'm over the limit.'

'Then make sure you don't get caught.'

Mr H's tone was hard and businesslike, and contained not a shred of empathy. Whatret felt a cold dread flush through his bloodstream, making him shiver involuntarily. He cursed himself silently for getting involved in this whole business.

'What do you need me to do with him?' he asked.

'Make him remember where the bodies are. I don't care how you do it, or how long it takes, so bring an overnight bag because you're staying with him until he coughs up the answer.'

'I can't just—'

'Shut up, Whatret. We're beyond "can'ts". We need that information, and you're going to get it for us. And I'll tell you something else. He's already remembering things, and he's certainly not the docile, spaced-out guy you reckoned he was yesterday when you saw him. He managed to escape the trained assassins who killed the other two and get all the way to London without too much trouble. As well as remembering his real name. So were you lying when you talked to me earlier?'

'No, of course not,' said Whatret a little too quickly, debating whether he should come clean about Sean's description of the dream, and immediately deciding against it. 'I wouldn't lie to you.'

'Good. You're ours now, Whatret. You do what we say. Understand?'

Mr H's words confirmed what Whatret had always suspected but never liked to admit to himself. By taking this job, he'd sold his soul, and the chances were he was never going to get it back. He took a deep breath, already sobering up. 'I understand,' he said. 'I'm on my way.'

*

Mr H replaced the phone in his trouser pocket. He was going to have to work out how they were going to kill Whatret once all this was over without raising suspicion. An alcoholic who was scared out of his wits couldn't be trusted not to shoot his mouth off to someone. It was possible they could do it tonight if he managed to get the information out of Egan. It would be convenient to kill the two of them together and bury them somewhere on the farm where their corpses would never be found. That way they could finally bring an end to this whole sorry saga. And not before time.

As he walked alongside the barn, Mr H heard Egan cry out in pain as his colleague, Balham, got to work on him. Mr H couldn't understand why anyone got a kick out of inflicting pain. Violence was sometimes necessary in order to restore equilibrium, but as far as Mr H was concerned, it was always regrettable, and if there was any other way to achieve the same result, then he preferred to take it.

'How's it going, Sean?' he asked, going inside and shutting the door behind him. Darkness was falling now and the overhead light was on, illuminating Egan as he sat slumped in the chair, bleeding from the lip and the nose, while Balham stood next to him with a pair of pliers in his hand.

Egan looked up at him wearily and Mr H noticed a cut running along his right eyebrow, which was oozing blood. 'I keep telling your friend, I don't know anything.'

'The bastard isn't talking,' said Balham, panting slightly. 'I was going to start on his front teeth.' He opened and closed the pliers a couple of times, trying hard not to look too excited. 'I'd stand well back. It's going to get a bit messy.'

Egan looked really scared now, and when he spoke he addressed Mr H. 'Please. I've told you all I know.'

'I don't think you have, Sean,' said Mr H calmly, waiting for a couple of seconds to see if he might break as Balham approached him with the pliers.

Egan moved his head rapidly from side to side letting out desperate moans from behind pursed lips until Balham got behind him and put him in a headlock, lifting the pliers to his mouth.

'All right, leave his teeth in for now,' said Mr H. 'We're going to give him another chance.'

Balham looked annoyed but knew better than to argue. He released Egan from the headlock and moved away.

Egan took a deep breath, keeping his mouth tightly shut, and looked at Mr H warily. 'Thank you.'

'I'm putting myself out for you, Sean, but rest assured, if we think you're holding back on us, you're going to lose your teeth. Maybe all of them.'

'I'm not holding back.'

'Do you want a drink?' He showed Egan the bottle of mineral water he was carrying.

Egan nodded eagerly. 'Yes please. I'm going to do everything I can to cooperate. I promise you.'

'Good. That's what I like to hear.'

Mr H had conducted plenty of interrogations in his time, some of which had been carried out with the threat of violence always in the background. Usually, he found that the threat was enough. He also knew that, given time, anyone could be broken down. Sometimes it took days, even weeks, and Mr H suspected that Egan would be harder than most, given that he'd spent more than a decade as an undercover police officer. But out here, on private land, far from prying eyes, they had all the time they needed to break him.

He crouched down beside Sean and placed the bottle gently to his lips but didn't let him drink. 'Are you sure you've told me the truth about everything, Sean?'

Egan nodded and Mr H smiled at him, letting him take a long gulp.

'That's enough for now,' he said, removing the bottle and standing back up. 'What do you say?'

Egan looked up at him with real gratitude in his eyes. 'Thanks,' he whispered.

Mr H nodded slowly, pleased at the response. Then he turned to Balham. 'Take a tooth.'

Nineteen

Tina parked her car in the shadows of a narrow stretch of woodland that, according to the map on her laptop, was about two
hundred metres east of the three buildings that made up Cherry
Tree Farm. The tracker she'd given Sean was designed to be
accurate to within five metres, and its location appeared to be the
westernmost building.

Tina closed the laptop, slipped it under the passenger seat, and
stepped out of the car, shutting the door quietly. A car drove past
on the road behind her but it was going fast and its headlights
had soon disappeared into the gloom. She looked at her watch.
8.20 p.m. About six hours since she'd dropped Sean off at A and
E. A lot could have happened to him in that time.

Tina had no idea what kind of situation she was walking into,
and the thought both unnerved and excited her. She'd come close
to dying more than once in the past few years, but those had been

days when her life was dark and directionless, when she'd had little to live for. Things had changed now. She was reasonably content with her cottage in the country, and her job as a private detective was bringing in a steady income. She didn't need to put her neck on the line any more, and it wasn't just herself she had to worry about either. Her mum had had a cancer scare at the end of the previous year, and her father had taken Tina aside one day and told her in as calm and loving a way as possible that part of the reason for the illness was her constant fear that Tina was going to end up killing herself. 'You can't keep doing this, love,' he'd said. 'It hurts both of us. I can take the pain. But your mum finds it very, very hard. Please think of her next time you find yourself doing these kinds of dangerous things. Because one day they're going to get you killed.'

Tina had always had a decent relationship with her parents. They'd always been good to her, and the self-destructive issues that had dogged her in the past had been the result of her time in the police force rather than any unresolved childhood trauma. 'It's OK, Dad,' she'd told him with a warm smile. 'Those days are behind me now.'

But they weren't. Because somehow trouble had sought Tina out once again, and now here she was creeping through woods in darkness, trying to help an amnesiac fugitive and convicted rapist who appeared to be mixed up with some very dangerous people. She'd thought again about involving the police but, in the end, she had no proof that anything bad had actually happened to Sean. It had seemed a better idea to investigate herself first. But as she came to the edge of the treeline and saw the ramshackle farm buildings directly in front of her – dark, empty and deserted

– and beyond them the imposing-looking barn at the far end with a faint slither of light escaping from inside, she knew that something was very wrong.

She paused and looked around. She couldn't see any parked cars or hear any voices. The night was cool and still. Everything was deadly quiet. She reached inside the pockets of her jacket, feeling the reassuring grip of her weapons: an illegal Taser bought in Belgium, a can of pepper spray from a hardware shop in France, and a small lead cosh she'd picked up in an antique shop in Camden, which was for when everything else failed. If she was caught with any of them, she'd face prosecution; caught with all three, she'd almost certainly end up with a long spell in prison. None of that bothered her, though, because in the end she'd always rather be able to defend herself, and worry about everything else afterwards.

An unwelcome vision of her dad trying to reason with her, the anxiety and disappointment clear in his eyes, crossed her mind, but she forced it away. It was time to move.

The adrenalin pumped through her and she felt the thrill of illicit excitement as she crept out from the trees and moved quickly but silently round the back of the first building, which looked to be little more than an outhouse. A low fence that might once have been part of a pigsty jutted out of the ground, and she had to step carefully over it before circumnavigating the rear of the second building – a single-storey house with a shallow slate roof that had partially caved in. Tina wondered who owned this place and why it had been left in such a state of disrepair. She made a mental note to check with the Land Registry when she got a chance because it seemed highly likely that it was no random coincidence Sean had been brought to a place as isolated as this one.

Twenty yards separated her from the barn now. A black Audi A6 was parked next to it, partially obscured by the stringy branches of a weeping willow, and beyond it was a high-wire fence with padlocked gates blocking access from the road.

Tina took the Taser from her pocket, her finger resting on the trigger, and listened hard. Thanks to the lack of ambient noise, she was sure she could hear muffled voices coming from inside the warehouse. She took a deep breath and stepped out from the cover of the building, creeping quietly across the yard towards the barn doors.

When she reached the doors, she stopped and put her ear against the wood. She could hear two men talking quietly but couldn't work out what they were saying. Neither of them was Sean, though, she was sure of that. She was trying to work out what to do next, and not coming up with any obvious ideas, when she heard the unmistakable sound of car tyres on gravel. She looked round the side of the barn and saw headlights approaching the locked gates, followed by the ringing of a phone inside the barn. One of the men answered the phone and his voice got louder as he approached the barn doors.

Without hesitating, Tina slipped out of sight round the blind side of the barn just as the door opened and the man emerged, no longer talking on the phone.

Robert Whatret pulled up at the gates to the rendezvous, wishing he could be any place rather than here. As a city man born and bred he wasn't used to the darkness and silence he was experiencing now. This was a lonely place where the trees rose up like grim sentinels and the night felt like it was enveloping him.

They could kill him here and no one would ever know. It would be easy. More worryingly, it would also be convenient. Whatret knew he knew too much. Mr H had all but told him so. This left him in a terrible quandary. If he didn't get the man he still knew as Matt to remember the exact details of what happened on the night of his car accident, then he was no use to the men wanting the information. Yet even if he did get them what they wanted, the net result would still be the same. His usefulness would have run out.

Whatret tried to slow his breathing, repeating the word 'calm' under his breath in that slow, melodious tone he'd always used with his patients in the days when the world had been at his feet and he'd been a man of substance.

It didn't work. He wanted to run. Grab his money and head somewhere they couldn't find him.

But a figure was already walking confidently towards him through the darkness, his face illuminated by the headlights.

Whatret swallowed. It was too late.

Twenty

It was strange. While I'd been sitting chained and helpless in this seat, as I'd been slapped, threatened and finally held down while one of my back teeth was torn out with a pair of pliers, something had happened. I'd had a vision of a tall, cadaverous man in his fifties with a bald head and the look of an undertaker sitting opposite me in an office somewhere. When the man spoke, his accent was plummy and patrician, but his words had hit me like stones. 'Always deny, Sean. Never admit to anything. Your legend is your lifeline. Keep to your story, no matter what they put you through. Because the moment you show weakness, you're dead.' A long time ago that man had been my boss in the police. I even knew his name – or at least what I'd called him behind his back. Captain Bob. Something bad had happened to him too, although I couldn't remember what it was.

But right now all that mattered were those words of advice

from long ago, and I'd used them to resist everything my two captors had thrown at me. I was in a lot of pain. The tooth was agony, and I was almost deliriously thirsty, but I could tell that Combover – the man in charge – was beginning to believe that I was telling the truth. Unfortunately, though, that was pretty irrelevant since I had no long-term strategy for getting out of there, and no idea about the location of the bodies they were after.

It sounded like Dr Bronson had arrived to try to move things along. Combover had just left the room to go and meet him, leaving Blackbeard staring at me sullenly from a few feet away. He didn't say anything. In fact, he looked quite bored. He'd enjoyed hurting me earlier, there was no doubt about that. He'd worn a tight bully's smile as he'd beaten me, and later, when he'd shown me the bloody tooth he'd removed with the pliers, holding it in front of me in the palm of his hand, he'd looked genuinely happy, as if he'd been showing me a trophy one of his kids had won. But it seemed that for now his sadism had been sated.

The hole where the tooth had been so rudely yanked out was still bleeding a little, but less so now. I spat out a mix of blood and saliva then felt round my mouth with my tongue, touching the hole gingerly, before exploring the other teeth, wondering, with less fear than I would have expected, which one they might go for next.

That was when I felt it. A filling in one of my back teeth that seemed to stick out just a little too much from the cavity. The texture didn't feel right either. I wondered why I'd never noticed it before. I also wondered what it was, because if it wasn't a filling, then it was something that had been placed in there artificially.

Like a tracking device.

'What are you doing?' demanded Blackbeard.

'Nothing,' I said, noticing the barn door opening ever so slightly behind him and a female figure slip inside. Even though I was concentrating on looking at Blackbeard rather than her, I knew it was Tina, and I had to work to keep a lid on the burst of hope and excitement that suddenly shot through me. 'Just checking the damage you did to me. You'd better hope the situation's never reversed, because if it is, I'll take you to pieces.'

He took a step forward, his face contorting into an angry sneer. 'They're never going to be reversed. Because you're not walking out of here.'

'We'll see,' I said, looking him right in the eye.

He raised a hand to hit me but at the last second he must have heard movement behind him because he turned round suddenly.

But it was too late. I heard what sounded like a crackle of electricity and Blackbeard grunted and fell to the floor, writhing and shaking wildly. And then Tina was standing over me, looking concerned.

'Shit, Sean. You look bad.'

'Quick,' I snapped. 'The keys are in his left pocket. It's a small silver one, does all of them.'

Tina crouched down, rummaged round and quickly produced a set of keys.

'That one, that one,' I said as she looked through them.

Tina didn't hesitate. Like me, she knew we hardly had any time, but her hands weren't shaking as she reached over and undid the wrist restraints. As she repeated the process with the ones securing my ankles, I reached down and grabbed the bloody pliers from the bucket, before turning my attention to the barn door, knowing that if Combover walked through we were finished.

I heard a car pull up directly outside the barn, which meant that they were going to be coming back in any second.

'Right, go!' hissed Tina, jumping to her feet.

There was no time for subtlety now. Nor any point in telling her that Combover had a gun. The only important thing was getting the hell out of there. I was on my feet in a second, stumbling at first from the stiffness in my legs, but quickly overcoming it. With Tina leading the way, we ran out of the doors and sprinted across the yard into the darkness.

I heard an angry shout not far behind us, followed by Combover's angry command of 'Stop or I'll shoot!'

But there was no way I was stopping now. And nor, it seemed, was Tina as she sprinted towards the cover of the nearest building, with me racing to keep up with her.

A shot rang out. I wasn't sure how close it came to me but the bullet ricocheted off the wall in front of me before zinging off into the darkness somewhere.

'Next shot's in your back, Sean!' screamed Combover, but there was desperation in his voice now and I was already ducking down as I ran round the back of the empty building and out of his line of fire.

We kept running. Up ahead, Tina jumped a small fence that popped up out of nowhere. I did the same, but stumbled and fell, hitting something hard. I rolled over, grunting in pain, but was on my feet in a second, feeling a wave of exhilaration at the fact I was suddenly free. Even as I ran I was already swearing to myself that I wouldn't get caught like this again. From now on I was going to stay free.

I followed Tina as she ran into a line of woodland that bordered the last of the buildings, risking a quick glance over my shoulder. There was no one coming but I knew they weren't going to let us go this easily. And I was almost certain that I was still wearing some kind of device they could use to track me. I pulled off my watch and threw it into some brambles. I remember being given it by Jane, which meant there was every chance it could contain the tracker. Even now, with everything else going on, I felt a sting of betrayal at what she'd done to me. For two long months she'd let me believe she was my sister, lying to me about our supposed upbringing, deliberately trying to keep me in a zombie-like state. Heartless bitch.

We emerged from the trees on to a narrow country road. Twenty yards further up a Ford Focus was parked on the bank. Tina ran up and unlocked it, and the two of us jumped inside.

'You're wearing a tracker, Sean,' she said urgently, switching on the engine.

'I know. It's the only way they could have found me. I think it might be my watch. I've thrown it away.'

'Good. Are you OK?'

'I've been better. You?'

'Well, I wasn't expecting to be shot at today,' she said, pulling away and accelerating fast, without putting her lights on.

'At least you didn't get hit.'

'That really isn't much consolation.'

After a couple of minutes, we came to a junction and Tina flicked on the headlights before pulling out on to a main road and putting her foot down, quickly catching up the car in front of us.

She glanced over at my hand. 'Why have you got those pliers?'

I was reluctant to tell her but knew I had to. 'Because the

tracker might not be in my watch. I was just feeling round in the back of my mouth with my tongue and there's a filling back there that doesn't feel right.'

She cursed. 'That's all we need. I can't afford to have people after me. We'll have to stop and take a look.'

A parking lane appeared up ahead with two stationary lorries in it and Tina pulled up behind them, switching on the car's interior light and producing a small torch from her jacket. I had to admit I liked her professionalism. There was no indecision where she was concerned. She just did what she had to do, and best of all, she did it fast.

'Open your mouth wide.'

I did as I was told and she leaned in and shone the light inside. She was so close that I could smell her hair and her natural scent, and I felt the stirrings of attraction as I breathed them in. She was a good-looking woman. Her coolness under pressure was just an added turn-on.

'Jesus, they made a mess in here. Did the bastards pull one of your teeth?'

I made a noise to signify yes but that was about all I could manage.

'OK, there's something in here that doesn't look right . . .' she murmured. Then: 'Oh shit, yeah. I think that might be it. It's going to have to come out. I'm sorry.' She pulled back from my mouth and looked me in the eye, still very close. 'Do you want me to do it?'

I handed her the pliers and took a deep breath, suddenly not so interested in what she looked like. 'Go for it,' I said.

Credit to Tina, she didn't bother saying anything along the

lines of 'this is going to hurt' or 'I'm sorry I have to do this to you'. Instead, she got me to open my mouth wide again and used the torch to orientate herself before clamping the pliers round the offending tooth and pulling me into a headlock.

I shut my eyes, knowing this was necessary, and tried to move my mind to another, gentler place. I thought of my brother John and tried to picture us together fishing on a summer's day many years ago. And as I thought this, another vision drifted into my consciousness. John and me in the local park. I was very young, maybe six years old, and he was teaching me how to ride a bike. He gave me a big push and I wobbled on the bike before finally balancing on my own for the first time. When I didn't fall off, the confidence seemed to bloom in me, and I could hear John's shouts of encouragement as I began to pedal—

The pain tore through me in a single sharp burst and I had to use all my self-discipline not to pull out of Tina's grip until the tooth came free.

When it did, I fell back in my seat, groped for the electric window controls, and spat a mouthful of blood through the opening gap.

'Here, have some water,' said Tina, handing me a plastic bottle.

I spat out some more blood then took a series of huge gulps, ignoring the fact that I was swallowing blood as well as water. I was too thirsty. I finished the bottle, wiped my mouth, and looked at the tooth in Tina's hand. It didn't look much out of the ordinary, but what was supposed to be the white filling was jutting out a couple of millimetres from the tooth as if it didn't quite fit properly, and the material appeared to be plastic rather than enamel.

'I think this is our tracker,' said Tina, poking the end of it with a nicely shaped fingernail. 'I'd love to take a closer look at it, but . . .' She threw it out of the window, and pulled back out on to the road. 'I don't think it would be such a good idea.'

I spat more blood into the water bottle before checking out the new hole at the back of my mouth. It was directly opposite to the tooth Blackbeard had yanked out, so at least it was symmetrical, although chewing wasn't going to be a lot of fun for a while yet.

But you know what? I didn't care. I was alive. I had hope. And I was having more memories.

I settled back in the seat, trying not to think about the pain that was coming in hot, intense waves and concentrating instead on thinking about Tina. Attractive, sexy, determined, and hard.

Jesus. She was definitely my kind of woman.

Twenty-one

After a long roundabout drive lasting a good half an hour, we pulled into a village which was little more than a street with a mix of modern and traditional houses on either side, and a pub.

'Is this where you live?' I asked as she slowed down in front of a row of quaint terraced cottages that looked like they'd been built when no one was taller than five foot three.

She gave me a stern look. 'That's right. And don't get any ideas, Sean. You're not staying.'

'Come on, Tina. Where else am I going to go? I'm hurt. And I've got no money. Well, not much.'

She switched off the engine and motioned for me to follow her inside. 'Whatever you might think, you're still a convicted rapist,' she said when she'd shut the door behind us and switched on the lights.

The words hit me a lot harder than the attack I'd been subjected to earlier, and immediately darkened my mood. 'But you know me,' I said, with more desperation in my voice than I would have liked.

'No, I don't know you,' she countered, walking into the kitchen and turning to face me. '*You* don't even know you.'

'I saved your life once.'

'And I've just saved yours, so that makes us quits. Now I'm going to clean you up, then book you into a hotel.' She searched in one of the cupboards before coming up with a bag of cotton-wool buds and some antiseptic. 'Sit down.'

I sat down at the small kitchen table and waited while she gently applied the antiseptic to the injuries on my face. It hurt, but then so did everything else, and I was beginning to get used to it. What I found harder was resisting the urge to lean forward and kiss Tina on the lips. Our faces were only a foot or two apart, and it was difficult not to look into her bright eyes and think of all the things we could be doing right now . . . Yet in her eyes I was a rapist, and for the moment I couldn't prove otherwise.

'How do I look?' I asked, with the beginnings of a smile.

'Not your best. They did a number on you back there. Is the inside of your mouth still bleeding?'

'Not enough to worry me. They were after the same information the people last night were after. The location of the bodies that I'm meant to know about. I'm still wondering if it has anything to do with my recurring dream.'

'And do you remember anything else about the dream?'

'Not at the moment, but my memory's beginning to come back. I'm getting flashbacks all the time. It's just a matter of piecing them all together. The stuff you printed out for me helped, but the guys who took me got hold of it before I finished reading.'

Tina's eyes narrowed. 'You didn't tell them where you got it from, did you?'

'No. That's why they were knocking me around. They didn't believe me when I told them that I'd found the information myself. I didn't give you up, Tina. I wouldn't do that.'

Her expression softened. 'Thanks. I appreciate that.' She picked up a tube of bonjela from the table. 'I don't know if this'll help but you might want to rub some round the area where the tooth was.'

'Teeth,' I corrected her, taking the bonjela and applying it to the affected areas, which just made everything hurt more.

'Jesus. They weren't messing about, were they? This whole thing's getting out of control, Sean. You need to speak to the police.'

'I can't. They *were* the police. Or at least they were carrying authentic police ID. That's how they managed to lift me from A and E. They even got hospital security to help.'

'I know a senior cop you can speak to who's incorruptible.'

I wasn't keen but I could see her point. 'OK, let's set up a meeting tomorrow. I can't face talking to anyone else tonight, and at least those guys can't find me any more.'

'I need to put a plaster on that cut above your eye,' she said, and came in close again as she cut off a thin strip and placed it over the wound.

This time I could smell the sweetness on her breath and, worryingly, felt myself getting aroused.

'Are you sure a hotel's going to let me in looking like this and paying in cash? I'd really appreciate it if you could just let me sleep on your sofa. I promise I won't let you down.'

Tina straightened up and took a pack of cigarettes from her jacket, lighting one without offering the pack. 'Let me tell you something, Sean. This place is my sanctuary. It's where I retreat from all the crap in the world. Some men tried to kill me in here once, and they almost succeeded. I came this close to moving out because of that, but I overcame my fears and swore I'd never let anything happen to me in here again. Only people I truly trust stay in my house. And right now, you're not one of them.'

I nodded. 'Fair enough. I understand. I hope at some point you'll learn to trust me.'

She shrugged. 'We'll see. There's a hotel ten minutes down the road from here who aren't too fussy who they let in. It's not the flashiest establishment in the world but it's clean, and it's safe.'

'And I guess it's better than being stuck in a barn with a couple of torturers.'

'That's for sure.' She took a drag on the cigarette and gave me a half smile through the smoke.

'I read about my brother,' I said, changing the subject. 'The way he got killed trying to stop an armed robbery. It's amazing. I'd forgotten I even had a brother.'

'Did reading it help you remember him?' Tina asked.

I nodded. 'Definitely. I keep getting flashbacks about growing up with him. They're vivid too. But, as I said, I didn't finish reading all that stuff you gave me. Did they ever catch the men who killed him?'

She frowned. 'You don't remember?'

I let out a hollow laugh. 'I don't remember much of anything, Tina.'

'Well, you got your revenge, Sean. It took you a long time but you got there in the end. It's how we met.'

'Care to tell me more?'

'It's a long story. I'll tell you another time.'

'Are the men who killed my brother dead?'

'Yes,' she said. 'They're all dead.'

'And did I kill them?'

'You killed at least one of them. In fact, you killed him in front of me. No one knows whether it was you who killed the other two – I guess, not even you – but you were never charged with any crime, although you had to leave the police.'

I sighed. I was pleased I'd killed at least one of them, and possibly all three. I had no idea who these men were who'd destroyed my family some twenty years ago, but they'd deserved to die for what they'd done to John. I just wished I could have remembered what had happened.

Tina put out her cigarette and opened her laptop on the kitchen table. 'Tell me something. In that recurring dream of yours, you said that you remembered seeing the woman I'm looking for, Lauren Donaldson, and also another woman. Can you remind me what she looked like?'

I could picture her immediately, as clear as day. 'Long, thick blonde hair. Very pretty. Late twenties.'

Tina picked up the laptop and handed it to me. 'Is this her?'

A photo of the top halves of three young women filled the screen. One of them was the dead girl in the dream; another I didn't recognize; but all my attention was on the third. I couldn't stop looking at her wide smile and deep blue eyes. I felt my mouth go dry and my stomach clench tight. 'Jesus Christ,' I said quietly. 'It *is* her.'

'Are you sure?'

I nodded. 'Positive.'

'What the hell is going on here, Sean?'

'I wish I knew. What's her name?'

'Jen Jones.'

It wasn't familiar but that didn't matter, because the girl was. I couldn't stop staring at the photo as an intense emotion so powerful it made me want to throw up swirled round my system like an infection.

'What's wrong?' asked Tina, staring at me.

I took a deep breath. 'This girl . . . Jen Jones. I was in love with her.' And for a second I was back in the dream, with her sat propped against the wall, bleeding from the head as she turned in my direction. And then the fear in her eyes as she saw me standing there.

Why? Why was she so terrified of me?

I handed back the laptop, suddenly feeling drained and very, very tired. 'I guess we'd better get me booked into this hotel. Maybe I'll remember more tomorrow.'

But even as I spoke the words, I was wondering if I actually wanted to.

Twenty-two

It was gone ten o'clock when Tina finally got home from dropping Sean at the hotel. She made herself a decaf coffee, sat at the table and lit another cigarette before making a note on the laptop that she'd lent him another two hundred pounds to cover hotel expenses and a change of clothes. At this rate she'd be broke in a week. It wasn't as if she made a huge amount of money from the detective work. She got by, but that was pretty much it, and she could ill afford to subsidize anyone, let alone a man like Sean who had little prospect of raising money from anywhere and whose presence in her life made things extremely dangerous.

The men at the barn tonight had been tracking him electronically ever since he'd fled the house in Wales. This meant that they'd know every place he'd been that day, including Tina's office, so it wouldn't take them long to put two and two together and ID her as the woman who'd rescued Sean.

So now she was in danger. She sighed, and dragged hard on the cigarette. It was the story of her life. The private detective work had been a way for her try to get some normality back in her life while still making use of some of the talents she'd picked up in the force, but nothing ever ran that smoothly for Tina Boyd. And tonight, when she'd emerged from the darkness and crept towards the barn with a Taser in her hand, knowing she was risking her life, the excitement had been incredible, the rush almost sexual.

She stubbed out the cigarette and finished her coffee before walking through the cottage and checking that all the doors and windows were locked, as she did every night. Tonight it felt like a lonely job – the lonely job of a lonely woman – and she found herself missing Sean's presence. She'd felt a definite stirring when she'd been tending his injuries earlier. A need for closeness, and a real desire to hold him, just so she could feel male contact again. But she'd fought it back down, and not just because she couldn't entirely trust him. It was more than that. It was because she always pushed men away. It was as if falling in love, even allowing herself to need someone, was a sign of weakness that could only damage her in the long run. She'd even started receiving counselling to deal with the problem, which was something she never thought she'd end up doing. Her therapist said that her intimacy issues stemmed from the violence she'd suffered at the hands of men during a long and unusually bloody police career. And Tina believed it. She'd come close to being killed on more than one occasion, and had killed others too. Three times. All men who'd deserved it. The scars those traumas had left her with were deep and permanent.

'Yet still I come back for more,' she said aloud as she readied herself for bed.

Through her bedroom window, she could hear the faint rumble of traffic on the M25 four miles away. Otherwise the world was silent. Ordinarily she enjoyed that silence, but tonight there was something foreboding about it.

She laid the Taser and the pepper spray on her bedside table, so they were close to hand, then got into bed and lay there for a few minutes with her eyes open, thinking about Lauren Donaldson, Jen Jones, and the enigmatic Sean Egan, the man who might yet be able to explain their disappearance.

Just before she let sleep take her, she asked herself a single question: 'Do I regret getting involved with Sean Egan?'

The answer came to her straight away.

Not yet.

Twenty-three

The dreams came again that night. A mad, seemingly never-ending jumble of snapshots: childhood on sunny afternoons; the angst-ridden days of youth; tragedy; undercover work; violence; sex; joy; despair. The whole shebang. It was like a heavy door being slowly forced open and my past pouring through the gap and flooding the present.

I woke up once at about three a.m., sweating and disorientated with a violent throbbing coming from my mouth and no idea where I was. It took me an unfeasibly long time to work out that I was in the crappy hotel room I'd checked into a few hours earlier, with one set of dirty clothes and two dirty great holes where two of my back teeth had once been. I got up, stumbled over to the toilet, and took a leak in the gloom, unable to resist looking at my reflection in the mirror. The glow from the streetlights outside allowed me to get a pretty good view of my battered face. My hair was greasy and wild, and I looked like shit.

'I'm Sean Egan,' I told the reflection. 'I was an undercover police officer. I worked for an outfit called CO10 in the Met. My boss was a man called Robin someone or other, but we all knew him as Captain Bob. He was an arsehole but he was good at his job.'

I stopped and smiled. My life was coming back to me, and fast now. Who knew what I'd find out about myself? It might not all be good, but it was so much better than living with no history and no identity. And somehow I knew things would be all right. I was a good man. I cared about people. I believed in justice.

I repeated those words to my reflection before heading back to my bed and my visions.

I didn't wake again until close to ten o'clock. The remainder of my sleep had been a restless series of visions but as I lay there in bed trying to piece them together, I found that I couldn't get things in order. Everything was still a jumble, and certain aspects of my life – particularly childhood, and my time as an undercover cop – were a lot more vivid than others. I could still remember nothing about the time I'd met Tina, or the supposed rape I'd committed, and my time in prison afterwards.

It was strange, though, because I remained convinced that I had a sister called Jane, even though she didn't appear in any of my dreams, and hadn't been mentioned in any of the material I'd read up on myself. In fact, rationally I knew she didn't exist, and that the woman who'd claimed to be her had been an impostor, but it didn't matter because, at a certain, very deep level, I believed I had a sister, and this certainty seemed to trump everything else.

It made me think about Dr Bronson and our hypnotherapy

sessions back in the house in Wales. Had he implanted false memories in me? Was that even possible?

I needed to talk to him, and urgently, because I had a feeling he could unlock a lot of my more recent memories if he was put under enough pressure. I was pretty sure Tina could find him. She'd given me another mobile number to reach her on plus her office number. I didn't have a mobile of my own any more but there was a hotel phone on the bedside table. I called Tina's numbers but she wasn't answering either, so I left messages on both, suggesting she think about tracking Bronson down, then clambered out of bed, feeling stiff from all the exertions of the previous thirty-six hours.

The room was small and box-like with a horrific floral carpet and thinly painted concrete walls, but at least it was clean. I pulled the curtains, opened the window, and looked out. My hotel was a cheap modern building that was already beginning to look tired, with a three-quarters-full car park out front. It was set on a main road with a retail park, consisting of a line of hangar-like warehouses, directly opposite. There was a fair amount of traffic about but surprisingly few pedestrians, even though it was a bright sunny day.

I stood there for a while watching the world go by, trying to work out what decisions I'd made to get myself into this position – a convicted felon all alone in the world, with enemies at every turn and only one potential friend, a woman who didn't even trust me. I couldn't believe I'd turned to the dark side. It just didn't fit with the view I had of myself.

'I'm a good man,' I whispered, repeating it again and again.

And then, almost as if my words were an ancient magic spell, I was effortlessly transported back to my first undercover role.

Twenty-four

Dylan Mackay lived in an apartment on the second floor of a Georgian townhouse on one of the less pretty roads just off the A4 in Kensington. But even with the slightly dilapidated state of the buildings and the smell of cooking coming from the cheap restaurants at either end of the street, it was still the kind of place only the well-off could afford to inhabit.

There was an up-to-date video entry system just inside the porch, and Tina pressed the button marked 3. It had just turned eleven and she was banking on Dylan being up and about. Otherwise she was going to have to find a suitable spot on the street and wait until he appeared.

A good minute passed before a man's voice came over the intercom. 'Yeah?' it demanded.

'Mr Mackay?' said Tina, looking up to the camera. 'DC Ann

Wright, Westminster CID. I'd like to speak to you for a few moments if I may.'

She held up a fake warrant card she'd bought over the internet. It wasn't perfect by any means, but it was designed to stand up to basic scrutiny, especially through a camera lens. The only problem, of course, would be if Mackay recognized Tina from the media – something that had happened to Tina more than once before.

But he didn't. 'What about?' he asked with a combination of belligerence and tiredness that reminded Tina of the tone her brother had adopted when he was an irritating teenager.

'I'd prefer not to discuss it over the intercom. Can you let me in please?' She kept her gaze firmly on the camera, allowing herself to pout just a little bit. She was dressed smartly in a trouser suit, with the top two buttons of her shirt undone, having figured that she might as well use all the weapons in her armoury to gain entrance.

It worked too. Mackay grunted something unintelligible but a second later, Tina was through the door.

'Bad move, Dylan,' she said to herself as she mounted the staircase, taking her time as she prepared herself for the interrogation ahead.

'So what is it you want?' said Mackay as he answered the door and with clear reluctance opened it further to let Tina inside.

It gave straight into a spacious lounge that was so white it made her want to squint.

'If it's the neighbours complaining again about the music, then they're bullshitting,' he continued. 'I haven't had people here in weeks.' He sat down heavily on a long white sofa that dominated the centre of the room and stared at Tina with undisguised impatience.

He was good-looking, but in a non-sexual way that was almost camp. He reminded her both in tone and appearance of one of the characters from *Made in Chelsea*. Tina preferred more rugged men, and there was no way you'd call Mackay that. He was medium height and medium build, with a boy band haircut that had been hastily pushed into shape with too much gel, and wore jeans and a linen shirt that was open to reveal a tanned, waxed chest. His feet were bare and it didn't look like he'd been up for that long.

Tina remained standing, looking down at him. 'It's not about the neighbours,' she said. 'It's about two missing girls, Lauren Donaldson and Jennifer Jones.'

'I don't know what you're talking about,' he said, shaking his head.

But he wasn't a good liar and she knew he did.

'Yes you do.' She reached into the inside pocket of her suit jacket and produced the two photos Sheryl Warner had emailed her. She took a step forward so she was standing right over him and held them out.

He gave them a cursory glance and shook his head again. 'Never seen them before in my life. Who told you I knew who they were?'

Tina ignored the question. 'I think you do know them, Mr Mackay. In fact, you encouraged them into prostitution. And now they're both missing. Which doesn't reflect very well on you at all.'

Suddenly Mackay was on his feet, furiously staring her down. 'Listen, back right off. You want to start throwing round accusations then I want my lawyer present. And I want your badge number as well. I'm not having you talking to me like that.'

Tina returned his stare. 'So you don't care what might have happened to those two girls?'

'I told you, I don't even know who they are. Who's been talking to you, eh? Because they're lying. Now get out. And if you want to talk to me, you do it through my lawyer. Capeesh?'

Tina didn't move. 'I don't believe you.'

'I don't give a fuck whether you do or not. Now, are you going to leave or am I going to have to call your boss?'

'I don't have a boss. I'm not a police officer, Dylan.'

Mackay snorted. 'Then who the fuck are you?'

'I'm working for Lauren Donaldson's father. One way or another, I'm going to find her. And you're going to help me.'

'No I'm not, you stupid bitch. Now get out of here before I beat your arse.'

Tina could see the rage building in Mackay. It was obvious he was contemplating trying to remove her forcibly from his apartment. In her three-inch heels she was roughly the same height as him, but he had more bulk. Although not that much more. Tina had been half expecting this kind of reaction, and she was ready for it. What she was less ready for was the rage that was also building in her.

'I know people who could really fuck you up, bitch,' continued Mackay in his irritatingly upper-class tones. 'You want that, do you?'

'Don't threaten me, Dylan.'

That was when he finally broke, grabbing Tina by the arm and starting to push her back towards the door.

Her reaction was instinctive and immediate. She swung round, moving in close, and drove a knee into his groin.

He gasped in pain, staggering backwards. He was now completely defenceless, so there was no excuse for what happened next. Tina grabbed him by his linen shirt with one hand and punched him in the face with the other, before getting a leg behind his and tripping him up. He fell backwards on to the tiled floor, landing heavily, and Tina placed a foot on his neck, holding him down.

The sudden burst of violence excited her. There was no denying it. This arsehole had treated her like dirt, deliberately holding back on information she knew he had on Lauren and her friend Jen, two girls who were missing, very possibly dead. For a long time as a police officer she'd been forced to uphold the law even when it meant treating suspects with kid gloves in the face of their blatant disrespect. In her old life she'd have been forced to put up with Mackay's denials and insults. No longer. Now her newfound power felt liberating.

She took out her mobile and put it to camera setting. 'Smile, Dylan,' she said sweetly, taking a shot of him lying humiliated on the floor, his face screwed up in pain. She replaced the phone and removed the shoe from his neck. 'I bet you've got drugs in here as well, haven't you? You look like the classic small-time dealer to me. The sort of guy who thinks he's really tough.' She crossed the room and pulled out the drawers on a cabinet next to the door to the kitchen, rifling through them until she found a battered tobacco tin. She opened it up and saw that it contained twenty or so single-gram wraps of what was almost certainly coke. 'Naughty, naughty. Look what I've found.' She strode back over and dropped the contents over Mackay, who was still lying on the floor, unwilling or unable to get up. 'You see, I've got contacts too, Dylan. A lot better ones than you. And if you don't tell me the truth I'm going to let them know about your little stash.'

'Listen,' he said, through gritted teeth. 'I honestly don't know what you're talking about.'

She stamped on his groin, and this time he let out a shriek of pure agony.

'Oh God,' he wailed, rolling over on to his side like a child, tears forming in his eyes.

Suddenly, Tina felt a pang of absolute disgust with herself. Jesus, what was she doing? She put a hand to her mouth and took a step back. She was deliberately and systematically assaulting a man she'd never met before, and inflicting real damage. She tried to think about Alan Donaldson, a broken man trying to find his estranged daughter before the cancer took him. She was doing this for him. Finding answers from a spoilt rich kid – a pimp and a drug dealer – who was being obstructive. And this was the only way.

But the justification felt hollow in her mind. She was better than this.

'God, you've really, really hurt me,' he whispered, the tears pouring freely down his face.

'And I'll keep hurting you until you tell me the truth,' she said, knowing that having started this, she couldn't stop now.

The information. It was all about the information.

'You hired Lauren Donaldson and Jen Jones out as prostitutes, didn't you?'

'No I didn't. I swear it.'

'Bullshit.' She loomed over him and raised her heeled foot again, hoping she wouldn't have to hurt him any more, but knowing she would if she had to.

'No, please . . .'

He raised a hand weakly, and she kicked it away.

'Answer honestly, because you know what? I can ruin you. I'll have cops on your back; I'll let everyone know you're a pimp; I'll post photos of you with my shoe in your face all over the place; I'll come back here and beat your arse. I'll make you wish you were dead. Do you understand?' She raised her foot again.

'Don't do this,' he pleaded. 'You don't know what you're getting involved in here.'

'I know I don't. You need to tell me. Now.'

'I can't.'

He knew something. But he was clearly more afraid of the consequences of imparting the information than he was of her.

She could have stopped there. Should have done. But she was close to a breakthrough, and right then she had to have it.

He started to move beneath her foot, slowly gaining confidence. 'Listen, if you go now, I won't say a—'

She kicked him hard in the ribs, then, as he doubled up in pain, took a step back and made a great play of donning a pair of surgical gloves before grabbing an empty wine glass from the coffee table and smashing it against the corner.

Dylan cried out and tried to roll away but Tina was on him in an instant, pinning his arms down with her knees. Her inner voice screamed at her to stop what she was doing but she ignored it, temporarily lost in the power of the moment, continuing to justify her actions to herself.

The fear in his eyes was clear and vivid. It made her feel sick but she kept her expression hard and indifferent. 'I don't think you're taking me seriously, Dylan, and that's a bad, bad move.'

'I am, I am!'

'I wonder how you'd look with a nice long scar across your face from ear to ear.' She held the jagged tip of the glass barely an inch from his face and drew a leisurely outline from the corner of his lip to his left eye. 'Shall we find out?'

'No! Please, please . . .'

'Then talk. You hired Lauren Donaldson and Jen Jones out as prostitutes, didn't you?'

'Yes, yes, I did,' he blurted out. 'I hired Lauren out a few times to guys, but I only hired Jen out once.'

'Did you ever hire them out together?'

He hesitated.

'Don't even think about lying,' she snarled, bringing her face close to his. She was scaring herself now so God alone knew what she was doing to him.

'Yes,' he said. 'Once.'

'And was that the last time you saw them?'

Hesitation.

Her eyes narrowed. 'Yes or no?'

'Yes.'

'When was this?'

'Months ago. Back in the spring.'

Only one more question now.

'Who did you hire them to?'

Sweat was dripping down Dylan's forehead. He looked absolutely terrified. Like a little boy. 'I can't tell you,' he whispered. 'Please don't make me.'

She couldn't let herself weaken. 'Tell me.'

'No.' He was weeping silently now, too scared to do anything but await his fate.

Tina felt her resolve weakening as the enormity of what she was doing hit her. There was no way she could continue this. 'I'm going to give you one more chance,' she said, but her heart was no longer in it, and that showed in her voice.

Dylan continued to weep. She'd broken him. It was a horrible feeling.

'Where's your phone?'

'In my jeans pocket.'

Still holding the glass close to his face, she rummaged inside until she found it, then slowly clambered off him. She put the glass on the table and pocketed the phone. 'I'm taking this,' she told him. 'And if you say a word about this to anyone, I'll break you. Do you understand?'

He nodded, and rolled on to his side so that he was facing away from her, like a scolded child, all the fight gone out of him. She was certain he wouldn't report her conduct to anyone in authority. He wouldn't want any inconvenient questions about what he knew about the disappearance of two young women. Because he knew something very important, even if he wasn't prepared to tell her what it was.

Tina left without another word and it was only when she was back inside her car, a ten-minute walk away, that she broke down, the tears coming in an intense flood. It was hard to come to terms with what she'd just done. She was a tough woman, far too used to violence. But even though she'd killed before, it had always been in the heat of the moment, and the men she'd killed had been killers themselves. What had happened with Dylan Mackay was different. He might have been an arrogant bastard but he was no killer. And Tina hadn't hurt him in the heat of the moment either. Her violence, and the threats of it, had been methodical. She'd tortured him. There was no other way of describing it, and it shamed her to think that this was what she'd become. Because for a few minutes she'd been out of control in his flat, and it would be a lie to say that a big part of her hadn't enjoyed the power she'd wielded over him, and the way she'd managed to drag out potentially key information about her case there was no way she'd have got using legitimate means. Because there was no question, she'd made a real breakthrough.

But at what cost? Her integrity? Certainly. Her sanity? Possibly. More worrying was the question that was burning through her tears.

How much further was she capable of sinking?

Twenty-five

It was one of the most relaxing mornings I'd had since . . . well, since I don't know when.

The thing was, I felt free. I could do what I wanted when I wanted. Admittedly, I didn't have much in the way of money – and what I did have, I owed to Tina – but for once I was my own man. It might have been only two days but already the months I'd spent at that isolated house in Wales felt like a lifetime ago. I'd been a prisoner then in all but name, fed a cocktail of drugs in order to keep me passive and helpless while Dr Bronson messed with my head as he tried to extract information I didn't know I had.

But that was behind me now, and my past was returning to me far faster than I could ever have anticipated. Every time a new memory popped up I stopped whatever it was I was doing and tried to fit it into place in the still scattered and only partially complete jigsaw that was my past life. Sometimes I was able to; other times the memories were random visions I filed away in my mind, hoping they'd slot in somewhere later. But it was a fantastic feeling knowing that I was finding myself once again after far too long in the wilderness.

I spent the morning wandering the streets round the hotel and doing some shopping. I bought a new shirt, new jeans and underwear, and threw away all the old stuff I'd been wearing, since most of it had been badly soiled by the events of the past couple of days. I also bought a cheap pre-paid mobile without leaving any details with the guy who sold it to me. That left me with about twenty quid, almost half of which I spent in McDonald's on two Big Macs, large fries, a hot apple pie and a strawberry milkshake. It was hardly the food of the gods but Christ, it tasted good, and I needed it.

Afterwards, feeling sated and tired, I headed back to the hotel figuring that a nice nap was in order. I thought about phoning Tina again since I hadn't heard back from her, but decided it could wait for later. Today, everything could wait. I was free. My belly was full. And I was alive. The world was good.

The door of the room next to mine was open and I saw the cleaner inside as I passed. I smiled and wished her a good afternoon, and she smiled back, nodding enthusiastically. She was young, early twenties, and pretty, and I felt a stirring somewhere down below. Jesus, I was horny, and there was very little I could do about it. Still, I wasn't going to let that, or anything else, dampen my mood.

The cleaner hadn't done my room yet. It smelled vaguely of sweat and the bed was unmade, just as I'd left it. I headed for the toilet, thinking I was going to need to hang a Do Not Disturb sign on the door so I could get some beauty sleep.

But the bathroom door opened before I got there and Combover stepped out holding the same revolver he'd had with him yesterday, pointing it at my chest. 'Hello again, Sean,' he said calmly as I backed away from him, quickly finding my retreat blocked by the room's bare wall.

He was no longer dressed in a suit but wearing a pair of neatly pressed jeans, a pink shirt and a sports jacket, as if he was just off out to a golf club lunch. He looked so unthreatening it would have been difficult to take him seriously if it hadn't been for the gun and the tense, impatient look in his eyes. Or the fact that he'd told his colleague to pull one of my teeth out with a pair of pliers the night before.

Behind him Blackbeard, the chief teeth puller, also emerged from the bathroom, wearing the same casually brutal expression. He was also dressed casually – though I didn't think he'd have been welcome at any golf club lunch.

I had no idea how they'd found me, but already my mind was working overtime, trying to figure out how I was going to get out of this.

Combover clearly sensed this. 'No funny business this time, OK?' he said, stopping a yard in front of me, the barrel of the gun now only a foot from my face. 'Otherwise I shoot you dead, in here. We want you alive, but if we have to, we'll take you dead. And we'll get away with it too. Understand?'

'I still don't know the information you're after.'

'But you will do. We know your memory's coming back.'

As he spoke, Blackbeard stopped alongside him and glared at

me. 'You're not getting away a second time,' he growled. 'Try it again and I'll cripple you.'

'Put the Do Not Disturb sign on the door,' Combover told him, without turning his gaze from me. 'We don't want any interruptions.'

Blackbeard looked displeased at being given a direct order but reluctantly peeled away.

'Right, Sean, I'm going to go through the drill now. You need to follow it to the letter or you die.'

He was interrupted by a knocking on the door coming from outside. It had to be the cleaner. Blackbeard still had the Do Not Disturb sign in his hand and, clearly surprised, Combover glanced briefly in the direction of the door as Blackbeard shouted for whoever was knocking to come back later.

I went for the gun, twisting Combover's wrist as I shoved his arm away from me. It went off with a loud retort, the bullet hitting the ceiling and releasing a cloud of plaster dust. Combover yelped in pain as I dug my thumb into the fleshy part of his palm where the hand meets the wrist, punching him in the ribs and knocking him off balance. He dropped the gun on the floor and I hit him again with an uppercut that caught him directly beneath the jaw. His head snapped back and he fell on to the unmade bed, rolling over.

The altercation had lasted barely three seconds, and Blackbeard had taken at least two to react. Now, though, he ran at me across the bed, his face a mask of pure rage, a roar beginning in his throat. In the background I could hear the cleaner shouting something from outside, but I was already scrabbling on the floor for the gun. I grabbed it and jumped back against the wall as

Blackbeard did a flying leap towards me. He struck me with full force, grabbing me by the hair with one hand as I gasped for air, but I was already pulling the trigger, and I could hear the gun's muffled retorts against his torso as I fired three times.

Immediately his grip on my hair weakened, and for a long couple of seconds the room was completely silent as he stared at me with a look of complete surprise. Then, with a hard shove, I pushed him away and he crumpled to the floor, clutching at the growing bloodstain on his shirt.

The shock of what I'd just done prevented me from moving for a few seconds. It was hard to believe I'd just shot someone, even if it was a man who'd been torturing me only hours before. I felt utterly numb, but when I looked down at my gun hand, it wasn't shaking. Outside, the cleaning woman was screaming, and I heard a number of slamming doors. Meanwhile, Combover was trying to get up off the bed and reaching towards the handle on the bathroom door.

I knew I had to get out, but first I needed answers. I grabbed Combover by the collar of his natty sports jacket and turned him over, pushing the still-smoking gun barrel into his cheek. He winced against the heat, looking scared for the first time.

'Who are you?' I demanded. 'Tell me or, so help me God, I'll blow your head off here and now.'

Outside in the corridor I heard a male voice shouting something about calling the police, then another door slamming.

'It's not what you think,' he stammered.

'I don't care what it is. Tell me. I've just shot your friend. Do you think I won't do the same to you? I will. You've got five seconds to start talking.' I pushed the barrel in harder, putting all my weight behind it, my finger tensing on the trigger. 'One. Two.'

I heard movement behind me then felt my leg being pulled hard. I had to work to keep my balance, and as I swung round, I saw Blackbeard up on his knees. He'd got hold of both my legs now and was trying to pull me over, his features taut with determination.

For a split second I just looked at him, thinking that he still had a surprising amount of strength for a man who'd just been shot three times. Then he lunged forward and I realized he was trying to bite me in the groin. His teeth clamped on the material of my new jeans, so I placed the barrel of the gun against his temple and pulled the trigger.

The bullet didn't exit from his head. Or at least there was no big cloud of blood and brains like there often is in the movies. But a thin trickle of red ran down his forehead and his eyes glazed over, and I knew he was dead even before I shoved him out of the way and turned round to face Combover.

But I was too late. He was already running into the bathroom and, as I took aim and yelled at him not to move, he slammed the door and I heard the lock being pushed across.

I thought about going in after him. I could kick down the door easily enough and I was certain he'd talk, but there wasn't time. The shouting in the corridor had stopped but I could still hear the faint echo of doors slamming and I was pretty sure the whole hotel knew by now that there'd been gunshots in Room 305. And now Blackbeard lay motionless and dead on the floor, and I was the man who'd killed him.

I reached down and patted his jeans pockets, quickly locating a wallet. I pocketed it without checking the contents and shoved the gun in the back of my jeans, barrel down, covering it with my untucked shirt.

There was no time to wipe the place down and remove any evidence of my stay. Instead, I pulled open the door, shoved my head out, and looked up and down the corridor. It was empty. No one wanted to be too close to gunfire. But as I ran down the staircase towards the ground floor I saw the cleaner standing in the second-floor stairwell with a male member of staff and a male guest. All three of them were looking up, and when they saw me, the cleaner screamed again. Still none of them moved.

I didn't have time to waste pleading my innocence or asking them nicely to make way. The priority was getting to safety, and the gun was out of my jeans and pointing at them before I even had time to think about it.

'Move! Move! Move!' I yelled.

And they moved. Fast. Almost falling over themselves to get through the door back on to the second floor.

I kept going, shoving the gun back in my jeans as I came out into the hotel's reception area where the previous night I'd checked in with Tina beside me. She'd had to use her credit card as collateral against any damage I might cause – something she'd been reluctant to do, and which in the light of the events of the past few minutes was perfectly justified. She was going to get in a lot of trouble for this, but not nearly as much as me. I'd just killed a man. And it could hardly be classed as manslaughter. I'd shot him four times, the last round a point-blank one to the head. There was no way I was going to be able to explain my way out of that one.

The same middle-aged woman who'd been at the reception desk when I'd walked past with a friendly hello five minutes earlier was now talking urgently into the phone. The moment she saw me, the words seemed to die in her mouth and she went as white as a sheet.

I walked across what passed for the hotel foyer, avoiding her eye and trying to look as casual as possible, as if all this commotion had nothing to do with me, even though I was sweating profusely and so pumped up with adrenalin that it was an actual physical effort to stop myself from breaking into a sprint.

As soon as I was out the front doors and into the bright sunshine of what was rapidly turning into a beautiful early autumn afternoon, I heard the insistent wail of a police siren, not that far away either. I started running across the car park, telling myself to keep calm and think of a way out of this.

That was when I saw the cheap blue car with white go-faster stripes pulling out of one of the parking spaces front first. The windows were down, letting out some very bad music, and a young guy with slicked black hair was behind the wheel. He was still turning the wheel as I ran in front of the car, blocking his exit.

His face contorted in anger and he started shouting something at me, but I couldn't hear what he was saying above the music, and anyway, he stopped the second he saw the gun in my hand.

'Get out!' I yelled, running round the driver's side and trying to pull open the door. It was locked so I put the gun against the side of his head and repeated the command.

'Don't shoot!' he cried, opening the door so fast he almost knocked me over in the process.

I grabbed him by the collar and literally threw him to the tarmac, realizing with a strange combination of elation and regret that I was a natural in the role of violent gunman. It was almost as if it was impossible to tell where the undercover cop in me stopped and the criminal began.

Jumping into the driver's seat, I put my foot down and raced to the car park exit, turning off the blaring music in the process. The siren was louder now, and it sounded as if it had been joined by a second. The traffic was moving at a steady pace, and thankfully there wasn't too much of it, but I didn't hang about, pulling out in front of a people carrier, forcing its driver, an irate-looking woman, to do an emergency stop. I turned a sharp right as she blasted on the horn, away from the sirens, and accelerated down the road, overtaking a car ahead that was going too slowly and forcing the one coming towards me to veer out of the way. The whole thing was surreal, like being flung into the middle of a Hollywood action movie, and I'd be lying if I didn't admit that a part of me was really enjoying the high of racing down a city street, muscling my way through the traffic, knowing that I had to get away.

But another part of me was far less excited. As I drove, getting further and further away from the hotel and my pursuers, a voice in my head told me loudly and insistently that I might have been in danger before, but now my situation was far worse. Because I was no longer just the target of a handful of shadowy figures.

Now I was wanted for murder too.

Twenty-six

It was gone two o'clock by the time Tina got back to the office. She'd stopped for coffee and sandwiches en route and eaten them in Hyde Park, allowing herself to calm down after the events of that morning. She'd also done a pretty good job of justifying her actions to herself. After all, Dylan Mackay was a nasty piece of work and she'd extracted important leads from him that he'd never have given up voluntarily. But a vague sense of shock still lingered as she sat down at her desk and thought about what she needed to do now.

Her first priority was to find out when Lauren and Jen's phones had gone out of service so she could then pinpoint an exact date they'd disappeared. She also needed their phone records, as well as the phone records for Dylan Mackay's number. That way she could work out the sequence of events and hopefully find a number for the man Dylan had hired the girls out to. This kind of information was impossible for a private detective to get hold of legally but it was easy for a police officer to access, and Tina had a contact in the Met who could provide her with it, albeit at a cost. His name was Jeff Roubaix, and she'd called him immediately after taking the Lauren Donaldson case, asking him to try to locate Lauren's phone records. That had been more than a week ago now and she hadn't heard back from him yet, which wasn't unusual. The process of finding out the mobile phone carrier a number was registered to, and then getting the carrier to provide the relevant information, sometimes took weeks. And if the number was unregistered, which plenty of them were, then it was even harder and more time-consuming.

But Tina was tired of waiting. She needed to move things forward, so she lit a cigarette, wandered out on to the street outside her building, and put in a call to Roubaix.

'Give me a moment,' he said when he picked up at the other end. She could hear office noise around him and then the sound of doors opening and closing. 'That's better,' he continued, sounding like he was now outside. 'How are you doing?'

Tina wasn't one for small talk but she knew Jeff from her long-ago days in Islington CID. He'd joined plainclothes a year after she had and they'd worked together for a while. He'd always been a nice guy, not bad-looking either, but with a predilection for gambling that hadn't been a problem then but had got worse over time.

'Not bad. Busy.'

'Just like us then. Although at least you're your own boss. Found that girl yet? Saw the article in the *Daily Mail*.'

Jeff's habit of talking in perfunctory half sentences had always irritated Tina and was actually the main reason she'd never fancied him. There was a kind of slapdash laziness about it that luckily didn't extend to his professional work. 'No, not yet. But I need those phone records for that number I gave you urgently.'

'I'm going fast as I can, Tina, but you know what it's like. Only found out who the carrier was yesterday, and that was quick by usual standards. Going to take longer for records.'

'But you can push it through faster if you try.'

'Yeah, but it's a hassle.'

'I'm paying you, Jeff. That should cover the hassle. I need to find out when and where it was turned off. I also need records on two other numbers urgently.'

Jeff made an exasperated noise down the phone. 'I can't just keep making comms data requests without some decent reason. You know that.'

She did. But she also knew about his gambling habit. 'Listen, I'll pay you double what I agreed to pay you for each number. That means if you get me the information fast – and by fast I mean within the next twenty-four hours – you'll be getting six times more than you thought. That should give you plenty of incentive to come up with as many good reasons as you need. And it'll be in cash.'

'That's a lot of money, Tina,' he said, his voice barely audible above the outside noise, but loud enough for her to hear the hunger in it.

'My client's wealthy and he's dying. He just wants to find his daughter, so he's not going to quibble about cash.'

'You know, if you've got an important lead on a missing person, you need to report it.'

'When I've got something concrete, I'll go straight to the police, but not before. And I promise I won't involve you, Jeff. I haven't got your name written down anywhere, and the phone I call you from is unregistered, so there'll never be a way to connect the two of us.'

He sighed. 'OK. I'll go in as urgent as I can without sounding too many alarm bells. May take longer than twenty-four hours though.'

'The faster you go the more money you get,' she told him, and having read out the numbers, she ended the call.

For a couple of minutes she stood in the sunshine, eyes closed, finishing off her cigarette and enjoying the thought that she was beginning to get closer to finding out what had happened to Lauren Donaldson, even though she had a strong feeling that the case wouldn't have a happy ending. She was also trying to work out what Sean's involvement in it was. He'd left a couple of messages for her earlier and she needed to call him back. She hoped he didn't want more money. He was bleeding her dry already and without, as far as she could see, any prospect of paying her back.

The office phone started ringing as she put out the cigarette, and she hurried back inside, seeing a mobile number she didn't recognize up on the screen.

It was Sean.

'This is good timing,' she said. 'I was just about to call you.'

'We've got a real problem,' he said breathlessly. It sounded like he was outside somewhere in a car. 'They found me.'

'Jesus. How? We removed the bug.'

'I don't know, but they were waiting in my hotel room for me when I came back this afternoon.'

That was when it dawned on Tina. Whoever these people were, they'd clearly identified her by checking the recent location history of Sean's tracking device and had traced him that way, probably through his phone call to her office that morning. Which meant her office, and her phone, were almost certainly bugged.

'Don't say another word,' she said, writing down his mobile number on a piece of paper. 'I'm going to call you back on your number in two minutes.'

Hanging up, Tina grabbed the slip of paper and hurried out the door, checking it briefly for any signs of a break-in. But nothing looked tampered with. Which scared her even more. Only professionals of the highest calibre would be able to break into this building without tripping the alarm, then get into her office and have the wherewithal and the technical gadgetry to bug her phone so they could trace the location of incoming calls. She might be wrong, of course. It was possible that there was another tracker somewhere on Sean's body, but she doubted it. It was hard enough implanting one without it being discovered; implanting two would have been near impossible. There just weren't enough locations.

There was a phone box about two hundred yards away on the next road along. Tina ran all the way down to it and dialled Sean's number. He answered immediately, still sounding like he was in a car.

'Where did you call me from this morning when you left the message on my office phone?' she demanded.

'My room. I didn't have a mobile.'

'There's only two ways they could have found you. One's if they've implanted you with a secondary tracking device.'

'No way,' he said. 'After last night, I checked every inch of my body. And I mean every inch. There's no way I'm carrying another. I'd have found it.'

She sighed. 'That's what I suspected. The only other way is if they've bugged my offices.' She explained how they could have done it.

'Shit,' he said when she'd finished. 'These guys are good.'

'Not that good. I'm assuming you got away.'

'Yeah. That's what I wanted to talk about.'

Something in his tone of voice put Tina on her guard. 'What happened?'

'There was an altercation in my room. They were trying to get me to go with them again but they got disturbed by the cleaner. One of them had a gun and I got hold of it.' There was a heavy pause. 'I shot the guy with the beard, the one you Tasered last night. Then I got the hell out of there. I had to borrow a car in the process.'

'The guy you shot. Is he . . . ?' Tina let the sentence trail off, not wanting to hear the answer.

'Yeah,' he said slowly. 'He's dead.'

'Oh for Christ's sake, Sean. You've got to go to the police.'

'Before I do, I need to speak to you. And not on the phone either. It's too dangerous.'

'Meeting you's just as dangerous after what's just happened.'

'Please, Tina. I'm begging.'

She took a deep breath. 'Where are you now?'

The Final Minute

'There's a layby about a mile north of Cheshunt on the A10. If you come off at junction twenty-six of the M25 it's about a ten-minute drive. I'm parked in a blue Ford Fiesta with white stripes on the side.'

'Classy,' said Tina. 'All right, I'll meet you there.'

Twenty-seven

It had just turned 3.30 when Tina pulled in behind the Ford Fiesta that Sean had somehow liberated from its rightful owner. She really didn't want to hear how he'd managed that. On the way there she'd driven past the hotel and the sight of the ambulance and dozen or so police vehicles in its car park had reminded her in the starkest terms that she couldn't keep her association with him secret any longer. It would only take the investigating officers a matter of hours, if that, to link the hotel's fugitive guest to her credit card, and then they'd be knocking on her door.

The layby was on a straight stretch of semi-rural dual carriageway, with fields on both sides, and aside from her car and Sean's, it was empty. Tina got out and walked over to the Fiesta, surprised to find there was no one in the driver's seat. Then she saw Sean waving at her from under a tree about twenty yards away. She had to climb over a fence to get to him, and as she approached she saw he was looking tired and dishevelled, even though he was wearing new clothes.

'Thanks for coming, Tina,' he said with a big smile. He seemed genuinely happy to see her.

'This can't carry on, Sean.'

He sighed. 'I can't go to the police yet. They'll never believe my story.'

'But you can't keep running. Where are you going to go?'

'I don't know, but my memory's coming back fast now, and if you can locate the psychotherapist who was treating me back at the place in Wales, then I think he can fill in some of the gaps. We used to have these hypnotherapy sessions and I think he was planting false memories in me to keep me confused. You know, I'm still convinced somewhere in my subconscious that Jane was my sister, even though I know in my head she can't have been. Because I know I had no sister.' He was talking fast, bouncing on his toes as he spoke, and constantly running his hand through his hair, giving Tina glimpses of the thick pink scar that ran across the top of his forehead, and which had snatched away the first thirty-eight years of his life in one life-changing instant.

'I'll see what I can do to find him, Sean.'

'His name's Dr Bronson, and he's in his mid-fifties. Big guy, black hair going slightly grey. Wears glasses. He's the one who's been trying to extract the information about the location of the bodies that all the people after me keep talking about, and I assume he's been doing that under hypnotherapy as well.'

'And you haven't had any further memories about that dream involving the girls?' Tina asked, deciding against telling Sean what she'd found out about Lauren and Jen's potential work as prostitutes.

He shook his head. 'I'm sure the women in the dream are the ones whose bodies they're after, though.'

Tina sighed, and thought of Alan Donaldson. 'I have a feeling you could be right. But why is their location so important?'

'I have no idea, but the couple who tortured and killed Tom and Jane at the house are working against the two guys who kidnapped me from A and E and who came after me today. And I have no idea who any of them are. I did manage to pull the wallet of the guy I shot, but there was no ID on him. Just some cash.'

'And you're going to spend that, right?'

He frowned. 'Look, I know how it looks, but it was self-defence. It was their gun. They were going to kidnap me. I resisted.'

'But you still found the time to rifle through your victim's pockets. That suggests to me you're either very cool under pressure or you're not actually that bothered that you've killed someone.'

'Look, Tina. I didn't ask for any of this. All I'm trying to do is find out why I'm being targeted. You know I'm not a cold-blooded killer. I was a copper for most of my adult life, for Christ's sake. I saved your life once, remember?'

'So you keep telling me,' she said, but she wasn't convinced. In fact, standing there out of sight of the traffic on the road, she realized that she was a little scared of the man in front of her. 'But people aren't going to believe you're innocent if you shoot a man dead, steal his wallet and then go on the run. Where's the gun?'

He gestured towards a thick tangle of bushes behind him. 'In there. I unloaded it, then buried it and the bullets separately.' He sighed. 'I will go to the police, I promise, but I want to face them knowing exactly who I am, and what I've done.'

'That's a laudable aim, Sean, but I'm not sure it's going to work out like that.'

'I won't involve you with anything, I promise.'

'You already have. I booked you into the hotel room on my credit card, remember?'

'But you haven't actually done anything wrong. I came to you asking for help, you tried to provide it, and now you can cut all your ties with me, and that'll be that.'

'You know I'm going to have to talk to the police.'

He nodded. 'Of course I do. Tell them whatever you want. It doesn't matter. You don't know where I'm going so you can't help them in that way.' He reached into his back pocket and pulled out the tracking device she'd given him. 'Take this. I don't need it any more. And I'm going to turn off the phone I'm carrying, and dump the car, so there's no way you can reach me. If I remember anything about Lauren Donaldson, I'll call you.'

'If you do, be careful about leaving messages. The police will be monitoring my phones. And so, I suspect, will the people after you.'

He took a deep breath. 'I'm sorry for getting you into all this. I didn't mean to get you into any trouble.'

She shrugged her shoulders. 'Sometimes these things happen. Especially to me.' She managed a smile. 'You've certainly provided some excitement.'

'And that's got to be a good thing, right?' He took a step closer. 'Thanks for everything, Tina. I'll pay you back the money too, I promise.'

Then, without warning, he moved right into her space, took her in his arms and started to kiss her.

The move was so sudden, Tina was caught completely off-guard, and for a second she was too shocked to react.

But only for a second.

'What the hell are you doing?' she snapped, shoving him away with both hands.

He stumbled backwards, looking as surprised as she was. 'I'm sorry. I didn't mean to do that.'

'Jesus, Sean. What's wrong with you?'

'I don't know, I'm just very attracted to you that's all. I have been since the moment we met.' He tried a boyish smile.

It didn't work. 'You're a convicted rapist, and a man who's got quite enough on his plate without alienating me.'

And with that she turned away and headed back to her car, without wishing him luck.

Twenty-eight

The Sunny View Hotel was bedlam when DCI Mike Bolt arrived. A whole section of the building including the reception area and the emergency staircase was now a crime scene, and its 180 rooms were in the process of being evacuated. Quite a few of those guests, some of them angry at being herded out on to the street and not being able to get to their cars, milled around the edges of the scene-of-crime tape that lined the central third of the car park, arguing with the uniforms protecting the crime scene's perimeter. There were also plenty of bystanders gathered at the car park entrance eager to see what all the fuss was about, while police vehicles lined the street on both sides, causing a traffic bottleneck that stretched for several hundred yards in both directions.

It had just turned 4.15 on a sunny afternoon, and any hope that Bolt had had of getting away on time that night had evaporated the minute they'd been given news of the fatal shooting in

Room 305. As the head of one of the Met's more local Murder Investigation Teams, this was always going to be his case.

He found a parking spot outside a giant B&Q about fifty yards further down the street, got himself kitted up inside the cordon and called his long-time colleague Mo Khan, who'd arrived separately half an hour earlier.

Mo met him on the front steps of the hotel and they shook hands, even though they'd seen each other earlier that day. It was a habit of theirs.

'What have we got exactly?' Bolt asked.

Mo opened up the notebook he always carried with him. 'It's a bit of a strange one, boss, to be honest. We've got an altercation in a hotel room. The cleaner's cleaning the room next door. She sees one of the guests walk back to his room, then when she knocks on his door to see if she can clean his room, she hears the sounds of a struggle, followed by a succession of gunshots. Next thing, the guest's running out the hotel with a gun leaving behind a dead male. There's a witness too. A guy who was in the room with the two of them.'

'And he's unhurt?'

'Yeah. He's sitting in the car over there.' He pointed at a patrol car on the far edge of the car park, away from the crowds. Two uniforms stood next to it. 'We've cuffed him to be on the safe side. He hasn't been searched.'

'We need to get an incident room set up at Barnet and get him down there ASAP.'

'I've got Grier on it now. We should be operational in the next hour.'

'Has anyone spoken to this witness yet?'

'Well, that's the strange thing, boss. He's refusing to speak to anyone below the rank of DCI. The DI from Barnet tried. So did I. But no go, and he's not saying why either.'

'What about the victim? What have we got on him?'

Mo shook his head. 'Nothing. He's an IC1 male, early to mid-forties, shot four times at pretty close range. He wasn't carrying any ID, but interestingly he was wearing gloves.'

'That *is* interesting,' Bolt agreed. Not many people wore gloves inside on a warm sunny day, and most people carried ID. 'What about the other guy? The witness. Did he have gloves on?'

'No, but if he's tried to get rid of them, we'll find them.'

'And when our suspect was walking past the cleaner back to his room, he was alone, right?'

'That's right. And apparently acting normally. He even said hello to her.'

'And how long after that did she think the shooting occurred?'

'Not long. She reckons she'd almost finished cleaning the room when she saw the suspect, and she was doing his one next. Only a couple of minutes. And she says she didn't hear any sound of an argument before that. In fact she said she heard nothing.'

Bolt nodded slowly. 'So these two guys were waiting for him in his room. He turns up, and a few minutes later one of them's dead and the suspect's charging through the hotel with a gun. Have we got an ID on the suspect yet?'

'A couple of guys from Barnet CID are talking to reception. I was just on my way to see if they'd got a name when you called.'

'OK, why don't you do that now? In the meantime, let me see if our witness fancies breaking his silence with me and telling us what the hell's going on.'

'I'll tell you something, boss,' said Mo as Bolt turned away. 'He doesn't look much like your average criminal.'

Bolt smiled. 'The best ones never do.'

But in truth, he was already a little perplexed. If their witness had been part of some kind of ambush, or dodgy business deal gone wrong, why had he hung around waiting to be questioned? Most criminals were stupid and their motives simple. Greed, jealousy or drunkenness generally covered the whole spectrum. If something went wrong during one of their crimes, and especially if someone ended up dead, they tended to panic and run. But this guy hadn't. Then again, by refusing to speak, he wasn't acting like a frightened witness either. Bolt was intrigued.

He was even more so when he opened the back door to the patrol car and looked down at a fairly ordinary-looking man of about fifty, dressed like he was sixty, with a badly fashioned comb-over that had clearly come somewhat askew during the events upstairs. His hands were cuffed behind his back but he didn't look remotely scared. There was a confidence about him that belied his appearance, and he looked more pissed off as Bolt introduced himself as a DCI and the SIO of the team that would be investigating the murder, and climbed inside next to him.

The witness asked to see Bolt's ID, and Bolt held the warrant card in front of him so he could read it properly.

'Can I have these restraints taken off?' he said in an educated accent that suggested he'd probably gone to a half-decent public school.

'Not until we establish who you are. I understand you didn't want to talk to any of the other officers.'

'I was waiting for the head of any investigation.'

'Well, you've got him now. So, who are you?'

'If you reach into the inside breast pocket of my jacket, you'll find my ID.'

Bolt did as requested, and pulled out a small plastic card. One look and he knew why the man in front of him, who according to his MI5 identity card was called Carl Hughie, wasn't talking.

Bolt sighed. 'You're a spook.'

'Yes. I'm going to give you the name and number of a man right at the top who can establish my bona fides. My colleague and I have been involved in a very sensitive operation. We were at the hotel room this afternoon to meet an individual of interest. However, the individual produced a handgun and shot my colleague before fleeing the scene.' He spoke the words calmly and matter-of-factly as if he'd been rehearsing them in the car.

'What was your colleague's name? And why was he carrying no ID?'

'I've said everything I'm prepared to say. You need to speak to my superior. You can have his number.'

'This is a murder investigation, Mr Hughie. You're a witness. In fact, right now you're actually a suspect. You can't just pick and choose the questions you answer.'

'I'm involved in a matter of national security, DCI Bolt, and there are very good reasons why I can't help you right now. My superior will give you, or your superiors, a more detailed explanation.'

Bolt took a deep breath. Hughie didn't come across like a man who was going to budge very easily. 'OK, at least tell me the name of the suspect we're meant to be chasing.'

Hughie shook his head. 'I'm sorry. I can't tell you anything more right now.'

'We're going to find out, so your lack of cooperation is just holding things up and allowing our suspect to escape – which I'm assuming, as this is a matter of national security, is something you don't want.'

Hughie said nothing.

'All right, have it your own way. You're going to be trans-ported to Barnet police station shortly, and we'll take a full statement there. In the meantime, I'm arresting you on suspicion of murder.' He gave Hughie his rights and started to get out of the car.

'Can you please remove the restraints now that you know who I am?' asked Hughie.

'No,' said Bolt, and slammed the door shut behind him.

That was when he saw Mo hurrying towards him, a puzzled expression on his face. At the same time, the mobile in Bolt's pocket rang. For the moment he ignored it, wanting to speak to his colleague. 'What is it?' he asked.

'This whole thing gets stranger, boss,' said Mo, breathing heavily from the effort of the brisk walk over. 'The suspect was booked into the hotel under the name Matthew Barron, but it's probably an alias because he gave a fictitious address. But it was paid for on someone else's credit card. You'll never guess who.'

'Go on, surprise me,' said Bolt, pulling the mobile free from his trouser pocket.

'Tina Boyd.'

The mere mention of her name brought out all kinds of

reactions in Bolt, none of them productive. Frowning, he looked down at the mobile screen, and put the phone to his ear.

'Hello Tina,' he said. 'That was good timing. I think you and I may need a little chat.'

Twenty-nine

I lied to Tina. I hadn't got rid of the pistol that I'd used to shoot Blackbeard. I still had it. I wasn't quite sure why. It wasn't for safety purposes. I'd already discovered that I could look after myself in a fight. But somehow, deep down, I knew that having it gave me options. There was only one bullet in the chamber but, if all else failed and I was facing arrest and certain imprisonment, it might offer a way out.

Still, that wasn't something I wanted to think about.

More interesting was the fact that there was an iPad on the front seat of the car I'd stolen. The only reason I knew anything about them was because Jane had owned one. She hadn't liked me looking at it – which in hindsight I could now understand – but I'd persuaded her to let me mess about with it a couple of times, so I knew the basic ins and outs. Like Jane's, it was locked with a four-digit passcode, but I remembered a crime prevention programme I'd seen on daytime TV the other week where the presenter bemoaned the fact that people used such obvious number combinations to secure their possessions, such as 1111 and 1234. So while I'd been waiting for Tina earlier, I'd tried 1111, and it had opened immediately.

Now, two hours later, I was parked on a residential back street in Bedford having put what I hoped was enough distance between me and the hotel to finally relax. I needed to get rid of the car. It wasn't exactly inconspicuous and I knew there'd be a major alert for it out by now, but with barely forty quid to my name (Blackbeard hadn't been carrying much cash in his wallet), I'd already decided I was going to sleep in it tonight. What happened after that was anyone's guess. My strategy was not to think too far ahead as, quite frankly, it was too depressing.

Instead, I decided to see if I could find out more about myself, so I typed in my real name and a whole bunch of results came up. The most recent ones referred to my rape trial and subsequent conviction. I wasn't strong enough to read about that yet. The memories that had come back had convinced me I was innocent, but it was also clear I wasn't backward in coming forward either, as my actions with Tina earlier had shown. The pass I'd made at her had come out of nowhere. It had been instinctive. I'd just wanted some human warmth, some physical contact with a woman. But she'd reacted like I was some kind of lunatic, and I felt a wave of embarrassment remembering it.

So I put it out of my mind.

Looking further down the list, I saw that the results turned to the undercover operation that had seen me fired from the police. I hadn't had a chance to read about that before, thanks to Combover and Blackbeard's intervention in the A and E department.

The undercover op had happened five years earlier, and it had been completely unofficial. While on long-term leave for stress I'd infiltrated the gang of armed robbers responsible for the murder of my brother back in the nineties, and become involved in the kidnapping of a murder suspect. All three of the gang had ended up dead, while I'd been shot twice while saving the life of a police officer, Tina Boyd. Although I'd shot dead one of the gang, it had been treated as self-defence as he was the one who'd shot me, and he'd also been trying to kill Tina.

After I'd finished reading, I tried to remember the events. They'd certainly been dramatic enough. For a while nothing came, and I almost gave up, but then a vision of a house on fire flashed across my mind, and I saw myself fighting with a man in the semi-darkness, looking up into his hate-filled eyes, knowing that he was doing everything he could to kill me. For a couple of seconds I could feel my own fear – the knowledge that I was only seconds from a bloody death – before the vision slipped away, back into the recesses of my mind, leaving me tense and shaking in the driver's seat.

Something else hit me before I could recover fully. A single jarring memory of my first day in prison. Standing in a room, handing over my possessions to a bored-looking prison officer with tattoos covering both his arms, while he made an inventory of them. Stripping off. Handing over my clothes. Waiting while he and another officer searched me in every orifice. The final thing the one with the tattoos said to me before I was led away in my new uniform to begin my time. 'It's going to be hard for you in here.' There was no sympathy in his voice. No anger either. He was simply stating a fact. At that moment I recalled those words perfectly. Remembered the fear I experienced as he said them. And the anger too, at the injustice of what was happening. As if the whole world had turned on me for no good reason, and all the good things I'd ever done suddenly counted for nothing. And then I was taken through a door and a key turned in the lock behind me – a signal that my life as I knew it was over.

I waited until the memory had faded before taking a gulp from the bottle of water on the seat beside me. I stared down at the iPad screen, wondering if I should read any more. In the end, I opened up a story from the Mail Online about my trial for rape and, with a thick sense of dread, began reading.

It was a short piece without photos stating that 'Disgraced ex-police officer Sean Egan' had been found guilty of rape and sentenced to five years in prison. There wasn't really anything in there that Tina hadn't already told me, except for the fact that I'd apparently been drunk at the time, and the woman I was supposed to have raped hadn't been. The article stated she'd been taking antibiotics that reacted extremely badly to being mixed with alcohol and, according to her own story, and that of two of her friends she'd been with earlier that evening, she hadn't been drinking at all on the night she'd met me. I wasn't sure this made any difference to anything but the tone of the article suggested it did. The victim wasn't named but the article finished with her saying that I'd ruined her life and that the sentence of five years was laughable. I didn't read it through a second time and I was relieved that it didn't dredge up any memories of what had happened.

I switched off the iPad and threw it in a black wheelie bin outside a house a few yards further down. I would have kept it but they'd said on the same programme where I'd learned about easily deciphered passcodes that iPads had a function that allowed their owner to locate them anywhere in the world, so I guessed it would be a lot easier to find than the car.

As I got back into the car and pulled away, it struck me that I'd been involved in some pretty heavy stuff over the years, so it was no real surprise that I'd found myself in the situation I was in now. I thought back to the dream that had started all this off. What the hell had happened that night with the blonde woman and her friend, the one Tina was searching for?

And where were the bodies?

Thirty

Back at home in her living room, a cigarette in one hand, a coffee in the other, Tina felt as if everything was running out of her control.

As soon as Sean had told her what had happened at the hotel, she knew she had to call the police and tell them what was going on. She'd given him an hour before she made the phone call. She wasn't sure why. It wasn't like he deserved it. His actions had risked getting her in a huge amount of trouble and then, to top it all, he'd made a seriously unwanted advance to her, barely any time after killing a man, which didn't say a huge amount about his empathy for his fellow human beings. But in the end, whether she liked it or not, he'd saved her life five years earlier, and for that reason she'd always owe him.

When Tina had eventually made the call, it had been to Mike Bolt, her former boss and one-time lover. As the head of one of the Met's Murder Investigation Teams, Mike had already been given the case of the man Sean had killed, and he'd known about her connection with it when she'd called. They'd talked for a few minutes and she hadn't held anything back. She'd given him Sean's name, and a brief rundown of what had happened since he'd come to see her the previous morning.

'We're going to need to take a statement,' Mike had said when she finished, not bothering to disguise the exasperation in his voice.

'Don't arrest me though, Mike. I haven't done anything wrong, and I don't deserve the bad publicity.'

'I'll do what I can, Tina, but you're going to have to be straight down the line with me. Try to hide anything and I'll come down on you hard.'

'I've got nothing to hide,' she'd told him. 'I promise.'

He hadn't said anything for a few seconds, and she'd been just about to fill the silence by asking if they'd ID'd the victim when he finally spoke. 'Why do you always get yourself involved with the wrong people?' His tone had reminded Tina of her father. 'Why don't you just . . . calm down?'

But that was the thing. If she'd known when Sean had walked through her door the trouble he was about to cause her, she'd have kicked him out there and then.

Or would she have done?

She put out the cigarette and picked up her laptop. Outside the window, night was beginning to fall. If her office was bugged, then it was possible her house was too. So she'd gone over every inch of both with the most sophisticated bug finder available on the market, although she was realistic enough to know that it was likely their equipment was going to be invisible to hers. Even so, she checked the outside of her laptop for keypad trackers and ran a series of virus checks on the hard drive before opening up her file on Lauren Donaldson.

She went through what she had so far, putting aside what Sean had told her, since his story was all conjecture. Both girls had gone missing around the same time. They'd been together in the last confirmed sighting Tina had, which was Sheryl's, and neither had been seen since, which strongly suggested they'd gone missing together. Dylan Mackay had admitted that he'd pimped them out to wealthy men, but had refused to name the last man he'd pimped them out to, even under extreme duress, and in Tina's opinion his silence was because he was scared of the guy. This meant two things. First, the guy was a nasty piece of work. Second, he had something to do with the girls' disappearance. So the important thing was to ID him and take it from there.

However, without Dylan's cooperation, that was going to be tricky. She plugged in the flash drive she'd used to extract the contents of his phone and browsed through his photos, notes and contacts list, without finding anything useful. He had a lot of photos: some showed him partying; others were of women, many in various stages of undress; and some looked to be of family and friends. There was one of Dylan holding up a boy of about three, both of them grinning at the camera, and it made Tina feel guilty because it showed him as a human being and not some archetypal bad guy.

In the end, though, none of the photos stood out; nor did any of the notes; and the contacts list was just that, a list, with 353 names on it, any one of whom could have been the person who'd last hired Lauren and Jen from Dylan. And of course it was eminently possible that his name wasn't on there at all any more, or might never have been. But at one time they must have spoken, and almost certainly on the phone, which meant that Tina's best chance of identifying him was going to be through Dylan's phone records, and she was going to have to wait for Jeff Roubaix to get hold of them.

In the meantime, she needed a last-known address for Lauren and Jen Jones. Sheryl had said they'd lived in a flat in Chalk Farm but a quick search of the Land Registry and the Electoral Register didn't turn up anything, which was no great surprise. This was one of the problems these days, thought Tina. Because everything was done by email and phone, people didn't tend to keep each other's postal addresses in the same way they'd done in the past, making them harder to track down.

Lighting another cigarette, Tina looked up Sheryl's number and called her.

'Did you go see Dylan?' Sheryl asked immediately.

'I did, but don't worry. I didn't mention you.'

'Thanks. I appreciate that. Did he help?'

'A little.'

'I'm surprised. You must have some serious powers of persuasion.'

You don't know the half of it, thought Tina.

'So what did he tell you?'

'He just gave me a few leads to follow up on,' said Tina carefully. 'I'll let you know how I get on.' She thought about advising Sheryl to keep out of Dylan's way in case he worked out that she was the one who'd given Tina his name, but decided against it. There was no point worrying her unduly. 'I'm trying to get an exact address for Lauren and Jen in Chalk Farm,' she continued. 'Do you know anyone who might be able to help me?'

'I can't think of anyone. We were all friends, but not that much, you know. Is there no other way of finding out? I mean, you're a detective, right?'

Tina sighed. 'I'll find it eventually, it's just easier if someone can tell me.'

There was a pause as Sheryl thought. 'I know Jen was seeing someone just before she went missing. Lauren told me about him. I never met him but I think he lived just down the road from them. Dylan might know him.'

'Do you have a name?'

'God, what was it?'

Tina waited again while Sheryl searched her memory banks on the other end of the phone.

'Sean. That was it.'

Tina felt a stab of excitement. 'Are you sure?'

'Yeah, totally. It was Sean.'

'Was his last name Egan?'

'She never told me his last name. I think he was a bit older than her. Late thirties maybe, and Lauren said he was good-look-ing. Look, I'm sorry. It's not much help, is it?'

But it was. As far as Tina was concerned there was simply no question that Jen's boyfriend and Sean weren't the same person. The age was about right, and Sean was undoubtedly a good-look-ing guy. It wasn't concrete evidence that he was connected – not by a long way – but it suddenly made her far more interested in his story, and the events surrounding it.

One thing was for sure: everything kept coming back to Sean.

Thirty-one

I ate dinner in a cavernous pub in Bedford town centre that could probably have fitted five hundred customers comfortably but had barely fifty, making it feel very empty, which suited me just fine. My plan was simple: have a decent meal and then head back to the car, which I'd moved to the other side of town from the spot where I'd abandoned the iPad, for a sleep. I figured I could think better on a full stomach.

I had fish, chips and mushy peas and it was surprisingly good. I ate the lot and washed it down with a pint of Foster's. Then I got profligate and ordered treacle sponge for pudding and another pint, which reminded me that I'd never been very good with money.

As I drank the second pint, settled in at a corner table a long way from anyone else, I relaxed and let my mind drift. When I'd been living at Jane's place I'd spent a lot of time on my own, yet the combination of the drugs and the fact that I had no memory from before the car accident had left me unable to think about all but the most basic of functions. The world had been a blank, confusing place. Now, suddenly, it had become exciting and new, and yet, ironically, it looked as if my newfound freedom would be over before I got a chance to fully appreciate it again.

The sounds of incarceration came back to me. The iron clank of cell doors; the tinkling of keys; the echoing shouts and cat-calls; the plaintive cries of the first-timers and the weak at night; the grunts of masturbation . . . And the smells: disinfectant in the corridors; the stale close-up odour of sweat on the prisoners; bad breath; cheap, mass-produced food.

In those moments, as I sat drinking my second pint in the comforting warmth of the pub, my conscious self soaking up memories from my subconscious, it was like opening up a book and beginning a story.

It's going to be hard for you in here.

And by God it was.

They came for me very early on in my stay. I'd helped to put away a lot of very bad people during my time as an undercover cop – gangsters, drug smugglers, armed robbers – and a lot of those people still had power and money, which was a very bad combination. Because of my background they had me on a wing with the so-called vulnerable inmates who needed protection: the paedophiles, the rapists, the terrified first-timers, the ex-cops who'd been caught out by the justice system they were supposed to be upholding. It didn't help, though.

When I first arrived, I had my own cell, and one morning I was standing at the sink cleaning my teeth when two of the wing's screws came in. The most senior of the two was called

Mr Crawley and he'd been the one who'd given me what they called a 'welcome briefing' when I'd first arrived. He was a big, cheery Yorkshireman with a crumpled, ruddy face that looked like it had been moulded out of playdough by a two-year-old and an air of real warmth about him – the kind of guy you'd end up talking to in a pub.

'Right, Sean,' he said, giving me a rueful smile. 'The governor needs to see you. We're on Amber Status at the moment so we're going to need to put the cuffs on, I'm afraid.'

'Any idea what it's about?' I asked, putting down the toothbrush. I was hoping that somehow it might be good news, like a quashed conviction.

'No idea,' he said, as the other one, whose name I couldn't recall, closed the cell door. 'You know what the bosses are like. They never talk to us plebs. You must have had that back in the police.'

We continued to chat amiably while he turned me round to face the wall and applied the cuffs, which was when I noticed that the other screw was filling up the sink with hot water, using his finger to gauge the heat. I said something light-hearted about the governor being a bit OCD if he needed me to wash twice before he saw me, but my instincts immediately told me that something was wrong.

And they were right to, because the next second Mr Crawley grabbed me from behind and swung me round, and he and the other screw forced my head into the sink, holding it underwater. The water was painfully hot, but not hot enough to scald. I struggled like a madman but Crawley was a lot stronger than I'd imagined, and anyway, there were two of them, so it was futile. I couldn't even cry out.

Because of the angle they were holding my head at, I could actually see them holding my head under and I looked up, desperately hoping they'd catch the panic in my eyes and have second thoughts about what they were doing. It was then that I saw the one whose name I couldn't remember had a phone in front of his face, and was actually filming what was happening.

Panic spread through me like a virus as the need to breathe grew stronger and stronger. My lungs felt like they were going to burst and yet still they held me under. I remember thinking I was going to drown. I struggled even harder, trying to lash out, but they had me pinned.

And then, just as suddenly as it had been shoved in, my head was yanked out of the hot water by my hair.

'Jason sends his love,' hissed Crawley in my ear as I gasped for breath.

I knew exactly who he was talking about: Jason Slade, a sadistic drug dealer who was one of the nastiest thugs I ever had to deal with. The irony of it was that I'd never even put Slade away. We'd tried to catch him out in an undercover op years before but he hadn't taken the bait and, because he was such a piece of shit, and because I knew he was guilty of some really heinous crimes, I'd let my anger get the better of me and had attacked him outside his home one night with a pair of makeshift knuckledusters. He hadn't managed to get his revenge at the time, but the nastiest criminals have long memories, as I was finding out to my cost.

Crawley gave me maybe ten seconds to get some breath back then he dunked me again, keeping me under even longer this time. He repeated the process twice more, and on the final time I actually took in a lungful of water. For a couple of seconds

I genuinely thought I was going to die before Crawley pulled me out and shoved a hand towel over my face to muffle my choking.

'Now I wouldn't have done that if you weren't a rapist,' he said in an almost regretful tone, 'but the fact is you are. So, just like the rest of them in here, you deserve what you get. Now, I can see you're a sensible man, so the best bet's not to say anything to anyone.' He sighed and gave me one of his rueful smiles. 'Because if you do, it'll be bad. Very bad.'

But it was going to be bad – very bad – anyway. I was sure of that. Jason Slade was nowhere near the most powerful man I'd crossed. There were others who'd pay good money to see me dead, and if Slade could get to me, they could too. After that incident, I could remember thinking that I was never going to make it out of there alive. That I was going to die in that hellhole.

And then something happened.

When I was a young undercover officer, there'd been a guy about ten years older than me who'd acted as my mentor. His name was Jack Duckford, and he was a good-looking London boy with a nice line in patter. We'd worked together on a number of assignments and had stayed friends on and off for some time afterwards. He'd moved away from undercover, joining the National Crime Squad and specializing in hunting down organized crime gangs, and one day, about a month into my time in prison – maybe a bit more – he came in to visit.

I could remember being shocked to see him. We hadn't talked in at least three years and most of my friends and former work colleagues were avoiding me like the plague, so I was happy that someone from my past had finally turned up to see me.

We didn't make much small talk. When he asked me how I was getting on I told him the truth. 'It's bad, Jack. I don't think I can do five years of this.' I explained what had happened with Crawley and the other screw, keeping my voice down because you never knew who was listening. 'Is there anything you can do to help?'

He looked at me very closely. 'Did you do it, Sean? Did you rape that woman?'

My answer was emphatic. 'No. I've never forced myself on any woman in my life. You know me. I wouldn't do that.'

He nodded slowly. 'Yeah, I know you wouldn't. I just had to hear it from you, that's all.' He looked around at the blank walls, taking in the soul-destroying blandness of the place. 'Jesus, they've fucked you, Sean. All the good work you've done over the years, and they repay you like this. Letting you rot in here with all the nonces.'

'You remember Jason Slade, don't you?'

'Yeah, I remember that lowlife arsewipe. Although I'd prefer not to.'

'He was the one behind the attack. And there are plenty of other people gunning for me too, and now they've got a way in through the screws. They're going to hurt me again, and bad.'

Jack frowned. 'I don't think I'll be able to do anything on an official level, Sean. People aren't exactly lining up to help you. But I'll ask around, see what I can do. I've got a lot of good contacts on both sides. They may be able to apply some pressure in the right places.'

I thanked him, and we continued talking for a few minutes about this and that. It was strange, because I couldn't really understand why he'd come. It wasn't as if we were great friends. But then, when the inevitable silence descended on the conversation, he leaned forward in his seat and said, 'Stay strong in here, Sean, and I'm sure you'll get out sooner than you think. And whatever happens, call me as soon as you do. I might have some work for you.'

'What kind of work?'

He smiled. 'The type you're good at.'

Thirty-two

Tina had developed an appreciation of food over the previous few months, and along with coffee and cigarettes it had become one of her most important pleasures. She'd learned to cook, and found the whole process therapeutic. Tonight, though, she'd taken the quicker option of a tuna and avocado salad with crusty homemade bread and hummus, and had only just finished eating when there was a loud knock on the front door.

She looked at her watch: 8.10. She was pretty sure it was Mike Bolt, but with everything going on at the moment she wanted to be on the safe side, so she went upstairs and looked down at the doorstep from the spare bedroom window.

There he was. Her former boss, sometime lover, and good friend. The man she'd come close to falling for more than once but never quite managing it. They hadn't seen each other for close to eighteen months now, after their one proper attempt at a relationship had fallen apart before it had even got going, courtesy mainly of Tina herself. Commitment issues, her therapist Debbie called it, but unfortunately Debbie had yet to come up with a cure.

Although she didn't like admitting it to herself, Tina missed Mike, and she was disappointed to see that he'd come with his colleague Mo Khan rather than alone. She went downstairs and let them in. There were formal handshakes all round. Mike managed a smile but there wasn't the usual gleam in his bright blue eyes.

She led them through to the lounge and asked if they'd like a drink but they both declined.

'Sorry about how late we are,' said Mike. 'But you know how it is.'

She smiled. 'No problem. I didn't have plans.' She sat down on her sofa and they both moved the armchairs so they were sitting opposite her. 'I hope you don't mind if I smoke. I've just finished dinner and that's always the cigarette I like the most.'

Mike smiled again. 'It's your house, you do what you want. OK with you, Mo?'

Mo made an 'I don't care' gesture as he sank into the chair, and Tina noticed that he'd put on even more weight since she'd last seen him several years earlier. He'd never been the skinniest of cops but another couple of pounds and they'd have to help him out of the chair.

'We've just come from the Sunny View Hotel,' said Mike formally, 'where a man was murdered earlier today in the room you rented in the name of Mr Matthew Barron.'

'Well, Matthew Barron, whose real name as I told you is Sean Egan, rented it. I just paid.'

'I want you to go through everything that's happened since Sean Egan – who's now our chief suspect in the murder – came to see you,' he continued, ignoring her interruption.

For the next ten minutes Tina went through the story in detail, avoiding any mention of her own missing persons case, since she still wasn't a hundred per cent sure it was relevant yet.

'It's a pretty outlandish story,' said Mo when she'd finished recounting what Sean had told her about why he was being chased by people he didn't know for a reason he'd yet to remember.

'I know,' said Tina with a sigh, 'and I'm still not entirely sure it adds up. He said the house where he was staying in Wales had been burned down by the couple who went there to kill him.'

'So why didn't you report the matter to the police immediately?'

'Because all I had was his story, which sounded even more outlandish when he first told it. I Googled articles about houses burning down near Pembroke, which was where he said it was, and one did burn down on Monday night as he claimed. But there was no mention of there being bodies inside. I asked Sean to hand himself in. I sent him to the hospital because he had amnesia, and that's where the two men who identified themselves as police officers – the two who, according to Sean, were in the hotel room today – abducted him.'

Mike frowned. 'And they wanted to know the location of some bodies?'

'That's what Sean said.'

'And he gave you no clue as to who those bodies might be?'

Tina could hear the scepticism in his voice. 'No,' she said, deciding to keep back the details of Sean's recurring dream. 'He claims he has no idea, although I've only got his word for that.'

'Mo, can you check if the local police found any bodies in that burned-out house?'

With an effort, Mo pulled himself out of his seat and went out into the hallway to make the call.

For a couple of seconds Tina and Mike just looked at each other. He was a good-looking guy, she thought. Big, broad-shouldered, with amazing eyes, and an air of kindness about him that had always attracted her. Yet somehow she'd managed to mess their relationship up.

'How are you getting on with the case?' she asked, breaking the silence.

Mike gave her a laconic smile and Tina realized the bond between them was still there. 'I'll level with you because you're levelling with us. Not very well. We can't ID the dead man at the moment because he wasn't carrying any, and the surviving witness, whose name's Carl Hughie, isn't cooperating. It looks like Hughie's involved with MI5 and he's got some very powerful friends because we're having real difficulty even getting to interview him. I've already had a call from my boss at Homicide Command telling me he's coming under pressure from on high to go easy on this guy. Apparently, whatever Hughie's involved in is a matter of national security. We've tested his hands and the gloves that we found on him for gunshot residue but so far nothing's shown up.'

'It won't,' said Tina. 'Sean admitted shooting Hughie's colleague. He said it was self-defence.'

'That's a lot of self-defence,' said Mo as he came back in the room and sat down. 'The victim was shot four times, including once in the head at point-blank range.'

Tina's expression didn't change, but the news concerned her. More and more she was beginning to realize how unpredictable Sean was.

'You also need to know that he fled the scene wielding the gun and threatening staff and guests,' continued Mo, 'before hijacking a car at gunpoint. They don't sound like the actions of an innocent man. We all know your history with him, and the fact that he saved your life, but if you hear anything from him, you've got to tell us.'

'I will,' said Tina, but she wasn't certain she would. She didn't like the fact that Mike's inquiry was being interfered with from on high before it had even properly begun. She thought of Dylan Mackay and the beating she'd given him that morning. It had been wrong. It had been illegal. It could even have been construed as torture. Yet it had got her at least some of the answers she was looking for – answers that Mike and Mo would never have got.

Mo's phone rang. 'That was Grier,' he said when he'd finished the call. 'There were two as yet unidentified bodies, a man and a woman, found in a burned-out house in rural Pembrokeshire on Monday night. They haven't yet got a definitive cause of death but initial findings suggest they both died violently.'

'I can help you ID the bodies,' said Tina. 'Sean gave me these.' She handed Mike the two driving licences Sean had taken from the house.

Mike inspected them carefully, before handing them to Mo. 'Where did he get these?'

'He took them from their wallets.'

'That's very interesting,' said Mo. 'We've got two dead bodies, and Sean Egan rifles through their possessions then tells a story about two mysterious hitmen killing them who no one else saw. It doesn't look good for him, does it?'

It was a fair point. 'I know,' said Tina. 'Which is why I'm talking to you now. Believe it or not, I got caught up in this completely by accident.'

'As usual,' said Mo.

Tina opened her mouth, then thought better of it. There was no point getting into an argument.

Mike gave Mo a look to say 'go easy' before turning back to her. 'OK, let me make things crystal clear for you, Tina. This is no longer anything to do with you, so you need to keep out of it, let us do our job, and we'll do our best to keep your link to an on-the-run murder suspect out of the papers. Deal?'

Tina nodded. 'Deal.'

But, as she let them out the door, she knew immediately that it was a promise she couldn't keep.

Thirty-three

Dylan Mackay wasn't good with stress. For a start, he wasn't used to it. Life had dealt him some pretty good cards. Rich parents who'd always given him what he wanted; a top-drawer education at one of London's premier public schools; enough superficial charm to get other people to give him what he wanted; and the kind of foppish bad-boy looks that women always seemed to go for. He could have been a millionaire by now if he'd applied himself. The problem was he never had. He'd scraped into Leicester Uni even though Ma and Pa had had their hearts set on Oxford, having already developed a taste for good drugs and high living. He'd dropped out after two years, done a gap year that had turned into three, spent a hell of a lot of money that wasn't his, and ended up as a DJ scraping a living at friends' parties. Because that was the thing about Dylan. He was never short of friends.

But friends don't pay the bills – not ones the size Dylan had run up anyway – and when the old man had cut him off a couple of years earlier after he'd turned up to a cousin's wedding off his head on a murderous combination of high-grade chang, champagne and MDMA and exposed himself to the bridesmaids at the reception (two of whom were under the age of twelve), he'd been forced to look for alternative forms of income. The problem was, when you started doing illegal stuff – and Dylan had been doing a lot of illegal stuff these past two years – you ended up dealing with some pretty dodgy people, which was how he'd got himself in the situation he was now in.

He should never have said a word to Tina Boyd. The moment he'd started talking he'd regretted it. He'd wanted to fight back – Christ, he had. Dylan was no coward, as more than one guy had found out to his cost, but she'd caught him by surprise, and when she'd held that broken glass to his face and threatened to cut him – and he knew she would have done it too – he'd had no choice but to cooperate. Even so, he hadn't given up the name she'd needed, and he was at least proud of that. Still, now that she'd taken his phone it was only a matter of time before she found out the name of the man he was protecting, and if that happened, then, put bluntly, he was finished.

He knew who'd put her on to him as well. It was that little slut Sheryl Warner. She'd been big buddies with Jen and Lauren, and he remembered the way she'd kept asking him loads of inconvenient questions when they disappeared off the scene so suddenly. She was lucky she wasn't made to disappear herself – thankfully, she'd shut up after a while, and things had settled down.

Until now.

He was looking forward to paying Sheryl back for her big mouth. He knew she fancied him, so he'd pop round her place one evening, all smiles, and when she let him in, he'd kick the shit out of her. The thought excited him, but his revenge was going to have to wait because at the moment Dylan had bigger fish to fry. He'd been instructed to call a certain number if anyone started asking too many questions about Jen and Lauren, and had been told in no uncertain terms what would happen to him if he didn't. What had stopped him from calling the number so far was fear. If the man he was meant to call knew that he'd cooperated with Tina and admitted his own role in pimping out Jen and Lauren, then Dylan was in real trouble. Which was why he'd spent the last twelve hours or so in a state of abject terror.

It was a no-win situation. Say something and risk being viewed as a liability, or keep quiet and definitely be seen as one. What sort of choice was that?

Dylan stood looking out of his bedroom window at the street below, his thirtieth cigarette of the day in one hand, mobile in the other, knowing that one way or another he was going to have to make the call. He wanted to throw up – the tension coursing through him was that bad. He could die for this, and it was all that bitch Sheryl's fault. God, he wished he could get his hands round her neck right now and throttle the life out of her. The same with Boyd. At least this call might mean the end for her. She really didn't know the people she was messing with here. For a couple of seconds an intense, hot rage overtook Dylan Mackay as he recalled the beating he'd received from her, and he pressed the speed dial button on the phone.

Holding it to his ear, he waited, almost unable to breathe, praying the call wouldn't be picked up at the other end.

And then a familiar voice came on the line: 'Long time no hear. What is it?'

Dylan swallowed. 'Someone's been asking questions.'

Thirty-four

It was a sunny morning when I finally woke up. I'd dreamed a lot but couldn't really remember anything, although as I sat up in the car seat, stiff, cold and tired, I had another flashback to prison, and almost with surprise I realized that I could remember more of my stay there now. Faces appeared in my mind of different screws and inmates, some whose names I remembered, others just passing and anonymous.

But I was filling in the gaps now. Childhood remained patchy, and I still had this nagging conviction that I had a sister, but adulthood, and particularly my time in the force, was becoming far more vivid and real.

I was on the mend. However, I was also on the run. I had next to no money and, worse, no plan. I was tempted to call Tina to ask how she was getting on tracking down Dr Bronson but I'd involved her too much already, and if she'd gone to the police, as she'd said she would, then they'd be tracking the mobile number I'd called her from yesterday. In fact they'd be able to track any number I called her from. I'd have to think of another way to contact her.

In the meantime, I switched on the car radio and searched through the stations until I found one that had the news. There was a big political story about an MP who'd been taking kickbacks from big business; another one about renewed violence in the Middle East; and finally a brief couple of sentences at the end about an incident at a north London hotel the previous day in which a man had been shot dead. The female newsreader said that police were appealing for witnesses, but no mention was made either of me or the identity of the dead man.

The story gave me just a glimmer of hope. If nothing else, I still had a little time before my face started appearing on TV screens and the hunt for me began in earnest. I knew I had to lose the car but decided to grab some breakfast first.

I found a roadside café just out of town and ate a fry-up washed down with a couple of cups of coffee. By the time I'd finished I wanted to go back to sleep, but there was no time for that, so I drove back into town and left the car on a back street not far from the main drag. By this time it was just after nine o'clock, so I walked round until I found the bus station, checked the different routes available, and finally jumped on one heading for Cambridge. I wanted to find somewhere isolated where I could lie low for a day or two until I worked out my next move.

After buying the bus ticket and a bottle of water, I had the sum total of six pounds to my name, so I was going to have to steal to survive. Once upon a time that thought would have bothered me, but not any more. This was about survival. I'd been dealt some bad cards by the world. Kicked out of the police, imprisoned for something I didn't do, and now hunted, it seemed, by a whole host of people I didn't know who either wanted to put me back in the slammer or in the ground. I was well and truly on my own. But I'd been in this position before and survived, and I was determined to survive again.

The bus meandered along a host of B-roads through flat Bedfordshire and Cambridgeshire countryside, passing through quaint villages and less quaint towns on its torturous, winding route. About an hour into the trip the bus stopped on a stretch of straight, tree-lined road with a sprinkling of houses backing on to rolling green farmland on either side, and I decided on a whim to get out and walk. There was something truly liberating about being able to stretch my legs on a sunny day, and I had this strange feeling that if I walked for long enough I'd get to where I wanted to be.

So that's what I did. Fortified by my high-carb breakfast, and taking advantage of this potentially last burst of freedom, I walked for hours, down forest tracks and across sweeping wheat fields, drinking in the smells and sights of the countryside and working constantly to keep down the fear of incarceration and death that was always there at the back of my mind.

After a long time, and with my water finished, I was heading down a bumpy single-track road when I came across a footpath that ran past a big wooden barn. The doors to the barn were open and I poked my head inside. It was empty, with hay bales stacked on both sides and a bed of loose hay covering much of the floor space. A wave of weariness suddenly washed over me. There were no other buildings nearby that I could see, and no people either, so I piled up some of the hay in the far corner where I couldn't be seen easily from the door, lay down on my back, placing the pistol beside me under a light covering of straw, and shut my eyes.

My last day in prison. That empty feeling of knowing so much time had been wasted, and the fear of what lay ahead. But, maybe thanks to Jack Duckford's contacts in the underworld, the remainder of my stay after that first incident had been largely uneventful. The same screw who'd signed me in gave me back the bag containing the meagre possessions I'd arrived with, then turned me over to a stern female probation officer called Sian who had wiry hair and the kind of pained smile that made it look like she was constipated. She drove me to the halfway house in the arse end of Balham where I was going to be staying for the next three months, because I didn't have any family who were prepared to take me in.

I remember that grim feeling walking into the building. The place stank a lot worse than prison. At least prison was clean. Here, it felt like the BO was encrusted in the grimy, cobweb-strewn walls, along with the deep stench of despair. The guests – the inmates, whatever the hell we were called – looked either listless and doped up or just plain confused. The staff, young and out of their depth for the most part, were run off their feet as they tried to keep everything and everyone under control, and as I walked into the reception and almost tripped over a mop and bucket standing next to an untouched pool of rancid-smelling piss, I knew there was no way I could last it out in there.

An hour later I used the payphone down the corridor from

the room I'd been allocated with three other men, to make a call to Jack. As I stood there with the phone to my ear, trying to ignore the drunken wailing and shouting of someone in one of the rooms, it hit me that right then he was pretty much my only hope, and if he didn't answer, then I didn't know what the hell I was going to do.

But he did answer, and by God I felt relief when I heard his voice.

'It's Sean,' I said. 'I've just got out. That job you were talking about when you came to see me. Is it still available?'

'Absolutely,' he said without a pause. 'In fact we need you more now than we did then.'

'Care to tell me about it?'

'Not over the phone. But I promise you this. It's right up your street.'

Thirty-five

Tina didn't enjoy working from home but there wasn't any alternative. Mike had told her that the colleague of the man Sean had killed had links to the security services, which would explain how they'd manage to bug her office, and why she'd been unable to find any of the devices with her bug finder. They were probably bugging her house as well, but somehow she felt safer here, and it was a lot easier to tell whether she was under surveillance in a sleepy village than in the middle of a city.

But what she still couldn't understand was why on earth they were after Sean and how this connected to the disappearance of Lauren Donaldson and Jen Jones. Because she was convinced that the two events were connected. There wasn't a lot she could do, though, until Jeff Roubaix came back with the details of their phone records and those of Dylan Mackay.

She finished her fourth coffee of the day and considered an

afternoon walk. She liked walking. It gave her time to contemplate the world without interruptions. Maybe it would also give her some ideas.

But as she got to her feet, she remembered Sean asking her to try to locate the psychotherapist who'd been treating him, Dr Bronson. Sean had been convinced that Bronson had been implanting false memories while he'd been under hypnotherapy, and was responsible for the recurring dream in which Lauren was dead and Jen injured. Tina didn't entirely trust Sean, but she agreed with him that if she could find Dr Bronson, he might be able to provide some answers.

She lit a cigarette and sat back down again. The walk could wait. She picked up her laptop, which she was pretty sure hadn't been bugged since it had been with her the whole time, and typed in the web address for the British Association for Counselling and Psychotherapy, or BACP for short, the approved organization for the nation's counsellors and therapists. A quick search revealed a page listing all those members who'd been struck off over the years. It was possible, of course, that the mysterious Dr Bronson worked for the security services, but Tina doubted it. Whatever was going on, it was definitely illegal. There was no way MI5 would officially sanction removing a vulnerable man from hospital and keeping him drugged in a house in the middle of nowhere for weeks on end. At least she hoped not. Either way, she felt sure that Bronson was a freelancer, and it was unlikely he'd agree to do something so unethical unless he was in trouble and couldn't make money any other way.

The list was a long one, and the misdemeanours varied from fraud to serious sexual assault. Concentrating on the previous five years and on men with Caucasian names, Tina came up with seventy-nine of them, which didn't narrow things down a huge amount. So she decided to focus on those who'd been struck off for the more serious crimes, reasoning that they were the kind of people who could be more easily bought. It wasn't an ideal search criterion but it did serve to whittle the list down to twenty-four.

Next it was a case of Googling the individuals and trying to find photos of each of them, and locations. The two men who'd abducted Sean from A and E two days ago had got Bronson to the Herts/Bucks border – to Cherry Tree Farm, where they were holding Sean – in a little over an hour, so he was most likely based somewhere in southern England. Sean had also described Bronson as being a big guy in his fifties with a thick head of dark hair and glasses, so these two things, taken together, were a help. Even so, it was still painstaking and extremely boring work, since photos weren't generally easy to come by.

However, an hour later Tina had images for four men in their fifties who to her mind best fitted the bill. Three lived in Greater London, the fourth in Suffolk. She took a deep breath and stretched in her chair, wondering what to do next. She couldn't just turn up on each man's doorstep and demand to know if he'd been illegally hypnotizing a man being held against his will. No one was ever going to admit it, and she couldn't do what she'd done with Dylan and knock the truth out of them either, not when at least three, and possibly all of them, were innocent.

In the end, she needed Sean's help to move forward, and right now he could be anywhere. She wondered how she'd react if he called. Would she tell Mike? Possibly, but not definitely.

She sighed and lit another cigarette while she thought about Sean. He was an enigma to her. A cop who'd been kicked off the force for carrying out an illegal undercover op during which he'd killed at least one man, and potentially others, and who'd ended up convicted of rape; and now he'd killed again, and it looked like he was the boyfriend of one of the missing girls at the time she'd gone missing. And yet she'd known him once as a decent guy who'd tried to bring his brother's killers to justice and who, more importantly, had saved her life. Did she trust him, or didn't she?

Her mobile rang, interrupting her thoughts. She'd changed the SIM card and given the new number to only two people. One was Sean; the other was Jeff Roubaix, and she recognized Jeff's number now.

To be on the safe side, Tina walked out into her back garden, notebook in hand, and sat down on the bench she'd put out there the previous summer, before answering the call.

'You owe me a lot of money, Tina,' said Jeff straight away.

'What have you got?'

'The first number you gave me, the one you said belonged to a Lauren Donaldson or Marano, was registered to an address in Chalk Farm, and the name was Marano.'

Tina wrote down the address, knowing that this was almost certainly where Lauren and Jen were living when they disappeared.

'I've got the phone records for the past year,' continued Jeff. 'I'll email them to you.'

'When was the phone last used?'

'Hold on, I'll check.'

She waited, listening to the clicking of a keyboard at the other end of the line, knowing that Jeff's next words would almost certainly tell her the day on which Lauren disappeared.

'April the seventh. The last call's at 18.43.'

The night before Sean's car accident.

'Is that a help?'

'Yes,' sighed Tina. 'It is.' It was also bad news because now it gave total credence to Sean's story of the dream, the one in which he'd seen a woman bearing a striking resemblance to Lauren lying lifeless on a bed. Someone had switched off Lauren's phone to prevent it being used to track her down. Tina felt a pang of sadness as she thought of Alan Donaldson, knowing his daughter was almost certainly dead. 'Can you triangulate the location to where it was last used?' she asked.

Jeff made a scoffing sound. 'Come on, Tina, be serious. That's way off my remit. You need to go a lot higher than me for that.'

'What about the first of the numbers I gave you yesterday, the one I believe belongs to a Jennifer Jones?'

'At the moment they can't find a carrier, and I told them to pull out all the stops as well. Which means it's almost certainly an unregistered pay-as-you-go.'

'Shit. That means it's going to be hard to track the records, doesn't it?'

'Very. And it'll need people with a lot more clout and resources than I've got to have a chance.'

'OK, thanks.' Tina was surprised that someone like Jen Jones had a pay-as-you-go. In her experience, the only people not on contracts were kids, technophobes and criminals trying to stay under the radar. 'And the other one I gave you for Dylan Mackay? Any joy tracking down the records for that?'

'Pulled out all the stops on that one too, just like you asked me to, and it is registered to Dylan Mackay at an address in Kensington. Haven't got a full year's records because he hasn't had the phone that long.'

'How long?'

Again there was the sound of tapping on the keyboard. 'Well, that's interesting,' Jeff said after a pause. 'Looks like the contract began on April the eighth.'

So Dylan had changed phones the day after Lauren disappeared and the same day that Sean had his car accident. But what Tina really needed to find out was who Dylan had been talking to in the days prior to 8 April because that might well tell her who he'd hired Lauren and Jen out to. And who'd killed them.

'Is there any way you can get the records for the phone Dylan owned before April the eighth?'

Jeff exhaled loudly. 'I can try, but it means more paperwork, and more hassle, and your bill's running up high already.'

'Do what you can and I'll pay you in cash the moment you need it.'

'How about tonight? Can meet up for a drink. Don't mind coming to your local.'

The last thing Tina wanted was for Jeff Roubaix, or any other business contact she had, to be within a few hundred metres of her front door, but she didn't fancy driving too far either, and she knew she was going to have to pay him now if she wanted any more favours.

They arranged to meet in her local pub – a place she rarely frequented due to the fact that she could no longer drink alcohol – at eight p.m., before ending the call.

For a few minutes Tina sat in the sunshine with her eyes closed, mulling over what she'd just learned. She thought about Alan Donaldson and his desperation to be reunited with his missing daughter. It hurt her to know there was going to be no happy ending to this story, but she could still achieve justice for Lauren if she continued on her present course. It would help if she spoke to Mike, because he had the authority to gather the information she needed on the various phones she was trying to track, but she knew he wouldn't help her. Sean would, though. She was sure of that. He was the key to this whole thing.

But where the hell was he?

Thirty-six

I woke with a start from a completely blank and very deep sleep and almost screamed out loud.

A figure was staring down at me, partly silhouetted by the barn's dim light, with a large dog next to it.

I sat up instinctively and the dog growled, tensing as if readying to pounce.

A woman of about forty, with curly shoulder-length hair and a kindly, attractive face, was bending over me. 'Calm down, Roman,' she said to the dog. Then to me, a not entirely unfriendly 'Who are you?'

I could see she didn't look particularly scared or angry – but then she did have a big German Shepherd right next to her – so I gave her my best smile. 'I'm sorry, I was taking a walk and I got a bit lost.'

'Where are you heading to?'

I rubbed my eyes. 'Anywhere. I've just split up from my wife. It hasn't been an easy few weeks. I just got on a bus and kept going. I guess I thought I'd keep walking until I found a place to stay.' I was surprised at how easy the lies came, but then lying had been a part of my job description for most of my adult life, so I really shouldn't have been. 'Anyway, I'm sorry. I didn't mean to trespass.' I slowly got to my feet, relieved that I'd covered the gun with some hay. 'I'll be on my way.'

'It's OK,' she said, stepping back to give me some space. 'No harm done.'

I walked out of the barn and into the sunshine, and looked at my watch. It was almost 4.30. Jesus, I'd been out for hours. The woman and her dog followed me a few feet back.

'It's this way back to the road, right?' I called over my shoulder, pointing in the general direction I'd come from, and thinking I'd wait a few minutes before I came back for the gun.

'Hang on a moment,' she called after me. 'Do you want a drink of water or something before you go? You'll need it in this heat.'

I knew I shouldn't. Far better just to keep walking and hoping she didn't remember me, but that was the thing about being on the run. It was so damned uncomfortable, and the idea of an ice-cold glass of water, or even a cup of tea and a sit-down, was simply too good an opportunity to pass up. I think I must have been a very short-term, impulsive person in my pre-accident life because I turned round with another smile. 'That would be great, thanks. I'm Matt, by the way.'

We shook hands and the dog growled again, keeping his beady eyes on me and leaving me in no doubt that he wouldn't hesitate to rip my throat out if given the order.

'I'm Luda,' she said.

'That's an unusual name,' I said, thinking that she had lovely blue eyes.

'It's Russian. It means "love of the people". A little bit ironic, given that I'm alone out here in the middle of nowhere.'

I followed her round the other side of the barn, through a thin strip of woodland, and into a field where half a dozen goats grazed and made goat noises in one corner.

'Is this all yours?' I asked her.

She nodded. 'I've got five acres. Prices are a lot cheaper round here.'

'It's a nice place.'

'Thank you. It's very peaceful.' She turned to me with a playful expression on her face. 'I don't usually do this, by the way. Offer strangers a glass of water, especially ones I find flat out in my barn.'

'I'm a nice boy, I promise.'

'Does your wife believe that?'

'You know, I think she does. She wanted us to stay together. It's me who wanted to split. She's been having an affair. And not her first either.'

'I'm sorry to hear that.'

I was sorry too to have to spin her so many lies, but now that I was here it was essential I turned myself into a man she could sympathize with. At this point, I didn't just want a glass of water. I wanted to sit down, have a cup of tea and, you know, maybe more . . .

'It's OK,' I told her with a vaguely rueful expression. 'These things happen.'

'I know,' she said. 'It happened to me a long time ago. Once someone close to you does that, it's hard to go back.'

By this time we'd come to a spacious modern farmhouse, clearly built when architects still cared about creating character and charm, with a decent-sized chicken coop on one side and a series of raised vegetable beds on the other. I had another memory then from my old life – a realization that I'd always wanted to grow vegetables. I'd discussed it with someone once – a woman. I concentrated on trying to remember who, but nothing came.

The farmhouse's back door was open and I followed Luda and Roman inside, into a big, traditional kitchen with oak worktops and an Aga. Recipe books, some of them ancient-looking, lined the walls. I immediately felt at home but remained in the doorway, striking a formal, unthreatening pose with my hands behind my back as she filled a glass with water and handed it to me.

She watched me as I downed it in one go, and I could tell she was pondering whether to invite me to stay a while. I had a feeling she was lonely out here and got very little company, particularly male. I wasn't a bad-looking guy, and although my clothes were a little dishevelled courtesy of sleeping in a car followed by a barn, they were still obviously new. I asked Luda for another glass to give her a bit more time to make her decision and drank that one more slowly.

Finally, she asked me if I'd like to stay for a cup of tea.

'I'd love one,' I said, and five minutes later we were sat at the kitchen table talking.

We talked a long time, and, like everything else, I'd forgotten how interested I was in other people and their stories. Luda told me that her husband had died six years earlier, the victim of a street mugging that went wrong while they'd been living in London. He'd been stabbed once when one of the muggers either panicked or decided he wasn't being compliant enough, and unfortunately the blade had pierced his heart. The story angered me. It seemed so unjust that a kind, young, attractive woman should have had her life snatched away from her like that, and it reminded me why I'd become a cop in the first place – to put away pieces of dirt like the one who'd killed her husband. Afterwards, with her dreams of starting a family with the man she loved in tatters, she'd been unable to stay in London, or in her job as a lawyer, and had sold up and moved out here to escape the memories. She'd been here ever since. Money, it seemed, wasn't a problem, but loneliness was.

'You won't believe this but I was a hugely social person,' she told me. 'Dan and I used to go out all the time – restaurants, parties . . .'

I asked her if she missed all that.

She thought about that for a while before answering. 'I miss company. I miss sharing things. When I came out here I was happy to be alone. I couldn't imagine anyone replacing Dan. Sometimes I still can't. But six years is a long time and I've been ready to meet someone for a while now. The problem is, there aren't that many men out here. But I can't really imagine living anywhere else.'

'It's pretty idyllic,' I said, meaning it. 'Growing your own food, breathing fresh air every day, a long way from all the crap.'

Luda gave me what I can only describe as a deep, probing look. 'How about you, Matt? What's your story?'

So I fed her a long, carefully embellished and perfectly believable lie about how I'd been a salesman in the IT industry for the best part of two decades (no one ever asks too many detailed questions about IT); how I'd married my childhood sweetheart, Sally; how things had been great until her first affair (which somewhat magnanimously I'd forgiven) before finally it had all fallen apart with her second, which had unfortunately coincided with me being made redundant, causing a perfect storm that had left me perilously close to coming off the rails. By the time I'd finished telling her all this, I was almost believing it myself.

I knew what I was doing was repugnant, but the thing was, I was desperate for Luda to like me enough to let me stay the night. I genuinely liked her; I liked her home; most of all, I liked the new, invented me. The ordinary guy fallen on hard times who wasn't a killer ex-con on the run. I also knew that the longer I stayed out of sight the more likely I was to get my memory back before the police got hold of me, and therefore potentially save myself from another much longer prison sentence. Because if I remembered what had happened to me before the accident, then I'd know why everyone was after me, and maybe – just maybe – I could prove my innocence.

'My God, it's 6.15,' said Luda, looking at her watch.

'Really? I guess I'd better get going.' I got to my feet, knowing this was the moment of truth. 'Thanks ever so much for the tea, and for listening to me. I really appreciate it.'

She didn't get up. Instead she gave me a clearly flirtatious look. 'Do you want to stay for supper?'

I tried to appear surprised but happy. 'Are you sure? I don't want to impose.'

She smiled. 'Yes, I'm sure. You seem a nice guy. Sit down.'

So I did.

Thirty-seven

Sheryl Warner was sitting in her front room watching *Coronation Street* and drinking a large vodka Red Bull to wake herself up when there was a knock on her door. She frowned, wondering who it was. She was meeting a couple of mates later at the All Bar One in Islington but that wasn't until ten p.m.

It immediately occurred to her that it might be Dylan. He knew where she lived and if he'd worked out that it had been her who'd spoken to Tina Boyd about Lauren and Jen, he might want to hurt her, although she wasn't sure how he'd got through the front door, which was always locked.

But when Sheryl looked through the spy hole, it wasn't Dylan standing there but a good-looking blonde woman of about thirty wearing a dress with a cool-looking leather jacket on top. Sheryl wondered if she'd met the woman before somewhere, then decided to answer the door and find out who she was.

It was a big mistake.

As soon as the door opened, Pen de Souza smiled and punched Sheryl Warner in the throat, before forcing her way inside, followed by Tank.

Sheryl was gasping for air but Pen knew the blow had only been enough to incapacitate her for a short while. For the moment, she and Tank needed her alive and conscious.

Pen gave Sheryl a hard shove so she fell backwards on to her sofa, still clutching her injured throat, her eyes wide with shock. They got even wider when Pen produced the pistol from inside her jacket and screwed the suppressor on to the end of the barrel. At the same time, Tank walked round the back of the sofa so that he was standing directly behind her. As Sheryl followed him with her eyes, he flexed his gloved fingers menacingly. The look on his face was cold and merciless, and Pen almost felt sorry for Sheryl as she visibly recoiled.

'Who are you?' Sheryl croaked. 'Did Dylan send you? I haven't done anything, I promise.' She was crying now.

Pen put a gloved finger to her lips. 'Calm down, Sheryl, and don't ask questions. If you do what we say, we won't hurt you.'

'What do you want?'

'Stop crying and I'll tell you. If you continue to make a noise, though, my friend here will put a gag round your mouth and then things will get unpleasant.'

Pen's words were delivered in a calm, measured tone designed to put her victim at ease, and it seemed to work. Sheryl wiped away her tears, cleared her throat and sat up. She still looked scared, but healthily so.

'That's better. Do you think you can act?'

'What do you mean?'

'I want you to phone Tina Boyd for me. I have a script for you to read. You have to convince her to come here. If you manage it, we'll let you go as soon as she arrives. If you don't, then we're not going to be very happy at all. Do you understand?'

'I don't know—'

Pen cut her off. 'I don't want any "I don't knows", Sheryl. You need to do this. For your own sake.'

Sheryl nodded, finally understanding that this was life and death for her.

Pen handed her the script.

It was time to set the trap.

Thirty-eight

Tina's meeting with Jeff Roubaix was always going to last longer than she'd wanted it to. He'd insisted on a few drinks in her local, saying he'd come a long way (which, to be fair, he had), and so for the last half an hour they'd been catching up on things, even though they'd never really been friends.

Jeff, though, seemed genuinely happy to see her, and was already on his second pint of lager, while Tina was coming towards the end of her orange juice and soda water, and not planning on drinking another. It wasn't that Jeff was bad company. He wasn't, and to be fair, he still looked pretty good for a man in his forties who spent too long behind a desk (and she could tell he fancied her as well, since he was making very little effort to hide the fact). But she really wasn't in the mood for chat, and the pub, with all its temptations, was making her feel uncomfortable. It was busy tonight, with laughing regulars packed round the bar, and the majority of tables taken up with diners. Out of the corner of her eye, Tina saw an older woman taking a sip from a big glass of red as she chatted to her husband, and the look of pleasure on the woman's face as the wine went down made Tina desperate to snatch the glass from her hand and down its contents in one.

Her phone rang.

'Sorry, Jeff, I need to take this,' she said, getting to her feet and heading for the door.

It was Sheryl Warner, and she sounded upset.

'What's wrong, Sheryl?' Tina asked, making her way into the car park.

'Dylan came round. He beat me up.'

Tina felt a rush of guilt and anger. 'Do you need an ambulance? I can call you one.'

'No, I'm OK . . . Can you come over? Dylan said something about Jen and Lauren. About the way they disappeared.'

'What did he say?'

'I can't talk about it over the phone. Can you come over?'

The last thing on earth Tina wanted to do right now was drive to Camden but she felt obligated.

'I think you'll want to hear it,' added Sheryl before Tina had a chance to answer.

'Sure. I'll be with you in about half an hour. Don't let anyone else in.'

'OK,' said Sheryl, and ended the call.

'Is she coming?' Pen asked Sheryl.

Sheryl nodded vigorously. 'She says she'll be here in half an hour.'

'Good. You've done well.' Pen smiled and leaned forward, brushing a lock of Sheryl's hair away from her face.

'What are you going to do to her?'

Pen laughed. 'What do they always say? If I tell you that, then I'll have to kill you. Let me give you a piece of advice for the future, Sheryl. Keep out of matters that don't concern you, and never ask awkward questions. That way you'll live a long and happy life.'

Sheryl managed a weak little smile and Pen could see the hope filling up in her eyes.

Poor little bitch, she thought.

For a good ten seconds after finishing the call, Tina stood in the car park staring down at the handset. Something about the conversation hadn't felt right. In fact, several things hadn't. Firstly, what information could Dylan have given Sheryl while beating her up? Surely the most he would have said was that if she wasn't careful she'd end up like Jen and Lauren, or words to that effect, and if that was the case then she could easily have told Tina that over the phone rather than get her to drive for half an hour to hear it. The wording Sheryl had used also rang an alarm bell. When she'd said 'I think you'll want to hear it', it hadn't sounded like a natural thing for a girl like her to say.

Tina pocketed the phone, wondering if she was just being paranoid. Probably, she concluded, although being paranoid had saved her life more than once. She went back inside and saw that Jeff had almost finished his pint.

'Everything all right?' he asked as she sat back down.

'I'm going to have to go. I might have a lead on the case I'm working.'

He smiled. 'That's not an excuse, is it? You know you can tell me if you just want to go home. I'd be disappointed, of course. I like your company.'

Tina knew he was hitting on her. 'No, Jeff, it's not an excuse. I do actually have a lead that needs sorting now.'

'Anything I can help with? I'm free all evening.' He said it as if he was expecting a brush-off and was just trying his luck, and ordinarily Tina would have turned him down flat, but on this particular occasion a bit of back-up was no bad idea.

'Well, now you mention it, I could actually use your services if you don't mind. But it's strictly gratis, right? I can't afford to pay you.'

Jeff didn't look quite so happy now. 'OK, but what is it you want me to do?'

'Nothing strenuous. The girl who just called me wants me to go round to her flat in Camden. She says she's got some information, but I think it might be a set-up.'

'What kind of set-up?'

'I had a run-in with a guy yesterday who's connected to her and it's possible he's round there with a couple of friends looking to give me some payback. It's unlikely, but I'd prefer to be on the safe side.'

'So you want me to go in there with you?'

'No. I'll call you on your mobile before I go in, and we'll keep the line open. You hang back, and if you hear down the phone that I'm in trouble, call 999, and maybe come to the door yelling "Armed police!" or something that scares them. I'll have some spray on me and a Taser but, as I said, I'm almost certainly being overcautious.'

'Can never be too overcautious. Sure I'll come with you. You're not going to be that long in there, are you?'

Tina shook her head. 'No. If it is legit, I'll just get the information and leave.'

'Maybe we can grab some dinner afterwards. I'm getting hungry, and there are a few good places round Camden.'

Tina gave him the kind of look which said don't push your luck, but she was smiling too. 'Maybe,' she said, 'but don't try to make any unwanted passes, not when I'm carrying a Taser and spray.'

He winked at her. 'I know you too well, Tina. I wouldn't dare.'

Thirty-nine

At that time in the evening, the journey to Camden took twenty-five minutes. Tina drove, promising to give Jeff a lift back to his car later. On the way, they chatted about the old days at Islington nick, the people they'd known, and what had become of them. Tina had forgotten what good company Jeff could be. He was funny and open, and, philanderer or not, he came across as refreshingly honest. He was based out of Holborn nick these days and still just plodding along, investigating what he was told to investigate, and presumably just counting the days until his retirement.

'Why did you never settle down and get married?' she asked him after a short break in the conversation.

'Hey, I'm not terminally ill. I still could. I just haven't found the right woman yet. And anyway, I could ask you the same question.'

'I got close once.'

'With John?' he said, referring to John Gallan, a man they'd both known.

She nodded. 'I think after what happened with him I got put off committing too much to one person.'

'Sometimes it's easier not to,' he said. 'That way you can't get hurt.'

And they fell silent once again, pondering that particular thought.

Tina found a spot only a few minutes' walk from Sheryl's flat. It had just turned nine p.m. and the streets were busy with people out for the night. Camden was a fashionable area these days, and the sight of full restaurants and groups of drinkers standing around outside the pubs enjoying the balmy temperatures calmed Tina and made her question her suspicions about Sheryl's phone call.

Leaving Jeff out of sight in the car, she made her way to the building's front door and rang the old-fashioned buzzer there. Sheryl let her through.

When she was inside, Tina used a couple of envelopes from the communal mailbox to prop open the door, then put a call through to Jeff.

'Any problems, you know what to do, right?' she whispered into the phone.

'Be in there like a shot, Tina, don't worry.'

Jeff was a big guy. He might have been running to fat a little, but Tina knew he could handle himself in a scrap.

'Thanks, Jeff, I really appreciate this.' She replaced the phone in her pocket and mounted the stairs.

It was empty and quiet, and Tina felt herself tense as she went up to Sheryl's door and knocked hard. The Taser was in her other jacket pocket and she gripped the trigger, ready to use it at a moment's notice.

The door opened and Sheryl stood there, a smile frozen on her face.

Two things struck Tina straight away. One: she was petrified. Two: she didn't have any injuries.

'Thanks for coming, Tina,' she said, moving aside to let her in.

The flat seemed empty behind Sheryl, and Tina hesitated for a second. 'Let's take a walk,' she said without stepping inside.

Sheryl was suddenly yanked to one side by someone just out of view, and almost at the same time a blonde woman appeared in her place, pointing a gun at Tina, the end of the barrel barely five feet from her head. Her gun hand was perfectly steady, like she knew exactly what she was doing.

It all happened too fast for Tina to get out of the way. 'Don't shoot!' she said, loudly enough for Jeff to hear in the car.

'Get inside and take your hands out of your pockets very slowly,' demanded the woman, in an American accent. 'Or I'll kill you right now.'

Tina didn't argue – she could see the woman meant it – and stepped over the threshold, taking her hands out of her pockets so they could be seen.

She was immediately grabbed by the same unseen hand that had pulled Sheryl away and flung across the floor in the direction of the sofa as the blonde closed the door behind her, trapping her inside.

Steadying herself, Tina turned back round to face her

adversaries, hands in the air, trying to look as calm and unthreatening as possible.

The man who'd grabbed her was huge. Ex-military for sure, with closely cropped hair and a square jaw, he was a good six feet two, with muscles that looked like they were trying to burst out of the clothes he was wearing. Tina hoped that Jeff didn't make a dramatic entrance, because this guy would break him in half.

Tina's eyes met Sheryl's. The poor girl was standing in the shadow of the man, who absolutely dwarfed her. She looked confused and terrified, and was clearly unable to understand what she'd got herself involved in. Tina gave her a supportive look, but she was close to panic herself.

'Sit down on the sofa, and keep your hands where we can see them,' the blonde woman said. 'Try anything stupid, and the first bullet goes through your kneecap.'

Tina did as she was told, the blonde woman following her with the gun.

The woman then motioned to the giant, and he walked round the sofa so he was standing behind Tina. Out of the corner of her eye, she saw him produce a gun of his own from the back of his trousers and slowly fit a suppressor to it.

When he'd finished, the blonde moved her gun away from Tina. 'Thanks for your help, Sheryl,' she said evenly, pointing it at Sheryl's head and pulling the trigger. Sheryl crumpled to the floor without a sound, blood pouring down her forehead, her eyes already closed.

Tina had seen violent death at close hand a number of times before but it never ceased to shock her. It was the suddenness of it, the way a whole life, full of experiences and memories, could be ended with the flick of a finger, and with barely a second's thought. It was debatable that the blonde had given it even that, because even as Sheryl fell she was turning the gun back on Tina.

'You need to answer our questions,' she said, walking over, gun arm outstretched. 'If you do, we'll make it quick. If you don't, it'll be very slow and very painful. Do you understand?'

For a second, Tina thought about telling them that she had police back-up outside, but just as quickly dismissed the idea. If they had to, they'd just kill her and leave. What she needed to do now was stay alive, appear to cooperate, and hope Jeff had called the cavalry. 'Yes, I understand,' she said, and this time there was no mistaking the fear in her voice.

'Good. You look like an intelligent woman. Under other circumstances we might have got on, but . . .' The blonde shrugged. 'I guess that's not going to happen. We're going to turn the music up a little bit. Just in case we need to hurt you.'

She motioned to the big guy again and he turned up the volume on an iPod player until the room was filled with the chilled, relaxed sound of a melodic female voice. Tina recognized the track as something by Zero 7, a band she normally liked. If she ever got out of here alive, she knew she'd never be able to listen to it again.

She swallowed, stared up at the blonde. Knowing she was talking for her life now.

They looked each other in the eye. The blonde's expression was hard and merciless, and sat wrongly on her pretty, youthful face. Monsters come in all forms, thought Tina, but she'd never have guessed this was one.

'Who else knows the details of your investigation?'

Fear seemed to fire up every nerve ending in Tina. She knew

that if she gave the wrong answer, they'd hurt her, and if she gave the right one, it took her a big step closer to death.

'No one knows the details,' she said quietly.

The blonde's finger tensed on the trigger. 'And where have you made a record of your investigations?'

Tina knew this was the last question they'd ask her. Once they had the information, she was gone.

Please, Jeff, if you're hearing this . . . do something.

'On my laptop.'

'Where's that?'

'In my car.'

'Where's your car parked?'

'I'm not sure.'

The blonde's expression darkened. 'What do you mean you're not sure?' She lowered the gun so it was pointed directly between Tina's legs. 'Maybe I should give you another hole for your boy-friend to fuck.'

'Armed police!' came an angry shout from beyond the front door. 'Open up now!'

The door shook alarmingly as it was kicked hard.

Tina recognized the voice as Jeff's, which wasn't good, because he wasn't armed. Then the sound of a wailing siren carried through an open window somewhere at the back of the flat, sounding like it wasn't that far away, and getting closer.

'Shit,' hissed the blonde, turning her head in the direction of the shouts.

The hiss of bullets being fired towards the door came from behind Tina. It was the giant, but Tina couldn't see if he was hitting it or not because her view was blocked by the blonde.

The Final Minute

All this happened in the space of a couple of seconds, which was all it took for Tina to make a decision. She knew she was about to be shot. The blonde was already turning back towards her. One more second and she'd end up like Sheryl.

She launched herself from the sofa, grabbing the gun and yanking it upwards just as the blonde pulled the trigger. She heard another shout of 'Armed police!', caught a glimpse of smoking holes in the door as the giant continued to fire into it, and then she had the blonde by the hair and was using her momentum to drag her round so her body was between Tina and the giant.

They both fell to the floor, crashing into the chair Tina had sat in when she'd come to see Sheryl a couple of days earlier, and knocking it backwards. Somehow the blonde ended up on top. She was snarling and trying to pull her gun hand free but Tina put all her strength into giving her attacker's wrist a single hard twist, digging her nails in.

The gun clattered to the carpet as the blonde let go of it, crying out in pain, and Tina used her hand to knock it out of reach. The blonde was fast, though. She immediately used her free hand to drive her palm into Tina's face, delivering a blow that caused excruciating pain. She then forced down Tina's arms and pinned them with her knees, before grabbing her round the neck with both hands and squeezing with real force.

'Shoot the bitch!' she yelled, and beyond her, Tina saw the giant looming into view, the gun in his hand, trying to find a good shot.

With her air cut off, Tina felt herself becoming light-headed. She kicked and bucked with everything she had beneath the blonde, but already her strength was fading, and the blonde's grip was like a vice. But she wouldn't give up . . . she couldn't.

The giant was only a few feet away now, already pointing the gun at Tina's head.

Then, from what felt like a long distance away, she heard the bang of the door being kicked open, and another scream of 'Armed police!'

The giant turned to where it was coming from, firing again, a look of intense concentration on his face. At the same time, Tina concentrated on wriggling her left arm free from under the blonde's knee, using all her remaining strength to lever it off.

As it came free, Tina punched the blonde in the side of the head and, as the grip on her throat momentarily loosened, drove herself upwards and raked her face with her nails. But in her peripheral vision she saw the giant was pointing the gun at her again.

He pulled the trigger.

It was over.

Except it wasn't. He'd run out of bullets. He cursed and reached into his pocket.

But Tina wasn't going to wait for him to reload. Already pressing her advantage, she yanked one of the blonde's hands from her neck and managed to knock her off balance. Kicking and struggling free, Tina scrambled across the floor in the direction of the gun, grabbed it, and swung round, finger already tensed on the trigger.

But the giant and the blonde were running towards the rear of the flat, slamming the door behind them and leaving Tina aiming at non-existent targets.

Suppressing a choking cough, she clambered unsteadily to her feet and looked towards the open front door.

'Oh Jesus,' she whispered as she saw Jeff Roubaix sprawled

on the hallway floor, his head propped up against the wall opposite. He'd been shot repeatedly in the upper body, and the blue shirt he'd been wearing that Tina remembered thinking she liked earlier was peppered with dark stains the shape of blooming roses. His eyes were closed and he looked dead, and she felt a hard wrench of shock and anger. Even though he'd been unarmed, he'd tried to save her, and it had cost him his life. She was responsible. This was her doing. Tina Boyd. The Black Widow. The woman no man wanted to work with because of the way they had a habit of dying around her.

She could hear heavy footfalls on the staircase and more shouts of 'Armed police!' These ones were real, though. The cavalry had arrived, but as so often, they were too late.

With the gun still in her hand, Tina ran through the flat in the direction the two assassins had taken. These were the two who'd come to kill Sean at the house in Wales, she was convinced of that, which now inextricably linked him to the disappearance of Lauren and Jen. But that was of no use to her if these bastards got away.

Passing through the kitchen, she ran into the back bedroom, gun arm outstretched. The room was empty and smelled of perfume, and the doors leading out to the narrow balcony were open.

The rear of the building looked out on to a residential street, and Tina ran on to the balcony and looked both ways. She was on the second floor, a good twelve feet above the ground, but the blonde and the giant had clearly jumped, because they weren't there now. And she couldn't see them either. They were gone.

Cursing and shaking, still holding the gun, Tina strode back into the lounge, almost straight into the guns of two cops sighting her down the barrels of their MP5s. Behind them she could see a third cop crouched down beside Jeff, trying to resuscitate him. 'It's no good,' she heard him call out. 'He's gone, he's gone.'

'Put the gun down now!' the cop on the left yelled at her. 'Now!'

She put it down.

'Get on your knees.'

She got down on her knees, as the one on the right kicked the gun away from her.

'Lie down on your front with your hands down by your side.'

'My name's Tina Boyd. I'm a private detective.'

'I don't give a fuck who you are, lady. Lie down or I'll shoot you.'

Tina lay down, level now with Sheryl's corpse, which was only a few feet away. Blood dripped slowly from the dead girl's head wound on to the carpet. Tina knew it could have been her, and she found herself shaking, knowing once again that she'd pushed her luck to the absolute limits.

But at least it was finished.

For now.

Forty

It was the nicest evening I could remember, which, given my general lack of memory and the shit I'd had to put up with over the last two months, probably wasn't saying too much. But the fact was I felt truly relaxed. Luda was a lovely woman. Kind, friendly, and a real conversationalist. During the course of dinner (a very tasty coq au vin with homemade bread and steamed veg from the garden) and two bottles of red wine, we really opened up to each other. Or perhaps more accurately, she opened up to me and I got into my role of the jilted salesman husband so well that I stopped thinking of it as a lie. It felt good, whereas being me just felt crap.

I think it was inevitable that we'd end up making love. Somewhere near the bottom of the second bottle she reached over the kitchen table and took my hand, we looked into each other's eyes, and that was pretty much it. I leaned forward and kissed her tenderly on the lips, and she kissed me back, but harder and with real passion, and then we were in each other's arms and trailing through the house and up the stairs, losing clothes on the way as we explored each other, mouths locked together in an almost desperate embrace.

When we got to the bedroom and were lying naked on the bed she turned to me with a nervous look on her face. 'I haven't done this for a long time,' she said quietly.

I propped myself up on one elbow and smiled down at her, gently pushing back a lock of hair from her face. 'Me neither,' I said, which was the truth.

'You and your wife didn't . . .'

I shook my head. 'Not for months. Listen, we don't have to do anything. I'm happy just to lie here with you.' This wasn't quite the truth but I was conscious of what I'd been sent to prison for and there was no way I was going to push myself on Luda. Not after everything she'd done for me.

She smiled. 'No. I want to do it with you.'

So, after some messing about with a condom from her bedside drawer, we did. It was wild, it was passionate, and it was going great. But then, just as we built up towards the climax, I found myself looking down not at Luda but at a beautiful blue-eyed woman with luscious lips, and thick blonde hair that seemed to cascade down on to the pillow. It was the girl from that recurring dream. Seeing her then, in place of Luda, I experienced an intense physical reaction that literally made me shake and, as the orgasm coursed through me and I buried my face in the crook of Luda's neck, all I could think about was this girl from the dream and how much I'd been in love with her.

Afterwards, we stayed in the same position for a long time before finally getting into bed. Luda switched off the lamp and snuggled up to me as I put a protective arm round her shoulder.

Lying there in the peaceful darkness, I was transported back to a busy bar. I couldn't remember who I was there with – I couldn't even remember the name of the place – but it was definitely the place where we'd met. I was just peeling away from the bar with a beer in one hand when I saw her. Jesus, she was gorgeous. Tall, young and glamorous, with the kind of face that's both sweetly pretty and sexually alluring at the same time. And she was smiling at me too.

It was like that feeling you get when you're so attracted to someone that the strength of it almost makes you fall over. It was – I swear it – love at first sight.

I walked straight up to her. 'Hi, my name's Sean. I'm trying to think of something cheesy to say, and I can't. So please just let me buy you a drink.'

She laughed then, a sweet, feminine sound. Although, to be honest, it wouldn't have mattered if she'd honked like a Canada goose. At that moment she could do no wrong. 'Sure, why not? My name's Jen, by the way.'

'Pleased to meet you, Jen,' I said, taking her hand in mine and shaking it gently. 'I bet you've got a really exotic surname as well.'

'Not really,' she said, still laughing. 'It's Jones.'

Jen Jones. The woman I'd been in love with.

I closed my eyes, and with Luda in my arms I fell asleep basking in memories of a time in my life when, for a few brief minutes at least, I'd felt truly happy.

Forty-one

It was a long night for Tina. She was formally arrested and taken straight from Sheryl's flat to Camden nick where she was forced to undergo a number of forensic tests designed to find out whether or not she'd fired the gun she was carrying, before being examined by a doctor who asked if she felt fit enough to be interviewed. Tina knew there was no point in delaying things so she said she was, and waived her right to legal counsel, which was something she'd never recommended to anyone being interviewed. But all she wanted to do was tell the truth and get the hell out of there.

The interview got underway at just after eleven p.m., and was conducted by two male detectives from the local Murder Investigation Team. It was clear they knew who she was, and her background as a Met police officer, but they didn't refer to any of this, and instead treated her first and foremost as a suspect, which was standard procedure. However, Tina kept solidly to her story, explaining why she'd gone to the flat, and the relevance of Sheryl Warner to her own investigation. The only part that wasn't the truth was the reason she gave for meeting Jeff Roubaix that evening, which she said had just been a friendly drink.

The point was, the story was plausible, and eventually the questioning softened as the two detectives admitted that Jeff had called 999 to say that she was in trouble and was being threatened with a firearm. They also confirmed that Jeff had died at the scene. Tina took this hard, and she had to work hard to stop herself from breaking down. They also told her that there was no sign of the two killers, although two men walking on the street behind the building had confirmed that they'd seen two people matching Tina's description running away from the scene.

Eventually, at just after two a.m., they let her go, the custody officer telling her that there was someone waiting for her in reception.

It was Mike Bolt, and he was on his own.

'What are you doing here?' she asked as they walked out of the building into the night.

'I heard about what happened. I wanted to check you were all right.'

She stopped and lit a cigarette with unsteady hands. 'Thanks. I appreciate that, but I'll be fine.'

'You don't look it.'

She didn't feel it either. The shock of the violence and the knowledge of how close she'd come to death filled her with an anxiety she was finding it hard to keep a lid on. For the first time in a while, she was desperate for a drink.

Mike's expression was sympathetic. 'I've spoken to my

bosses and they're organizing twenty-four-hour protection for you because it's clear you were the target of the killers.'

'I don't need twenty-four-hour protection, Mike. I'd appreciate a couple of officers outside my house so I feel safe there, but I've got a missing woman to find, and I don't want to be trailed everywhere I go.'

'You're still in danger, Tina.'

'I don't think they'll try it again. It's too risky.'

Mike raised a sceptical eyebrow. 'Let me give you a lift home. You don't look like you're up to driving tonight. There's already an ARV outside your place so you'll definitely be safe there. You can pick up your car in the morning.'

Tina looked at him and saw the concern in his bright blue eyes. He was a good man and he cared for her, and right then, that felt good. 'Sure, I'd like that,' she said.

When they were in the car and driving through the silent night streets, she asked him about progress on their case with the mysterious Carl Hughie.

'Slow. He's still not cooperating, and he got himself lawyered up with some high-level representation. What he did do, though, finally, was give us the name of his colleague, the murder victim. He's William Balham, and he's on the payroll at MI5, so it looks like it might be one of their ops went wrong.'

'What kind of op does MI5 conduct which involves abducting a British citizen on British soil, taking him to an isolated farmhouse, and then torturing him? You know that William Balham pulled out one of Sean's teeth? I was there. I saw it. They might work for MI5 but I'm telling you, they work for someone else too. Someone who wants some information from Sean Egan very badly.'

Mike sighed. 'That may well be true, and if Hughie and Balham have been working for someone else, we'll find out who. But right now we've got the Home Office and even the Home Secretary involving themselves and putting pressure on us to drop everything against Hughie.'

'So have you let him go?'

'We've released him on bail. We didn't really have a lot of choice.'

'Any sign of Sean?'

Mike shook his head. 'Not yet. But we've got CCTV footage of him at the scene, plus the mugshot taken of him when he was nicked for rape, and we're releasing images of him to the media at a press conference first thing tomorrow. We got a positive ID on the footage from his ex-wife so we can officially name him as a suspect as well.'

'What's his ex-wife like?'

'She seems nice. She's agreed to make an appeal for Sean to give himself up, but she took a lot of persuading. I think she'd prefer to keep him in the past, and she's naturally worried about their daughter finding out too much of what's going on. Do you think he'll try to make contact with her?'

'To be honest, I'm not even sure he knows she exists. I didn't tell him about her when he came to see me because I guessed she probably wouldn't want to see him.'

'He's the key to all this, isn't he?'

'He's definitely connected to these missing girls.' Tina told him about the timing of Sean's car accident coinciding with Lauren Donaldson's phone being switched off for the last time. 'And the man and woman who tried to kill me tonight sound and look like the same ones who tried to kill him three nights ago. Have you found out any more about the two people who were looking after Sean in Wales, by the way?'

Mike nodded. 'The woman's a jobbing actress who's had a few bit parts over the years, but nothing major. She's single with an address in New Malden. The man's an ex-con with convictions for violence and burglary. Single, no dependants, and an address in Chelmsford. There's no obvious connection between the two of them.'

'So they were hired to babysit Sean. You need to check their bank accounts and see who was paying them.'

'We've already done that. They were both receiving fortnightly payments from an offshore company based in the Bahamas. We're still trying to find out who owns it, but the authorities over there aren't being too cooperative.' Mike rubbed his eyes. It had obviously been a long night for him too. 'I get the feeling something big's happening here, but we're still no closer to finding out what Egan's part in it is.' He paused, then looked at Tina. 'So, what questions have you been asking that makes you so dangerous to the people who tried to kill you tonight?'

Tina knew she was going to have to come a lot cleaner than she had been the first time she'd talked to Mike, so she told him about Dylan Mackay, the way he'd been pimping out the girls, how he'd refused to tell her the names of the men who were his customers, and how one of them was almost certainly something to do with Lauren and Jen's disappearance. 'I think the two people who tried to kill me tonight work for whoever that customer is. They were definitely pros. They knew what they were doing.'

'But where does Egan fit in?'

She told him about Sean's recurring dream involving Lauren and Jen.

'It seems you're holding back quite a lot, Tina,' Mike said. 'Anything else you'd like to share?'

She gave him a rueful smile. 'No, that's it,' she replied. 'Look, it's possible Sean was somehow involved with the man behind Lauren and Jen's disappearances, but when I last spoke to him that part of his memory hadn't come back.' She considered telling him about the psychotherapist Dr Bronson, and how he might be able to shed more light on what Sean was involved in, but held back. Without evidence implicating him – and there wasn't any – there was no way Bronson would talk to the police. He might talk to her if she deployed the same techniques she'd used on Dylan Mackay, but Tina wasn't at all sure she had the stomach for that. She'd experienced too much violence these past two days.

'OK,' said Mike, when she'd finished speaking. 'We'll pick up Mackay and see if we can get him to reveal the names of his clients. We'll go through his phone records as well.'

'He changed phones the day after Lauren Donaldson's phone was switched off, and the same day that Sean had the car accident that wiped out his memory. I don't think that's a coincidence.'

'No,' said Mike with a sigh. 'Neither do I.'

A little later they were coming into Tina's village, with its single meandering high street. All was silent, the only light provided by the white glow of the streetlights and the illuminated sign on the pub where Tina had taken the call from Sheryl a few hours earlier. 'I think that's Jeff's car,' she said, pointing to the lone vehicle in the pub's car park as they drove past, slowing down as they came to Tina's house. Parked a few yards further on, on the same side of the road, was a marked police car with at least two people inside.

'Have you been seeing Jeff?' Mike asked, trying to make his tone sound matter-of-fact but not quite pulling it off.

She shook her head. 'No, I was using him to get the phone records I needed. But I'd appreciate it if you kept that information to yourself. There's no point blackening his name now.'

'Fair enough,' he said, pulling up to the kerb and stopping the car. 'So what were you meeting him for tonight?'

'To pay him for the information he'd got for me. Then, when I got the call from Sheryl, I had a feeling it was a set-up so I asked him to come along in case I got into trouble. Typical, isn't it? He helps me out and it costs him his life. The latest in a long line of men unfortunate enough to get paired up with me.' She laughed hollowly. 'The media are going to love this, aren't they? The Black Widow strikes again. In fact, I'm amazed you're risking riding in a car with me.'

A wave of emotion passed over her, and once again she had to fight to hold back the tears.

'Don't be foolish, Tina,' Mike said. 'You're just unlucky, that's all. You're a good detective, and you're determined, which is why you come to the attention of the wrong sorts of people.' He put a hand on her shoulder and gave it a squeeze. 'Try and take things easy for a while. If your missing persons case is tied up with our inquiry, then I promise we'll find out what happened to Lauren so you can give your client some closure. I've got a good team. And I'm a good detective too.'

She smiled, touching his arm. 'I know you are.'

There was a couple of seconds' silence while they both just

looked at each other. More than anything, Tina wanted him to hold her, but then she saw a uniformed cop approaching the car, a suspicious look on his face, and the moment was gone.

'Well, at least they're paying attention,' said Mike with a smile, and they both got out of the car.

Tina thanked him for the lift and, as Mike showed his warrant card to the cop, let herself into the house.

Only when she was safely upstairs in her bedroom with the window closed did she allow the tears to come, weeping and shaking in near silence until finally exhaustion overwhelmed her.

Forty-two

I was always going to sleep late. It had been a seriously stressful few days, and Luda's bed was soft, warm and comfortable. Add to this the fact that I was absolutely shattered and it was no surprise that when my eyes finally opened the following morning, it was almost 10.30. The space beside me was empty and I could hear Luda pottering about downstairs.

After a couple of minutes of just lying there and enjoying the comparative luxury of my surroundings, I finally clambered out of bed and had a long, hot shower in Luda's en suite bathroom while I worked out what I was going to do next. I could probably stay here for a few days – although at some point I was going to have to get a change of clothes – but I couldn't do it permanently, however attractive the idea seemed. Because the thing was, at some point I was going to have to face the music. I considered phoning Tina to see how she was getting on tracking down Dr

Bronson but decided to leave it until the next day. First things first. I needed to eat.

Having dried myself and borrowed some pleasant-smelling deodorant, I got dressed and headed downstairs, hoping that Luda would offer me something tasty for breakfast.

But as soon as I walked into the kitchen my heart plummeted.

There was a TV connected to the wall above the kitchen table and the screen was frozen on an image. It looked like it had been taken two days ago back at the hotel. I was looking away from the camera but you could quite clearly see the gun in my hand. Worse still, you could also quite clearly see it was me.

Luda was standing on the other side of the kitchen table, the dog by her side, a very hard expression on her face. 'You lied to me, Sean,' she said quietly, but with real venom.

'Look, whatever they're saying about me on there, it's not true. I didn't kill anyone.'

I took a step towards her and she immediately bent down and produced a shotgun from behind the table. She pointed it at my chest.

'I've called the police, Sean.'

'This isn't what you think it is.'

'It's exactly what I think it is. Which is that you're a murderer, just like the men who murdered Dan. You've betrayed me, and if you come a foot closer, so help me God, I'll shoot you.'

'I haven't betrayed you. I didn't tell you the truth because you wouldn't have believed me. I'm being chased. The man I killed was trying to kill me. It was self-defence.'

'The report said you're a convicted rapist. How do you explain that one away?'

'I didn't do it, I promise.'

'Liar. Stay exactly where you are.'

'I didn't try to rape you, did I?'

'You didn't have to, you bastard. I let you make love to me. And do you know how that makes me feel now? Unclean.'

'I'm sorry,' I said, because I honestly couldn't think of anything else to say. 'All I want to do is walk out of here, because there's no way I'm going back to prison.'

As I spoke the words, I walked over to the kitchen top and slipped a carving knife from the rack.

'I told you to stand still,' she hissed angrily. 'I'll set Roman on you.' As if on cue, the dog growled menacingly.

'I'm not going to hurt you, I promise, but if you set your dog on me, I'll stab him, and I really don't want to have to do that. I'm sorry for the pain I've caused you, and I truly hope at some point you'll realize I'm not the man they say I am.'

I'd noticed a key rack next to the door the previous evening, and I turned and looked for it now.

'What are you doing?' demanded Luda.

'I need to borrow your car,' I said, pocketing her car keys. 'I'll leave it as I found it.'

'Try to leave here with my keys and I'll shoot you!' Her voice was much louder now, verging on hysterical.

With the carving knife still in my hand, I began my retreat through the door.

Luda's breathing intensified, and I saw her finger tensing on the shotgun's trigger. At the same time, Roman's growl became even more pronounced. He looked desperate to take a chunk out of me.

'Don't do anything you'll regret, Luda,' I said, taking another step backwards. 'For your own sake.'

'You lying, criminal bastard. You think you can just walk all over me . . .' The emotion and anger in her voice were almost physical in their intensity, and her hands were beginning to shake. 'Stay exactly where you are, or I will fucking shoot you.'

She meant it too, I could see that. But I was in the doorway and the front door was twenty feet behind me across the hall. My eyes met hers. I tried to look as honest and reasonable as possible, a man who empathized with her feelings.

And then, in one movement, I turned and bolted into the hall, slamming the kitchen door behind me and chucking the knife before dropping into a roll as a shotgun blast rang out, sending splinters of wood flying over my head. *I'll probably get the blame for that as well*, I thought briefly as I leapt back to my feet. Behind me I could hear the dog's paws scraping madly at the ruined door as he unleashed a series of blood-curdling barks.

The front door was bolted and I'd just released the bolt and yanked it open when the dog came hurtling down the hall towards me, mouth curled back in a vicious snarl.

I slammed the front door in his face and ran on to a driveway that looked out on to open fields, with trees in the far distance. But I wasn't concentrating on the view. I was far more interested in the two cop cars on the horizon, driving fast down the road in my direction. Their lights and sirens were off but I knew that was only because they were planning on surprising me.

I ran over to Luda's old VW Golf, opening it using the stolen keys, jumped inside and started it up just as Luda appeared at the front door, still holding the shotgun, the dog at her side. I shoved the car into reverse and backed out of the driveway in a screech of tyres, keeping my head down just in case Luda decided to take another potshot at me.

Thankfully she thought better of it and, pulling on to the road, I turned the car in the opposite direction to the approaching cop cars, both of which were barely a hundred metres away, and put my foot down.

Almost immediately the road, which was pretty poor anyway, gave way to a potholed track, which swung round at almost ninety degrees. The car lurched and whined as I tried to avoid the worst of the holes while continuing to up my speed. Trees sprang up on either side of me and the track got even narrower until it was little more than a wide path which I could only just fit through.

And then, fifty metres on, it widened suddenly before coming to a dead end next to a barn I immediately recognized as the one where I'd been discovered by Luda the previous afternoon. My gun, with its one bullet, was still in there. Caught with it, I'd be adding yet another major crime to the ones I'd already supposedly committed. But it also offered me a way out. A bullet in the head was preferable to prison for the next God knew how many years because, in the end, no one was ever going to believe my story. Jesus, half the time I wasn't even sure I believed it myself.

I stopped the car, scrambled out of the driver's door, deliberately leaving it open, retrieved the gun from the barn, shoving it in the back of my jeans, then doubled back on myself, running into the trees on the passenger side of the car, figuring they'd expect me to head the other way. The sirens had started up now and I doubted if the cops were more than thirty seconds behind me. There'd be others coming too. I might have been one of them once, but to them I was now the worst kind of police officer – one who'd dishonoured the service. I could expect no mercy, although in a strange way it was that thought which gave me impetus.

I was a survivor. I'd survived everything the world had thrown at me so far, and I wasn't going to make it easy for them now.

The trees gave way to a field of chest-high wheat, and I tore through it, keeping my head down, grateful for the cover it provided me with. In the distance I could hear more sirens coming from different directions, their insistent wails filling the still, clear air as they closed in on me. I kept running, ignoring the burning in my lungs, thinking I'd had more exercise this week than I'd had in the previous two months.

The wheat field was huge, half a mile across at least, with a line of trees marking the border at the far end. As I got further in, slowed down by the tilled earth beneath my feet, a cluster of caravans and mobile homes appeared in the distance to my right, partially obscured by the trees. There were a number of cars and vans parked up among them, and smoke rose from somewhere in the middle. It looked to me like a travellers' camp. I had a vague memory of going to one once before as an undercover cop trying to set up a deal to buy stolen 4×4s, and things not ending too well. But I wasn't so worried about that now, and straight away I turned in its direction.

Out of the corner of my eye I saw two uniformed cops armed with guns appearing out of the woodland from which I'd emerged barely a minute earlier. They were staring out across the field, but it didn't look like they'd spotted me. Keeping my head down as much as possible, I ploughed on, telling myself not to panic. As far as they were concerned I could be armed, which meant they'd have to secure the area and, if necessary, evacuate it before they moved in. All that took time, which worked in my favour.

The travellers' camp loomed in front of me. It didn't look that big – the caravans, mobile homes, 4×4s and vans numbered about twenty – but what caught my eye was a large flatbed truck used for hauling plant that was parked behind one of the caravans, out of sight of the rest of the camp. There weren't that many people around. I could see a group of about half a dozen kids playing around the remnants of the fire that was producing all the smoke, while a couple of guys in overalls worked on an ancient Ford Cortina, and a big middle-aged woman hung washing on a line that ran between two camper vans.

I slowed as I approached, taking a quick look round. I couldn't see the two armed cops any more and, although the sirens still sounded far too close, there was no sign of the cars. A fence separated the field from the camp, and there was about thirty yards of exposed wasteland I was going to have to cross before I got to the truck I wanted. It was a big risk trying to nick a truck from under the noses of a bunch of witnesses, but it was an even bigger one staying put, so, taking a deep breath, I hopped the fence and bolted towards it, hoping like hell that the doors weren't locked. At almost exactly the same time, two police cars hurtled up the track, skidding to a halt in the middle of the camp, scattering the kids but not the two men working on the Cortina, who turned and stood their ground, joined almost immediately by several others.

The truck's cab was only a few feet from one of the mobile homes, and only a few feet more from the woman hanging out her washing. To avoid being seen by her or anyone else, I crept round the passenger side, passing perilously close to the mobile home's windows. I glanced inside and saw a big guy with a bald head, an impressive white moustache and more tattoos than naked skin watching TV. All he had to do to see me was turn round, but he looked pretty engrossed in whatever was on so I stood on the passenger step of the truck and tried the door, silently thanking God when it opened. I slipped inside, quietly closing the door, and manoeuvred my way through a pile of burger wrappers and empty junk food containers into the driver's seat. From this new position I could see the uniformed cops, who didn't appear to be armed, remonstrating with the men.

I could feel the adrenalin kick of excitement, and I loved it. I must always have done. It must have been why I spent so much time as an undercover cop. Even though this was a game that was always going to end badly for me at some point, I was enjoying it. I just knew I was going to go down fighting.

Keeping my head down, I checked the ignition. No keys. No surprise. Ignoring the stale smell of cheap old food and body odour, I got to work on hotwiring the engine. Like a lot of things, I had no specific memory of learning how to hotwire a vehicle. I just knew. As I touched the wires together and pumped the accelerator, the engine kicked into life with an angry grumble. The noise did the inevitable and made everyone turn round in surprise.

I released the handbrake and found reverse gear. The truck lurched backwards and immediately stalled. The woman was yelling something and, as I touched the wires together again, kicking the engine into life a second time, the bald guy with the tache and tattoos came running into view, making for the driver's side with alarming speed. The cops were running towards me too, as were the rest of the men, so I accelerated backwards across the grass until I was almost at the fence, then swung the wheel round so I was facing away from my many pursuers, before putting the truck into first.

But for a big man, the guy with the tache was fast, and as I pulled away he jumped up on the step and yanked open the driver's door. I managed to get the truck into second before the guy shoved a beefy arm inside the cab and grabbed me round the neck. He was hanging half in, half out the door, trying to drag me out before I could pick up too much speed, his fingers squeezing into my neck. But there was no way I was stopping for him or anyone, so I swung round, keeping my foot flat down on the accelerator, and punched him twice in the face.

His grip loosened and he wobbled a bit, cursing me in a thick Irish accent, but he didn't let go and instead tried to yank me out of my seat. Unable to reach round and grab the gun in the position I was in, I punched him again and swung the wheel a hard left, then right, driving towards the edge of one of the far caravans. He wobbled again, holding on to the doorframe for support, and changed tactics, hitting me in the side of the head. It was a good shot too but I ignored the pain and kept my foot hard on the accelerator, aiming straight for the back of the caravan.

The outswinging driver's door struck the caravan as I skirted past it and immediately slammed shut on my attacker. He cried out and I took my chance, leaning over and giving him a single hard shove. This time he fell out of the doorway and disappeared from view, and I grabbed the wheel with both hands as the truck lurched on to the track, turning hard in the direction of a road about twenty yards away. I could see a bare-chested guy racing towards me swinging a pickaxe handle. He grabbed at the door with his free hand but I continued accelerating, the engine making a high-pitched scream as the rev counter hit dangerous levels, and he was dragged along for about five yards before falling over into the dirt.

I took a rapid glance in my rear-view mirror. Two cops were running after me, both looking knackered already, while one of the locals had a third cop in a headlock. It was only when I looked back ahead that I saw flashing blue lights through the hedge bordering the road, and then a cop car appeared right in front of me, blocking off the end of the track.

It was a bad move on their part. I kept going, still picking up speed, aiming for the bonnet, not wanting to hurt anyone but knowing there was no way I was going to surrender either. Doors flew open on either side of the car and two cops emerged holding pistols. They were still in the process of pointing them in my direction when I hit the bonnet head on, shunting the car out of the way. I kept my head down as two shots rang out amid angry, unintelligible shouts, and the truck mounted the bank on the other side of the road, taking out a chunk of the hedge. But I kept control of the wheel and the truck slammed back down on to the tarmac amid another volley of shots as they tried to blow out the tyres.

But momentum was on my side now, and I kept driving, putting the truck into third. And as the cops, and their battered patrol car, disappeared in my rear-view mirror, I laughed out loud.

I was on my way.

Forty-three

The first call to Tina's landline came at 8.20 a.m., and it woke her from a deep slumber. It was a journalist from the *Daily Mirror* wanting to do an exclusive interview about her relationship with Sean Egan.

Tina hung up on him without comment.

When the next call, from a *Guardian* reporter, came through at 8.35, she took her phone off the hook, switched all three of her mobiles on to silent and went back to sleep, confident that the police on duty outside wouldn't allow any journalists to come knocking on her door.

It was another gloriously sunny day, and her police guard were still in their car outside the house when Tina finally rose at about eleven. She showered and ate, trying to put the memories of the previous night behind her, before checking her phones again. She had seven missed calls on her main mobile but only recognized one of the numbers, that of Lauren's father, Alan Donaldson. The others were probably journalists. She listened to Donaldson's message. He told her that he'd read in that morning's newspaper that Tina was linked to the disappearance of a murder suspect, and that the TV was carrying unconfirmed reports that she'd been at the scene of a double murder the previous night, and had been arrested, then released – all of which was true. He finished by saying he hoped she was all right, and asking her to call him.

As her sole paying client, Tina felt she must return his call, but she was pleased when he didn't answer. She didn't want to have to go into a lengthy explanation about what had happened, or how it impacted on her search for Lauren, so she left a brief message saying she was fine and would talk to him later before heading outside into her garden with a coffee and a cigarette.

But she'd barely sat down when she got a call from Mike Bolt.

'How are you feeling today?' he asked her.

'I'm still here, and right now that's a bonus.'

'You're always going to be here, Tina. I'm beginning to think you're indestructible.'

'I wish I had your confidence.'

'Have you seen the news today?'

'No, but I've heard I'm on it. You weren't able to keep my connection to Sean out of the public domain, then.'

'I'm sorry. You know how it goes. These things tend to leak, especially when they're newsworthy stories, which they always are when you're involved.'

'What are they saying about me?'

'Not a lot yet, although the Scotland Yard press office has

confirmed you were arrested but then released without charge after the incident last night.'

Tina sighed, wondering how her poor parents were going to react to this. 'I guessed as much.'

'That's not why I phoned, though. We requested local CID to pick up Dylan Mackay this morning. They had to break down the door because there was no answer.'

'Oh shit,' said Tina, knowing what was coming next. 'How did he die?'

'They found him hanging from a light fitting. No signs of a struggle, but no suicide note either.'

'He was murdered.'

'It looks that way, but it was a professional job. Apparently there are no signs of a struggle on the body.'

'The people we're dealing with are professionals, Mike. To them, Dylan was just a loose end. If you can get hold of his phone records from around April the seventh and find out who he was talking to, you'll be able to track down who's behind all this, and hopefully connect them to your murder victim from the hotel.'

'We're doing that right now,' he said, 'although I'm having difficulty explaining to my team what the relevance of Dylan Mackay to our case is.'

'They're connected, you know that.'

Mike sighed. 'Did you hear there was a confirmed sighting of Sean Egan at a house in Cambridgeshire earlier today? The local cops tried to arrest him but he got away in a truck he stole from a travellers' camp. You almost have to admire the guy.'

It didn't surprise Tina that Sean had got away again. He was nothing if not resourceful.

'Did you find out any more about the company who were paying those two people to look after Sean?' she asked.

There was a pause down the other end of the line. 'I'm not sure how much I should be telling you, Tina,' Mike said eventually. 'We've come across some very sensitive information.'

'This is me, Mike. I don't blab. Unlike some members of your team.'

'Fair enough. You remember I told you that Sean's minders were being paid by a shell company based in the Bahamas? Well, we got some people from the SFO to find out who owns it. There was something of a money trail heading back through more than one offshore company, but eventually they traced it to a UK outfit called Secure Solutions who, according to their company blurb, provide cyber security and counter-espionage services to industry.'

The news surprised Tina. 'So why would they have been involved with an ex-con like Sean Egan?'

'I have no idea. But that's not all. This company has direct links to the Home Secretary, Garth Crossman.' Mike paused. 'Whatever Egan was involved in, it was something very, very big.'

Forty-four

It didn't take long for the euphoria of my escape to wear off. Having dumped the truck in a village about five miles from Luda's farm, I hotwired an old Datsun that was parked round the back of someone's house and drove it into the centre of Cambridge, which was where I was now. I'd managed to locate some spare change in the truck and now had the sum total of nine pounds twenty to my name. It was enough for one meal and then I was back to square one again.

I found a pub offering a combination of chicken curry, naan bread and a pint of beer for £4.99, which seemed as good a deal as any I was going to get, so I went inside and ordered from a bored barmaid who thankfully didn't bother looking me in the eye, before finding a seat a long way from everyone else.

The food came and I ate hungrily, wondering whether this was going to be my final meal as a free man. Now that my face was out there in the public domain, it was only a matter of time before the police finally caught up with me, and the longer this whole saga went on, the less likely it was that anyone was going to believe my story. I didn't deserve to be in this situation, yet I still couldn't remember what had happened to me after I'd left prison and taken the job with Jack Duckford. It had to have been some kind of undercover role, one that had led me to that house in the dream.

It struck me then that Jack Duckford could help fill in the gaps in my memory. Whether he'd want to help a killer on the run was another thing entirely, but it had to be worth a try. I didn't have his number, nor any obvious means of getting hold of it, but Tina would be able to find it. Calling her was a major risk, but it was only a matter of hours, days at most, before I was caught. I had to use whatever opportunities were available to me.

As if to drum home the point, I looked up from my half-empty glass to see the big screen at the end of the bar showing aerial views of a building I immediately recognized as Luda's farmhouse. The footage was being taken from a helicopter hovering overhead, and there were a dozen or so police vehicles lined up on the road outside, and various black-clad figures milling about. I even saw one guy appearing to search the chicken coop, although what he was expecting to find there was anyone's guess. Maybe he wanted some free-range eggs. As I watched, the camera panned away, moving across fields and woodland until it came to the travellers' camp where I'd stolen the truck. The police car I'd hit was still in the same position, just outside the entrance, and even from a distance you could see that a huge piece appeared to have been sheared off one side of the bonnet. More cops, some of them armed, stood around aimlessly while clusters of travellers watched them from a distance. The breaking news headline rolling across the bottom of the screen said simply that shots had been fired in an operation to arrest wanted murder suspect Sean Egan, and that one officer had sustained minor injuries. I was guessing he'd been in the car I'd hit, and I hoped he was OK.

A different photo from the one I'd seen earlier on Luda's kitchen TV popped up in the corner of the screen. It was a police mugshot, doubtless taken when I'd been charged with rape. I was staring morosely at the camera, looking every inch the criminal I was supposed to be. I'd put on weight since then, and my hair was longer now, but it was a good enough likeness to make me feel distinctly uncomfortable being inside a pub. A couple of middle-aged drinkers at a table near the bar were watching intently and the barmaid who'd served me earlier was pouring a drink only ten feet away from the screen. If she saw my picture, there was a very good chance she'd recognize me.

The important thing was not to panic. I remembered that from undercover. You hold your ground and act with total confidence, because that's the most effective way of making others doubt their own instincts. So I took another sip of my pint, making it last, and settled back in the seat as my mug disappeared from the screen and the camera returned to the news studio where the male anchor continued with his report. The sound was right down and I couldn't hear what he was saying, so I waited another minute, took a casual look round to check no one was staring at me, then finished my drink and stood up.

I was just passing one of the wall-mounted speakers on my way to the door, and realizing I could now hear what the anchor was saying, when he suddenly announced something that stopped me in my tracks.

'Earlier, Egan's former wife appeared at a police press conference to plead with her former husband to give himself up.'

Reflexively, I turned towards the screen where an attractive dark-haired woman with a nervous look on her face sat between a couple of senior-looking cops, a microphone on the desk in front of her.

'Sean,' she said, her voice steady yet full of tension, 'if you can hear this, please give yourself up. If you're innocent, then the best thing you can do is hand yourself in and explain the truth of what happened. I know you won't do it for me, but please do it for your daughter. Milly's really worried about you, and she needs a father.'

I couldn't believe what I was hearing. Or seeing. Here was a woman on TV to whom I was meant to have been married. The more I stared at her, the more familiar she became, yet I had no real tangible memory of her, nor of the girl who was supposed to be my daughter.

Milly.

My ex-wife – on the TV it gave her name as Claire Nixon – stopped speaking and one of the cops next to her took over, but I was no longer listening. Out of the corner of my eye I saw the barmaid looking at me just a little too closely, but I kept walking as casually as possible, and sped up as soon as I was on the street.

Now more than ever I was convinced that I had to see Dr Bronson again. It was clear he'd been manipulating my mind when he'd been giving me the hypnotherapy because, although my memory was returning, key parts of my life were missing, as if they'd been locked out. I also urgently needed to speak to Jack Duckford.

Somehow I had to get to both of them, and for that I needed Tina. I pulled out the piece of paper with her number scrawled on it, and switched on the mobile phone I was carrying.

It was time to play my last card.

Forty-five

Tina owned three mobile phones. One was registered in the company name and was used for official, above-the-board work; the other two were unregistered pay-as-you-go models for calls she didn't want traced back to her. She was in the kitchen making her third coffee of the day, and contemplating making a trip to Camden to pick up her car, when the unregistered phone she used the least rang. As far as she knew, only one person had the number of the current SIM card inside this one, and that was Sean Egan.

She walked into the back garden before answering.

Sean's voice was thick with tension. 'Are you on your own?'

Tina kept walking, going out of her back gate and along the narrow alleyway that led to the hill that rose beyond her house. 'I am now. And this line's secure.'

'Have you seen the news?'

'I heard you had a run-in with the police, if that's what you mean.'

But it wasn't. 'You must have known about my wife and daughter, so why didn't you tell me about them?'

'Because they might not have wanted to see you.'

'Isn't that up to them to decide?'

Tina sighed. 'I was going to talk to them, but what with everything else going on, I haven't had a chance.'

'What do you know about them?' he asked, a desperation in his voice that she hadn't heard before. 'How old's my daughter?'

'She's three, I think.'

'Her name's Milly. That's what my ex said on the TV.' He took a deep breath. 'You know, Tina, I had no idea. I was a family man, married with a daughter, and I had no fucking idea. I still don't have any memories of either of them.'

'Your wife was pregnant when you were arrested for the rape,' Tina told him. 'I read it somewhere.'

'Jesus. What have I done with my life?'

'I really don't know, Sean, but it's looking pretty bad right now. You need to give yourself up.'

'I will, I told you, but not until I've remembered everything. How are things your end?'

'Nearly as dramatic as yours. I almost got killed last night.' As she started up the hill, away from the houses, Tina told him about the events at Sheryl's flat.

'Jesus,' Sean said when she'd finished, sounding genuinely concerned. 'Are you OK?'

'I'm talking to you, aren't I?'

'They're definitely the same people who killed Jane and Tom

back at the house. A good-looking American woman and a big, ugly guy built like an ox. So they're after you as well.'

'Something else. Jen Jones, the blonde-haired woman who went missing with Lauren, the one who appeared in your dream. I think she was your girlfriend.'

'You're right,' said Sean. 'I've got that memory chunk back since I last saw you. I remember meeting her in a bar. I was in love with her, Tina. I can feel it. But at the moment I still can't remember anything about our relationship.'

'What about the dream? Any idea what you were doing in that?'

'I'm almost certain I was in an undercover role, and that's what I was doing in the house, but that's as far as I've got with it. But I do have a new lead. I was working for an old police colleague of mine called Jack Duckford. The last I knew he was working with SOCA. Can you get me a number for him?'

'You're going to contact him? I'm not sure that's a good idea, Sean. If you were working for him, he may well be connected to the man you killed at the hotel.'

'I've known him a long time. I remember we were friends once. I think if I call him, he'll talk to me. Don't worry, I'm not an idiot. I won't do anything stupid like arrange to meet up with him. I just want to ask him a couple of questions over the phone.'

Tina sighed and dragged a hand through her hair. 'OK, I'll try to find his number for you, as long as you promise not to tell anyone where you got it from.'

'You have my word,' he said solemnly. 'And have you had any luck tracking down Bronson? I'm sure he's responsible for at least some of the gaps in my memory.'

'I've got some photos of men who may or may not be your Dr Bronson. If you can ID him then we might be able to locate him. I'm guessing you haven't got an internet connection where you are.'

Sean grunted derisively. 'I've got nothing, Tina. I don't even have any money any more.'

'If you can find an internet café and create an email account, I can mail you the pictures.'

'I don't think you're hearing me. I have nothing. Nothing at all.'

'Then give yourself up, Sean. You can't keep running.'

'If I do that, we'll never find Bronson, I'll never talk to Jack, and we'll never solve the mystery of those two missing girls.'

There was a long silence as they both thought this through.

'Can we meet somewhere?' Sean said at last. 'I can take a look at those pictures, and if one of them's Bronson, then we can track him down.'

'No way, Sean. I can't implicate myself in your case any more than I have done already. If I meet you, I'm leaving myself open to some very serious charges.'

'You're doing that already, aren't you? Please, Tina. Help me, one last time.'

She didn't say anything for a few seconds as she looked back down the hill to the village where she'd lived for the past five years. She could see two old ladies talking outside the corner shop where they sold fruit and vegetables direct from New Covent Garden, recognizing one as her next-door-but-one neighbour, a widow called Mrs Maybury who always smiled at her. A mother pushed her child in a pushchair along the pavement outside the pub while a group of hikers walked in a narrow trail like ants across the hill that rose on the other side. It was a scene of utter normality, made all the more so by the fact that she couldn't see the marked patrol car parked outside her house.

'Tell me something,' she said eventually. 'You said your memory's coming back in pieces, so answer me this question honestly. Did you rape that woman?'

'No,' he answered emphatically. 'I didn't. I slept with her. I remember that. And I knew she was married too because she told me. But it was consensual, I promise you that.'

He could have been lying. He was, after all, an undercover cop by trade. Even so, Tina believed him.

'Where are you now?'

Now it was his turn to hesitate. 'I'm trusting you here, Tina. Please don't let me down.'

'Ditto, Sean.'

'I saved your life once, remember?'

'You're not letting me forget it.'

'I'm in Cambridge. Can you come and meet me?'

'You need to get back into London. It'll be easier for me to meet you there on neutral ground. If I drive out of here and head straight for Cambridge, I may arouse suspicion.'

'I've got no money.'

'You'll find a way. When you're back in London, call me on this number and we'll arrange to meet. In the meantime, I'll try to track down a number for Jack Duckford, but if you have to talk to him, do it from a phone box. Somewhere they won't be able to trace you.'

'Thanks, Tina. I really appreciate this.'

'You'd better,' she said, ending the call and taking a deep breath before lighting a cigarette, not even wondering any more why she was doing this.

The powerful sense of anticipation she was experiencing had already given her the answer.

Forty-six

Pen de Souza was nineteen years old when they released her from Juvie for the attack on her father, a year before the official end of her sentence. She'd been a model prisoner, and had convinced all those who came into contact with her that she was a reformed character who wanted to make amends for the terrible crime she'd committed as a child, in a temporary moment of insanity. This was 2002, in the still-fresh aftermath of 9/11, when the whole of America's world had been turned upside down, and a new spirit of patriotism was in the air. Like many others, Pen had asked to be given the opportunity to serve her country. The prison chaplain, Reverend Bower, a pious and influential man whose brother was a local politician, had formed a significant emotional bond with Pen, fuelled in part by the incredible blowjobs she regularly gave him, and he'd petitioned the authorities on her behalf, and done more than anyone to get her a place in the US army.

Four years in Juvie was perfect preparation for the military. Institutionalized already, Pen had fitted in perfectly, and over the course of the next five years, during which time she did two tours of Iraq, she rose to the rank of lieutenant. But the army was never going to be enough. She was a good-looking and highly intelligent young woman who'd shown herself to be cool under pressure, and with a streak of ruthlessness that would be a liability in civilian life but in certain professions was a real asset. So it was no surprise that she eventually came to the attention of the CIA.

At the time, certain sections of the CIA were heavily involved in so-called 'black ops' – secret and often illegal operations designed to destabilize America's enemies and keep the country safe. And so began a new and more lethal phase of Pen's career: one of clandestine meetings in dusty Middle Eastern back streets, romantic trysts in five-star hotels, blackmail, and finally murder. Pen was excellent at her job. People – especially men – trusted her. They underestimated her too, not realizing what they were up against until it was far too late. She became a proficient assassin and in the space of less than two years did more to destabilize Iran's burgeoning nuclear programme than sanctions could ever do by killing two of the country's most gifted young scientists in separate incidents: one in London by poison, the other in Mumbai in what was meant to look like a bungled street robbery. No one ever suspected her.

The problem was, she eventually became a liability to her bosses. Pen knew too much, and the way the CIA operated was changing as Obama took over from Bush. A male colleague she trusted tried to set her up for her own assassination in Prague but she got out, making her own way back to the States and resigning from the CIA before disappearing off the grid for a couple of years.

During this time she was offered work by a former agency man who'd set up a niche outfit that specialized in various clandestine services, including murder, for any company or government with deep enough pockets. That man had been Bryan Coombs, aka Tank, and the rest was history. Over the years they'd killed off the other employees, and now it was just the two of them working and building a future together.

Soon they'd have enough money to retire and get married, and then she'd become Pen Coombs. She liked that name. There was something sweet and suburban about it. She and Mr Coombs would buy a beach house somewhere in the Caribbean. She liked the idea of St Thomas or St John, maybe even Puerto Rico, but with their budget it was more likely to be Panama. Their plan was to have enough money to while away their days in the sunshine, making love and living off the land and the sea. She and Tank together. The fairytale ending.

First, though, they had to make enough cash, which was why they needed this current job to work. Kill the man identified as Sean Egan before he was detained by the police and they'd be half a million richer – money that could immediately be invested in property. But things had already gone badly wrong. First they'd missed their chance to kill Egan, and then they'd failed to take out the new target they'd been given, Tina Boyd. It was the first real run of misfortune they'd had in five years of working together, and now the client was furious. Worse still, they didn't know how to find Egan, and if the police got him before they did

– which by now was highly likely – the job was off, and their reputation for getting things done would suffer permanent damage.

Pen had been through enough in her life not to worry unduly, though, and right now she was relaxing in bed, enjoying the warm post-coital glow of an intense lovemaking session with her husband-to-be. It was difficult to describe how satisfied Tank made her feel, and impossible even to think what she'd do without him.

On the hotel room TV, Sean Egan's ex-wife was talking at a police press conference, encouraging her former husband to surrender to the police for the sake of their young daughter who, apparently, was very worried about him.

Pen looked up as Tank came into the room, a towel wrapped round his waist, beads of water still clinging to the perfect contours of his body, and immediately she felt another stab of pure desire.

He motioned towards the TV. 'What's happening?'

'That's Egan's ex-wife. Apparently they have a kid together.'

Tank nodded. 'Yeah, I saw that in the dossier. I wonder if he even remembers he's a dad.'

Pen smiled. 'It doesn't matter if he does or not. As soon as he sees this, he's going to want to get in touch with her.'

Tank shrugged. 'The cops will know that though, won't they? They'll have people watching the ex-wife's house in case he shows up. Standard practice.'

'True, but it still gives us an avenue. A parent will do anything for their child. Don't you remember that doctor back in Vermont? The one who went underground and wouldn't show his face until we sent him footage of his son with the razor?'

'Oh yeah,' said Tank with what looked to Pen like a slight shudder. 'I still can't believe you did that to him.'

'It worked though, didn't it? Daddy came running even though he knew what was going to happen to him.'

'Yeah, but we were able to get a message to that guy. We've got no way of contacting Egan.'

'So what? We don't need to. Remember. If we take the wife and kid and get the client to keep them alive somewhere, we can get an anonymous message to Egan, even if he's in custody, to let him know that if he opens his mouth to anyone, they die. He hears that, he won't say a damn word, I can guarantee it. The beauty is, the wife and kid can be kept like that for weeks, months even, while we work out a way to finish off Egan.' She looked up at him. 'It's foolproof. And we get to keep our money.'

Tank whistled through his teeth, then ran the back of a hand softly down her cheek. 'Jeez, sweetcheeks, I've got to hand it to you. You think of everything.'

Pen leaned over and pulled his towel away. 'It's all for us, baby,' she whispered. 'It's all for us.'

Forty-seven

Tina wasn't sure giving Sean the contact details for Jack Duckford was a particularly good idea, but she was intrigued to find out more about Duckford's background. With the death of Jeff Roubaix, she'd lost her best inside contact in the force, but she still had people who owed her favours.

Two calls and twenty minutes later she had a direct line for Duckford at his current place of work, the NCA's Organized Crime Arm. Duckford was a vet. Forty-eight years old, with the full thirty years' service, he had an unblemished record, which included a citation for bravery during the arrest of a knife-wielding robber fifteen years earlier.

Could Duckford and his NCA colleagues have been running an unofficial undercover operation using a disgraced ex-con, Tina wondered? Sean certainly seemed to think so, and Tina knew from past experience that such things, though certainly illegal, did occasionally happen. However, even if this was one such case, Duckford was unlikely to want to help Sean now. Friend or not, he was already eligible for retirement with a full pension, and if he was involved in something illegal he was going to want to keep it very quiet.

Sitting up on the hill behind her house, with the sun on her face, she took a few moments simply to enjoy the view, knowing that by aiding and abetting a known offender she was risking all of this. But that was who Tina was. She took risks. She had the kind of dogged determination that meant she'd do whatever it took to find out what had happened to Lauren Donaldson, and make whoever was behind her disappearance face some sort of justice, regardless of the cost to herself.

So she picked up the phone and called Sean.

I was on the slow train heading from Cambridge to St Pancras when Tina called. The carriage was almost empty and there was no sign of a ticket inspector, but I was still jittery. It was hard work continually breaking the law, whether it be shooting a man dead or dodging the fare on public transport, because the end result was always the same: if I was caught, it was prison, no question, and I'd regained enough of my memory to know that I couldn't go back there again.

'I've got a number for Jack Duckford,' said Tina when I picked up. 'I'm assuming you haven't got a pen so I'm going to text it to you when I finish the call. Where are you now?'

I told her. 'The train's due in at St Pancras at 17.19. Can we meet as soon as possible after that?'

'There's a church called St Mary Magdalene on Osnaburgh

Street. Take a right out of the station and keep walking for about ten minutes. The turning's on the right just past Warren Street tube station. If the main door's locked, go down the steps into the garden and wait for me there. And if you call Duckford, remember to do it from a phone he can't trace you to, OK? A call box or something, and not one right round the corner from the church.'

'I'm not a fool, Tina. Are you going to bring those photos of the struck-off therapists?'

'I am. But if none of the men in the photos are your Dr Bronson, and your man Duckford can't, or won't, shed any light on what's going on, then that's it, Sean. I can't give you any more help.'

'Sure,' I said quietly. 'I understand.'

I put the phone in my pocket and sat back in the seat, keeping my head down as I looked out the window at the passing countryside. Hitching a free ride on a train had been my last resort. I'd rejected the idea of using the car I'd stolen earlier in the day to get to London in case the police were actively looking for it. I did try to steal two others but failed both times and set off the alarm on one, so in the end I hadn't really had a lot of choice. If you took away the fact that I was in constant fear of being recognized, it wasn't actually a bad way to travel.

Since leaving the pub my thoughts had been dominated by the fact that I'd been married, and had a three-year-old daughter. I tried to dredge up an image of my ex-wife's face from my memory but couldn't, and I still had no recollection of Milly. I wondered if she'd ever been brought in to see me in prison. I wondered, in fact, if I'd ever seen her before. The thought once again weighed heavily on me like a dark cloud and I had to force myself to snap out of it.

The Final Minute

The train stopped at a station and two teenage girls who'd been chatting away a few seats down got off. No one got on, and I realized, with a sense of relief, that apart from a single middle -aged man in a suit who was asleep at the far end, I was the only person left in the carriage.

My phone pinged. It was a text message containing a phone number and nothing else. I stared at the screen and remembered the call I'd made to Jack Duckford from the bail hostel just after I'd been released from prison.

'That job you were talking about when you came to see me. Is it still available?'

'Absolutely,' he'd said. 'In fact we need you more now than we did then.'

But what had Jack needed me for? And how had it ended?

I knew Tina was right about me not calling him from a traceable phone. But my memory was also telling me from my undercover days that the authorities could only track mobile phones when they were switched on. All I had to do was switch mine off when I ended the call and, since I was on a moving train, I'd be miles away before they got people to the phone's last-known location.

As if to emphasize the point the train picked up speed, clattering noisily down the tracks.

I remembered an undercover job Jack and I had done together years ago. I'd spent the best part of three months posing as a professional car thief to get close to a group of Lebanese businessmen who sold luxury cars into the Middle Eastern market, and we'd set up a meeting where I was introducing Jack to them as my senior partner who had dozens of stolen vehicles for sale. The problem was, when we went to the meeting place, a house in Ladbroke Grove, one of the main Lebanese guy's bodyguards recognized Jack from an earlier undercover role and all hell broke loose. There were six of their people in the room, including four who were muscle, and only two of us, which are never good odds.

Being recognized has got to be an undercover cop's worst nightmare, and it couldn't have happened in a worse place. As it was a first meeting with Jack we had no back-up, so no one even knew we were there. But you never panic. And you never, ever admit you're a cop, whatever the provocation. So Jack told the guy he was mistaken. So did I. We really argued our case.

But the guy had been adamant.

Three of the muscle held Jack down on the floor and beat him, while the fourth – a huge black guy with arms thicker than my legs – produced a piece of lead piping and let it be known that if I intervened, it would be the last active thing I did for a long time. As they beat and questioned Jack, trying to get him to break, I pleaded with my Lebanese contacts, telling them there was no way Jack was undercover, that I'd known him for years. But they weren't having any of it. We were split up, and I was locked alone in an upstairs room for more than an hour. Occasionally I'd hear Jack scream in pain. I had no idea what they were doing to him but whatever it was, it was bad.

I can still remember the terror of being trapped in a tiny room in a strange place, knowing that I might never get out of there alive. That's how bad it was.

Finally, after a long period when there'd just been silence, my main Lebanese contact unlocked the door and told me that Jack had admitted to being an undercover cop, and had told them that I was one too. If I just admitted it, they'd let us both go.

I was tempted. God, I was tempted. The idea of being held down and subjected to whatever it was Jack had been subjected to scared the living crap out of me. But you don't take the easy option. In life, it's usually the worst one. Instead, I went on the offensive. I screamed; I shouted; I told him that there was no way on earth Jack was a cop, and if they'd got him to say that he was, it was because he was being tortured. And it was an insult of the highest degree even to suggest that I was one too.

For the first time I could see my contact thinking that perhaps his bodyguard had made a mistake. So, with a flurry of apologies, he reunited me with Jack who'd been locked in the basement and who, incredibly, wasn't too badly hurt. He had plenty of cuts and bruises, but the reason for his screams, he told me afterwards, was because they'd heated up a knife until it was red hot and then repeatedly held it only inches away from his eyes, threatening to burn them out.

Afterwards, we'd headed straight for the pub and both got hopelessly pissed. We'd talked in awe about our lucky escape, and I have a vivid memory of Jack laughing uproariously at how close we'd come to really serious injury, and suddenly that laughter turning to floods of tears as he broke down. I broke down too, and we sat in a forgotten corner of the pub, off our heads, crying together as all the emotions of that day came surging out.

We'd bonded that night – the kind of bond that a civilian who's never done this kind of work couldn't possibly understand.

I looked at my watch. 4.45. In just over half an hour I'd be in London. If I was going to call Jack, it would be easier to do it now while I was still on the move. With a deep breath, I keyed his number into the phone and waited.

Forty-eight

'Duckford,' said a clear, deep voice just as I was about to put down the phone.

'Jack? It's me, Sean Egan.'

He literally gasped. 'Sean, what the . . . ? Listen, let me call you back from my other phone. It's more private. What's your number?'

'Sorry, that doesn't work for me. Just talk quietly.'

'Where are you?'

'Come on, Jack, don't treat me like an idiot. I'm not going to tell you that.'

'What do you want?' There was an edge to his voice now, as if he expected me to be the bearer of bad news.

'I need your help. I was in a car accident a few months back and I lost my memory. I've got a lot of it back now but I need to know about the work I was doing for you when I left prison.'

There was a heavy silence down the other end of the phone for a good five seconds.

I broke it. 'I know you came to visit me in prison offering me work. And I know I was working for you when I left. I just don't remember what I was doing. So please, for old times' sake, help me out here. I'll remember what it was eventually, so even if you don't tell me, it's all going to come out in the wash.'

'I'm going to have to transfer you through to another number,' he whispered. 'I can't talk in here. Give me twenty seconds.'

'Twenty seconds. No more.'

I counted in my head as I waited, wondering if I was making a mistake. By the time I got to nineteen, he came back on the line. It sounded like he was in a corridor somewhere.

'We need to meet,' he said quickly. 'You were doing under-cover work, infiltrating a group of very dangerous people. I'm going to have to give you a thorough debriefing, then I'm going to go with you when you hand yourself in. Because you're going to have to give up, Sean, you know that.'

The automatic doors at the end of the carriage hissed open and a ticket inspector walked in. There was only the sleeping man in the suit between us, and I was in the last carriage, which meant there was no way I could avoid him.

'Give me the names of the people in this group,' I hissed into the phone. 'Now.'

'We need to meet,' he said firmly. 'I'll tell you then.'

The train slowed. We were approaching a station. The ticket inspector woke the sleeping man and asked to check his ticket.

'Please, Jack,' I said. 'Names.'

'It's big, Sean. Really big.' He sighed. 'The person we really wanted you to find out about was the Home Secretary.'

That shocked me. I'd expected the name of some big-time criminal. The Home Secretary was one of the few politicians I could actually put a name to: I'd seen him on TV at Jane's a couple of times. Garth Crossman was a charismatic, silver-haired guy who sounded like he actually understood the problems of the voters. Jesus, what had I been doing investigating him?

I looked up. The ticket inspector was approaching me now, a dour expression on his face, as if some sixth sense had already told him I didn't have a ticket.

Jack was still telling me I needed to meet him as soon as possible.

'I'm going to have to call you back,' I said, and ended the call, switching off the phone as the inspector stopped in front of me.

'Tickets, please,' he said, looking down at me. He was a tall, thin guy in his mid-fifties who looked like he'd make a good undertaker.

Beyond him, I could see that the guy in the suit had already closed his eyes again. The brakes squealed as the train continued to slow, and the announcer said that we were approaching Stevenage. 'Sorry, it's in here,' I said, getting to my feet and acting like I was going to reach into my back pocket. I still wasn't sure exactly what I was going to do until I suddenly grabbed him, swung him round and applied a chokehold, rapidly upping the pressure so he couldn't cry out, while all the time staring at the sleeping passenger, hoping he didn't hear what was going on.

Outside the window the station's platform appeared. The inspector made a choking noise, then went limp in my arms.

Moving quickly, I dragged him the few feet to the carriage toilet and manoeuvred us both inside, shutting the door behind me. He was moaning quietly but still pretty much out, so I propped him up on the toilet seat and relieved him of his peaked cap, jacket and ID, before hastily donning them. The train had stopped now and I heard people coming on board, so I squeezed out of the door, dressed in my new outfit, and, pushing the cap down so it covered my features as much as possible, walked down the carriage.

A noisy group of students were streaming on board but they moved out of my way as I made for the doors before they closed, careful not to hurry, even though I knew the inspector was going to wake up any second and raise the alarm. The students must have woken up the guy in the suit, because he glanced up at me as I passed, looked vaguely surprised at the fact that my face appeared to have changed, but not surprised enough to do any-thing about it, then shut his eyes again.

Two minutes later I was on a different train, heading non-stop into London.

For now, it seemed, my luck was holding.

Forty-nine

Mike Bolt was sitting in his office in the incident room at Barnet police station when Mo Khan walked in, a sheaf of papers in his hand. It had just turned five p.m. and Bolt was beginning to think about finishing up for the day. The forty-eight hours since they'd been called to the murder at the Sunny View Hotel had been both frenetic and frustrating, and he hadn't got to bed until three a.m. that morning. He needed a rest.

Mo sat down and put the papers on the desk. 'I've got some interesting information about our two MI5 men, Mr Hughie and the late Mr Balham. We've been through both their bank accounts and everything's in order. All they've been receiving is their government salaries. However, they both live in decent-sized houses and own nice cars.'

'So how have they financed them?'

'Well, Hughie's single, but his brother pays his mortgage,

and his car payments. He also books and pays for a couple of Hughie's long-haul holidays. Whereas Mrs Balham's the big earner in the Balham household. And it turns out that Hughie's brother and Mrs Balham are consultants for the same company. Secure Solutions.'

Bolt sat up in his chair, no longer tired. 'The same company that was paying the two people babysitting Sean Egan in Wales, and who are both now dead. A company that's linked directly to the Home Secretary, Garth Crossman, the man who's currently trying to stop our investigation into Balham's murder. You know, this is a very strange case. Because for the life of me I cannot understand why Crossman or any of his people are interested in an ex-con like Sean Egan. And no one in MI5 seems to want to enlighten us either.' He looked at Mo. 'Any ideas?'

'Nothing springs out, boss, I've got to admit.'

Bolt shook his head and let out a long breath. He needed to leave and grab himself a drink in his local back in Clerkenwell. 'Have we got the records back for Dylan Mackay's phone yet? Tina's convinced his murder's linked to what's been happening with Egan.'

Mo grunted. 'I'm not so sure of that.' He'd never been a fan of Tina Boyd and made little secret of his disdain for Bolt's more sympathetic attitude towards her. 'But I've got the records here.' He sorted through the bundle of papers he'd brought in with him, and slid the relevant ones across the desk. 'I checked through the calls he made and received on his old phone, the one he stopped using the day of Egan's car accident.'

'Anything stand out?'

'I'll be honest, boss, not really. I think a team from Area West are going to be taking the Mackay case as well, so it'll be out of our hands soon.'

'Fair enough. Thanks for getting it sorted for me anyway.'

When Mo had gone back to the incident room, Bolt had a brief scan of the records. Mackay had used the SIM card for his previous phone for more than four years before he'd stopped using it, at 1.11 a.m. on the morning of 8 April. A few hours later, an anonymous man carrying no ID, who Tina claimed was Sean Egan, had hit a tree in his car and ended up in a coma. Mo might not have been convinced of any connection but Bolt thought it was too much of a coincidence to have been an accident, and he trusted Tina's judgement. Whatever her faults – and Bolt would be the first to admit she had a fair few – she'd always been a good detective.

The last call Dylan Mackay had received had lasted four minutes and seventeen seconds, and had come from a mobile number. Bolt looked back over the fifty or so calls Mackay had made or received during the five days running up to when the phone was switched off for the last time, looking for that same number, and saw that it appeared twice more: Mackay had received a call from it on 6 April lasting five minutes and twenty-eight seconds and had then made a call on 7 April lasting seven minutes and thirty-one seconds. The fact that it was the last number Dylan had received a call from before changing his phone and SIM card for the first time in four years told Bolt that it was worth finding out who it belonged to.

Tracking the ownership of mobile numbers could take weeks if standard procedures were followed, but in emergencies that time could be reduced to hours, sometimes even minutes. There was no way this was an emergency, but neither was it a regular case. Four people had been murdered in the previous forty-eight hours in wildly different circumstances; Bolt couldn't afford to wait for weeks for an answer. He had a feeling that Sean Egan would be in prison, or possibly even dead, by then and the whole inquiry would grind to a very convenient halt.

He called the liaison officer at Homicide and Serious Crime Command whose job it was to deal with the UK's mobile phone carriers, and gave him the number and a rapid-fire spiel of why he needed the name of the registered owner right now, and how it could tie up several separate murder inquiries, then sat back in his seat, figuring that it was going to be a while before he had that pint.

But the liaison officer was fast. Just forty minutes later he phoned Bolt back and told him that the number was registered to a publicly listed company. Thanking him, Bolt wrote down the number and Googled the company.

It took him less than two minutes to establish a connection between the company and the Sean Egan murder inquiry, and maybe another ten before he finally began to work out what had really been going on.

'Jesus Christ,' he whispered to himself. No wonder Sean Egan was such a hunted man.

Fifty

St Mary Magdalene parish church was an old stone building set on a quiet back street a hundred metres away from the busy hubbub of the Euston Road, and almost in the shadows of the gleaming office blocks of the brand-new Regents Place development. In her younger years, when she'd been living in and around Camden, Tina had enjoyed going for long walks and exploring the city, which is how she'd come to find this place. It was a peaceful spot with a pretty little sheltered garden that could be reached down a short flight of stone steps.

The sun was shining and children played in the small park opposite as Tina walked up to the front entrance. Churches in London tended to be locked, even in the day, in order to keep out thieves and the homeless, which seemed to Tina to be a sad indictment of modern society, but the door to St Mary Magdalene opened when she tried it. She was almost certain she hadn't been followed there, but she took a last look round anyway just to make sure before slipping inside and taking a seat at the end of one of the rows of pews.

The church was empty and quiet, and Tina immediately felt at peace. It was hard to believe that barely two minutes ago she'd been fighting her way through the armies of commuters swarming along the Euston Road, and it made her wonder why more people didn't take sanctuary in places like these, where they could escape from the modern world, even if it was for a few minutes, and just . . . contemplate.

Tina closed her eyes and concentrated on her breathing, taking herself back to childhood. Neither of her parents had been religious, but she remembered going to church with her maternal grandma when she'd been a little girl, and her grandma telling her that if she was good, then God would look after her. The vicar at the church had been a kindly old man and Tina had always felt very welcome. It had seemed like a place of pure goodness, and maybe to her it still was.

Her grandma had been a loving, stable influence in Tina's life but she'd been gone for close to twenty years now, having passed away when Tina was in her second year of university. Sitting there in the musty cool, she could picture her grandma perfectly, and the image calmed her.

'Penny for your thoughts,' said Sean Egan as he shuffled along the pew towards her. He was dressed in an ill-fitting grey suit jacket and a peaked cap, with a photo ID tag hanging from a lanyard around his neck.

'What *are* you wearing?' she asked as he sat down beside her.

'It's a long story,' he said with a rueful smile. 'And a good disguise. No one looks at you twice when you're dressed like this.'

Tina raised her eyebrows but didn't ask where he'd got the outfit from. Right now, she didn't want to know. 'OK Sean, I spent a long time searching through the list of struck-off therapists looking for candidates for your Dr Bronson, and I've narrowed it down to four people. I wasn't operating from an exhaustive list, though, so he might not be one of them. For all we know he may not even be struck off, but it's the best I can do. And it's the last thing I'm doing too. We're quits after this. I'm not risking my neck for you any more.'

'I understand.' He pulled the kind of face men pull when they want a woman to sympathize with them, but it didn't look real. Sean was a manipulator. Tina had come to realize that.

She produced four folded A4 sheets from inside her jacket and handed them to him.

He glanced at the first photo and shook his head, placing it at the bottom of the pile.

As she watched him, Tina realized that she really wanted Bronson's face to be in there because, with him, another piece of the puzzle fell into place, and she came that bit closer to finding out what had happened to Lauren Donaldson. She was certain the news wasn't going to be good, but she needed to give Lauren's father closure.

'That's him,' said Sean, pointing at a black and white photo showing an upper body shot of a middle-aged man in a suit, with dark hair and glasses. 'One hundred per cent. That's Bronson.'

Tina had numbered each of the photos. Bronson was number 3. She consulted her notebook. 'His real name's Robert Whatret, and he was a well-qualified and highly regarded psychotherapist until he was struck off and imprisoned for sexually assaulting his patients.'

'Have you got an address?'

This was where it got tricky for Tina. 'If I give you his address, and then you hurt him and it gets back to me, I'm suddenly in a lot of trouble I don't need. Like I told you, Sean. I consider us quits now.'

Sean looked her squarely in the eye. 'I need your help on this, Tina. Because this guy knows what's happened to the girl you're looking for. It may be that he has to put me under to get my memory back, and if he does that, I need you there to make sure he doesn't implant any other false memories. I can't do this alone.'

'Jesus, Sean. And how are we going to get him to cooperate? He's not going to want to talk and I don't see how we can force him.' She thought of Dylan Mackay, the young man she'd tortured information out of who'd ended up dead within a day of her visit, and doubtless as a direct result. It made her feel dirty and in no mood to do the same thing again to someone else.

'I haven't got much time, Tina, and this bastard helped keep me in a near-catatonic state for two months just so he could extract some information, knowing that as soon as he got it, the people he was working for would almost certainly kill me. He's not a good man.'

'You haven't answered my question.'

Sean took a deep breath and let it out slowly. Then he reached round behind his back and pulled something out from under his jacket.

As soon as Tina saw it, her breath stopped in her throat. 'That's the gun from the hotel room, isn't it? The one you used to shoot that MI5 man. You told me you'd buried it.' She started to get to her feet, sick of his lies.

'Please Tina, don't go. I'm not going to use it. It's not even loaded. I just need to scare him, that's all.' He replaced the gun under his jacket and stood up, blocking her way back to the aisle.

'You mean *I* need to scare him, because if he puts you under, it's going to be me holding the gun. You're using me, Sean, and I don't like that.'

'I'm your only hope of finding that girl,' he stated simply. 'You know that.'

For a few seconds, they stood there staring at each other. The terrible thing was, Tina knew he was right. She'd run out of leads and she couldn't rely on Mike. Lauren Donaldson wasn't even his case, and it sounded like every effort was being made from on high – maybe even as high as the Home Secretary – to scupper his investigation. Sean was her only leverage.

'I saved your life once, Tina. Now's your chance to save mine.'

'I told you. We're even.'

'Are we? You've gone out of your way to help me, no question, but you wouldn't even be breathing now if it wasn't for me. And I hate to use this on you, I really do, but I've got no choice.' The words were rushing out of him now in an urgent burst. 'Unless you help me, I'm finished. I may not even be alive in a week. This is our last chance.'

Tina had known it would come to this from the moment she'd agreed to meet him here. But the full consequences of her actions were only now dawning on her. If they got Bronson to put Sean under, Tina knew she'd have to stand there pointing a gun at him, and the fact that it would be unloaded wasn't going to help her if it ever came out in court. She'd still go down for a long time, the prospect of which terrified her.

But Sean was right. This could be their last chance.

He stood staring at her now, the desperation clear in his eyes.

'OK,' said Tina at last. 'But we're going to do it my way.'

Fifty-one

Robert Whatret, the man I'd always known as Dr Bronson in the short and rather unproductive time we'd known each other, lived in the basement flat of a ramshackle 1950s townhouse in an equally ramshackle street in one of the less salubrious parts of Acton.

As we stepped out of Tina's car I was hit by the strong and not entirely unpleasant smell of fried food in the air, courtesy of the fast-food takeaway on the corner. It was 6.40 p.m. and the sun was beginning to set in the west. Rap music played through an open window on the other side of the street and the sound of slow-moving rush-hour traffic from the A40 were loud in my ears. Somehow it disappointed me that the distinguished-looking therapist I'd spent so many afternoons with lived in a rundown place like this. I guess it just added to the lie that had been the last two months of my life.

The Final Minute

We'd already decided how we were going to do this. Tina would ring on the bell, looking official, while I waited out of sight. Our theory was that he'd answer it because she looked unthreatening, and as soon as she was inside I'd come down the steps and she'd let me in. There was, of course, no guarantee that he was at home, or even for that matter alive. We'd know soon enough.

We crossed the road in the same silence we'd endured during the journey there. I could tell Tina was hugely uncomfortable doing this, and I felt bad having used emotional blackmail to get her to help me, but not bad enough to regret it.

The steps to Whatret's place went straight down from the street and were covered in splats of pigeon turd. I watched from out of sight of his front door and cobweb-encrusted front window while Tina went down and rang. The street was empty bar a couple of scraggy-looking kids messing about outside the fast-food place a good thirty yards away, but I felt conspicuous hanging around in full view of the other houses. I was still wearing my ticket inspector disguise but it wasn't exactly foolproof, and all it would take was one eagle-eyed curtain twitcher getting a half-decent look at me and the whole thing was over.

Tina rang Whatret's bell a second time, then I heard her mutter a curse. 'Get down here, Sean,' she hissed. 'I can see him in there. He's heading out the back.'

I hurried down the steps and saw that Tina had a set of picks out and was carefully picking the lock. She pushed open the door and stepped back. 'He's all yours.'

I ran through the dingy living room and into the long, narrow kitchen. Whatret was at the back door, hurriedly trying to unlock it. He turned when he saw me coming, a look of abject terror on his face, and threw up his arms in surrender. But I wasn't in a very forgiving mood, and I batted them aside and punched him in the face. His head hit the doorframe and he let out a painful grunt as I grabbed him round the neck, dragged him back through the kitchen and shoved him down on one of his chairs. Tina had come inside and shut the door but was standing in the shadows, a scarf pulled up over her face. We'd agreed that she'd play as minimal a part in this as possible.

'I think we need to talk, Doc,' I said, glaring down at him. 'And don't look at her. Look at me.'

'Matthew, please . . .' he gasped, resetting his glasses and trying to regain some composure. His hair was a mess and his nose was bleeding where I'd hit him, but the terror in his expression was no longer there.

That changed when I produced the gun and pointed it down at him. 'I think we can dispense with the Matthew now, Mr Whatret. I know who I am now and, more importantly, I know exactly who you are too. A disgraced ex-con, just like me.'

'Please don't point that thing at me. I have a heart problem.'

'Answer my questions and we'll leave you in peace. But mess me around and I'll kill you. You must understand that. I have nothing to lose, and I've killed before.'

He looked up at me, and I saw that his hands were shaking. 'I believe you. Can I have a drink, please?'

'No. Who were you working for when you used to visit me?'

'I only know his name as Mr H. I didn't even meet him until the other night when he brought me to that barn where they were keeping you. I know nothing about him, I promise you.'

'When did he hire you?'

'Two months ago. He said you'd just come out of a coma lasting three months, and there was information that you had that he badly needed but, because you were suffering from retrograde amnesia, this information was going to have to be . . .' He paused. 'Extracted from you. We agreed that it would have to be done under hypnosis.'

'And this information was the location of bodies, wasn't it?'

He looked nervous. 'Yes. That's right.'

'Whose bodies?'

'I don't know. I really don't.'

I let him see my finger tighten on the trigger, and my expression darkened. 'You're lying.'

He lifted his hands, terrified. 'I'm not, Sean. You have to believe me. I didn't want to do any of this. I was blackmailed. I've got no money, no prospects. I had no choice.' His face crinkled up with emotion and I thought he was going to burst into tears. 'Please. I had no choice.'

In spite of myself, I felt a little sorry for him. 'So how did it all work? I know you implanted false memories in me. I was convinced I had a sister, and I still can't remember anything about the undercover job I was doing when I had my accident.'

Whatret removed his glasses and ran a hand across his face. 'It was a very delicate procedure. I needed to convince you that you were someone else with a whole different set of memories. What you almost certainly don't remember was that probably eighty per cent of our session time involved hypnotherapy, and yes, I'm sorry to have to admit that I did implant false memories in your subconscious. I also had to work very hard to stop other memories coming out, particularly the work you were involved in immediately prior to your accident. Mr H didn't want you working out what had happened to you before I got the information they needed. That was why the two individuals looking after you, who incidentally I never knew by name, kept you regularly supplied with a cocktail of a number of inhibiting drugs, leaving you in a permanently passive state.'

He sighed. 'The problem was that in a delicate procedure such as this, things will almost certainly go wrong. Mr H told me that you' – he emphasized the 'you' – 'had buried three bodies somewhere, having been to a house with another man, whose name I was never told, to collect them. To find out where you'd buried them I had to continually try to walk you through what happened that night under hypnotherapy, while making sure you remembered nothing when the session ended. But when you hit your head in the cellar the other week you started having flashbacks to that night with the bodies, and dreaming about it. I think we were getting very close to finding out what happened, but then you escaped. And now . . . Now you're here and you can see me for what I really am. You may not believe it, Sean, but I'm truly sorry for my part in all this.'

He no longer looked terrified as he spoke these last words. He looked unburdened and genuinely remorseful. Then again, he'd looked a pretty genuine, caring guy when we'd done our sessions together.

'You know, I actually liked you,' I told him, making no effort to lower the gun. 'You disappoint me.'

'I disappoint myself. I've been doing that a long time.'

'I can't believe I would have knowingly buried people's

bodies.' I was also surprised at the number. Three? Who'd been the third person then?

'I'm only repeating what I was told by Mr H. You never confirmed whether you did or not to me. In fact, regarding your account of what happened in the house with the dead bodies, I only know as much as you do.'

I took a deep breath. 'You need to hypnotize me. I have to find out exactly who I was and what I was doing before my car accident.'

He frowned. 'Are you sure about this? I can do it, but you might not like what you find.'

'So be it. At least then I'll know who I am.' But inside I was feeling real doubt. Yes, I'd done good things in my life. Yes, I believed I was a good man. But I also knew, when I was brave enough to admit it to myself, that I was capable of doing some pretty bad things too.

I turned and walked over to where Tina stood impassively, handing her the gun and giving her a nod to tell her I knew what I was doing, even though I wasn't at all sure I did.

Then I sat down opposite the man I used to know as Dr Bronson and looked him right in the eye. 'Do it,' I said.

Fifty-two

Tina stood to one side of Whatret and Sean, the gun down by her side at Whatret's request, since he'd claimed – with some justification – that he couldn't work effectively with a gun to his head.

He started off by talking to Sean in soothing tones, not unlike a parent talking to a child. His voice was soft and sonorous and Tina had to concentrate hard not to become entranced by it herself. She would have liked just to leave the room but she didn't trust Whatret not to try something, so instead she thought about her grandma – of happy childhood times; of tea and cakes and Christmases; of the unconditional love she'd felt for her.

She could see Sean going, his head starting to tilt a little from side to side, and then he slumped back in the chair, his eyes shut, a peaceful expression on his face. She half expected Whatret to glance over to check whether she too had succumbed to his mantra, but he didn't. Instead he continued to talk to Sean, bringing up each of the false memories he'd clearly implanted over a number of sessions, and explaining that they were, indeed, false, and that when Sean woke up he would have forgotten them. It all seemed incredibly simple and Tina couldn't see how it could possibly work, but she hoped to God it did. There was no shortage of fake memories either. They ranged from having a sister and not a brother to a career spent in teaching, and plenty in between. There were also real memories that had been removed. It seemed that Whatret had convinced Sean he'd never married, or fathered children, and had also deliberately blocked him from remembering what had happened to him after he'd left prison.

Whatret kept Sean under for almost half an hour, and Tina had long since mentally drifted away when he finally paused, took a deep breath, and told Sean that he was going to count to five and when he'd finished he would wake up.

As he counted, Tina's finger tensed on the gun's trigger. When he reached five, she watched as Sean's eyes opened and he sat up in the chair, looking over at Whatret as if nothing had happened. And then his eyes narrowed.

'When are you going to put me under?' he demanded.

'I have done,' said Whatret uncertainly. 'Your memory, or at least part of it, will return. It may take a few minutes, though. It's a lot for your mind to suddenly take on board.'

For a long time, Sean simply sat there, his eyes closed, as if he was meditating. Tina looked at Whatret, wondering if he was playing some sort of trick, but he remained impassive, and she could see his hands were shaking.

'Do you mind if I have a drink?' he asked Tina.

'In a minute. I want to see whether your little act worked or not first. Are you OK, Sean?' she asked him.

He didn't answer. Then suddenly his face contorted wildly and he sat bolt upright, staring straight ahead, his breaths coming in rapid-fire bursts.

The room fell silent. No one said anything.

Finally Sean's breathing slowed. He got to his feet and looked at Tina with one of the most haunted expressions she'd ever seen on a human being.

'I remember it all,' he said wearily, his words as heavy as tombstones. 'I remember it all.'

Having those memories come back was like a tidal wave hitting me. I'd been told for months that I'd lived one life, and now I'd found out that I'd lived another entirely. The memories were big and overwhelming: marriage, love and childbirth; arguments and infidelities; the shame of prison; the job after I'd left, and the huge and irreversible effect my fall from grace had had on my life. All hitting me one after the other. I staggered on my feet, punch drunk, not sure what to do, only vaguely aware of Tina staring at me from beneath her pulled-up red scarf, until finally the emotions passed and the sea became calm once again.

I gave Tina a weak smile. 'Can I have my gun back?'

'I don't think that's a good idea, Sean,' she said. 'Not right now.'

I nodded slowly, unsurprised, and then, as the full gravity of what had been done to me hit home, I jumped on Whatret, Bronson, whatever the hell his name was and grabbed him round the throat with both hands, squeezing hard. 'You bastard. You stole my life. You stole my fucking life!' His eyes bulged and a horrible rasp rose from his throat but still I squeezed harder.

'Let him go, Sean,' hissed Tina in my ear. 'Do not do this. It won't help. We need him alive to testify.'

The anger subsided to a more controlled simmering point, and I released my grip. 'What you did to me was unforgivable,' I said, pointing accusingly down at him, ignoring his strangled chokes.

'I know it was,' he said when he'd recovered and could finally bring himself to look up at me. I saw then that he had tears in his eyes, and not just from where I'd half strangled him. The guy was crying. 'I know I did wrong and I am so, so sorry.'

It was Tina who spoke next, lifting the scarf above her lips so she could be heard clearly. 'You can save yourself, Mr Whatret, and bring the people behind all this to justice. Mr H, the man you work for – his real name is Carl Hughie, and he's currently on police bail in connection with the murder of one of his colleagues. He might avoid the murder charge but if you testify in court that he was the man who hired you, he'll go down for a long time, and you might be treated far more leniently than you deserve. Sean here will say you restored his memory out of guilt, when he came to you here in your home, and you'll conveniently forget ever seeing a gun.' As she spoke these last words, she slipped the weapon under her jacket.

Whatret looked at Tina with a puzzled expression. 'Who are you? And how do you know all this?'

'No questions. Just remember this. If you hire a lawyer and try to go down the ignorance route, you'll go to prison for a lot longer than you did last time.' She turned away. 'Come on, Sean. Let's get out of here.'

'Wait,' said Whatret urgently. 'What happens if they come for me? They might kill me.'

'Then go to the nearest police station, hand yourself in, and tell them exactly what I've just told you.'

I took one last look at Whatret, sitting broken on the sofa with shaking hands, then turned and followed Tina back outside on to the street.

Night was falling fast now and we didn't speak until we were safely inside Tina's car.

She lit a cigarette and turned to me. 'What happened to Lauren Donaldson?'

I ran a hand through my hair, my fingers touching the rough contours of the scar across the top of my forehead, trying to piece together what had happened. 'The recurring dream I've been having . . . it wasn't a dream. Lauren, the woman you're looking for, is dead. The other woman, Jen Jones, is also dead.'

Tina sighed, took a thoughtful pull on the cigarette and blew a line of smoke out of her half-open window. 'I thought as much. It's still a shock though. And are those the bodies everyone seems to want to know the location of?'

'Yes. But I still don't know where they are. And I didn't kill them either. I know what I was doing at that house, I know who I went there with, and I know who killed them, and why he did it.'

'Who?'

'I can picture him but I'm not sure I ever knew his name. If I did, it'll come to me, but everything feels incredibly strange right now. It's like the memories are overwhelming me and I'm not entirely sure what's real and what isn't. There are also a lot of gaps. Still, I'm beginning to build up a picture of what happened in the months before my accident.'

'Whatret mentioned three bodies,' Tina reminded me. 'Who did the third belong to?'

'I don't know yet. It's still a bit of a blur.'

'I think we need to make this official now, Sean. It's not helping your case to stay on the run any longer. I'm going to call my main police contact, DCI Mike Bolt. He's the SIO in charge of the investigation into the shooting in your hotel room. I'll get him to meet us somewhere and then I'm going to hand you over to him. In the meantime, you can start at the beginning and tell me everything.' She put a reassuring hand on my shoulder. 'It's the best way, Sean. In fact, it's the only way.'

She was right. I knew that. But there was something I had to do first.

'I know it's the only way, Tina,' I said, 'and I'll give myself up as long as you come with me when I do it. I'll also tell you everything. But on one condition: I want to see my wife and daughter. I want to see Claire and Milly. I remember them now.'

'Sean, I don't know how to get hold of them.'

'I do.' I grinned at her suddenly, feeling incredibly liberated. 'I can remember Claire's mobile number.'

Tina shrugged. 'OK, deal. I'm going to call Mike now and say we're going to meet him.'

I nodded and pulled out the phone I'd been using, feeling nervous as I turned it on. I knew it was a long time since I'd spoken with Claire. I vaguely remembered her visiting me when I'd first been held in custody but I had no memory of her coming after I'd been found guilty. But I remembered our first meeting,

341

on a dating website of all things, and the whirlwind romance that followed. For a time we'd been happy, and then she'd got pregnant, and things had begun to change. I hadn't been easy to live with. I hadn't wanted a child because I'd known that it would mess up our relationship. I'd been jealous. I'd been an arsehole.

Now I wanted to make amends. More than that, I wanted to see my daughter for the first time.

I looked down at the screen and saw I had a new message. It read CALL THIS NUMBER IMMEDIATELY, followed by a mobile number.

But it was what was immediately below it that caught my attention. It was an image of a woman and a young girl, both blindfolded. I recognized Claire immediately, and knew that the girl was my daughter Milly – the child I'd never seen.

I dropped the phone in my lap and stared straight ahead. The last five days had been full of shocks to my system, but none had struck me as hard as this. It was a sledgehammer blow. In the background I could hear Tina talking, then I heard her end the call and ask me if I was all right.

Finally I turned to her, my mouth dry, the fight temporarily driven out of me. When I spoke, my words were barely a croak. 'They've got my family, Tina.'

Fifty-three

'That was Tina Boyd,' said Bolt to Mo Khan as he came off the phone. 'She's going to bring Sean Egan here in the next hour. He wants to see his daughter first, though, so can you get someone to call the people watching his ex-wife's place and tell them to expect Egan and Tina?'

Mo nodded. 'I'll get on to it.'

It was 7.35 p.m. For the last two hours Bolt had been in his office discussing with Mo the significance of what Bolt had found in Dylan Mackay's phone records, and trying to piece together a combined motive for the killings in the house in Wales, Tina Boyd's two missing women, and the murders of Sheryl Warner and DC Jeff Roubaix the previous night. Bolt had a theory that fitted the facts, but when he and Mo tried to fill in the gaps it quickly became obvious that they needed to interview Sean Egan, and now it looked as if they were going to. But Bolt's excitement was tempered by the fact that Tina had told him that Sean had lost his memory, so there might still be a long wait for answers.

Mo poked his head back round the open door, a concerned expression on his face. 'We've got two plainclothes from local CID watching Egan's ex-wife's place, and neither of them are answering their phones.'

'Have we got a landline number for the ex?'

'Yeah. And a mobile. And she's not answering either. I don't like this, boss. The last contact we had with the cops on the scene was only half an hour ago to tell us that she'd arrived back home with her daughter. Apparently, they tend to stay put for the evenings.'

'OK. Send a patrol car over there and get them to report back. I'll call Tina, and get her to bring Egan in right now. He can see his family later.'

But when he called Tina back it went straight to voicemail. He waited two minutes and called again. Still no answer. He wondered what the hell she was doing, and left a message asking her to return his call immediately. He put the phone back down on his desk and closed his eyes, experiencing an unpleasant feeling that he was somehow on the periphery of major events that were happening all around him, and yet of which he knew nothing.

It wasn't a situation he was prepared to tolerate for long.

'Jesus, Sean. How did they get this number?' said Tina, turning her head away from the phone's screen.

I was finding it hard to think straight. 'Whoever they are, I need to call them. This message was left fifteen minutes ago.'

'We can do this through the police, you know. Track that number, find out where your family are.'

'I'm not prepared to trust anyone else with this. It was me who put them in danger. It'll be me who gets them out.'

'Come on, Sean, you know what'll happen. They'll tell you to meet them somewhere if you ever want to see your family alive again. You'll go, and they'll kill you. There's not even any guarantee that it'll save your family.'

She was right. Of course she was. But what the hell else was I supposed to do? 'I need to call them, Tina. Can't you understand that?'

She must have seen the anguish on my face because for once she didn't argue. 'I'll wait here,' she said as I opened the passenger door.

I stepped out on to the night street. Across the other side of the road, a young couple were walking in the direction of the fast-food joint. They looked like students and they were holding hands and laughing, and I wondered at what point in each of their lives the world would come crashing down on their shoulders, like it was crashing down on mine.

I called the number and put the phone to my ear, every nerve ending in my body on fire, waiting.

The call was picked up before the end of the first ring by the man I was expecting. 'I'm sorry, Sean,' he said without preamble.

'You fucking bastard, Jack,' I hissed, shaking with rage.

'I never wanted it to turn out this way.'

'You kidnapped my wife and my daughter. Why, for Christ's sake? I trusted you.'

'So you remember who they are then? I was hoping you would.'

'I remember enough,' I said coldly.

'Listen, they're OK and unharmed. Your daughter thinks it's a game.'

'If you hurt them—'

'No one's going to hurt anyone, Sean. Not if you do what I say. Where are you?'

'In London.'

'I need a more exact location because here's what's going to happen. I'm going to come and pick you up in my car and take you on a little drive just so we can make sure no one's following. Then I'm going to deliver you to an associate of mine and you're going to be exchanged for your wife and daughter. You will see them. You'll even get a chance to say goodbye to them. I will then personally drive them back home, and you have my word on that. And that'll be the end of it.'

'What happens to me?'

'It's your life for theirs, Sean. You may not believe me but I'm really sorry it has to be like this. I've always liked you. You were just really unlucky that things panned out like they did.' He sounded sorry too, but then so had Bronson. Everyone was really sorry, but it didn't seem to stop any of them doing some pretty terrible things.

'Let me tell you something, Jack. That's not how it's going to happen. I remember what happened at the house that night with Lauren Donaldson and Jennifer Jones. And I remember your part in it too.'

He was silent for a few seconds as he thought this through. When he spoke again, there was a note of warning in his voice:

'Is your life worth as much as your kid's?'

I wanted to kill him then, but I kept my temper under control. 'You tell me a place to meet and I'll come there alone.'

'Have you got a car?'

'I've just stolen one. I can get to you.'

'Bullshit, Sean. You don't call the shots here.'

'I do. I've got enough to fuck you completely, Jack. Now I'm prepared to sacrifice myself for my family, but only if I know they're going to be safe.'

'Where are you? I'm coming to pick you up. It's the only way we're dealing with this.'

I had to be strong. If he picked me up, I was dead, no question, and with no guarantee my family would be safe. 'No,' I said firmly. 'Give me a location.'

The line went dead and I was left standing alone on the street, my heart thumping in my chest, wondering if I'd just made a terrible mistake. I waited a minute, pacing the pavement, no longer caring how suspicious I looked.

In the car, I could see Tina staring at me. She made a 'what's happening?' gesture but I ignored it. Another minute passed. Still no call back from Jack. I'd played games of bluff before in my undercover days, when the stakes were incredibly high – Jesus, Jack had been with me some of those times – but nothing like this. The lives of a woman I'd once loved and a daughter I'd never met depended on me making the right decision and, as a third minute passed without a call, the doubts and fears were hitting me like well-aimed punches.

Four minutes. I told myself to hold on. They needed me. Jack was bluffing. He had to be.

My family. A chance to start again. To live a normal life just like everyone else. Where I was needed and valued.

Five minutes. My heart was hammering in my chest. I stared down at the phone, counted to five, and called Jack back.

I'd lost the game.

Fifty-four

Tina drummed her fingers on the dashboard and lit another cigarette as she waited for Sean to finish on the phone. During that time Mike Bolt had phoned three times, leaving two messages. Tina was tempted to talk to him but she'd promised Sean she wouldn't do anything until he came back, even though he'd now disappeared from view. She looked in the rear-view mirror and saw him walking back towards the car, the phone no longer to his ear. He looked like he'd aged ten years.

This new development had changed everything. Tina had never had children but she could imagine the terror Sean must be feeling. If she'd seen a photo of her parents or nieces blindfolded like that, she'd be exactly the same.

The passenger door opened and Sean got inside. He took a deep breath. His forehead was covered in a sheen of sweat.

'They're going to pick me up and take me to my wife and daughter. It's not what I wanted, but it's the only way.'

This was exactly what Tina had feared. 'They'll kill you.'

He nodded. 'I know.'

'So, you're just going to your death?'

He turned to her. 'That tracking device I gave back to you at the layby when I went on the run. Have you still got it?'

Tina thought for a moment. 'It's in the glove compartment.' She rummaged inside until she'd found it.

'If you track me, you'll be able to see where I'm going.'

'I can't do anything on my own, Sean. I'm one person, and I'm unarmed. You need to let the professionals handle this. They've got the resources.'

'I haven't got time to let the professionals handle this, Tina. They're picking me up from the end of the road. I don't know when. They didn't say. They just told me to wait. It might be in two minutes. It might be in an hour. It depends where they are, I suppose.' He sighed. 'How much influence have you got over your police contact?'

'Not a lot. Why?'

'Call him while you're tracking me if you have to but I need you to do everything you can to hold them back from doing anything that puts my family in danger.'

Tina pulled hard on her cigarette, the taste unusually acrid in her mouth. If she gave him the tracker, she was supporting his suicidal decision to go to his death. There was a selfish reason for holding back too. If Sean died, then so would any chance of finding Lauren's body and bringing whoever had killed her to justice.

'Look, Sean—'

The Final Minute

'Look what, Tina? Are you going to help me or not?' He had a manic look in his eyes, and Tina wasn't at all sure he wouldn't try and take the tracker off her forcibly if he had to.

'OK,' she said at last. 'But this is your call, Sean, and yours alone.'

'Yeah, I know that. And I appreciate everything you've done for me, Tina.' He took the tracker and pushed it down one of his socks. 'Can I have my gun back?'

'Aren't they just going to take it off you?'

'Maybe. But I figure I don't have a lot to lose.'

Reluctantly, Tina handed the gun over, knowing she was committing another crime to add to the ones she'd already committed on Sean's behalf that week.

He took it, flicked open the chamber and placed a single bullet inside. 'That's all I've got,' he said, shoving the gun into the back of his jeans and covering it with his shirt.

He turned to go, but something was bugging Tina.

'How did they know your number, Sean?' she asked. 'I thought I was the only person who knew it.' She sighed. 'You called Jack Duckford on it, didn't you? Even though I told you not to.'

Sean nodded. 'Yeah. He's the one who's picking me up. Sadly, he's not on the side of the angels.'

'But if you were working undercover for him, why's he kidnapping your family?'

'Well, that's the problem,' said Sean, after a pause that was just a little too long. 'I wasn't undercover.'

The words hung heavy in the silence of the car as Tina took in this new piece of information. It made her feel a little sick. 'What job were you doing for him then?'

'Jack Duckford works on the side for a gangster. He hired me to work for the same gangster too. I guess I wasn't on the side of the angels either.'

Tina leaned forward urgently. 'And what's this gangster's name?'

'Only Jack's got the answer to that.' And with that, Sean got out of the car and started walking, leaving her sitting alone and feeling utterly betrayed.

Fifty-five

The next twenty-three minutes were the longest of my life. I stood on the street corner opposite the fast-food takeaway with my head down, bathed in the orange glow of the streetlight, wishing I could be any place rather than here, and wishing too that I could step back in time to when I didn't know I had a family. This time the previous night I'd been sitting at Luda's kitchen table laughing and chatting over a bottle of wine and good food. Now, twenty-four hours later, I was waiting for a car that was going to take me on a journey that would almost certainly lead to my death, to save the life of a daughter I'd never met.

But you know what? Though the fear was coursing through me, I knew I was doing the right thing. I thought of my brother, John. The man I'd always looked up to. I wondered if he was watching me now from somewhere up above, and if he was, whether or not he'd be proud. I hoped so. I didn't believe in God – I never had

– but I'd always thought there was a place our souls went to when we departed this life, where we somehow lived on, and if I did have to die tonight, I clung to the hope that at least we might meet again.

A black 4×4 with tinted rear windows pulled up at the kerb and, although I hadn't seen him for a long time, I recognized Jack Duckford behind the wheel. I glanced briefly at the street outside the fast-food place, saw it was temporarily empty, then opened the front passenger door and looked inside.

Straight away, I saw in the back seat the huge guy with the buzz cut who'd tried to kill me four nights earlier back at the house in Wales. He glared at me impassively, and I saw he had a gun with suppressor attached down by his side.

'Get in, Sean,' Jack said hurriedly. 'It's illegal to stop here.'

I'd already slipped the gun from the back of my jeans, and before the big guy could raise his, I'd leaned inside the car and shot him in the face. The shot made a loud noise in the confines of the car but, as the gun was only a .22 and the street was empty, I was pretty confident it wasn't loud enough to be heard by anyone.

The big guy cried out in shock and his head snapped to one side. Blood poured from the penny-shaped hole in his upper right cheek, and he began to sway drunkenly in the seat, but even so he was still a fair way from being dead. Worse than that, he was trying to raise his gun and I had no bullets left.

I jumped inside and shut the door, shoving the still-smoking gun against Jack's temple. 'Drive!' I hissed.

He opened his mouth to say something but I think he must have caught a glimpse of the look on my face because he pulled away from the kerb in silence, picking up speed as he joined the light flow of traffic.

I swung the gun round in the direction of the big guy. There was blood all over the collar of his shirt now and he was pawing uselessly at the wound on his face with his free hand, but he'd managed to lift his own gun so that the barrel was at a forty-five-degree angle to the floor.

'Drop it!' I screamed. 'Or I'll shoot you again! Last chance!'

But this guy was one stubborn fool and he kept lifting it, his eyes narrowing in defiance. A couple more inches and the gun would be pointing directly at my groin. Out of the corner of my eye I saw Jack reaching towards me, looking for a way to relieve me of my own gun. I was in a very dangerous situation but I knew from experience that any hesitation was fatal. I had to keep them on the back foot.

I lunged forward, grabbed the barrel of the big guy's gun, catching him completely by surprise, and yanked it out of his hand, careful to keep the end pointed away from me. He pulled the trigger at the same time, the bullet making a festive pop like a champagne cork as it left the gun and ricocheted round the car, ending up God knew where. I dropped the .22 and turned the big guy's pistol round, pointing at both of them in turn.

But the big guy was slumped in the seat now, weakening fast, so I turned my attention, and the gun, on Jack. 'Where are Claire and Milly, you bastard?'

'You've just made a big mistake, Sean,' he said. His hands had the steering wheel in a death grip and he looked suitably terrified.

'Really? Maybe I should make another one and shoot you in the face as well.'

'Kill me and you've got no chance of seeing your family again. You know that.'

'That's true,' I said evenly. 'But I can still hurt you very badly. And you know I'll do it too.' I lowered the gun so it was pointed at his leg. 'Now, answer my question. Where are Claire and Milly?' We stopped at traffic lights at the A40 junction. Cars pulled up alongside us but I ignored them. 'Answer me, you piece of shit,' I hissed into his ear, 'or I'll blow your fucking kneecap off.'

'All right, all right,' he said hurriedly. 'They're about fifteen miles from here at a disused airfield.'

I sat back in my seat. 'So that's where we're going now. Who's holding them?'

'His girlfriend.' He gestured over his shoulder towards the big guy. 'We were just going to take you out there, you arsehole, give you a chance to say goodbye to your family.'

I laughed. 'You know the most important lesson I've learned these past few days, Jack? Everyone's a fucking liar. So forgive me if I take that with a pinch of salt.'

'You know, those two are engaged. When she finds out what you've done to her fiancé she's . . . I don't know . . .' He shook his head, letting the sentence trail off, then turned west on to the A40 as the lights turned green.

Jack didn't have to tell me what that bitch was capable of. I'd seen her handiwork on Jane. I looked over at the big guy. His eyes were flickering and his skin had gone an unpleasant greyish pallor, but the bleeding had slowed to a constant trickle, and he still looked as though he'd live, which was something I realized I could use to my advantage. 'Let me worry about that,' I told him. 'In the meantime, tell me about the job you hired me for.'

'I thought your memory had come back.'

'It has, but I want to hear it from you.'

'I gave you a chance, Sean,' he said bitterly. 'When no one else would touch you.' He shot me an angry sideward glance, as if somehow I was to blame for everything that had happened. 'I set you up with a nice little pad in London and a salary of fifty grand a year, and all you had to do was provide some consultancy.'

'I was working for a gangster, I know that much.'

'You were working for a businessman.'

'What's his name?'

'It's best you don't know.'

'No, it's best I do know,' I said firmly.

'OK. Alexander Hanzha. He's a Ukrainian oligarch. Your job was to help me provide his people with security and counter-espionage advice. A lot of them are Russian and Ukrainian and don't know the way things work over here. All you had to do was help them make their business run smoothly. No bad shit, like this.'

'Except there was bad shit, wasn't there?' There always was when you worked with gangsters, and I'd known that when I'd taken the job. Yet still I'd taken it, because Jack was right. At that time, no one else would touch me. 'What happened that night, Jack? Why were we at that house? It was his, wasn't it? Hanzha's.'

Jack sighed and shook his head. 'Oh Jesus, that was a fuck-up. No, it belonged to Hanzha's son, Victor. He'd hired these two prostitutes with his friend and taken them back to his country pad. Except one of them wasn't a prostitute. She was an industrial spy. Hanzha's company have been trying to conduct a hostile takeover of a big British IT company for the past year. It's always been a controversial deal because the company is partly owned by the family of the Home Secretary, Garth Crossman. Crossman hasn't been able to block the deal legitimately, so his people have resorted to trying to dig up dirt on Hanzha.'

Something clicked into place for me then. My girlfriend before the accident – Jen Jones. Maybe our chance meeting in the bar hadn't been a chance meeting after all. Maybe she was just looking for a way into Hanzha through me. 'The blonde one. She was the industrial spy, wasn't she?'

'The girl's name was Jennifer Jones. She worked for Crossman's company,' he said, confirming my suspicions. 'Victor caught her planting a bug in his room. According to his story, he confronted her; she denied everything and tried to leave; then he started hitting her. Things got out of hand and he thought he'd killed her, so he felt he had no choice but to kill the other prostitute, who was there with his friend. From what I gather, the friend helped him with the killing to prove he could be trusted not to say anything.' Jack sighed. 'Then Victor called me in a panic, as you would do when you've got two dead whores in your house. I called you, and we went over there to try to sort out the mess.'

As Jack spoke, I began to remember how nervous I'd been in the car with Jack on the way over there, because he wouldn't tell me what was going on. Then the shock I'd had when I'd first seen Lauren Donaldson lying dead on that bed with her head smashed in. Even now, it made me feel sick.

'When we arrived, you went upstairs to check everything out while I called Victor's old man and told him what had happened. He was pissed off but he didn't lose his temper. He's that kind of guy. He stays calm. But what he did say was that we couldn't have any witnesses.' Jack paused for a moment. 'That meant you had to die as well. You might not believe it but I was gutted. I've always liked you, Sean, whatever you may think now.'

I didn't say anything.

'Mr Hanzha knew I didn't want to kill you, so he said he'd send over his bodyguard and you and he would take the bodies away for burial. Except the plan was that you wouldn't come back.'

'And you decided to go along with that?'

'No,' he said, 'I didn't. I was trying to think of ways to save you and when I went upstairs looking for you, a way presented itself. You see, Jennifer Jones wasn't dead. She'd taken a real beating from that sadistic bastard Victor, but somehow she'd managed to get to her feet and walk around. When I got upstairs she was leaning against the landing wall, bleeding all over the place but still conscious, and you were just standing there, staring at her. I think you were in shock.'

'I was. I was in love with her, so to find her half naked in someone else's house, and dying too . . .' I shuddered at the intensity of the memory.

'You remember what I told you to do?'

I shook my head and swallowed. I could remember my emotions: the anger, the jealousy, the sense of doom. But I couldn't remember what had happened next. 'No, I don't. Tell me.'

Jack's face creased into a tight frown that showed a lot of new lines on his face, and for the first time it occurred to me how much older he looked since I'd seen him last. He took a deep breath. 'I handed you a knife, and I told you to kill her. I did it because I thought it would show Hanzha that, like Victor's friend, you could be trusted. I did it so you could live, and I'll tell you this, I'm not proud of it, but at least it gave you a chance.'

Still the memory wouldn't come to me. I wondered if my mind had deliberately suppressed it.

'And did I? Finish her off?'

The car slowed in traffic, and Jack turned to me. 'No,' he said. 'You didn't.'

The moment he said those words, I took a deep breath, feeling a surge of relief.

I'm not a bad man.

'You couldn't do it,' he continued. 'Neither could I. I've never killed anyone in my life. We had to wait for Mr Hanzha's man. I dragged you into another room while he shot her. Then you both took the bodies of the two girls away for disposal.' He sighed. 'Only you know what happened after that, Sean, because the next time I heard from you was five hours later in the middle of the night. You phoned and called me a double-crossing bastard. You said you'd killed Mr Hanzha's bodyguard and buried all three of the bodies, and that you were going to deliver a letter to your solicitor to be opened in the event of anything happening to you, which would detail everything that had gone on that night, and give the location of the bodies. You told me you wanted a hundred grand in cash to ensure your silence. I actually said that we could do that, and you finished the call by saying you'd be back in touch. Except you weren't, because that was the last time we spoke before today.'

'But you knew I was alive, right?'

'Not right away we didn't. Not until the blackmail started.'

I frowned. 'Blackmail?'

Jack nodded. 'Yeah. The Home Secretary, Crossman – his people made contact a few months later. They said they had you alive in a safe place. They even supplied us with footage of you, although you looked out of it. They said that the Crossman group was going to launch a counter-bid for Mr Hanzha's company, and that if he didn't accept the offer, they'd release the information on what happened, and give up the location of the bodies of the whores. They claimed there would still be enough DNA evidence on them to link their murders to Victor.'

'But what I can't understand is how Crossman's people knew anything about the bodies.'

'I've thought about that a lot, and the best explanation is that their spy, Jennifer Jones, had bugged your flat, so when you made the threatening call to me they heard everything you said. I don't know what happened next but I reckon they were trying to inter-cept you when you had your accident. For all we know, they were responsible for it, and that would conveniently explain your lack of ID and how they knew what hospital you were in.'

I shook my head in exasperation. 'Jesus, I can't believe this whole thing's just about a company takeover.'

'It's big profits, Sean. The Crossman group stood to make a hundred million pounds if Mr Hanzha played along and sold his company to them on the cheap. People will do a lot for that kind of money. That's why we had to pull out all the stops to find you. It took a long time but we finally tracked down one of Crossman's people in St Lucia who knew where you were being held, and he coughed up the information. Then we brought in these two to deal with you once and for all.' Jack paused. 'Except they didn't, which is why we're here now.'

'Help me get my family back, Jack,' I said. 'You're better than this.'

'I'm sorry, Sean, I can't. You're thinking of your family. I'm thinking of mine.'

A mobile phone started ringing in the back. It was the big guy's. He made a moaning sound but made no move to get it.

'That'll be his girlfriend,' said Jack.

The big guy's mobile stopped ringing and Jack's started. He looked at me. 'I'm going to have to answer this. If I don't, she'll know something's wrong and she might hurt your family. She's not a nice woman, Sean. Not a nice woman at all.'

'I know. I've met her. Take out the phone and give it to me.'

He did as he was told and I put the phone to my ear. 'This is Sean Egan,' I said. 'If anything's happened to my wife and daughter, I'll kill your boyfriend nice and slowly.'

'Let me speak to him,' she hissed, but I could hear the fear in her voice.

'No. He's hurt, but he's going to live if we get him to a hospital. Let my family go, and you get him back.'

'You don't make demands on me, you worm. I'll cut your daughter's eyes out unless you let me speak to Tank right now.'

I swallowed hard, knowing I had to stay strong. Knowing too that I was gambling with my child's life. 'No,' I said with a cold edge to my voice that I had to work far too hard to produce. 'I'm going to send you a short video of him to prove he's alive but that's all you're going to get. Then we're going to meet and exchange your boyfriend for my family.'

She started to say something but I ended the call, found the camera setting on the phone, and turned it on the big hulk in the back. As if on cue, he moved in his seat and his eyes flickered open. He gave me a vaguely puzzled look, as if I'd just disturbed his sleep, before closing them again. The blood had completely drenched the top half of his white dress shirt now, and he didn't look in a good way, so I knew I was taking a big risk sending the film. Unfortunately, I didn't have a lot of choice.

'How much is she willing to sacrifice for this guy?' I asked Jack as I finished filming. I still had the gun trained on him but he looked more relaxed now, as if he knew I wasn't going to shoot him.

'Shit, Sean, I don't know. I only met these people twice.'

'Take a guess,' I snapped.

He shrugged. 'They're engaged, and the way she looks at him makes me think they're pretty close. But she has a reputation as one of the most cold-hearted people in the business.' He turned to look at me. 'Listen, acting like this isn't going to work, Sean. It'll just get your daughter killed.'

'If she dies, so do you, Jack. Tonight. I will kill you. Do you understand?'

He glanced at me and nodded. 'Yeah,' he said wearily. 'I understand.'

I pressed the send button on Jack's phone and watched as the text containing the film was sent to the number the woman had just called from.

A minute later the phone rang again, but this time all I could hear down the line was a woman screaming in the background. I recognized the voice immediately as belonging to Claire, my ex-wife, but it was the words coming out of her mouth that caught my attention: 'Please don't hurt her! She's only a child!'

'What the hell's going on?' I shouted into the phone. 'Talk to me now, you bitch, or I swear to God I will cut your boyfriend's nuts off right now.'

'I'm about to cut your daughter,' she said, coming on the line, her voice calm now. 'And I'm going to film it for you.'

'Touch her and I kill him now,' I came back, just as calmly. 'I guarantee it. All I want's a straight swap. My family for your boyfriend.'

'It's not a straight swap, is it? You've hurt my man.'

'I shot him with a .22. It's not a big-calibre bullet, and it hasn't caused a life-threatening injury. He'll be as good as new when he's had the right medical attention.'

'So will your daughter. I'm only going to cut her face. And your ex-wife's. They won't be life-threatening injuries either.'

She ended the call.

I called back immediately, my fingers fumbling on the buttons, the sweat pouring down my face.

It rang once.

Twice.

My hands were shaking now and I had a sudden, desperate urge to put the gun against my own temple and pull the trigger, just to end all this terrible stress once and for all.

She picked up on the third ring. All I could hear was terrified screaming. A woman's. And a child's.

'You can have me!' I shouted. 'You can have me as long as you don't hurt them!'

'That's more like it,' she said as the screaming subsided. 'And good timing. I hadn't actually started cutting. Is Mr Duckford still driving the car?'

'Yes.'

'Put him on.'

'No. You can have me, and you can have your boyfriend – exactly what you wanted – but only when I see that my family are free and unharmed. I know you're holding them at an airstrip and we're coming directly there now. We'll contact you when we arrive. Is that a deal?'

She was silent for a good five seconds. 'Deal. But if you do anything else, I will hurt them real bad.'

'I know,' I said, and ended the call.

Fifty-six

Tina was following the car that had picked up Sean along the A40, keeping about a quarter of a mile back, when she finally put a call into Mike Bolt. She'd ignored his calls until Sean was safely in the car and driving, knowing that if she got the police involved too quickly then it might compromise the safety of Sean's family.

Bolt answered straight away, and he wasn't happy. 'Why haven't you been answering the phone? I've just received word that the two detectives watching Egan's ex-wife's place are lying in their car with their throats cut and the house is empty.'

'That's because his ex and kid have been abducted. The deal is Sean's got to go to a rendezvous where the kidnappers will let the wife and kid go and take Sean in their place.'

'How did they manage to contact him?'

'An NCA man, Jack Duckford, knows Sean from the past. Sean got in touch with him and Duckford set him up.'

'Shit.' There was a short pause at Bolt's end. 'Where's Egan now?'

'In a car travelling west on the A40, just going past the Swakeleys Road turn-off now.' She read out the registration number. 'I'm following them.'

'You should have called me straight away, Tina.'

'I called you as soon as I could,' she lied. 'But the important thing is I'm following Sean now and he's wearing a tracking device. I can give you its serial number and code so you can track it too. You can also track my phone signal.'

'Do we even know he's still alive? If I were them, I'd kill him straight away.'

'I don't know. I couldn't get close enough to check, but he was armed with the same gun he shot the guy in the hotel with, so I don't think he's going to go down without a fight.'

'Jesus, Tina, this is a total bloody mess.' He paused again, and Tina could picture him in his office with a face like thunder. 'Give me the details of the tracker.'

She knew the information by heart and reeled it out. 'We've got to play this carefully though, Mike. If the people holding Sean get wind of what's going on, they're not going to hesitate to kill their hostages.'

'You don't have to tell me. I've met Claire and Milly. What can you tell me about the people holding them? Do we have any idea of their numbers? The location of the hostages?'

Tina sighed, knowing she'd put herself in a hugely compromising situation. 'No, I've got nothing, except what I've told you.'

'OK, but stay back and wait for us, Tina. And whatever you do, keep your phone on and make sure you answer it.'

'Sure,' she said, once again agreeing on a course of action she had no intention of following.

Up ahead, the car carrying Sean accelerated so that it was now travelling at more than eighty miles per hour.

Tina kept her distance, biding her time.

Fifty-seven

The clock on the dashboard said 20:39 as Jack turned into a private road.

The car was so silent I could hear the hammering of my heart. It had been like that for the past twenty minutes of the journey, ever since the last phone call from the woman holding what was left of my family. I still had my gun trained on Jack while the guy in the back moaned softly in a state of semi-consciousness. His complexion had gone a fish-scale grey, and if he didn't get help soon, he was going to die.

'This is the place,' said Jack as he drove us slowly down the access road past a Keep Out – Private Property sign, and another stating that the land was going to be developed for executive and starter homes by some company I really didn't care about. Thick, overgrown bushes sprouted up on either side of the road, and up ahead I could see a high mesh gate that looked like it had been pulled open in a hurry. It was dark here.

'Stop the car,' I said, leaning back in the seat, conscious that this was a good spot for an ambush. 'What's the layout?'

'There's a single runway, and a two-storey terminal building with a tower attached across the other side. This road takes us straight up to the runway. The building's then straight opposite us, about fifty metres away. That's where your ex-wife and daughter are being held.'

I thought fast. 'Drive very slowly up to the runway then stop and kill the lights,' I said, crouching right down in the seat so I would no longer be visible from the outside. 'But keep the engine running. And remember this,' I added as he put the car into gear and moved forward. 'If this is an ambush, I'll still have time to kill you.'

He didn't say anything, and thirty seconds later we'd stopped again, having driven down a slight incline. He killed the lights. 'We're here.'

Slowly, I sat back up in the seat, half expecting to get a bullet in the head from somewhere outside but keeping my gun trained on Jack.

We were in a wide open space, and in the distance I could see the silhouette of the terminal building and tower. There were no lights on, and no one around, and right then I was the most scared I'd ever been – or could remember being, anyway – because it wasn't just myself I was trying to save, it was the only family I had left in the world, and I couldn't see how the hell I was going to do it.

Still keeping pretty low in the seat, I called the woman.

She answered straight away.

'Where are you?' I demanded.

'We're here,' she said calmly. 'I can see you.'

I felt a flash of fear as I realized she could be right beside us.

'Put Claire on the line.'

'You can see her.'

I squinted through the windscreen, which was when I saw three figures emerging from the shadows of the building and making their way towards us. I could see that it was a woman and child in front, holding hands, while another person followed just behind them.

I turned to Jack. 'Turn the lights on and drive up to meet them. Slowly.'

Tina stopped her car at the entrance to the disused airfield. The laptop on the passenger seat clearly showed the tracker on Sean moving very slowly across the runway towards the old terminal building. She wished she'd given him some kind of recording device so she'd at least have some idea what was going on, but from the speed the car was moving, it looked like some kind of exchange was going to take place. Which meant Sean was alive.

She turned on to the access road, switched off her headlights, and slowed her pace to a crawl, before calling Mike Bolt.

'The car Egan's travelling in looks like it's reached the rendezvous.'

'Yeah, I can see that too.'

'How far are you guys behind?'

'Me and Mo are probably less than ten minutes, but we're unarmed. We've got six ARVs converging on a rendezvous point directly north of the airfield on the A412, as well as armed surveillance and the locals, but they're not going to be ready to move for at least ten minutes.'

'Sean may well be dead by then.'

Bolt sighed. 'I know, but I still want you to stay back and wait for us. And don't do anything stupid. I mean that. I will arrest you if you get in the way of a police operation.'

'Understood,' she said, ending the call. But she kept driving, through the open gates, cutting her engine as she reached a gentle incline in the road. What was it her therapist had said about her once? She had a need for attention, which manifested itself in an unhealthy addiction to dangerous situations.

Well, she couldn't argue with that.

Fifty-eight

I could see the figures clearly in the headlights now. I focused on the terrified expressions on the faces of the woman I'd once loved and the daughter I'd never met. My daughter . . . she seemed so small and vulnerable. Only three years old and being put through this. I had a huge and sudden yearning to take her in my arms and hold her, tell her that everything would be all right.

And then behind her, a figure in a black balaclava, a silenced pistol in one hand, a knife glinting in the other.

It took every ounce of willpower I possessed to stay calm.

'Stop the car and keep the lights and the engine on.'

Jack stopped the car and I could see he was as nervous as I was. Sweat gleamed on his brow and his hands were clenched tight on the wheel. 'What now?'

I tried to think. All I had to do was make one mistake and we all died. I could feel the pressure bearing down on me.

'We both get out, nice and slowly. You first.'

Jack started to get out, and I pointed the gun directly at the head of the figure in the balaclava before slowly getting out of the car myself, using the passenger door as a shield, trying to work out my next move. The problem was, as I could remember now from my undercover days, you can never control the situation when there's only one of you. People react unpredictably; plans can unravel in the blink of an eye.

My plan simply consisted of keeping my gun pointed at the woman in the balaclava, so that's exactly what I did. I could see Jack standing by the other side of the car, but I could no longer see his hands, and it struck me that the search I'd given him had been cursory at best.

The woman addressed him now as she stopped five yards away from us, touching the gun to Claire's head and keeping the knife far too close to Milly. 'Is he alive?' she demanded in her American accent, and I was immediately reminded about what she'd done to Jane only four nights ago.

'Yeah, he's alive,' said Jack. 'But he's hurt.'

Claire was staring straight ahead into space, an expression of shock and resignation on her face. I glanced at Milly, careful not to take my eyes off the woman for too long. She looked scared too but she was looking up at me with . . . I don't know what it was with. Maybe hope.

'It's going to be OK, I promise,' I said, amazed at the confidence in my voice. Then, to the woman: 'I'm here. Let them go.'

She pushed the end of the pistol's barrel against Claire's temple. 'You know the deal. Put the gun down.'

'Not until you let them go. You need to give them a head start too. Three minutes. We'll wait here. I'll even lower my gun a little.'

Somewhere in the distance, across the night sky, I could hear a siren.

The woman cocked her head in its direction. 'What's that?' she demanded.

'That is nothing to do with me,' I said. 'I promise.'

To be honest, I had no idea if this was true or not. I'd given Tina permission to call the police as long as they kept back, but what guarantee did I have that they would? That was when I noticed that the blonde's knife was a good few inches from Milly. I could shoot her in the face now, just as I'd shot her boyfriend. The gun would probably go off in her hand, killing Claire, and I debated with myself whether I could make that sacrifice, knowing in my heart that I could.

But then I saw Jack pull a gun from the back of his trousers, and it hit me with a grim finality that there was no way he could afford to let my family go. Claire had just seen his face, thanks to me. So had Milly.

The siren faded into the distance. It was over.

'Put the gun down,' said the woman.

Behind her mask, I could almost see her calculating whether she could take me out with a single shot. With my family as a shield, she'd know I'd hesitate to fire back. If she got me, that was it. We'd all be dead.

I realized my hand was no longer shaking. I was suddenly, inexplicably, calm. 'Let my family go or I pull the trigger and take you with me.' I could see Jack pointing the gun at me now but remembered him telling me he'd never killed anyone, and I could sense his heart wasn't in it. 'Are you going to shoot me, Jack? Have you got the balls for it?'

The knife moved in the woman's hand. Now the edge of the blade was touching my daughter's face. Milly visibly cringed. 'If you don't lower the gun now, I'm going to disfigure your daughter for life with just one flick of my wrist.' As she spoke, she crouched lower behind Claire, making herself a near-impossible target. 'You have three seconds to comply. One . . .'

'Lower the gun, Sean,' said Jack urgently.

'She's going to kill them, Jack,' I said. 'You want that on your conscience?'

'Two. Daddy wants you to bleed, baby. He wants you to suffer.'

'Sean, do as she says, for God's sake!' pleaded Claire, speaking for the first time.

I lowered the gun.

Slowly.

Then pulled the trigger.

I was aiming for her right shoulder area, which was partly exposed to allow her to hold the knife to Milly's face. It was unbelievably risky. But what else was there for me to do?

The woman stumbled backwards out of view with a yelp and I swung round, already shouting for Claire and Milly to run, turning the gun on Jack on the other side of the car. He had the gun in his hand and he was staring at me with a startled expression but making no move to fire, so I shot him twice in the chest, then swung back round to face the woman, knowing I'd only wounded her.

I got a fleeting glimpse of her lying on her back on the tarmac, the knife no longer in her hand, but the gun very much so and pointing at me, then the barrel lit up and I felt a huge weight like a punch hitting me somewhere in the sternum, then another, and another, each one harder than the last, and suddenly I was lying on my back on the tarmac too, staring up into space as the world seemed to wobble and blur around me.

I tried to sit up but all my strength was gone, and I could just make out the woman getting to her feet, still holding the gun, although her knife arm hung limply down at her side.

So this was it. She was going to kill me.

But she didn't. Instead, she turned in the direction Claire had run with Milly and, as I lay there helpless and defeated, she raised the gun to fire.

Fifty-nine

Tina had been watching events on the runway unfold from bushes thirty metres away. She couldn't hear what was being said but the 4×4's headlamps had illuminated the scene well enough, and she could guess. From the angle she was at she was able to recognize Sean, and thought she could make out both Claire and Milly. She didn't know the man on the other side of the car holding a gun but guessed it was Jack Duckford. The figure in the balaclava was definitely a woman, which meant it was almost certainly the one who'd murdered Sheryl Warner in her apartment the previous night, although there was no sign of her Neanderthal sidekick.

And then, just like that, the shooting had started and suddenly everyone was falling down and a single outsize silhouetted figure – a mother carrying her child – was running in Tina's direction across the tarmac. Then she saw the figure in the balaclava in the glare of the headlights, aiming her gun at them.

'Keep running!' screamed Tina, breaking cover. 'And keep your heads down!' She'd parked her car about twenty yards further back, behind the wall of bushes lining the access road, and she sprinted for it now, hearing shots ringing out behind her, and praying that the woman firing hadn't hit her targets.

Switching the headlights to full beam, she gunned the engine and drove on to the runway, relieved to see Claire and Milly still running towards her. She accelerated past them, bearing down on the woman in the balaclava, who'd taken up a crouched one-handed firing position a few yards in front of the 4×4. Tina could see she was hurt by the way one arm hung at her side, but she still ducked her head as the woman fired at her. A bullet flew through the middle of the windscreen, missing her by inches, and then the woman was jumping up and darting to one side, clearly hoping to take Tina through the passenger window when she came past and hit the 4×4, which was an inevitability on her current course.

Tina swung the wheel hard, braking at the same time, chasing down her target. The woman's gun arm flailed as she tried to get out of the way and a second shot rang out, but this time it didn't even hit the car and Tina kept driving, clipping the woman's legs with the edge of the bonnet and sending her flying out of view. She kept spinning the wheel in a screech of tyres until she'd turned round 180 degrees.

The woman in the balaclava was getting to her feet, unsteadily. She'd lost the gun and was trying to shield her eyes from the glare of Tina's headlights with her one good arm. She looked disorientated and, as Tina watched, she staggered over to the 4×4. Tina saw the gun lying on the tarmac and she drove forward, putting the car between it and the woman, then jumped out and picked it up.

The woman had opened the back door of the 4×4 and was leaning inside with her back to Tina.

'Put your hands in the air!' Tina called out, coming round the front of her car, holding the gun.

But the woman didn't seem to be listening. Instead Tina could hear her talking softly to someone inside the 4×4.

Tina repeated her command. Only three or four yards separated them now. She needed to neutralize the woman but had no idea how she was going to do it. She could hardly shoot her, even though she was sorely tempted, and she had no handcuffs, nor any sign of assistance.

And then the woman yanked off her balaclava, revealing her long blonde hair, and cried out – a terrible keening sound, like that of an animal in distress. She turned towards Tina, her face twisted in anguish, and for the first time Tina saw the prone body of the Neanderthal in the back of the car, his head hanging over the end of the seat.

'No!' screamed the woman, her voice echoing across the vast emptiness of the airfield, and, almost as if in answer, a siren wailed, followed by a second, close by, and coming closer.

Something flashed in the woman's gloved hand. A blade of some sort. Then she was running at Tina, the anguish transformed in an instant to pure white rage.

Tina pulled the trigger and fired two shots into her heart, stopping her in her tracks.

The woman wobbled on her feet, looking momentarily surprised, and it struck Tina for the first time how beautiful she was – a woman who could have had everything yet who'd ended up like this, dying young, violently and alone in a foreign land.

She fell to the tarmac with a dull, empty thud, leaving Tina the last person standing.

One Month Later

Sixty

Somehow I survived that night.

The blonde woman shot me three times in the upper body causing extensive internal damage. I suffered a collapsed lung, lost three inches of my small intestine, two of my ribs were shattered, and I no longer have a spleen. But somehow my most important organs were missed, and I've been told I'm likely to make a full recovery. I understand that Tina Boyd, who turned up like a slightly tardy version of the Seventh Cavalry, administered emergency first aid until the ambulance crew arrived. She also killed the woman who shot me and saved Claire and Milly, so I guess we're evens now. In fact, I probably owe her. I'd have liked to thank her personally for what she did but she hasn't been to see me here at the hospital, where I remain under police guard. And sadly under arrest. As soon as I leave here I'm being transferred to prison to await trial on a number of charges.

Claire hasn't visited me either. Nor Milly – about the only good thing, it seems, I've ever produced in my life. Claire has let it be known that she wants nothing more to do with me, and doesn't want me to contact her or Milly, and I guess under the circumstances I can understand her position.

I was finally well enough to be interviewed by the police a week back. Two men came to talk to me; one was DCI Mike Bolt, the guy Tina had told me about. He was a big presence, the kind of man who could intimidate if he wanted to, but also someone you felt you could trust. The other was his colleague, DS Mo Khan, who looked like he ate too much.

I asked them a lot of questions, none of which they seemed interested in answering. What they were interested in was finding out what had happened that night at Victor Hanzha's house. And, like everyone else, they wanted to know the location of the bodies.

By that point I'd remembered pretty much everything that had happened that night and, if I'm honest, they were memories I'd rather not have accessed. I was in love with Jen Jones, so to have to load her bloodied, still-warm corpse into the back of a car, along with that of an equally young woman, was one of the worst experiences of my life. I came close to being physically sick, and feel nauseous now just thinking about it. That night, I knew I'd been marked for death as well. So when Jack sent me off with Hanzha's bodyguard – a big Russian guy with an expressionless face – to bury the girls, it was obvious I was going to be joining them in the ground.

The Russian's sense of local geography was limited so it was up to me to find a final resting place for the girls. I chose Epping

Forest. It was a good forty miles around the M25 from Victor Hanzha's house and undeniably risky to be driving any distance with two bodies in the car, but I knew that at least we'd have a good chance of making them disappear permanently there. Don't get me wrong. I felt awful about what we were doing, but genuinely thought I had no other option. I knew the Russian was armed: I'd seen a gun in a shoulder holster underneath his jacket while we were loading the bodies. So I had to go along with it. But all the time I was thinking about how I was going to survive.

I'd picked up a small cutting knife from the kitchen before I left and it was in my back pocket. I figured that like almost all criminals I'd known, the Russian would be intrinsically lazy, and wouldn't even think about killing me until I'd helped him dig the grave, so when we finally reached a suitable place deep in the woods and were part way through digging a hole big and deep enough for the bodies, I put down my shovel, wiped my brow with a sigh and, as he told me in broken English to keep going, I whipped out the knife and shoved it in his neck. The whole thing was over in seconds. I got out of the way as the man who'd coldly finished off the girl I'd been in love with staggered round the hole, blood pouring from his neck, before falling into it, dead.

I spent another hour digging. It would have been much longer but it had rained a lot in recent weeks – I remember that now – and the ground was soft. When I'd finished, I buried all three of them, covered the bodies in the quicklime the Russian had thoughtfully brought with him to aid decomposition, and then filled the hole in with as much earth as possible.

I performed the whole exercise in a state of shock, but by the time I'd finished I'd realized that as long as I remained in the country, I was a dead man. So I had to get out fast, and for that I needed money. As soon as I got home, I called Jack Duckford, just like he'd said I had. Having thrown a heap of abuse at him for betraying me and demanding a hundred grand for my silence, I told him I'd photographed the girls' bodies in the house, as well as recording Victor Hanzha talking about the killings on my phone mike, and uploaded the footage to a memory stick, which I'd then placed in a letter along with a map showing where they were buried. I told him I was just about to post the letter to my solicitor with instructions that the letter be opened only in the event of my death. It was all bullshit, of course, but believable enough, and I remember Jack telling me that he'd get me the money.

After that, things are a bit sketchy. I knew I couldn't stay in my flat any longer – it was too dangerous – and I remember driving out of town, heading for the south coast where we used to holiday when I was a kid. It must have been four or five a.m. by this time, pitch black and with virtually no traffic on the road, and I have only the vaguest recollection of headlights on full beam in my rear-view mirror, dazzlingly bright as they bore down on me . . . then nothing until I woke up three months later and looked into the eyes of a woman who claimed to be my sister and who said she was going to look after me.

So who ran me off the road that night? My guess is that it was Combover and Blackbeard. I now know, thanks to Jack, that Jen Jones - the magnificent blonde I was in love with - was working for them, and was only interested in me to get nearer Alexander Hanzha. At some point she would have bugged my flat, and on that fateful night when I got back home and called Jack, I reckon that Combover and Blackbeard were listening. They heard me say that I had a letter with all this dynamite information on and when I left the flat, they picked up my trail at some point, wanting to intercept the letter, and ended up causing the accident. I'm guessing they checked the car, found no letter but, seeing that I was still alive, pulled me free and called 999, before setting the car on fire and removing all my ID, so that Hanzha's people wouldn't be able to find me. Then while I lay in hospital in a coma, they set up the whole thing with my fake sister, so that when I woke up, they could extract the information they needed from me.

It's all conjecture of course, but the pieces fit, and it's the best I've got.

So there I was, back in hospital, talking to DCI Mike Bolt and DS Mo Khan about my memories of that night at Victor Hanzha's house and, as you can imagine, I had a pretty major dilemma. If I told them the truth and gave them the approximate location of the burial ground, I'd almost certainly face murder charges. So far I'd only been charged with three counts of aggravated vehicle taking and a further count of assault causing ABH on a police officer – the result of the collision at the travellers' camp. I'd claimed self-defence with the shooting of Blackbeard, and it seemed my story hadn't been entirely discounted as fiction. With just those charges I might have been able to avoid too long a stretch, especially given the extenuating circumstances. But unlawfully burying three bodies, and with no proof that I hadn't murdered all of them . . . that was a different kettle of fish altogether.

But if I didn't give them a truthful account of what had happened then Victor Hanzha, the man who'd killed Lauren Donaldson, and as good as killed Jen Jones, would get off scot-free, and the girls would be denied a proper burial, leaving their grieving families in limbo.

What would you have done?

I'm a good man. I genuinely believe that.

But maybe not good enough.

In the end, I saved myself twenty years in prison by telling them I couldn't remember anything concrete about that night.

Sometimes you've got to think about number one. Especially when number one's all you've got left.

Sixty-one

It was an unseasonably warm October day and the sun was high in the sky as Tina and Mike Bolt stood at the top of the hill that ran up behind her house, admiring the view of the sleepy village below.

'I can't see why you like it here,' he said. 'It's far too peaceful for you.'

She laughed. 'I like peace and quiet as much as anyone else. As long as there's a bit of excitement mixed in now and again.'

Mike grunted. 'A bit of excitement. Is that what you call what happened with Sean Egan?' He gave her a smile which made her wonder why they'd never worked out. 'It's nice of you to invite me up here, but I'm guessing it's not entirely a social call.'

'It is a social call. I like seeing you. And I'm grateful for what you've done on my behalf.' Mike had done a lot to make sure Tina avoided charges for aiding and abetting a fugitive. 'But now you mention it, it would be nice to find out what was really going on behind the scenes.'

'It's all quite murky,' said Mike. 'Especially as a lot of powerful people won't talk to us. Our best bet of confirming what really happened is Carl Hughie. We know he's one of Crossman's people, but he's keeping completely shtum.'

'Didn't the psychotherapist, Whatret, implicate Hughie as the man paying him to get the information about the bodies from Sean?'

Mike shook his head. 'Under questioning, Whatret said he didn't know what we were talking about. He denied ever meeting Carl Hughie, or Sean Egan for that matter, and he wouldn't budge.'

'Sean had this recurring dream that Jennifer Jones and Lauren Donaldson were murdered at a house somewhere by someone close to Hanzha,' said Tina as they walked along the brow of the hill away from the village.

'But did he ever give you any more details than that?'

'No,' she said reluctantly. 'He didn't.'

'Because Sean says he can't remember anything about the night of his accident. In fact he's vague on pretty much everything after he left prison, and he's doing everything he can to avoid incriminating himself.'

Tina thought of her client, Mr Donaldson. In her final meeting with him three days earlier she'd had to tell him his daughter was almost certainly dead, and that it was unlikely they were ever going to find a body. The police had already told him the same thing, but it hadn't stopped him breaking down in front of her. She'd tried to comfort him but it had been half hearted because ultimately she knew she'd failed. It might not have been her fault but that didn't matter. She'd failed.

She stopped and looked up at Mike with a flash of anger in her eyes. 'So no one's going to be brought to justice for killing those girls? And everything's just going to carry on like before?'

'Well, Hanzha's already under investigation, and MI5 and the NCA are going to be looking at him a lot more closely now. And all the publicity's making Crossman look toxic as Home Secretary. There's talk he's going to be demoted.'

'But it's not enough, is it?'

Mike sighed. 'It's all we're going to get. A lot of the other people we'd like to talk to are dead, like Jack Duckford, and those two American contract killers. Incidentally, Egan might still face charges over the killing of the male contract killer. The same gun from the hotel killing was used, and Egan's explanation that it was self-defence doesn't really hold water.'

'You know, I went to see the woman Sean supposedly raped,' said Tina after a few minutes.

Mike looked annoyed, just as she knew he would. 'Jesus. How the hell did you find her?'

'I'm a detective, remember?'

'But it's illegal, Tina. Why do you keep helping Egan?'

'He saved my life once, Mike. When someone does that, it's hard to let it go when you see them in trouble. He was a good cop once too. All his problems, from the broken marriage to working for the bad guys, came from that one accusation. I wanted to find out whether it was true or not.'

'And what did she say?'

Tina remembered the meeting. She'd turned up unannounced

and Holly Verran, a well-dressed woman in her forties who'd had too much work done to her face, had recognized her from her recent appearances on the news, and let her in without a problem. In fact she'd been all smiles until Tina had told her what her visit was about. Then she'd gone from angry to upset as Tina had confronted her with everything that had happened to Sean and his family since he'd been charged with the rape.

'She still said it was rape,' said Tina. 'But I don't believe her.'

Holly Verran had come close to admitting the truth, but at the last second had stopped herself, then threatened to have Tina arrested for illegally approaching her and making wild, unfounded accusations, until Tina had told her that if she did that she'd be back, and would be a lot less friendly next time. It was a cheap shot, and Tina didn't feel good about herself for doing it, though clearly it had worked because she'd heard nothing since.

'There's nothing that can be done about that now, Tina,' said Mike, looking at her with something more than sympathy in his bright blue eyes. She knew he cared for her, and right now, that felt good. 'You can't solve the world's problems on your own. Sometimes you've just got to let go.'

'I know,' she said. She'd tried her best to help Alan Donaldson find his daughter, and Sean Egan to find out who was after him and why, and she could do no more.

She stopped, took a deep breath, and stared up at the almost cloudless blue sky, her hand tentatively finding Mike's. It really was a gorgeous day and, for once, it felt as if it might get better.

Also by Simon Kernick

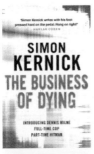

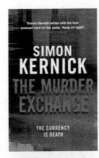

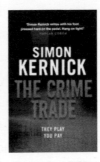

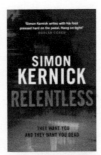

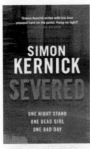

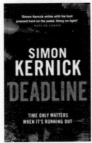

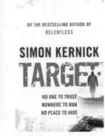

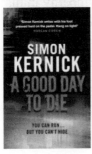

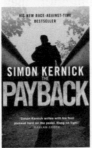

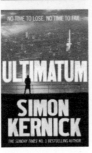

FIND OUT MORE ABOUT
SIMON AND HIS BOOKS ONLINE AT

www.simonkernick.com

 /SimonKernick

@simonkernick